ROBERT LOUIS STEVENSON

STRANGE CASE OF
DR. JEKYLL AND MR. HYDE
AND OTHER STORIES

KÖNEMANN

🙵 Notes (on pp. 316 to 324)
are keyed thus in the margin

© 1995 for this edition
Könemann Verlagsgesellschaft mbH
Bonner Straße 126, D–50968 Köln

Series and volume editor: Michael Hulse
Cover design: Peter Feierabend
Layout and typesetting: Birgit Beyer
Printed in Hungary
ISBN 3-89508-079-9

CONTENTS

STRANGE CASE OF
DR. JEKYLL AND MR. HYDE

STORY OF THE DOOR

Mr. Utterson the lawyer was a man of a rugged countenance, that was never lighted by a smile; cold, scanty and embarrassed in discourse; backward in sentiment; lean, long, dusty, dreary, and yet somehow lovable. At friendly meetings, and when the wine was to his taste, something eminently human beckoned from his eye; something indeed which never found its way into his talk, but which spoke not only in these silent symbols of the after-dinner face, but more often and loudly in the acts of his life. He was austere with himself; drank gin when he was alone, to mortify a taste for vintages; and though he enjoyed the theatre, had not crossed the doors of one for twenty years. But he had an approved tolerance for others; sometimes wondering, almost with envy, at the high pressure of spirits involved in their misdeeds; and in any extremity inclined to help rather than to reprove. "I incline to Cain's heresy," he used to say quaintly: "I let my brother go to the devil in his own way." In this character, it was frequently his fortune to be the last reputable acquaintance and the last good influence in the lives of down-going men. And to such as these, so long as they came about his chambers, he never marked a shade of change in his demeanour.

No doubt the feat was easy to Mr. Utterson; for he was undemonstrative at the best, and even his friendships seemed to be founded in a similar catholicity of good nature. It is the mark of a modest man to accept his friendly circle ready-made from the hands of opportunity; and that was the lawyer's way. His friends were those of his own blood, or those whom he had known the longest; his affections, like ivy, were the growth of time, they implied no aptness in the object. Hence, no doubt, the bond that united him to Mr. Richard Enfield, his distant kinsman, the well-known man about town. It was a nut to crack for many, what these two could see in each other or what subject they could find in common. It was reported by those who encountered them in their Sunday walks that they said nothing, looked singularly dull, and would hail with obvious relief the appearance of a friend. For all that, the two men put the greatest store by these excursions, counted them the chief jewel of each week, and not only set aside occasions of pleasure, but even resisted the calls of business, that they might enjoy them uninterrupted.

It chanced on one of these rambles that their way led them down a by-street in a busy quarter of London. The street was small, and what is called quiet, but it drove a thriving trade on the week-days. The inhabitants were all doing well, it seemed, and all emulously hoping to do better still, and laying out the surplus of their gains in coquetry; so that the shop-fronts stood along that thoroughfare with an air of invitation, like rows of smiling saleswomen. Even on Sunday, when it veiled its more florid charms and lay comparatively empty of passage, the street shone out in contrast to its dingy neighbourhood, like a fire in a forest; and with its freshly painted shutters, well-polished brasses, and general cleanliness and gaiety of note, instantly caught and pleased the eye of the passenger.

Two doors from one corner on the left hand going east, the line was broken by the entry of a court; and just at that point a certain sinister block of building thrust forward its gable on the street. It was two stories high; showed no window, nothing but a door on the lower story and a blind forehead of discoloured wall on the upper; and bore in every feature the marks of prolonged and sordid negligence. The door, which was equipped with neither bell nor knocker, was blistered and distained. Tramps slouched into the recess and struck matches on the panels; children kept shop upon the steps; the schoolboy had tried his knife on the mouldings; and for close on a generation no one had appeared to drive away these random visitors or to repair their ravages.

Mr. Enfield and the lawyer were on the other side of the by-street, but when they came abreast of the entry, the former lifted up his cane and pointed.

"Did you ever remark that door?" he asked; and when his

companion had replied in the affirmative, "it is connected in my mind," added he, "with a very odd story."

"Indeed?" said Mr. Utterson, with a slight change of voice, "and what was that?"

"Well, it was this way," returned Mr. Enfield: "I was coming home from some place at the end of the world, about three o'clock of a black winter morning, and my way lay through a part of town where there was literally nothing to be seen but lamps. Street after street, and all the folks asleep — street after street, all lighted up as if for a procession and all as empty as a church — till at last I got into that state of mind when a man listens and listens and begins to long for the sight of a policeman. All at once I saw two figures: one a little man who was stumping along eastward at a good walk, and the other a girl of maybe eight or ten, who was running as hard as she was able down a cross street. Well, sir, the two ran into one another naturally enough at the corner; and then came the horrible part of the thing; for the man trampled calmly over the child's body and left her screaming on the ground. It sounds nothing to hear, but it was hellish to see. It wasn't like a man; it was like some damned Juggernaut. I gave a view-holloa, took to my heels, collared my gentleman, and brought him back to where there was already quite a group about the screaming child. He was perfectly cool, and made no resistance, but gave me one look, so ugly that it brought out the sweat on me like running. The people who had turned out were the girl's own family; and pretty soon, the doctor, for whom she had been sent, put in his appearance. Well, the child was not much the worse, more frightened, according to the Sawbones; and there you might have supposed would be an end to it. But there was one curious circumstance. I had taken a loathing to my gentleman at first sight. So had the child's family, which was only natural. But the doctor's case was what struck me. He was the usual cut-and-dry apothecary, of no particular age and colour, with a strong Edinburgh accent, and about as emotional as a bagpipe. Well, sir, he was like the rest of us; every time he looked at my

9

prisoner, I saw that Sawbones turn sick and white with the desire to kill him. I knew what was in his mind, just as he knew what was in mine; and killing being out of the question, we did the next best. We told the man we could and would make such a scandal out of this as should make his name stink from one end of London to the other. If he had any friends or any credit, we undertook that he should lose them. And all the time, as we were pitching it in red-hot, we were keeping the women off him as best we could, for they were as wild as harpies. I never saw a circle of such hateful faces; and there was the man in the middle, with a kind of black, sneering coolness – frightened, too, I could see that – but carrying it off, sir, really like Satan. 'If you choose to make capital out of this accident,' said he, 'I am naturally helpless. No gentleman but wishes to avoid a scene,' says he. 'Name your figure.' Well, we screwed him up to a hundred pounds for the child's family; he would have clearly liked to stick out; but there was something about the lot of us that meant mischief, and at last he struck. The next thing was to get the money; and where do you think he carried us but to that place with the door? – whipped out a key, went in, and presently came back with the matter of ten pounds in gold and a cheque for the balance on Coutts's, drawn payable to bearer and signed with a name that I can't mention, though it's one of the points of my story, but it was a name at least very well known and often printed. The figure was stiff; but the signature was good for more than that, if it was only genuine. I took the liberty of pointing out to my gentleman that the whole business looked apocryphal, and that a man does not, in real life, walk into a cellar-door at four in the morning and come out of it with another man's cheque for close upon a hundred pounds. But he was quite easy and sneering. 'Set your mind at rest,' says he, 'I will stay with you till the banks open and cash the cheque myself.' So we all set off, the doctor, and the child's father, and our friend and myself, and passed the rest of the night in my chambers; and next day, when we had breakfasted, went in a body to the bank. I gave in the cheque myself, and said I had every reason to believe it was a forgery. Not a bit of it. The cheque was genuine."

"Tut-tut," said Mr. Utterson.

"I see you feel as I do," said Mr. Enfield. "Yes, it's a bad story. For my man was a fellow that nobody could have to do with, a really damnable man; and the person that drew the cheque is the very pink of the proprieties, celebrated too, and (what makes it worse) one of your fellows who do what they call good. Blackmail, I suppose; an honest man paying through the nose for some of the capers of his youth. Black Mail House is what I call that place with the door, in consequence. Though even that, you know, is far from explaining all," he added, and with the words fell into a vein of musing.

From this he was recalled by Mr. Utterson asking rather suddenly: "And you don't know if the drawer of the cheque lives there?"

"A likely place, isn't it?" returned Mr. Enfield. "But I happened to have noticed his address; he lives in some square or other."

"And you never asked about — the place with the door?" said Mr. Utterson.

"No, sir: I had a delicacy," was the reply. "I feel very strongly about putting questions; it partakes too much of the style of the day of judgment. You start a question, and it's like starting a stone. You sit quietly on the top of a hill; and away the stone goes, starting others; and presently some bland old bird (the last you would have thought of) is knocked on the head in his own back garden and the family have to change their name. No, sir, I make it a rule of mine: the more it looks like Queer Street, the less I ask."

"A very good rule too," said the lawyer.

"But I have studied the place for myself," continued Mr. Enfield. "It seems scarcely a house. There is no other door, and nobody goes in or out of that one but, once in a great while, the gentleman of my adventure. There are three windows looking on the court on the first floor; none below; the windows

11

are always shut, but they're clean. And then there is a chimney which is generally smoking; so somebody must live there. And yet it's not so sure; for the buildings are so packed together about that court that it's hard to say where one ends and another begins."

The pair walked on again for a while in silence; and then, "Enfield," said Mr. Utterson, "that's a good rule of yours."

"Yes, I think it is," returned Enfield.

"But for all that," continued the lawyer, "there's one point I want to ask: I want to ask the name of that man who walked over the child."

"Well," said Mr. Enfield, "I can't see what harm it would do. He was a man of the name of Hyde."

"H'm," said Mr. Utterson. "What sort of a man is he to see?"

"He is not easy to describe. There is something wrong with his appearance; something displeasing, something downright detestable. I never saw a man I so disliked, and yet I scarce know why. He must be deformed somewhere; he gives a strong feeling of deformity, although I couldn't specify the point. He's an extraordinary-looking man, and yet I really can name nothing out of the way. No, sir; I can make no hand of it; I can't describe him. And it's not want of memory; for I declare I can see him this moment."

Mr. Utterson again walked some way in silence and obviously under a weight of consideration. "You are sure he used a key?" he inquired at last.

"My dear sir — " began Enfield, surprised out of himself.

"Yes, I know," said Utterson; "I know it must seem strange. The fact is, if I do not ask you the name of the other party it is because I know it already. You see, Richard, your tale has gone home. If you have been inexact in any point, you had better correct it."

"I think you might have warned me," returned the other with a touch of sullenness. "But I have been pedantically exact, as you call it. The fellow had a key; and what's more, he has it still. I saw him use it not a week ago."

Mr Utterson sighed deeply but said never a word; and the young man presently resumed. "Here is another lesson to say nothing," said he. "I am ashamed of my long tongue. Let us make a bargain never to refer to this again."

"With all my heart," said the lawyer. "I shake hands on that, Richard."

That evening Mr. Utterson came home to his bachelor house in sombre spirits and sat down to dinner without relish. It was his custom of a Sunday, when this meal was over, to sit close by the fire, a volume of some dry divinity on his reading-desk, until the clock of the neighbouring church rang out the hour of twelve, when he would go soberly and gratefully to bed. On this night, however, as soon as the cloth was taken away, he took up a candle and went into his business-room. There he opened his safe, took from the most private part of it a document endorsed on the envelope as Dr. Jekyll's Will, and sat down with a clouded brow to study its contents. The will was holograph, for Mr. Utterson, though he took charge of it now that it was made, had refused to lend the least assistance in the making of it; it provided not only that, in case of the decease of Henry Jekyll, M.D., D.C.L., LL.D., F.R.S, &c., all his possessions were to pass into the hands of his "friend and benefactor Edward Hyde," but that in case of Dr. Jekyll's "disappearance or unexplained absence for any period exceeding three calendar months," the said Edward Hyde should step into the said Henry Jekyll's shoes without further delay and free from any burthen or obligation, beyond the payment of a few small sums to the members of the doctor's household. This document had long been the lawyer's eyesore. It offended him both as a lawyer and as a lover of the sane and customary sides of life, to whom the fanciful was the immodest. And hitherto it was his ignorance of Mr. Hyde that had swelled his indignation; now, by a sudden turn, it was his knowledge. It was already bad enough when the name was but a name of which he could learn no more. It was worse when it began to be clothed upon with detestable attributes; and out of the shifting, insubstantial mists that had so long baffled his eye, there leaped up the sudden, definite presentment of a fiend.

"I thought it was madness," he said, as he replaced the obnoxious paper in the safe, "and now I begin to fear it is disgrace."

With that he blew out his candle, put on a great-coat, and set forth in the direction of Cavendish Square, that citadel of medicine, where his friend, the great Dr. Lanyon, had his house and received his crowding patients. "If any one knows, it will be Lanyon," he had thought.

The solemn butler knew and welcomed him; he was subjected to no stage of delay, but ushered direct from the door to the dining-room, where Dr. Lanyon sat alone over his wine. This was a hearty, healthy, dapper, red-faced gentleman, with a shock of hair prematurely white, and a boisterous and decided manner. At sight of Mr. Utterson, he sprang up from his chair and welcomed him with both hands. The geniality, as was the way of the man, was somewhat theatrical to the eye; but it reposed on genuine feeling. For these two were old friends, old mates both at school and college, both thorough respecters of themselves and of each other, and, what does not always follow, men who thoroughly enjoyed each other's company.

After a little rambling talk, the lawyer led up to the subject which so disagreeably preoccupied his mind.

"I suppose, Lanyon," said he, "you and I must be the two oldest friends that Henry Jekyll has?"

"I wish the friends were younger," chuckled Dr. Lanyon. "But I suppose we are. And what of that? I see little of him now."

"Indeed?" said Utterson. "I thought you had a bond of common interest."

"We had," was the reply. "But it is more than ten years since Henry Jekyll became too fanciful for me. He began to go wrong, wrong in mind; and though of course I continue to take an interest in him for old sake's sake, as they say, I see and I have seen devilish little of the man. Such unscientific balderdash," added the doctor, flushing suddenly purple, "would have estranged Damon and Pythias."

This little spirt of temper was somewhat of a relief to Mr. Utterson. "They have only differed on some point of science," he thought; and being a man of no scientific passions (except in the matter of conveyancing) he even added: "It is nothing

15

worse than that!" He gave his friend a few seconds to recover his composure, and then approached the question he had come to put. "Did you ever come across a protégé of his—one Hyde?" he asked.

"Hyde," repeated Lanyon. "No. Never heard of him. Since my time."

That was the amount of information that the lawyer carried back with him to the great, dark bed on which he tossed to and fro, until the small hours of the morning began to grow large. It was a night of little ease to his toiling mind, toiling in mere darkness and besieged by questions.

Six o'clock struck on the bells of the church that was so conveniently near to Mr. Utterson's dwelling, and still he was digging at the problem. Hitherto it had touched him on the intellectual side alone; but now his imagination also was engaged, or rather enslaved; and as he lay and tossed in the gross darkness of the night and the curtained room, Mr. Enfield's tale went by before his mind in a scroll of lighted pictures. He would be aware of the great field of lamps of a nocturnal city; then of the figure of a man walking swiftly; then of a child running from the doctor's; and then these met, and that human Juggernaut trod the child down and passed on regardless of her screams. Or else he would see a room in a rich house, where his friend lay asleep, dreaming and smiling at his dreams; and then the door of that room would be opened, the curtains of the bed plucked apart, the sleeper recalled, and lo! there would stand by his side a figure to whom power was given, and even at that dead hour he must rise and do its bidding. The figure in these two phases haunted the lawyer all night; and if at any time he dozed over, it was but to see it glide more stealthily through sleeping houses, or move the more swiftly and still the more swiftly, even to dizziness, through wider labyrinths of lamplighted city, and at every street corner crush a child and leave her screaming. And still the figure had no face by which he might know it; even in his dreams, it had no face, or one that baffled him and melted before his eyes; and thus it was that there sprang up and grew apace in the lawyer's mind a singularly strong, almost an inordinate, curiosity to behold the features of the real Mr. Hyde. If he could but once set eyes on him, he thought the mystery would lighten and perhaps roll altogether away, as was the habit of mysterious things when well examined. He might see a reason for his friend's strange preference or bondage (call it which you please) and even for the startling clauses of the will. And at least it would be a face worth seeing: the face of a man who was without bowels of mercy: a face which had but to show itself to raise up, in the mind of the unimpression-able Enfield, a spirit of enduring hatred.

From that time forward, Mr. Utterson began to haunt the door in the by-street of shops. In the morning before office hours, at noon when business was plenty and time scarce, at night under the face of the fogged city moon, by all lights and at all hours of solitude or concourse, the lawyer was to be found on his chosen post.

"If he be Mr. Hyde," he had thought, "I shall be Mr. Seek."

And at last his patience was rewarded. It was a fine dry night; frost in the air; the streets as clean as a ballroom floor; the lamps, unshaken by any wind, drawing a regular pattern of light and shadow. By ten o'clock, when the shops were closed, the by-street was very solitary and, in spite of the low growl of London from all round, very silent. Small sounds carried far; domestic sounds out of the houses were clearly audible on either side of the roadway; and the rumour of the approach of any passenger preceded him by a long time. Mr. Utterson had been some minutes at his post, when he was aware of an odd, light footstep drawing near. In the course of his nightly patrols he had long grown accustomed to the quaint effect with which the footfalls of a single person, while he is still a great way off, suddenly spring out distinct from the vast hum and clatter of the city. Yet his attention had never before been so sharply and decisively arrested; and it was with a strong, superstitious pre-vision of success that he withdrew into the entry of the court.

17

The steps drew swiftly nearer, and swelled out suddenly louder as they turned the end of the street. The lawyer, looking forth from the entry, could soon see what manner of man he had to deal with. He was small and very plainly dressed, and the look of him, even at that distance, went somehow strongly against the watcher's inclination. But he made straight for the door, crossing the roadway to save time; and as he came, he drew a key from his pocket like one approaching home.

Mr. Utterson stepped out and touched him on the shoulder as he passed. "Mr. Hyde, I think?"

Mr. Hyde shrank back with a hissing intake of the breath. But his fear was only momentary; and though he did not look the lawyer in the face, he answered coolly enough: "That is my name. What do you want?"

"I see you are going in," returned the lawyer. "I am an old friend of Dr. Jekyll's—Mr. Utterson of Gaunt Street—you must have heard my name; and meeting you so conveniently, I thought you might admit me."

"You will not find Dr. Jekyll; he is from home," replied Mr. Hyde, blowing in the key. And then suddenly, but still without looking up, "How did you know me?" he asked.

"On your side," said Mr. Utterson, "will you do me a favour?"

"With pleasure," replied the other. "What shall it be?"

"Will you let me see your face?" asked the lawyer.

Mr. Hyde appeared to hesitate, and then, as if upon some sudden reflection, fronted about with an air of defiance; and the pair stared at each other pretty fixedly for a few seconds. "Now I shall know you again," said Mr. Utterson. "It may be useful."

"Yes," returned Mr. Hyde, "it is as well we have met; and *à propos,* you should have my address." And he gave a number of a street in Soho.

"Good God!" thought Mr. Utterson, "can he too have been thinking of the will?" But he kept his feelings to himself and only grunted in acknowledgment of the address.

"And now," said the other, "how did you know me?"

"By description," was the reply.

"Whose description?"

"We have common friends," said Mr. Utterson.

"Common friends?" echoed Mr. Hyde, a little hoarsely. "Who are they?"

"Jekyll, for instance," said the lawyer.

"He never told you," cried Mr. Hyde, with a flush of anger. "I did not think you would have lied."

"Come," said Mr. Utterson, "that is not fitting language."

The other snarled aloud into a savage laugh; and the next moment, with extraordinary quickness, he had unlocked the door and disappeared into the house.

The lawyer stood awhile when Mr. Hyde had left him, the picture of disquietude. Then he began slowly to mount the street, pausing every step or two and putting his hand to his brow like a man in mental perplexity. The problem he was thus debating as he walked was one of a class that is rarely solved. Mr. Hyde was pale and dwarfish. He gave an impression of deformity without any nameable malformation, he had a displeasing smile, he had borne himself to the lawyer with a sort of murderous mixture of timidity and boldness, and he spoke with a husky, whispering and somewhat broken voice; all these were points against him, but not all of these together could explain the hitherto unknown disgust, loathing, and fear with which Mr. Utterson regarded him. "There must be something else," said the perplexed gentleman. "There *is* something more, if I could find a name for it. God bless me, the man seems hardly human! Something troglodytic, shall we say? or can it be the old story of Dr. Fell? or is it the mere radiance of a foul soul that thus transpires through, and transfigures, its clay continent? The last, I think; for O my poor old Harry Jekyll, if ever I read Satan's signature upon a face, it is on that of your new friend."

Round the corner from the by-street there was a square of ancient, handsome houses, now for the most part decayed from their high estate and let in flats and chambers to all sorts

and conditions of men: map-engravers, architects, shady law-
yers, and the agents of obscure enterprises. One house, however, second from the corner, was still occupied entire; and at
the door of this, which wore a great air of wealth and comfort,
though it was now plunged in darkness except for the fan-light,
Mr. Utterson stopped and knocked. A well-dressed elderly
servant opened the door.

"Is Dr. Jekyll at home, Poole?" asked the lawyer.

"I will see, Mr. Utterson," said Poole, admitting the visitor, as
he spoke, into a large, low-roofed, comfortable hall, paved with
flags, warmed (after the fashion of a country house) by a
bright, open fire, and furnished with costly cabinets of oak.
"Will you wait here by the fire, sir? or shall I give you a light in
the dining-room?"

"Here, thank you," said the lawyer, and he drew near and
leaned on the tall fender. This hall, in which he was now left
alone, was a pet fancy of his friend the doctor's; and Utterson
himself was wont to speak of it as the pleasantest room in
London. But tonight there was a shudder in his blood; the face
of Hyde sat heavy on his memory; he felt (what was rare with
him) a nausea and distaste of life; and in the gloom of his
spirits, he seemed to read a menace in the flickering of the fire-
light on the polished cabinets and the uneasy starting of the
shadow on the roof. He was ashamed of his relief, when Poole
presently returned to announce that Dr. Jekyll was gone out.

"I saw Mr. Hyde go in by the old dissecting-room door,
Poole," he said. "Is that right, when Dr. Jekyll is from home?"

"Quite right, Mr. Utterson, sir," replied the servant. "Mr. Hyde
has a key."

"Your master seems to repose a great deal of trust in that
young man, Poole," resumed the other musingly.

"Yes, sir, he do indeed," said Poole. "We have all orders to
obey him."

"I do not think I ever met Mr. Hyde?" asked Utterson.

"O dear no, sir. He never *dines* here," replied the butler.
"Indeed, we see very little of him on this side of the house; he

mostly comes and goes by the laboratory."

"Well, good night, Poole."

"Good night, Mr. Utterson."

And the lawyer set out homeward with a very heavy heart. "Poor Harry Jekyll," he thought, "my mind misgives me he is in deep waters! He was wild when he was young; a long while ago, to be sure; but in the law of God there is no statute of limitations. Ay, it must be that; the ghost of some old sin, the cancer of some concealed disgrace: punishment coming, *pede claudo*, years after memory has forgotten and self-love condoned the fault." And the lawyer, scared by the thought, brooded awhile on his own past, groping in all the corners of memory, lest by chance some Jack-in-the-Box of an old iniquity should leap to light there. His past was fairly blameless; few men could read the rolls of their life with less apprehension; yet he was humbled to the dust by the many ill things he had done, and raised up again into a sober and fearful gratitude by the many that he had come so near to doing, yet avoided. And then, by a return on his former subject, he conceived a spark of hope. "This Master Hyde, if he were studied," thought he, "must have secrets of his own: black secrets, by the look of him; secrets compared to which poor Jekyll's worst would be like sunshine. Things cannot continue as they are. It turns me cold to think of this creature stealing like a thief to Harry's bedside; poor Harry, what a wakening! And the danger of it; for if this Hyde suspects the existence of the will, he may grow impatient to inherit. Ay, I must put my shoulder to the wheel—if Jekyll will but let me," he added, "if Jekyll will only let me." For once more he saw before his mind's eye, as clear as a transparency, the strange clauses of the will.

DR. JEKYLL WAS QUITE AT EASE

A fortnight later, by excellent good fortune, the doctor gave one of his pleasant dinners to some five or six old cronies, all intelligent, reputable men, and all judges of good wine; and Mr. Utterson so contrived that he remained behind after the others had departed. This was no new arrangement, but a thing that had befallen many scores of times. Where Utterson was liked, he was liked well. Hosts loved to detain the dry lawyer, when the light-hearted and the loose-tongued had already their foot on the threshold; they liked to sit awhile in his unobtrusive company, practising for solitude, sobering their minds in the man's rich silence after the expense and strain of gaiety. To this rule Dr. Jekyll was no exception; and as he now sat on the opposite side of the fire—a large, well-made, smooth-faced man of fifty, with something of a slyish cast perhaps, but every mark of capacity and kindness—you could see by his looks that he cherished for Mr. Utterson a sincere and warm affection.

"I have been wanting to speak to you, Jekyll," began the latter. "You know that will of yours?"

A close observer might have gathered that the topic was distasteful; but the doctor carried it off gaily. "My poor Utterson," said he, "you are unfortunate in such a client. I never saw a man so distressed as you were by my will; unless it were that hide-bound pedant, Lanyon, at what he called my scientific heresies. Oh, I know he's a good fellow—you needn't frown—an excellent fellow, and I always mean to see more of him; but a hide-bound pedant for all that; an ignorant, blatant pedant. I was never more disappointed in any man than Lanyon."

"You know I never approved of it," pursued Utterson, ruthlessly disregarding the fresh topic.

"My will? Yes, certainly, I know that," said the doctor, a trifle sharply. "You have told me so."

"Well, I tell you so again," continued the lawyer. "I have been learning something of young Hyde."

The large handsome face of Dr. Jekyll grew pale to the very lips, and there came a blackness about his eyes. "I do not care to hear more," said he. "This is a matter I thought we had agreed to drop."

"What I heard was abominable," said Utterson.

"It can make no change. You do not understand my position," returned the doctor, with a certain incoherency of manner. "I am painfully situated, Utterson; my position is a very strange—a very strange one. It is one of those affairs that cannot be mended by talking."

"Jekyll," said Utterson, "you know me: I am a man to be trusted. Make a clean breast of this in confidence; and I make no doubt I can get you out of it."

"My good Utterson," said the doctor, "this is very good of you, this is downright good of you, and I cannot find words to thank you in. I believe you fully; I would trust you before any man alive—ay, before myself, if I could make the choice; but indeed it isn't what you fancy; it is not so bad as that; and just to put your good heart at rest, I will tell you one thing: the moment I choose, I can be rid of Mr. Hyde. I give you my hand upon that; and I thank you again and again; and I will just add one little word, Utterson, that I'm sure you'll take in good part: this is a private matter, and I beg of you to let it sleep."

Utterson reflected a little, looking in the fire.

"I have no doubt you are perfectly right," he said at last, getting to his feet.

"Well, but since we have touched upon this business, and for the last time I hope," continued the doctor, "there is one point I should like you to understand. I have really a very great interest in poor Hyde. I know you have seen him; he told me so; and I fear he was rude. But I do sincerely take a great, a very great interest in that young man; and if I am taken away, Utterson, I wish you to promise me that you will bear with him and get his rights for him. I think you would, if you knew all; and it would be a weight off my mind if you would promise."

"I can't pretend that I shall ever like him," said the lawyer.

"I don't ask that," pleaded Jekyll, laying his hand upon the other's arm; "I only ask for justice; I only ask you to help him for my sake, when I am no longer here."

Utterson heaved an irrepressible sigh. "Well," said he, "I promise."

THE CAREW MURDER CASE

Nearly a year later, in the month of October 18—, London was startled by a crime of singular ferocity, rendered all the more notable by the high position of the victim. The details were few and startling. A maidservant living alone in a house not far from the river had gone upstairs to bed about eleven. Although a fog rolled over the city in the small hours, the early part of the night was cloudless, and the lane, which the maid's window overlooked, was brilliantly lit by the full moon. It seems she was romantically given, for she sat down upon her box, which stood immediately under the window, and fell into a dream of musing. Never (she used to say, with streaming tears, when she narrated that experience), never had she felt more at peace with all men or thought more kindly of the world. And as she so sat she became aware of an aged and beautiful gentleman with white hair drawing near along the lane: and advancing to meet him another and very small gentleman, to whom at first she paid less attention. When they had come within speech (which was just under the maid's eyes) the older man bowed and accosted the other with a very pretty manner of politeness. It did not seem as if the subject of his address were of great importance; indeed, from his pointing, it sometimes appeared as if he were only inquiring his way; but the moon shone on his face as he spoke, and the girl was pleased to watch it, it seemed to breathe such an innocent and old-world kindness of disposition, yet with something high too, as of a well-founded self-content. Presently her eye wandered to the other, and she was surprised to recognise in him a certain Mr. Hyde, who had once visited her master, and for whom she had conceived a dislike. He had in his hand a heavy cane, with which he was trifling; but he answered never a word, and seemed to listen with an ill-contained impatience. And then all of a sudden he broke out in a great flame of anger, stamping with his foot, brandishing the cane, and carrying on (as the maid described it) like a madman. The old gentleman took a step back, with the air of one very much surprised and a trifle hurt; and at that Mr. Hyde broke out of all bounds and clubbed him to the earth. And next moment, with ape-like fury, he was trampling his victim under foot, and hailing down a storm of blows, under which the bones were audibly shattered and the body jumped upon the roadway. At the horror of these sights and sounds the maid fainted.

It was two o'clock when she came to herself and called for the police. The murderer was gone long ago; but there lay his victim in the middle of the lane, incredibly mangled. The stick with which the deed had been done, although it was of some rare and very tough and heavy wood, had broken in the middle under the stress of this insensate cruelty; and one splintered half had rolled in the neighbouring gutter—the other, without doubt, had been carried away by the murderer. A purse and a gold watch were found upon the victim; but no cards or papers, except a sealed and stamped envelope, which he had been probably carrying to the post, and which bore the name and address of Mr. Utterson.

This was brought to the lawyer the next morning before he was out of bed; and he had no sooner seen it, and been told the circumstances, than he shot out a solemn lip. "I shall say nothing till I have seen the body," said he; "this may be very serious. Have the kindness to wait while I dress." And with the same grave countenance he hurried through his breakfast and drove to the police station, whither the body had been carried. As soon as he came into the cell he nodded.

"Yes," said he, "I recognise him. I am sorry to say that this is Sir Danvers Carew."

"Good God, sir," exclaimed the officer, "is it possible?" And the next moment his eye lighted up with professional ambition. "This will make a deal of noise," he said. "And perhaps you can help us to the man." And he briefly narrated what the maid had seen, and showed the broken stick.

Mr. Utterson had already quailed at the name of Hyde; but when the stick was laid before him he could doubt no longer;

broken and battered as it was, he recognised it for one that he had himself presented many years before to Henry Jekyll.

"Is this Mr. Hyde a person of small stature?" he inquired.

"Particularly small and particularly wicked-looking, is what the maid calls him," said the officer.

Mr. Utterson reflected; and then, raising his head, "If you will come with me in my cab," he said, "I think I can take you to his house."

It was by this time about nine in the morning, and the first fog of the season. A great chocolate-coloured pall lowered over heaven, but the wind was continually charging and routing these embattled vapours; so that as the cab crawled from street to street, Mr. Utterson beheld a marvellous number of degrees and hues of twilight; for here it would be dark like the back-end of evening; and there would be a glow of a rich, lurid brown, like the light of some strange conflagration; and here, for a moment, the fog would be quite broken up, and a hag-gard shaft of daylight would glance in between the swirling wreaths. The dismal quarter of Soho seen under these chang-ing glimpses, with its muddy ways, and slatternly passengers, and its lamps, which had never been extinguished or had been kindled afresh to combat this mournful re-invasion of dark-ness, seemed, in the lawyer's eyes, like a district of some city in a nightmare.

The thoughts of his mind, besides, were of the gloomiest dye; and when he glanced at the companion of his drive, he was conscious of some touch of that terror of the law and the law's officers which may at times assail the most honest.

As the cab drew up before the address indicated, the fog lift-ed a little, and showed him a dingy street, a gin-palace, a low French eating-house, a shop for the retail of penny numbers and twopenny salads, many ragged children huddled in the doorways, and many women of many different nationalities passing out, key in hand, to have a morning glass; and the next moment the fog settled down again upon that part, as brown as umber, and cut him off from his blackguardly surroundings.

This was the home of Henry Jekyll's favourite; of a man who was heir to a quarter of a million sterling.

An ivory-faced and silvery-haired old woman opened the door. She had an evil face, smoothed by hypocrisy; but her manners were excellent. Yes, she said, this was Mr. Hyde's, but he was not at home; he had been in that night very late, but had gone away again in less than an hour; there was nothing strange in that; his habits were very irregular, and he was often absent; for instance, it was nearly two months since she had seen him till yesterday.

"Very well then, we wish to see his rooms," said the lawyer; and when the woman began to declare it was impossible, "I had better tell you who this person is," he added. "This is Inspector Newcomen of Scotland Yard."

A flash of odious joy appeared upon the woman's face. "Ah!" said she, "he is in trouble! What has he done?"

Mr. Utterson and the inspector exchanged glances. "He don't seem a very popular character," observed the latter. "And now, my good woman, just let me and this gentleman have a look about us."

In the whole extent of the house, which but for the old woman remained otherwise empty, Mr. Hyde had only used a couple of rooms; but these were furnished with luxury and good taste. A closet was filled with wine; the plate was of silver, the napery elegant; a good picture hung upon the walls, a gift (as Utterson supposed) from Henry Jekyll, who was much of a connoisseur; and the carpets were of many plies and agreeable in colour. At this moment, however, the rooms bore every mark of having been recently and hurriedly ransacked; clothes lay about the floor, with their pockets inside out; lockfast drawers stood open; and on the hearth there lay a pile of grey ashes, as though many papers had been burned. From these embers the inspector disinterred the butt-end of a green cheque-book, which had resisted the action of the fire; the other half of the stick was found behind the door; and as this clinched his suspicions, the officer declared himself delighted. A visit to the bank, where several thousand pounds were found to be lying to the murderer's credit, completed his gratification.

"You may depend upon it, sir," he told Mr. Utterson: "I have him in my hand. He must have lost his head, or he never would have left the stick or, above all, burned the cheque-book. Why, money's life to the man. We have nothing to do but wait for him at the bank, and get out the handbills."

This last, however, was not so easy of accomplishment; for Mr. Hyde had numbered few familiars—even the master of the servant-maid had only seen him twice; his family could nowhere be traced; he had never been photographed; and the few who could describe him differed widely, as common observers will. Only on one point were they agreed; and that was the haunting sense of unexpressed deformity with which the fugitive impressed his beholders.

INCIDENT OF THE LETTER

It was late in the afternoon when Mr. Utterson found his way to Dr. Jekyll's door, where he was at once admitted by Poole, and carried down by the kitchen offices and across a yard which had once been a garden to the building which was indifferently known as the laboratory or the dissecting-rooms. The doctor had bought the house from the heirs of a celebrated surgeon; and, his own tastes being rather chemical than anatomical, had changed the destination of the block at the bottom of the garden. It was the first time that the lawyer had been received in that part of his friend's quarters; and he eyed the dingy windowless structure with curiosity, and gazed round with a distasteful sense of strangeness as he crossed the theatre, once crowded with eager students and now lying gaunt and silent, the tables laden with chemical apparatus, the floor strewn with crates and littered with packing straw, and the light falling dimly through the foggy cupola. At the farther end, a flight of stairs mounted to a door covered with red baize; and through this, Mr. Utterson was at last received into the doctor's cabinet. It was a large room, fitted round with glass presses, furnished, among other things, with a cheval-glass and a business-table, and looking out upon the court by three dusty windows barred with iron. The fire burned in the grate; a lamp was set lighted on the chimney shelf, for even in the houses the fog began to lie thickly; and there, close up to the warmth, sat Dr. Jekyll, looking deadly sick; he did not rise to meet his visitor, but held out a cold hand and bade him welcome in a changed voice.

"And now," said Mr. Utterson, as soon as Poole had left them, "you have heard the news?"

The doctor shuddered. "They were crying it in the square," he said. "I heard them in my dining-room."

"One word," said the lawyer. "Carew was my client, but so are you, and I want to know what I am doing. You have not been mad enough to hide this fellow?"

"Utterson, I swear to God," cried the doctor, "I swear to God I will never set eyes on him again. I bind my honour to you that I am done with him in this world. It is all at an end. And indeed he does not want my help; you do not know him as I do; he is safe, he is quite safe; mark my words, he will never more be heard of."

The lawyer listened gloomily; he did not like his friend's feverish manner. "You seem pretty sure of him," said he; "and for your sake, I hope you may be right. If it came to a trial your name might appear."

"I am quite sure of him," replied Jekyll; "I have grounds for certainty that I cannot share with any one. But there is one thing on which you may advise me. I have—I have received a letter; and I am at a loss whether I should show it to the police. I should like to leave it in your hands, Utterson; you would judge wisely, I am sure; I have so great a trust in you."

"You fear, I suppose, that it might lead to his detection?" asked the lawyer.

"No," said the other. "I cannot say that I care what becomes of Hyde; I am quite done with him. I was thinking of my own character, which this hateful business has rather exposed."

Utterson ruminated awhile; he was surprised at his friend's selfishness, and yet relieved by it. "Well," said he at last, "let me see the letter."

The letter was written in an odd, upright hand and signed "Edward Hyde": and it signified, briefly enough, that the writer's benefactor, Dr. Jekyll, whom he had long so unworthily repaid for a thousand generosities, need labour under no alarm for his safety, as he had means of escape on which he placed a sure dependence. The lawyer liked this letter well enough; it put a better colour on the intimacy than he had looked for; and he blamed himself for some of his past suspicions.

"Have you the envelope?" he asked.

"I burned it," replied Jekyll, "before I thought what I was about. But it bore no postmark. The note was handed in."

"Shall I keep this and sleep upon it?" asked Utterson.

"I wish you to judge for me entirely," was the reply. "I have lost confidence in myself."

"Well, I shall consider," returned the lawyer.—"And now one word more: it was Hyde who dictated the terms in your will about that disappearance?"

The doctor seemed seized with a qualm of faintness; he shut his mouth tight and nodded.

"I knew it," said Utterson. "He meant to murder you. You have had a fine escape."

"I have had what is far more to the purpose," returned the doctor solemnly: "I have had a lesson—O God, Utterson, what a lesson I have had!" And he covered his face for a moment with his hands.

On his way out, the lawyer stopped and had a word or two with Poole. "By the by," said he, "there was a letter handed in to-day: what was the messenger like?" But Poole was positive nothing had come except by post; "and only circulars by that," he added.

This news sent off the visitor with his fears renewed. Plainly the letter had come by the laboratory door; possibly, indeed, it had been written in the cabinet; and if that were so, it must be differently judged, and handled with the more caution. The newsboys, as he went, were crying themselves hoarse along the footways: "Special edition. Shocking murder of an M.P." That was the funeral oration of one friend and client; and he could not help a certain apprehension lest the good name of another should be sucked down in the eddy of the scandal. It was, at least, a ticklish decision that he had to make; and, self-reliant as he was by habit, he began to cherish a longing for advice. It was not to be had directly; but perhaps, he thought, it might be fished for.

Presently after, he sat on one side of his own hearth, with Mr. Guest, his head clerk, upon the other, and midway between, at a nicely calculated distance from the fire, a bottle of a particular old wine that had long dwelt unsunned in the foundations of his house. The fog still slept on the wing above the drowned city, where the lamps glimmered like carbuncles; and through the muffle and smother of these fallen clouds, the procession of the town's life was still rolling on through the great arteries with a sound as of a mighty wind. But the room was gay with fire-light. In the bottle the acids were long ago resolved; the imperial dye had softened with time, as the colour grows richer in stained windows; and the glow of hot autumn afternoons on hillside vineyards was ready to be set free and to disperse the fogs of London. Insensibly the lawyer melted. There was no man from whom he kept fewer secrets than Mr. Guest; and he was not always sure that he kept as many as he meant. Guest had often been on business to the doctor's; he knew Poole; he could scarce have failed to hear of Mr. Hyde's familiarity about the house; he might draw conclusions: was it not as well, then, that he should see a letter which put that mystery to rights? and above all since Guest, being a great student and critic of handwriting, would consider the step natural and obliging? The clerk, besides, was a man of counsel; he would scarce read so strange a document without dropping a remark; and by that remark Mr. Utterson might shape his future course.

"This is a sad business about Sir Danvers," he said.

"Yes, sir, indeed. It has elicited a great deal of public feeling," returned Guest. "The man, of course, was mad."

"I should like to hear your views on that," replied Utterson. "I have a document here in his handwriting; it is between ourselves, for I scarce know what to do about it; it is an ugly business at the best. But there it is; quite in your way: a murderer's autograph."

Guest's eyes brightened, and he sat down at once and studied it with passion. "No, sir," he said; "not mad; but it is an odd hand."

"And by all accounts a very odd writer," added the lawyer.

Just then the servant entered with a note.

"Is that from Dr. Jekyll, sir?" inquired the clerk. "I thought I knew the writing. Anything private, Mr. Utterson?"

"Only an invitation to dinner. Why? do you want to see it?"

"One moment. I thank you, sir"; and the clerk laid the two sheets of paper alongside and sedulously compared their contents. "Thank you, sir," he said at last, returning both; "it's a very interesting autograph."

There was a pause, during which Mr. Utterson struggled with himself. "Why did you compare them, Guest?" he inquired suddenly.

"Well, sir," returned the clerk, "there's a rather singular resemblance; the two hands are in many points identical: only differently sloped."

"Rather quaint," said Utterson.

"It is, as you say, rather quaint," returned Guest.

"I wouldn't speak of this note, you know," said the master.

"No, sir," said the clerk. "I understand."

But no sooner was Mr. Utterson alone that night than he locked the note into his safe, where it reposed from that time forward. "What!" he thought. "Henry Jekyll forge for a murderer!" And his blood ran cold in his veins.

REMARKABLE INCIDENT OF DR. LANYON

Time ran on; thousands of pounds were offered in reward, for the death of Sir Danvers was resented as a public injury; but Mr. Hyde had disappeared out of the ken of the police as though he had never existed. Much of his past was unearthed, indeed, and all disreputable: tales came out of the man's cruelty, at once so callous and violent, of his vile life, of his strange associates, of the hatred that seemed to have surrounded his career; but of his present whereabouts, not a whisper. From the time he had left the house in Soho on the morning of the murder, he was simply blotted out; and gradually, as time drew on, Mr. Utterson began to recover from the hotness of his alarm, and to grow more at quiet with himself. The death of Sir Danvers was, to his way of thinking, more than paid for by the disappearance of Mr. Hyde. Now that that evil influence had been withdrawn, a new life began for Dr. Jekyll. He came out of his seclusion, renewed relations with his friends, became once more their familiar guest and entertainer; and whilst he had always been known for charities, he was now no less distinguished for religion. He was busy, he was much in the open air, he did good; his face seemed to open and brighten, as if with an inward consciousness of service; and for more than two months the doctor was at peace.

On the 8th of January Utterson had dined at the doctor's with a small party; Lanyon had been there; and the face of the host had looked from one to the other as in the old days when the trio were inseparable friends. On the 12th, and again on the 14th, the door was shut against the lawyer. "The doctor was confined to the house," Poole said, "and saw no one." On the 15th he tried again, and was again refused; and having now been used for the last two months to see his friend almost daily, he found this return of solitude to weigh upon his spirits. The fifth night he had in Guest to dine with him; and the sixth he betook himself to Dr. Lanyon's.

There at least he was not denied admittance; but when he

came in, he was shocked at the change which had taken place in the doctor's appearance. He had his death-warrant written legibly upon his face. The rosy man had grown pale; his flesh had fallen away; he was visibly balder and older; and yet it was not so much these tokens of a swift physical decay that arrested the lawyer's notice, as a look in the eye and quality of manner that seemed to testify to some deep-seated terror of the mind. It was unlikely that the doctor should fear death; and yet that was what Utterson was tempted to suspect. "Yes," he thought; "he is a doctor, he must know his own state and that his days are counted; and the knowledge is more than he can bear." And yet when Utterson remarked on his ill-looks, it was with an air of great firmness that Lanyon declared himself a doomed man.

"I have had a shock," he said, "and I shall never recover. It is a question of weeks. Well, life has been pleasant; I liked it; yes, sir, I used to like it. I sometimes think if we knew all we should be more glad to get away."

"Jekyll is ill too," observed Utterson. "Have you seen him?"

But Lanyon's face changed, and he held up a trembling hand. "I wish to see or hear no more of Dr. Jekyll," he said in a loud, unsteady voice. "I am quite done with that person; and I beg that you will spare me any allusion to one whom I regard as dead."

"Tut-tut," said Mr. Utterson; and then, after a considerable pause, "Can't I do anything?" he inquired. "We are three very old friends, Lanyon; we shall not live to make others."

"Nothing can be done," returned Lanyon; "ask himself."

"He will not see me," said the lawyer.

"I am not surprised at that," was the reply. "Some day, Utterson, after I am dead, you may perhaps come to learn the right and wrong of this. I cannot tell you. And in the meantime, if you can sit and talk with me of other things, for God's sake, stay and do so; but if you cannot keep clear of this accursed topic, then, in God's name, go, for I cannot bear it."

As soon as he got home, Utterson sat down and wrote to

Jekyll, complaining of his exclusion from the house, and asking the cause of this unhappy break with Lanyon; and the next day brought him a long answer, often very pathetically worded, and sometimes darkly mysterious in drift. The quarrel with Lanyon was incurable. "I do not blame our old friend," Jekyll wrote, "but I share his view that we must never meet. I mean from henceforth to lead a life of extreme seclusion; you must not be surprised, nor must you doubt my friendship, if my door is often shut even to you. You must suffer me to go my own dark way. I have brought on myself a punishment and a danger that I cannot name. If I am the chief of sinners, I am the chief of sufferers also. I could not think that this earth contained a place for sufferings and terrors so unmanning; and you can do but one thing, Utterson, to lighten this destiny, and that is to respect my silence." Utterson was amazed; the dark influence of Hyde had been withdrawn, the doctor had returned to his old tasks and amities; a week ago, the prospect had smiled with every promise of a cheerful and an honoured age; and now in a moment, friendship and peace of mind and the whole tenor of his life were wrecked. So great and unprepared a change pointed to madness; but in view of Lanyon's manner and words, there must lie for it some deeper ground.

A week afterwards Dr. Lanyon took to his bed, and in something less than a fortnight he was dead. The night after the funeral, at which he had been sadly affected, Utterson locked the door of his business-room, and sitting there by the light of a melancholy candle, drew out and set before him an envelope addressed by the hand and sealed with the seal of his dead friend. "PRIVATE: for the hands of G.J. Utterson ALONE, and in case of his predecease *to be destroyed unread*," so it was emphatically superscribed; and the lawyer dreaded to behold the contents. "I have buried one friend today," he thought: "what if this should cost me another?" And then he condemned the fear as a disloyalty, and broke the seal. Within there was another enclosure, likewise sealed, and marked upon the cover as "not to be opened till the death or disappearance of

Dr. Henry Jekyll." Utterson could not trust his eyes. Yes, it was disappearance; here again, as in the mad will which he had long ago restored to its author, here again were the idea of a disappearance and the name of Henry Jekyll bracketed. But in the will that idea had sprung from the sinister suggestion of the man Hyde; it was set there with a purpose all too plain and horrible. Written by the hand of Lanyon, what should it mean? A great curiosity came on the trustee, to disregard the prohibition and dive at once to the bottom of these mysteries; but professional honour and faith to his dead friend were stringent obligations; and the packet slept in the inmost corner of his private safe.

It is one thing to mortify curiosity, another to conquer it; and it may be doubted if, from that day forth, Utterson desired the society of his surviving friend with the same eagerness. He thought of him kindly; but his thoughts were disquieted and fearful. He went to call indeed; but he was perhaps relieved to be denied admittance; perhaps, in his heart, he preferred to speak with Poole upon the doorstep and surrounded by the air and sounds of the open city, rather than to be admitted into that house of voluntary bondage, and to sit and speak with its inscrutable recluse. Poole had, indeed, no very pleasant news to communicate. The doctor, it appeared, now more than ever confined himself to the cabinet over the laboratory, where he would sometimes even sleep; he was out of spirits, he had grown very silent, he did not read; it seemed as if he had something on his mind. Utterson became so used to the unvarying character of these reports, that he fell off little by little in the frequency of his visits.

INCIDENT AT THE WINDOW

It chanced on Sunday, when Mr. Utterson was on his usual walk with Mr. Enfield, that their way lay once again through the by-street; and that when they came in front of the door, both stopped to gaze on it.

"Well," said Enfield, "that story's at an end at least. We shall never see more of Mr. Hyde."

"I hope not," said Utterson. "Did I ever tell you that I once saw him, and shared your feeling of repulsion?"

"It was impossible to do the one without the other," returned Enfield. "And by the way, what an ass you must have thought me, not to know that this was a back way to Dr. Jekyll's! It was partly your own fault that I found it out, even when I did."

"So you found it out, did you?" said Utterson. "But if that be so, we may step into the court and take a look at the windows. To tell you the truth, I am uneasy about poor Jekyll; and even outside, I feel as if the presence of a friend might do him good."

The court was very cool and a little damp, and full of premature twilight, although the sky, high up overhead, was still bright with sunset. The middle one of the three windows was half-way open; and sitting close beside it, taking the air with an infinite sadness of mien, like some disconsolate prisoner, Utterson saw Dr. Jekyll.

"What! Jekyll!" he cried. "I trust you are better."

"I am very low, Utterson," replied the doctor drearily, "very low. It will not last long, thank God."

"You stay too much indoors," said the lawyer. "You should be out, whipping up the circulation like Mr. Enfield and me. (This is my cousin—Mr. Enfield—Dr. Jekyll.) Come now; get your hat and take a quick turn with us."

"You are very good," sighed the other. "I should like to very much; but no, no, no, it is quite impossible; I dare not. But indeed, Utterson, I am very glad to see you; this is really a great pleasure; I would ask you and Mr. Enfield up, but the place is really not fit."

"Why then," said the lawyer good-naturedly, "the best thing we can do is to stay down here and speak with you from where we are."

"That is just what I was about to venture to propose," returned the doctor, with a smile. But the words were hardly uttered, before the smile was struck out of his face and succeeded by an expression of such abject terror and despair as froze the very blood of the two gentlemen below. They saw it but for a glimpse, for the window was instantly thrust down; but that glimpse had been sufficient, and they turned and left the court without a word. In silence, too, they traversed the by-street; and it was not until they had come into a neighbouring thoroughfare, where even upon a Sunday there were still some stirrings of life, that Mr. Utterson at last turned and looked at his companion. They were both pale; and there was an answering horror in their eyes.

"God forgive us, God forgive us!" said Mr. Utterson.

But Mr. Enfield only nodded his head very seriously, and walked on once more in silence.

THE LAST NIGHT

Mr. Utterson was sitting by his fireside one evening after dinner, when he was surprised to receive a visit from Poole.

"Bless me, Poole, what brings you here?" he cried; and then, taking a second look at him, "What ails you?" he added, "is the doctor ill?"

"Mr. Utterson," said the man, "there is something wrong."

"Take a seat, and here is a glass of wine for you," said the lawyer. "Now, take your time, and tell me plainly what you want."

"You know the doctor's ways, sir," replied Poole, "and how he shuts himself up. Well, he's shut up again in the cabinet; and I don't like it, sir—I wish I may die if I like it. Mr. Utterson, sir, I'm afraid."

"Now, my good man," said the lawyer, "be explicit. What are you afraid of?"

"I've been afraid for about a week," returned Poole, doggedly disregarding the question, "and I can bear it no more."

The man's appearance amply bore out his words; his manner was altered for the worse; and except for the moment when he had first announced his terror, he had not once looked the lawyer in the face. Even now, he sat with the glass of wine untasted on his knee, and his eyes directed to a corner of the floor. "I can bear it no more," he repeated.

"Come," said the lawyer, "I see you have some good reason, Poole; I see there is something seriously amiss. Try to tell me what it is."

"I think there's been foul play," said Poole hoarsely.

"Foul play!" cried the lawyer, a good deal frightened, and rather inclined to be irritated in consequence. "What foul play? What does the man mean?"

"I daren't say, sir," was the answer; "but will you come along with me and see for yourself?"

Mr. Utterson's only answer was to rise and get his hat and great-coat; but he observed with wonder the greatness of the relief that appeared upon the butler's face, and perhaps with no less, that the wine was still untasted when he set it down to follow.

It was a wild, cold, seasonable night of March, with a pale moon, lying on her back as though the wind had tilted her, and a flying wrack of the most diaphanous and lawny texture. The wind made talking difficult, and flecked the blood into the face. It seemed to have swept the streets unusually bare of passengers, besides; for Mr. Utterson thought he had never seen that part of London so deserted. He could have wished it otherwise; never in his life had he been conscious of so sharp a wish to see and touch his fellow-creatures; for, struggle as he might, there was borne in upon his mind a crushing anticipation of calamity. The square, when they got there, was all full of wind and dust, and the thin trees in the garden were lashing themselves along the railing. Poole, who had kept all the way a pace or two ahead, now pulled up in the middle of the pavement, and, in spite of the biting weather, took off his hat and mopped his brow with a red pocket-handkerchief. But for all the hurry of his coming, these were not the dews of exertion that he wiped away, but the moisture of some strangling anguish; for his face was white, and his voice, when he spoke, harsh and broken.

"Well, sir," he said, "here we are, and God grant there be nothing wrong."

"Amen, Poole," said the lawyer.

Thereupon the servant knocked in a very guarded manner; the door was opened on the chain; and a voice asked from within, "Is that you, Poole?"

"It's all right," said Poole. "Open the door."

The hall, when they entered it, was brightly lighted up; the fire was built high; and about the hearth the whole of the servants, men and women, stood huddled together like a flock of sheep. At the sight of Mr. Utterson, the housemaid broke into hysterical whimpering; and the cook, crying out "Bless God! it's Mr. Utterson," ran forward as if to take him in her arms.

"What, what? Are you all here?" said the lawyer peevishly. "Very irregular, very unseemly; your master would be far from pleased."

"They're all afraid," said Poole.

Blank silence followed, no one protesting; only the maid lifted up her voice and now wept loudly.

"Hold your tongue!" Poole said to her, with a ferocity of accent that testified to his own jangled nerves; and indeed, when the girl had so suddenly raised the note of her lamentation, they had all started and turned towards the inner door with faces of dreadful expectation. "And now," continued the butler, addressing the knife-boy, "reach me a candle, and we'll get this through hands at once." And then he begged Mr. Utterson to follow him, and led the way to the back garden.

"Now, sir," said he, "you come as gently as you can. I want you to hear, and I don't want you to be heard. And see here, sir, if by any chance he was to ask you in, don't go."

Mr. Utterson's nerves, at this unlooked-for termination, gave a jerk that nearly threw him from his balance; but he recollected his courage and followed the butler into the laboratory building and through the surgical theatre, with its lumber of crates and bottles, to the foot of the stair. Here Poole motioned him to stand on one side and listen; while he himself, setting down the candle and making a great and obvious call on his resolution, mounted the steps and knocked with a somewhat uncertain hand on the red baize of the cabinet door.

"Mr. Utterson, sir, asking to see you," he called; and, even as he did so, once more violently signed to the lawyer to give ear.

A voice answered from within: "Tell him I cannot see any one," it said complainingly.

"Thank you, sir," said Poole, with a note of something like triumph in his voice; and taking up his candle, he led Mr. Utterson back across the yard and into the great kitchen, where the fire was out and the beetles were leaping on the floor.

"Sir," he said, looking Mr. Utterson in the eyes, "was that my master's voice?"

"It seems much changed," replied the lawyer, very pale, but giving look for look.

"Changed? Well, yes, I think so," said the butler. "Have I been twenty years in this man's house, to be deceived about his voice? No, sir; master's made away with; he was made away with eight days ago, when we heard him cry out upon the name of God; and *who's* in there instead of him, and *why* it stays there, is a thing that cries to Heaven, Mr. Utterson!"

"This is a very strange tale, Poole; this is rather a wild tale, my man," said Mr. Utterson, biting his finger. "Suppose it were as you suppose, supposing Dr. Jekyll to have been—well, murder-ed, what could induce the murderer to stay? That won't hold water; it doesn't commend itself to reason."

"Well, Mr. Utterson, you are a hard man to satisfy, but I'll do it yet," said Poole. "All this last week (you must know) him, or it, or whatever it is that lives in that cabinet, has been crying night and day for some sort of medicine and cannot get it to his mind. It was sometimes his way—the master's, that is—to write his orders on a sheet of paper and throw it on the stair. We've had nothing else this week back; nothing but papers, and a closed door, and the very meals left there to be smuggled in when nobody was looking. Well, sir, every day, ay, and twice and thrice in the same day, there have been orders and complaints, and I have been sent flying to all the wholesale chemists in town. Every time I brought the stuff back, there would be another paper telling me to return it, because it was not pure, and another order to a different firm. This drug is wanted bitter bad, sir, whatever for."

"Have you any of these papers?" asked Mr. Utterson.

Poole felt in his pocket and handed out a crumpled note, which the lawyer, bending nearer to the candle, carefully examined. Its contents ran thus: "Dr Jekyll presents his compli-ments to Messrs. Maw. He assures them that their last sample is impure, and quite useless for his present purpose. In the year 18—, Dr. J. purchased a somewhat large quantity from Messrs. M. He now begs them to search with the most sedulous care, and should any of the same quality be left, to forward it to him at once. Expense is no consideration. The importance of this to Dr. J. can hardly be exaggerated." So far the letter had run composedly enough, but here, with a sudden splutter of the pen, the writer's emotion had broken loose. "For God's sake," he had added, "find me some of the old."

"This is a strange note," said Mr. Utterson; and then sharply, "How do you come to have it open?"

"The man at Maw's was main angry, sir, and he threw it back to me like so much dirt," returned Poole.

"This is unquestionably the doctor's hand, do you know?" resumed the lawyer.

"I thought it looked like it," said the servant rather sulkily; and then, with another voice, "But what matters hand-of-write?" he said. "I've seen him!"

"Seen him?" repeated Mr. Utterson. "Well?"

"That's it!" said Poole. "It was this way. I came suddenly into the theatre from the garden. It seems he had slipped out to look for this drug, or whatever it is; for the cabinet door was open, and there he was at the far end of the room digging among the crates. He looked up when I came in, gave a kind of cry, and whipped upstairs into the cabinet. It was but for one minute that I saw him, but the hair stood up on my head like quills. Sir, if that was my master, why had he a mask upon his face? If it was my master, why did he cry out like a rat, and run from me? I have served him long enough. And then ..." the man paused and passed his hand over his face.

"These are all very strange circumstances," said Mr. Utterson, "but I think I begin to see daylight. Your master, Poole, is plainly seized with one of those maladies that both torture and deform the sufferer; hence, for aught I know, the alteration of his voice; hence the mask and his avoidance of his friends; hence his eagerness to find this drug, by means of which the poor soul retains some hope of ultimate recovery—God grant that he be not deceived! There is my explanation; it is sad enough, Poole, ay, and appalling to consider; but it is plain and natural, hangs well together, and delivers us from all exorbitant alarms."

"Sir," said the butler, turning to a sort of mottled pallor, "that thing was not my master, and there's the truth. My master"—here he looked round him and began to whisper—"is a tall, fine build of a man, and this was more of a dwarf." Utterson attempted to protest. "O sir," cried Poole, "do you think I do not know my master after twenty years? do you think I do not know where his head comes to in the cabinet door, where I saw him every morning of my life? No, sir, that thing in the mask was never Dr. Jekyll—God knows what it was, but it was never Dr. Jekyll; and it is the belief of my heart that there was murder done."

"Poole," replied the lawyer, "if you say that, it will become my duty to make certain. Much as I desire to spare your master's feelings, much as I am puzzled by this note which seems to prove him to be still alive, I shall consider it my duty to break in that door."

"Ah, Mr. Utterson, that's talking!" cried the butler.

"And now comes the second question," resumed Utterson: "Who is going to do it?"

"Why, you and me, sir," was the undaunted reply.

"That is very well said," returned the lawyer; "and whatever comes of it, I shall make it my business to see you are no loser."

"There is an axe in the theatre," continued Poole; "and you might take the kitchen poker for yourself."

The lawyer took that rude but weighty instrument into his hand, and balanced it. "Do you know, Poole," he said, looking up, "that you and I are about to place ourselves in a position of some peril?"

"You may say so, sir, indeed," returned the butler.

"It is well, then, that we should be frank," said the other. "We both think more than we have said; let us make a clean breast. This masked figure that you saw, did you recognise it?"

"Well, sir, it went so quick, and the creature was so doubled up, that I could hardly swear to that," was the answer. "But if you mean, was it Mr. Hyde?—why, yes, I think it was! You see, it was much of the same bigness; and it had the same quick light way with it; and then who else could have got in by the laboratory door? You have not forgot, sir, that at the time of the murder he had still the key with him? But that's not all. I don't know, Mr. Utterson, if ever you met this Mr. Hyde?"

"Yes," said the lawyer, "I once spoke with him."

"Then you must know as well as the rest of us that there was something queer about that gentleman—something that gave a man a turn—I don't know rightly how to say it, sir, beyond this: that you felt it in your marrow kind of cold and thin."

"I own I felt something of what you describe," said Mr. Utterson.

"Quite so, sir," returned Poole. "Well, when that masked thing like a monkey jumped from among the chemicals and whipped into the cabinet, it went down my spine like ice. Oh, I know it's not evidence, Mr. Utterson; I'm book-learned enough for that; but a man has his feelings, and I give you my Bible-word it was Mr. Hyde!"

"Ay, ay," said the lawyer. "My fears incline to the same point. Evil, I fear, founded—evil was sure to come—of that connection. Ay, truly, I believe you; I believe poor Harry is killed; and I believe his murderer (for what purpose, God alone can tell) is still lurking in his victim's room. Well, let our name be vengeance. Call Bradshaw."

The footman came at the summons, very white and nervous.

"Pull yourself together, Bradshaw," said the lawyer. "This suspense, I know, is telling upon all of you; but it is now our intention to make an end of it. Poole, here, and I are going to force our way into the cabinet. If all is well, my shoulders are broad enough to bear the blame. Meanwhile, lest anything should really be amiss, or any malefactor seek to escape by the back, you and the boy must go round the corner with a pair of good sticks, and take your post at the laboratory door. We give you ten minutes to get to your stations."

As Bradshaw left, the lawyer looked at his watch. "And now,

Poole, let us get to ours," he said; and taking the poker under his arm, he led the way into the yard. The scud had banked over the moon, and it was now quite dark. The wind, which only broke in puffs and draughts into that deep well of building, tossed the light of the candle to and fro about their steps, until they came into the shelter of the theatre, where they sat down silently to wait. London hummed solemnly all around; but nearer at hand, the stillness was only broken by the sound of a footfall moving to and fro along the cabinet floor.

"So it will walk all day, sir," whispered Poole; "ay, and the better part of the night. Only when a new sample comes from the chemist, there's a bit of a break. Ah, it's an ill conscience that's such an enemy to rest! Ah, sir, there's blood foully shed in every step of it! But hark again, a little closer—put your heart in your ears, Mr. Utterson, and tell me, is that the doctor's foot?"

The steps fell lightly and oddly, with a certain swing, for all they went so slowly; it was different indeed from the heavy creaking tread of Henry Jekyll. Utterson sighed. "Is there never anything else?" he asked.

Poole nodded. "Once," he said. "Once I heard it weeping!"

"Weeping? how that?" said the lawyer, conscious of a sudden chill of horror.

"Weeping like a woman or a lost soul," said the butler. "I came away with that upon my heart that I could have wept too."

But now the ten minutes drew to an end. Poole disinterred the axe from under a stack of packing straw; the candle was set upon the nearest table to light them to the attack; and they drew near with bated breath to where that patient foot was still going up and down, up and down, in the quiet of the night.

"Jekyll," cried Utterson, with a loud voice, "I demand to see you." He paused a moment, but there came no reply. "I give you fair warning, our suspicions are aroused, and I must and shall see you," he resumed; "if not by fair means, then by foul—if not of your consent, then by brute force!"

"Utterson," said the voice, "for God's sake have mercy!"

"Ah, that's not Jekyll's voice—it's Hyde's!" cried Utterson. "Down with the door, Poole."

Poole swung the axe over his shoulder; the blow shook the building, and the red baize door leaped against the lock and hinges. A dismal screech, as of mere animal terror, rang from the cabinet. Up went the axe again, and again the panels crashed and the frame bounded; four times the blow fell; but the wood was tough and the fittings were of excellent workmanship; and it was not until the fifth, that the lock burst in sunder and the wreck of the door fell inwards on the carpet.

The besiegers, appalled by their own riot and the stillness that had succeeded, stood back a little and peered in. There lay the cabinet before their eyes in the quiet lamplight, a good fire glowing and chattering on the hearth, the kettle singing its thin strain, a drawer or two open, papers neatly set forth on the business-table, and, nearer the fire, the things laid out for tea: the quietest room, you would have said, and, but for the glazed presses full of chemicals, the most commonplace that night in London.

Right in the midst there lay the body of a man sorely contorted, and still twitching. They drew near on tiptoe, turned it on its back, and beheld the face of Edward Hyde. He was dressed in clothes far too large for him, clothes of the doctor's bigness; the cords of his face still moved with a semblance of life, but life was quite gone; and by the crushed phial in the hand and the strong smell of kernels that hung upon the air, Utterson knew that he was looking on the body of a self-destroyer.

"We have come too late," he said sternly, "whether to save or punish. Hyde is gone to his account; and it only remains for us to find the body of your master."

The far greater proportion of the building was occupied by the theatre, which filled almost the whole ground story and was lighted from above, and by the cabinet, which formed an upper story at one end and looked upon the court. A corridor joined the theatre to the door on the by-street; and with this, the cabinet communicated separately by a second flight of stairs. There were besides a few dark closets and a spacious cellar. All these they now thoroughly examined. Each closet needed but a glance, for all were empty, and all, by the dust that fell from their doors, had stood long unopened. The cellar, indeed, was filled with crazy lumber, mostly dating from the times of the surgeon who was Jekyll's predecessor; but even as they opened the door, they were advertised of the uselessness of further search, by the fall of a perfect mat of cobweb which had for years sealed up the entrance. Nowhere was there any trace of Henry Jekyll, dead or alive.

Poole stamped on the flags of the corridor. "He must be buried here," he said, hearkening to the sound.

"Or he may have fled," said Utterson, and he turned to examine the door in the by-street. It was locked; and lying near by on the flags, they found the key, already stained with rust.

"This does not look like use," observed the lawyer.

"Use!" echoed Poole. "Do you not see, sir, it is broken? much as if a man had stamped on it."

"Ay," continued Utterson, "and the fractures, too, are rusty." The two men looked at each other with a scare. "This is beyond me, Poole," said the lawyer. "Let us go back to the cabinet."

They mounted the stair in silence, and, still with an occasional awe-struck glance at the dead body, proceeded more thoroughly to examine the contents of the cabinet. At one table there were traces of chemical work, various measured heaps of some white salt being laid on glass saucers, as though for an experiment in which the unhappy man had been prevented.

"That is the same drug that I was always bringing him," said Poole; and even as he spoke, the kettle with a startling noise boiled over.

This brought them to the fireside, where the easy-chair was drawn cosily up, and the tea-things stood ready to the sitter's elbow, the very sugar in the cup. There were several books on a shelf; one lay beside the tea-things open, and Utterson was amazed to find it a copy of a pious work, for which Jekyll had several times expressed a great esteem, annotated, in his own hand, with startling blasphemies.

Next, in the course of their review of the chamber, the searchers came to the cheval-glass, into whose depths they looked with an involuntary horror. But it was so turned as to show them nothing but the rosy glow playing on the roof, the fire sparkling in a hundred repetitions along the glazed front of the presses, and their own pale and fearful countenances stooping to look in.

"This glass have seen some strange things, sir," whispered Poole.

"And surely none stranger than itself," echoed the lawyer in the same tones. "For what did Jekyll"—he caught himself up at the word with a start, and then conquering the weakness: "what could Jekyll want with it?" he said.

"You may say that!" said Poole.

Next they turned to the business-table. On the desk, among the neat array of papers, a large envelope was uppermost, and bore, in the doctor's hand, the name of Mr. Utterson. The lawyer unsealed it, and several enclosures fell to the floor. The first was a will, drawn in the same eccentric terms as the one which he had returned six months before, to serve as a testament in case of death and as a deed of gift in case of disappearance; but, in place of the name of Edward Hyde, the lawyer, with indescribable amazement, read the name of Gabriel John Utterson. He looked at Poole, and then back at the paper, and last of all at the dead malefactor stretched upon the carpet.

"My head goes round," he said. "He has been all these days in possession; he had no cause to like me; he must have raged to see himself displaced; and he has not destroyed this document."

He caught up the next paper; it was a brief note in the doctor's hand, and dated at the top. "O Poole!" the lawyer cried, "he was alive and here this day. He cannot have been disposed of in so short a space, he must be still alive, he must have fled! And then, why fled? and how? and in that case, can we venture to declare this suicide? Oh, we must be careful. I foresee that we may yet involve your master in some dire catastrophe."

"Why don't you read it, sir?" asked Poole.

"Because I fear," replied the lawyer solemnly. "God grant I have no cause for it!" and with that he brought the paper to his eyes and read as follows:

"My dear Utterson,—When this shall fall into your hands, I shall have disappeared, under what circumstances I have not the penetration to foresee, but my instinct and all the circumstances of my nameless situation tell me that the end is sure, and must be early. Go then, and first read the narrative which Lanyon warned me he was to place in your hands; and if you care to hear more, turn to the confession of

"Your unworthy and unhappy friend,
"Henry Jekyll."

"There was a third enclosure?" asked Utterson.

"Here, sir," said Poole, and gave into his hands a considerable packet sealed in several places.

The lawyer put it in his pocket. "I would say nothing of this paper. If your master has fled or is dead, we may at least save his credit. It is now ten; I must go home and read these documents in quiet; but I shall be back before midnight, when we shall send for the police."

They went out, locking the door of the theatre behind them; and Utterson, once more leaving the servants gathered about the fire in the hall, trudged back to his office to read the two narratives in which this mystery was now to be explained.

DR. LANYON'S NARRATIVE

On the ninth of January, now four days ago, I received by the evening delivery a registered envelope, addressed in the hand of my colleague and old school-companion, Henry Jekyll. I was a good deal surprised by this; for we were by no means in the habit of correspondence; I had seen the man, dined with him, indeed, the night before; and I could imagine nothing in our intercourse that should justify the formality of registration. The contents increased my wonder; for this is how the letter ran:—

"10th December, 18—

"Dear Lanyon,—You are one of my oldest friends; and although we may have differed at times on scientific questions, I cannot remember, at least on my side, any break in our affection. There was never a day when, if you had said to me, 'Jekyll, my life, my honour, my reason, depend upon you,' I would not have sacrificed my fortune or my left hand to help you. Lanyon, my life, my honour, my reason, are all at your mercy; if you fail me tonight, I am lost. You might suppose, after this preface, that I am going to ask you for something dishonourable to grant. Judge for yourself.

"I want you to postpone all other engagements for tonight—ay, even if you were summoned to the bedside of an emperor; to take a cab, unless your carriage should be actually at the door; and with this letter in your hand for consultation, to drive straight to my house. Poole, my butler, has his orders; you will find him waiting your arrival with a locksmith. The door of my cabinet is then to be forced; and you are to go in alone; to open the glazed press (letter E) on the left hand, breaking the lock if it be shut; and to draw out, with all its contents as they stand, the fourth drawer from the top or (which is the same thing) the third from the bottom. In my extreme distress of mind I have a morbid fear of misdirecting you; but even if I am in error, you may know the right drawer by its contents: some powders, a phial, and a paper book. This drawer I beg of you to carry back with you to Cavendish Square exactly as it stands.

"That is the first part of the service: now for the second. You should be back, if you set out at once on the receipt of this, long before midnight; but I will leave you that amount of margin, not only in the fear of one of those obstacles that can neither be prevented nor foreseen, but because an hour when your servants are in bed is to be preferred for what will then remain to do. At midnight, then, I have to ask you to be alone in your consulting-room, to admit with your own hand into the house a man who will present himself in my name, and to place in his hands the drawer that you will have brought with you from my cabinet. Then you will have played your part and earned my gratitude completely. Five minutes afterwards, if you insist upon an explanation, you will have understood that these arrangements are of capital importance; and that by the neglect of one of them, fantastic as they must appear, you might have charged your conscience with my death or the shipwreck of my reason.

"Confident as I am that you will not trifle with this appeal, my heart sinks and my hand trembles at the bare thought of such a poss-ibility. Think of me at this hour, in a strange place, labouring under a blackness of distress that no fancy can exaggerate, and yet well aware that, if you will but punctually serve me, my troubles will roll away like a story that is told. Serve me, my dear Lanyon, and save

"Your friend,
"H.J.

"P.S. — I had already sealed this up when a fresh terror struck upon my soul. It is possible that the post office may fail me, and this letter not come into your hands until tomorrow morning. In that case, dear Lanyon, do my errand when it shall be most convenient for you in the course of the day; and once more expect my mess-enger at midnight. It may then already be too late; and if that night passes without event, you will know that you have seen the last of Henry Jekyll."

Upon the reading of this letter I made sure my colleague was insane; but till that was proved beyond the possibility of doubt, I felt bound to do as he requested. The less I understood of this farrago, the less I was in a position to judge of its importance; and an appeal so worded could not be set aside without a grave responsibility. I rose accordingly from table, got into a hansom, and drove straight to Jekyll's house. The butler was awaiting my arrival; he had received by the same post as mine a registered letter of instruction, and had sent at once for a locksmith and a carpenter. The tradesmen came while we were yet speaking; and we moved in a body to old Dr. Denman's surgical theatre, from which (as you are doubtless aware) Jekyll's private cabinet is most conveniently entered. The door was very strong, the lock excellent; the carpenter avowed he would have great trouble and have to do much damage, if force were to be used; and the locksmith was near despair. But this last was a handy fellow, and after two hours' work the door stood open. The press marked E was unlocked; and I took out the drawer, had it filled up with straw and tied in a sheet, and returned with it to Cavendish Square.

Here I proceeded to examine its contents. The powders were neatly enough made up, but not with the nicety of the dispensing chemist; so that it was plain they were of Jekyll's private manufacture; and when I opened one of the wrappers, I found what seemed to me a simple, crystalline salt of a white colour. The phial, to which I next turned my attention, might have been about half-full of a blood-red liquor, which was highly pungent to the sense of smell and seemed to me to contain phosphorus and some volatile ether. At the other ingredients I could make no guess. The book was an ordinary version-book, and contained little but a series of dates. These covered a period of many years, but I observed that the entries ceased nearly a year ago, and quite abruptly. Here and there a brief remark was appended to a date, usually no more than a single word: "double" occurring perhaps six times in a total of several hundred entries; and once very early in the list, and followed by several marks of exclamation, "total failure!!!" All this, though it whetted my curiosity, told me little that was definite. Here was a phial of some tincture, a paper of some salt, and a record of a series of experiments that had led (like too many of Jekyll's investigations) to no end of practical usefulness. How could the presence of these articles in my house affect either the honour, the sanity, or the life of my flighty colleague? If his messenger could go to one place, why could he not go to another? And even granting some impediment, why was this gentleman to be received by me in secret? The more I reflected, the more convinced I grew that I was dealing with a case of cerebral disease; and though I dismissed my servants to bed, I loaded an old revolver that I might be found in some posture of self-defence.

Twelve o'clock had scarce rung out over London, ere the knocker sounded very gently on the door. I went myself at the summons, and found a small man crouching against the pillars of the portico.

"Are you come from Dr. Jekyll?" I asked.

He told me "yes" by a constrained gesture; and when I had bidden him enter, he did not obey me without a searching backward glance into the darkness of the square. There was a policeman not far off, advancing with his bull's-eye open; and at the sight I thought my visitor started and made greater haste.

These particulars struck me, I confess, disagreeably; and as I followed him into the bright light of the consulting-room, I kept my hand ready on my weapon. Here, at last, I had a chance of clearly seeing him. I had never set eyes on him before, so much was certain. He was small, as I have said; I was struck besides with the shocking expression of his face, with his remarkable combination of great muscular activity and great apparent debility of constitution, and—last but not least—with the odd, subjective disturbance caused by his neighbourhood. This bore some resemblance to incipient rigor, and was accompanied by a marked sinking of the pulse. At the time, I set it down to some idiosyncratic, personal distaste, and merely wondered at the acuteness of the symptoms; but I have since had reason to believe the cause to lie much deeper in the nature of man, and to turn on some nobler hinge than the principle of hatred.

This person (who had thus, from the first moment of his entrance, struck in me what I can only describe as a disgustful curiosity) was dressed in a fashion that would have made an ordinary person laughable: his clothes, that is to say, although they were of rich and sober fabric, were enormously too large for him in every measurement—the trousers hanging on his legs and rolled up to keep them from the ground, the waist of the coat below his haunches, and the collar sprawling wide upon his shoulders. Strange to relate, this ludicrous accoutrement was far from moving me to laughter. Rather, as there was something abnormal and misbegotten in the very essence of the creature that now faced me—something seizing, surprising, and revolting—this fresh disparity seemed but to fit in with and to reinforce it; so that to my interest in the man's nature and character there was added a curiosity as to his origin, his life, his fortune and status in the world.

These observations, though they have taken so great a space to be set down in, were yet the work of a few seconds. My visitor was, indeed, on fire with sombre excitement.

"Have you got it?" he cried. "Have you got it?" And so lively was his impatience that he even laid his hand upon my arm and sought to shake me.

I put him back, conscious at his touch of a certain icy pang along my blood. "Come sir," said I. "You forget that I have not yet the pleasure of your acquaintance. Be seated, if you please." And I showed him an example, and sat down myself in my customary seat and with as fair an imitation of my ordinary manner to a patient as the lateness of the hour, the nature of my preoccupations, and the horror I had of my visitor, would suffer me to muster.

"I beg your pardon, Dr. Lanyon," he replied civilly enough. "What you say is very well founded; and my impatience has shown its heels to my politeness. I come here at the instance of your colleague, Dr. Henry Jekyll, on a piece of business of some moment; and I understood ..." he paused and put his hand to his throat, and I could see, in spite of his collected manner, that he was wrestling against the approaches of the hysteria—"I understood, a drawer..."

But here I took pity on my visitor's suspense, and some perhaps on my own growing curiosity.

"There it is, sir," said I, pointing to the drawer, where it lay on the floor behind a table and still covered with the sheet.

He sprang to it, and then paused, and laid his hand upon his heart; I could hear his teeth grate with the convulsive action of his jaws; and his face was so ghastly to see that I grew alarmed both for his life and reason.

"Compose yourself," said I.

He turned a dreadful smile to me, and as if with the decision of despair, plucked away the sheet. At sight of the contents he uttered one loud sob of such immense relief that I sat petrified. And the next moment, in a voice that was already fairly well under control, "Have you a graduated glass?" he asked.

I rose from my place with something of an effort and gave him what he asked.

He thanked me with a smiling nod, measured out a few minims of the red tincture and added one of the powders. The mixture, which was at first of a reddish hue, began, in proportion as the crystals melted, to brighten in colour, to effervesce audibly, and to throw off small fumes of vapour. Suddenly and at the same moment, the ebullition ceased and the compound changed to a dark purple, which faded again more slowly to a watery green. My visitor, who had watched these metamorphoses with a keen eye, smiled, set down the glass upon the table, and then turned and looked upon me with an air of scrutiny.

"And now," said he, "to settle what remains. Will you be wise? will you be guided? will you suffer me to take this glass in my hand and to go forth from your house without further parley? or has the greed of curiosity too much command of you? Think before you answer, for it shall be done as you decide. As you decide, you shall be left as you were before, and neither richer nor wiser, unless the sense of service rendered to a man in mortal distress may be counted as a kind of riches of the soul.

Or, if you shall so prefer to choose, a new province of know-ledge and new avenues to fame and power shall be laid open to you, here, in this room, upon the instant; and your sight shall be blasted by a prodigy to stagger the unbelief of Satan."

"Sir," said I, affecting a coolness that I was far from truly poss-essing, "you speak enigmas, and you will perhaps not wonder that I hear you with no very strong impression of belief. But I have gone too far in the way of inexplicable services to pause before I see the end."

"It is well," replied my visitor. "Lanyon, you remember your vows: what follows is under the seal of our profession. And now, you who have so long been bound to the most narrow and material views, you who have denied the virtue of trans-cendental medicine, you who have derided your superiors—behold!"

He put the glass to his lips and drank at one gulp. A cry followed; he reeled, staggered, clutched at the table and held on, staring with injected eyes, gasping with open mouth; and as I looked there came, I thought, a change—he seemed to swell—his face became suddenly black and the features seem-ed to melt and alter—and the next moment I had sprung to my feet and leaped back against the wall, my arm raised to shield me from that prodigy, my mind submerged in terror.

"Oh God!" I screamed, and "O God!" again and again; for there before my eyes—pale and shaken, and half fainting, and groping before him with his hands, like a man restored from death—there stood Henry Jekyll!

What he told me in the next hour I cannot bring my mind to set on paper. I saw what I saw, I heard what I heard, and my soul sickened at it; and yet now when that sight has faded from my eyes, I ask myself if I believe it, and I cannot answer. My life is shaken to its roots; sleep has left me; the deadliest terror sits by me at all hours of the day and night; I feel that my days are numbered, and that I must die; and yet I shall die incredulous. As for the moral turpitude that man unveiled to me, even with tears of penitence, I cannot, even in memory, dwell on it without a start of horror. I will say but one thing, Utterson, and that (if you can bring your mind to credit it) will be more than enough. The creature who crept into my house that night was, on Jekyll's own confession, known by the name of Hyde, and hunted for in every corner of the land as the murderer of Carew.

HASTIE LANYON

HENRY JEKYLL'S FULL STATEMENT
OF THE CASE

I was born in the year 18— to a large fortune, endowed besides with excellent parts, inclined by nature to industry, fond of the respect of the wise and good among my fellow-men, and thus, as might have been supposed, with every guarantee of an honourable and distinguished future. And indeed the worst of my faults was a certain impatient gaiety of disposition such as has made the happiness of many, but such as I found it hard to reconcile with my imperious desire to carry my head high, and wear a more than commonly grave countenance before the public. Hence it came about that I concealed my pleasures; and that when I reached years of reflection, and began to look round me and take stock of my progress and position in the world, I stood already committed to a profound duplicity of life. Many a man would have even blazoned such irregularities as I was guilty of; but from the high views that I had set before me, I regarded and hid them with an almost morbid sense of shame. It was thus rather the exacting nature of my aspirations than any particular degradation in my faults, that made me what I was, and, with even a deeper trench than in the majority of men, severed in me those provinces of good and ill which divide and compound man's dual nature. In this case, I was driven to reflect deeply and inveterately on that hard law of life, which lies at the root of religion and is one of the most plentiful springs of distress. Though so profound a double-dealer, I was in no sense a hypocrite; both sides of me were in dead earnest; I was no more myself when I laid aside restraint and plunged in shame, than when I laboured, in the eye of day, at the furtherance of knowledge or the relief of sorrow and suffering. And it chanced that the direction of my scientific studies, which led wholly towards the mystic and the transcendental, reacted and shed a strong light on this consciousness of the perennial war among my members. With every day, and from both sides of my intelligence, the moral and the intellectual, I thus drew steadily nearer to that truth, by whose partial discovery I have been doomed to such a dreadful shipwreck: that man is not truly one, but truly two. I say two, because the state of my own knowledge does not pass beyond that point. Others will follow, others will outstrip me on the same lines; and I hazard the guess that man will be ultimately known for a mere polity of multifarious, incongruous and independent denizens. I for my part, from the nature of my life, advanced infallibly in one direction, and in one direction only. It was on the moral side, and in my own person, that I learned to recognise the thorough and primitive duality of man; I saw that of the two natures that contended in the field of my consciousness, even if I could rightly be said to be either, it was only because I was radically both; and from an early date, even before the course of my scientific discoveries had begun to suggest the most naked possibility of such a miracle, I had learned to dwell with pleasure, as a beloved day-dream, on the thought of the separation of these elements. If each, I told myself, could but be housed in separate identities, life would be relieved of all that was unbearable; the unjust might go his way, delivered from the aspirations and remorse of his more upright twin; and the just could walk steadfastly and securely on his upward path, doing the good things in which he found his pleasure, and no longer exposed to disgrace and penitence by the hands of this extraneous evil. It was the curse of mankind that these incongruous fagots were thus bound together—that in the agonised womb of consciousness these polar twins should be continuously struggling. How, then, were they dissociated?

I was so far in my reflections when, as I have said, a side-light began to shine upon the subject from the laboratory table. I began to perceive more deeply than it has ever yet been stated, the trembling immateriality, the mist-like transience, of this seemingly so solid body in which we walk attired. Certain agents I found to have the power to shake and to pluck back that fleshy vestment, even as a wind might toss the curtains of a pavilion. For two good reasons, I will not enter deeply into this scientific branch of my confession. First, because I have been made to learn that the doom and burthen of our life is bound for ever on man's shoulders, and when the attempt is made to cast it off, it but returns upon us with more unfamiliar and more awful pressure. Second, because as my narrative will make, alas! too evident, my discoveries were incomplete. Enough, then, that I not only recognised my natural body for the mere aura and effulgence of certain of the powers that made up my spirit, but managed to compound a drug by which these powers should be dethroned from their supremacy, and a second form and countenance substituted, none the less natural to me because they were the expression, and bore the stamp, of lower elements in my soul.

I hesitated long before I put this theory to the test of practice. I knew well that I risked death; for any drug that so potently controlled and shook the very fortress of identity, might by the least scruple of an overdose or at the least inopportunity in the moment of exhibition, utterly blot out that immaterial tabernacle which I looked to it to change. But the temptation of a discovery so singular and profound at last overcame the suggestions of alarm. I had long since prepared my tincture; I purchased at once, from a firm of wholesale chemists, a large quantity of a particular salt which I knew, from my experiments, to be the last ingredient required; and late one accursed night, I compounded the elements, watched them boil and smoke together in the glass, and when the ebullition had subsided, with a strong glow of courage drank off the potion.

The most racking pangs succeeded; a grinding in the bones, deadly nausea, and a horror of the spirit that cannot be exceeded at the hour of birth or death. Then these agonies began swiftly to subside, and I came to myself as if out of a great sickness. There was something strange in my sensations, something indescribably new and, from its very novelty, incredibly sweet. I felt younger, lighter, happier in body; within I was conscious of a heady recklessness, a current of disordered sensual images running like a mill-race in my fancy, a solution of the bonds of obligation, an unknown but not an innocent freedom of the soul. I knew myself, at the first breath of this new life, to be more wicked, tenfold more wicked, sold a slave to my original evil; and the thought, in that moment, braced and delighted me like wine. I stretched out my hands, exulting in the freshness of these sensations; and in the act I was suddenly aware that I had lost in stature.

There was no mirror, at that date, in my room; that which stands beside me as I write was brought there later on, and for the very purpose of these transformations. The night, however, was far gone into the morning—the morning, black as it was, was nearly ripe for the conception of the day—the inmates of my house were locked in the most rigorous hours of slumber; and I determined, flushed as I was with hope and triumph, to venture in my new shape as far as to my bedroom. I crossed the yard, wherein the constellations looked down upon me, I could have thought, with wonder, the first creature of that sort that their unsleeping vigilance had yet disclosed to them; I stole through the corridors, a stranger in my own house; and, coming to my room, I saw for the first time the appearance of Edward Hyde.

I must here speak by theory alone, saying not that which I know, but that which I suppose to be most probable. The evil side of my nature, to which I had now transferred the stamping efficacy, was less robust and less developed than the good which I had just deposed. Again, in the course of my life, which had been, after all, nine-tenths a life of effort, virtue, and control, it had been much less exercised and much less exhausted. And hence, as I think, it came about that Edward Hyde was so much smaller, slighter, and younger than Henry Jekyll. Even as good shone upon the countenance of the one, evil was written broadly and plainly on the face of the other. Evil besides (which I must still believe to be the lethal side of man) had left on that body an imprint of deformity and decay. And yet when I looked upon that ugly idol in the glass, I was conscious of no repugnance, rather of a leap of welcome. This, too, was myself.

It seemed natural and human. In my eyes it bore a livelier image of the spirit, it seemed more express and single, than the imperfect and divided countenance I had been hitherto accustomed to call mine. And in so far I was doubtless right. I have observed that when I bore the semblance of Edward Hyde, none could come near to me at first without a visible misgiving of the flesh. This, as I take it, was because all human beings, as we meet them, are commingled out of good and evil: and Edward Hyde, alone in the ranks of mankind, was pure evil.

I lingered but a moment at the mirror: the second and conclusive experiment had yet to be attempted; it yet remained to be seen if I had lost my identity beyond redemption and must flee before daylight from a house that was no longer mine; and, hurrying back to my cabinet, I once more prepared and drank the cup, once more suffered the pangs of dissolution, and came to myself once more with the character, the stature, and the face of Henry Jekyll.

That night I had come to the fatal cross roads. Had I approached my discovery in a more noble spirit, had I risked the experiment while under the empire of generous or pious aspirations, all must have been otherwise, and from these agonies of death and birth I had come forth an angel instead of a fiend. The drug had no discriminating action; it was neither diabolical nor divine; it but shook the doors of the prison-house of my disposition; and like the captives of Philippi, that which stood within ran forth. At that time my virtue slumbered; my evil, kept awake by ambition, was alert and swift to seize the occasion; and the thing that was projected was Edward Hyde. Hence, although I had now two characters as well as two appearances, one was wholly evil, and the other was still the old Henry Jekyll, that incongruous compound of whose reformation and improvement I had already learned to despair. The movement was thus wholly toward the worse.

Even at that time I had not yet conquered my aversion to the dryness of a life of study. I would still be merrily disposed at times; and as my pleasures were (to say the least) undignified, and I was not only well known and highly considered, but growing towards the elderly man, this incoherency of my life was daily growing more unwelcome. It was on this side that my new power tempted me until I fell in slavery. I had but to drink the cup, to doff at once the body of the noted professor, and to assume, like a thick cloak, that of Edward Hyde. I smiled at the notion; it seemed to me at the time to be humorous; and I made my preparations with the most studious care. I took and furnished that house in Soho, to which Hyde was tracked by the police; and engaged as housekeeper a creature whom I well knew to be silent and unscrupulous. On the other side, I announced to my servants that a Mr. Hyde (whom I described) was to have full liberty and power about my house in the square; and to parry mishaps, I even called and made myself a familiar object, in my second character. I next drew up that will to which you so much objected; so that if anything befell me in the person of Doctor Jekyll, I could enter on that of Edward Hyde without pecuniary loss. And thus fortified, as I supposed, on every side, I began to profit by the strange immunities of my position.

Men have before hired bravos to transact their crimes, while their own person and reputation sat under shelter. I was the first that ever did so for his pleasures. I was the first that could thus plod in the public eye with a load of genial respectability, and in a moment, like a schoolboy, strip off these lendings and spring headlong into the sea of liberty. But for me, in my impenetrable mantle, the safety was complete. Think of it—I did not even exist! Let me but escape into my laboratory-door, give me but a second or two to mix and swallow the draught that I had always standing ready; and whatever he had done, Edward Hyde would pass away like the stain of breath upon a mirror; and there in his stead, quietly at home, trimming the midnight lamp in his study, a man who could afford to laugh at suspicion, would be Henry Jekyll.

The pleasures which I made haste to seek in my disguise were, as I have said, undignified; I would scarce use a harder term. But in the hands of Edward Hyde they soon began to turn towards the monstrous. When I would come back from these excursions, I was often plunged into a kind of wonder at my vicarious depravity. This familiar that I called out of my own soul, and sent forth alone to do his good pleasure, was a being inherently malign and villainous; his every act and thought centred on self; drinking pleasure with bestial avidity from any degree of torture to another; relentless like a man of stone. Henry Jekyll stood at times aghast before the acts of Edward Hyde; but the situation was apart from ordinary laws, and insidiously relaxed the grasp of conscience. It was Hyde, after all, and Hyde alone, that was guilty. Jekyll was no worse; he woke again to his good qualities seemingly unimpaired; he would even make haste, where it was possible, to undo the evil done by Hyde. And thus his conscience slumbered.

Into the details of the infamy at which I thus connived (for even now I can scarce grant that I committed it) I have no design of entering; I mean but to point out the warnings and the successive steps with which my chastisement approached. I met with one accident which, as it brought on no consequence, I shall no more than mention. An act of cruelty to a child aroused against me the anger of a passer-by, whom I recognised the other day in the person of your kinsman; the doctor and the child's family joined him; there were moments when I feared for my life; and at last, in order to pacify their too just resentment, Edward Hyde had to bring them to the door, and pay them in a cheque drawn in the name of Henry Jekyll. But this danger was easily eliminated from the future, by opening an account at another bank in the name of Edward Hyde himself; and when, by sloping my own hand backward, I had supplied my double with a signature, I thought I sat beyond the reach of fate.

Some two months before the murder of Sir Danvers, I had been out for one of my adventures, had returned at a late hour, and woke the next day in bed with somewhat odd sensations. It was in vain I looked about me; in vain I saw the decent furniture and tall proportions of my room in the square; in vain that I recognised the pattern of the bed-curtains and the design of the mahogany frame; something still kept insisting that I was not where I was, that I had not wakened where I seemed to be, but in the little room in Soho where I was accustomed to sleep in the body of Edward Hyde. I smiled to myself, and, in my psychological way, began lazily to inquire into the elements of this illusion, occasionally, even as I did so, dropping back into a comfortable morning doze. I was still so engaged when, in one of my more wakeful moments, my eye fell upon my hand. Now the hand of Henry Jekyll (as you have often remarked) was professional in shape and size: it was large, firm, white, and comely. But the hand which I now saw, clearly enough, in the yellow light of a mid-London morning, lying half shut on the bed-clothes, was lean, corded, knuckly, of a dusky pallor, and thickly shaded with a swart growth of hair. It was the hand of Edward Hyde.

I must have stared upon it for near half a minute, sunk as I was in the mere stupidity of wonder, before terror woke up in my breast as sudden and startling as the crash of cymbals; and bounding from my bed, I rushed to the mirror. At the sight that met my eyes my blood was changed into something exquis-itely thin and icy. Yes, I had gone to bed Henry Jekyll, I had awakened Edward Hyde. How was this to be explained? I asked myself; and then, with another bound of terror—how was it to be remedied? It was well on in the morning; the servants were up; all my drugs were in the cabinet—a long journey, down two pairs of stairs, through the back passage, across the open court and through the anatomical theatre, from where I was then standing horror-struck. It might indeed be possible to cover my face; but of what use was that, when I was unable to con-ceal the alteration in my stature? And then, with an overpower-ing sweetness of relief, it came back upon my mind that the servants were already used to the coming and going of my second self. I had soon dressed, as well as I was able, in clothes of my own size: had soon passed through the house, where

Bradshaw stared and drew back at seeing Mr. Hyde at such an hour and in such a strange array; and ten minutes later Dr. Jekyll had returned to his own shape, and was sitting down, with a darkened brow, to make a feint of breakfasting.

Small indeed was my appetite. This inexplicable incident, this reversal of my previous experience, seemed, like the Babylonian finger on the wall, to be spelling out the letters of my judgment; and I began to reflect more seriously than ever before on the issues and possibilities of my double existence. That part of me which I had the power of projecting had lately been much exercised and nourished; it had seemed to me of late as though the body of Edward Hyde had grown in stature, as though (when I wore that form) I were conscious of a more generous tide of blood; and I began to spy a danger that, if this were much prolonged, the balance of my nature might be permanently overthrown, the power of voluntary change be forfeited, and the character of Edward Hyde become irrevocably mine. The power of the drug had not been always equally displayed. Once, very early in my career, it had totally failed me; since then I had been obliged on more than one occasion to double, and once, with infinite risk of death, to treble the amount; and these rare uncertainties had cast hitherto the sole shadow on my contentment. Now, however, and in the light of that morning's accident, I was led to remark that whereas, in the beginning, the difficulty had been to throw off the body of Jekyll, it had of late gradually but decidedly transferred itself to the other side. All things therefore seemed to point to this: that I was slowly losing hold of my original and better self, and becoming slowly incorporated with my second and worse.

Between these two, I now felt I had to choose. My two natures had memory in common, but all other faculties were most unequally shared between them. Jekyll (who was composite) now with the most sensitive apprehensions, now with a greedy gusto, projected and shared in the pleasures and adventures of Hyde; but Hyde was indifferent to Jekyll, or but remembered him as the mountain bandit remembers the cavern in which he conceals himself from pursuit. Jekyll had more than a father's interest; Hyde had more than a son's indifference. To cast in my lot with Jekyll was to die to those appetites which I had long secretly indulged, and had of late begun to pamper. To cast it in with Hyde was to die to a thousand interests and aspirations, and to become, at a blow and for ever, despised and friendless. The bargain might appear unequal; but there was still another consideration in the scales; for while Jekyll would suffer smartingly in the fires of abstinence, Hyde would be not even conscious of all that he had lost. Strange as my circumstances were, the terms of this debate are as old and commonplace as man; much the same inducements and alarms cast the die for any tempted and trembling sinner; and it fell out with me, as it falls with so vast a majority of my fellows, that I chose the better part, and was found wanting in the strength to keep to it.

Yes, I preferred the elderly and discontented doctor, surrounded by friends and cherishing honest hopes; and bade a resolute farewell to the liberty, the comparative youth, the light step, leaping pulses, and secret pleasures, that I had enjoyed in the disguise of Hyde. I made this choice perhaps with some unconscious reservation, for I neither gave up the house in Soho, nor destroyed the clothes of Edward Hyde, which still lay ready in my cabinet. For two months, however, I was true to my determination; for two months I led a life of such severity as I had never before attained to, and enjoyed the compensations of an approving conscience. But time began at last to obliterate the freshness of my alarm; the praises of conscience began to grow into a thing of course; I began to be tortured with throes and longings, as of Hyde struggling after freedom; and at last, in an hour of moral weakness, I once again compounded and swallowed the transforming draught.

I do not suppose that, when a drunkard reasons with himself upon his vice, he is once out of five hundred times affected by the dangers that he runs through his brutish, physical insensibility; neither had I, long as I had considered my position, made enough allowance for the complete moral insensibility and insensate readiness to evil, which were the leading characters of Edward Hyde. Yet it was by these that I was punished. My devil had been long caged, he came out roaring. I was conscious, even when I took the draught, of a more unbridled, a more furious propensity to ill. It must have been this, I suppose, that stirred in my soul that tempest of impatience with which I listened to the civilities of my unhappy victim; I declare at least, before God, no man morally sane could have been guilty of that crime upon so pitiful a provocation; and that I struck in no more reasonable spirit than that in which a sick child may break a plaything. But I had voluntarily stripped myself of all those balancing instincts, by which even the worst of us continues to walk with some degree of steadiness among temptations; and in my case, to be tempted, however slightly, was to fall.

Instantly the spirit of hell awoke in me and raged. With a transport of glee I mauled the unresisting body, tasting delight from every blow; and it was not till weariness had begun to succeed, that I was suddenly, in the top fit of my delirium, struck through the heart by a cold thrill of terror. A mist dispersed; I saw my life to be forfeit; and fled from the scene of these excesses, at once glorying and trembling, my lust of evil gratified and stimulated, my love of life screwed to the topmost peg. I ran to the house in Soho, and (to make assurance doubly sure) destroyed my papers; thence I set out through the lamplit streets, in the same divided ecstasy of mind, gloating on my crime, light-headedly devising others in the future, and yet still hastening and still hearkening in my wake for the steps of the avenger. Hyde had a song upon his lips as he compounded the draught, and as he drank it, pledged the dead man. The pangs of transformation had not done tearing him, before Henry Jekyll, with streaming tears of gratitude and remorse, had fallen upon his knees and lifted his clasped hands to God. The veil of self-indulgence was rent from head to foot, I saw my life as a whole: I followed it up from the days of childhood, when I

had walked with my father's hand, and through the self-deny-
ing toils of my professional life, to arrive again and again, with
the same sense of unreality, at the damned horrors of the evening. I could have screamed aloud; I sought with tears and
prayers to smother down the crowd of hideous images and
sounds with which my memory swarmed against me; and still,
between the petitions, the ugly face of my iniquity stared into
my soul. As the acuteness of this remorse began to die away, it
was succeeded by a sense of joy. The problem of my conduct
was solved. Hyde was thenceforth impossible; whether I
would or not, I was now confined to the better part of my existence; and oh how I rejoiced to think it! with what willing
humility I embraced anew the restrictions of natural life! with
what sincere renunciation I locked the door by which I had so
often gone and come, and ground the key under my heel!

The next day came the news that the murder had been overlooked, that the guilt of Hyde was patent to the world, and that
the victim was a man high in public estimation. It was not only
a crime, it had been a tragic folly. I think I was glad to know it;
I think I was glad to have my better impulses thus buttressed
and guarded by the terrors of the scaffold. Jekyll was now my
city of refuge; let but Hyde peep out an instant, and the hands
of all men would be raised to take and slay him.

I resolved in my future conduct to redeem the past; and I can
say with honesty that my resolve was fruitful of some good.
You know yourself how earnestly in the last months of last
year, I laboured to relieve suffering; you know that much was
done for others, and that the days passed quietly, almost happily for myself. Nor can I truly say that I wearied of this benefi-
cent and innocent life; I think instead that I daily enjoyed it
more completely; but I was still cursed with my duality of purpose; and as the first edge of my penitence wore off, the lower
side of me, so long indulged, so recently chained down, began
to growl for licence. Not that I dreamed of resuscitating Hyde;
the base idea of that would startle me to frenzy: no, it was in my
own person that I was once more tempted to trifle with my

conscience; and it was as an ordinary secret sinner that I at last fell before the assaults of temptation.

There comes an end to all things; the most capacious measure is filled at last; and this brief condescension to evil finally destroyed the balance of my soul. And yet I was not alarmed; the fall seemed natural, like a return to the old days before I had made my discovery. It was a fine, clear, January day, wet under foot where the frost had melted, but cloudless overhead; and the Regent's Park was full of winter chirrupings and sweet with spring odours. I sat in the sun on a bench; the animal within me licking the chops of memory; the spiritual side a little drowsed, promising subsequent penitence, but not yet moved to begin. After all, I reflected, I was like my neighbours; and then I smiled, comparing myself with other men, comparing my active goodwill with the lazy cruelty of their neglect. And at the very moment of that vainglorious thought a qualm came over me, a horrid nausea and the most deadly shuddering. These passed away, and left me faint; and then, as in its turn the faintness subsided, I began to be aware of a change in the temper of my thoughts, a greater boldness, a contempt of danger, a solution of the bonds of obligation. I looked down; my clothes hung formlessly on my shrunken limbs; the hand that lay on my knee was corded and hairy. I was once more Edward Hyde. A moment before I had been safe of all men's respect, wealthy, beloved—the cloth laying for me in the dining-room at home; and now I was the common quarry of mankind, hunted, houseless, a known murderer, thrall to the gallows.

My reason wavered, but it did not fail me utterly. I have more than once observed that, in my second character, my faculties seemed sharpened to a point and my spirits more tensely elastic; thus it came about that, where Jekyll perhaps might have succumbed, Hyde rose to the importance of the moment. My drugs were in one of the presses of my cabinet; how was I to reach them? That was the problem that (crushing my temples in my hands) I set myself to solve. The laboratory door

I had closed. If I sought to enter by the house, my own servants would consign me to the gallows. I saw I must employ another hand, and thought of Lanyon. How was he to be reached? how persuaded? Supposing that I escaped capture in the streets, how was I to make my way into his presence? and how should I, an unknown and displeasing visitor, prevail on the famous physician to rifle the study of his colleague, Dr. Jekyll? Then I remembered that of my original character, one part remained to me: I could write my own hand; and once I had conceived that kindling spark, the way that I must follow became lighted up from end to end.

Thereupon I arranged my clothes as best I could, and summoning a passing hansom, drove to a hotel in Portland Street, the name of which I chanced to remember. At my appearance (which was indeed comical enough, however tragic a fate these garments covered) the driver could not conceal his mirth. I gnashed my teeth upon him with a gust of devilish fury; and the smile withered from his face—happily for him—yet more happily for myself, for in another instant I had certainly dragged him from his perch. At the inn, as I entered, I looked about me with so black a countenance as made the attendants tremble; not a look did they exchange in my presence; but obsequiously took my orders, led me to a private room, and brought me wherewithal to write. Hyde in danger of his life was a creature new to me: shaken with inordinate anger, strung to the pitch of murder, lusting to inflict pain. Yet the creature was astute; mastered his fury with a great effort of the will; composed his two important letters, one to Lanyon and one to Poole; and that he might receive actual evidence of their being posted, sent them out with directions that they should be registered.

Thenceforward, he sat all day over the fire in the private room, gnawing his nails; there he dined, sitting alone with his fears, the waiter visibly quailing before his eye; and then, when the night was fully come, he set forth in the corner of a closed cab, and was driven to and fro about the streets of the city. He,

I say—I cannot say, I. That child of Hell had nothing human; nothing lived in him but fear and hatred. And when at last, thinking the driver had begun to grow suspicious, he discharged the cab and ventured on foot, attired in his misfitting clothes, an object marked out for observation, into the midst of the nocturnal passengers, these two base passions raged within him like a tempest. He walked fast, hunted by his fears, chattering to himself, skulking through the less frequented thoroughfares, counting the minutes that still divided him from midnight. Once a woman spoke to him, offering, I think, a box of lights. He smote her in the face, and she fled.

When I came to myself at Lanyon's, the horror of my old friend perhaps affected me somewhat: I do not know; it was at least but a drop in the sea to the abhorrence with which I looked back upon these hours. A change had come over me. It was no longer the fear of the gallows, it was the horror of being Hyde that racked me. I received Lanyon's condemnation partly in a dream; it was partly in a dream that I came home to my own house and got into bed. I slept after the prostration of the day, with a stringent and profound slumber which not even the nightmares that wrung me could avail to break. I awoke in the morning shaken, weakened, but refreshed. I still hated and feared the thought of the brute that slept within me, and I had not, of course, forgotten the appalling dangers of the day before; but I was once more at home, in my own house and close to my drugs; and gratitude for my escape shone so strong in my soul that it almost rivalled the brightness of hope.

I was stepping leisurely across the court after breakfast, drinking the chill of the air with pleasure, when I was seized again with those indescribable sensations that heralded the change; and I had but the time to gain the shelter of my cabinet, before I was once again raging and freezing with the passions of Hyde. It took on this occasion a double dose to recall me to myself; and alas! six hours after, as I sat looking sadly in the fire, the pangs returned, and the drug had to be re-administered. In short, from that day forth it seemed only by a great effort as of gymnastics, and only under the immediate stimulation of the drug, that I was able to wear the countenance of Jekyll. At all hours of the day and night I would be taken with the premonitory shudder; above all, if I slept, or even dozed for a moment in my chair, it was always as Hyde that I awakened. Under the strain of this continually impending doom and by the sleeplessness to which I now condemned myself, ay, even beyond what I had thought possible to man, I became, in my own person, a creature eaten up and emptied by fever, languidly weak both in body and mind, and solely occupied by one thought: the horror of my other self. But when I slept, or when the virtue of the medicine wore off, I would leap almost without transition (for the pangs of transformation grew daily less marked) into the possession of a fancy brimming with images of terror, a soul boiling with causeless hatreds, and a body that seemed not strong enough to contain the raging energies of life. The powers of Hyde seemed to have grown with the sickliness of Jekyll. And certainly the hate that now divided them was equal on each side. With Jekyll, it was a thing of vital instinct. He had now seen the full deformity of that creature that shared with him some of the phenomena of consciousness, and was co-heir with him to death: and beyond these links of community, which in themselves made the most poignant part of his distress, he thought of Hyde, for all his energy of life, as of something not only hellish but inorganic. This was the shocking thing; that the slime of the pit seemed to utter cries and voices; that the amorphous dust gesticulated and sinned; that what was dead, and had no shape, should usurp the offices of life. And this again, that that insurgent horror was knit to him closer than a wife, closer than an eye; lay caged in his flesh, where he heard it mutter and felt it struggle to be born; and at every hour of weakness, and in the confidence of slumber, prevailed against him, and deposed him out of life. The hatred of Hyde for Jekyll was of a different order. His terror of the gallows drove him continually to commit temporary suicide, and return to his subordinate

station of a part instead of a person; but he loathed the
necessity, he loathed the despondency into which Jekyll was
now fallen, and he resented the dislike with which he was himself regarded. Hence the ape-like tricks that he would play me,
scrawling in my own hand blasphemies on the pages of my
books, burning the letters and destroying the portrait of my
father; and indeed, had it not been for his fear of death, he
would long ago have ruined himself in order to involve me in
the ruin. But his love of life is wonderful; I go further: I, who
sicken and freeze at the mere thought of him, when I recall the
abjection and passion of this attachment, and when I know
how he fears my power to cut him off by suicide, I find it in my
heart to pity him.

It is useless, and the time awfully fails me, to prolong this
description; no one has ever suffered such torments, let that
suffice; and yet even to these, habit brought—no, not allevia-
tion—but a certain callousness of soul, a certain acquiescence
of despair; and my punishment might have gone on for years,
but for the last calamity which has now fallen, and which has
finally severed me from my own face and nature. My provision
of the salt, which had never been renewed since the date of the
first experiment, began to run low. I sent out for a fresh supply,
and mixed the draught; the ebullition followed, and the first
change of colour, not the second; I drank it and it was without
efficiency. You will learn from Poole how I have had London
ransacked; it was in vain; and I am now persuaded that my first
supply was impure, and that it was that unknown impurity
which lent efficacy to the draught.

About a week has passed, and I am now finishing this statement under the influence of the last of the old powders. This,
then, is the last time, short of a miracle, that Henry Jekyll can
think his own thoughts or see his own face (now how sadly
altered!) in the glass. Nor must I delay too long to bring my
writing to an end; for if my narrative has hitherto escaped
destruction, it has been by a combination of great prudence
and great good luck. Should the throes of change take me in

the act of writing it, Hyde will tear it in pieces; but if some time shall have elapsed after I have laid it by, his wonderful selfishness and circumscription to the moment will probably save it once again from the action of his ape-like spite. And indeed the doom that is closing on us both has already changed and crushed him. Half an hour from now, when I shall again and for ever re-indue that hated personality, I know how I shall sit shuddering and weeping in my chair, or continue, with the most strained and fearstruck ecstasy of listening, to pace up and down this room (my last earthly refuge) and give ear to every sound of menace. Will Hyde die upon the scaffold? or will he find the courage to release himself at the last moment? God knows; I am careless; this is my true hour of death, and what is to follow concerns another than myself. Here then, as I lay down the pen and proceed to seal up my confession, I bring the life of that unhappy Henry Jekyll to an end.

THE BODY-SNATCHER

THE BODY-SNATCHER

Every night in the year, four of us sat in the small parlour of the George at Debenham—the undertaker, and the landlord, and Fettes, and myself. Sometimes there would be more; but blow high, blow low, come rain or snow or frost, we four would be each planted in his own particular armchair. Fettes was an old drunken Scotchman, a man of education obviously, and a man of some property, since he lived in idleness. He had come to Debenham years ago, while still young, and by a mere continuance of living had grown to be an adopted townsman. His blue camlet cloak was a local antiquity, like the church spire. His place in the parlour at the George, his absence from church, his old, crapulous, disreputable vices, were all things of course in Debenham. He had some vague Radical opinions and some fleeting infidelities, which he would now and again set forth and emphasise with tottering slaps upon the table. He drank rum—five glasses regularly every evening; and for the greater portion of his nightly visit to the George sat, with his glass in his right hand, in a state of melancholy alcoholic saturation. We called him the Doctor, for he was supposed to have some special knowledge of medicine, and had been known, upon a pinch, to set a fracture or reduce a dislocation; but beyond these slight particulars, we had no knowledge of his character and antecedents.

One dark winter night—it had struck nine some time before the landlord joined us—there was a sick man in the George, a great neighbouring proprietor suddenly struck down with apoplexy on his way to Parliament; and the great man's still greater London doctor had been telegraphed to his bedside. It was the first time that such a thing had happened in Debenham, for the railway was but newly open, and we were all proportionately moved by the occurrence.

"He's come," said the landlord, after he had filled and lighted his pipe.

"He?" said I. "Who?—not the doctor?"

"Himself," replied our host.

"What is his name?"

"Doctor Macfarlane," said the landlord.

Fettes was far through his third tumbler, stupidly fuddled, now nodding over, now staring mazily around him; but at the last word he seemed to awaken, and repeated the name "Macfarlane" twice, quietly enough the first time, but with sudden emotion at the second.

"Yes," said the landlord, "that's his name, Doctor Wolfe Macfarlane."

Fettes became instantly sober; his eyes awoke, his voice became clear, loud, and steady, his language forcible and earnest. We were all startled by the transformation, as if a man had risen from the dead.

"I beg your pardon," he said, "I am afraid I have not been paying much attention to your talk. Who is this Wolfe Macfarlane?" And then, when he had heard the landlord out, "It cannot be, it cannot be," he added; "and yet I would like well to see him face to face."

"Do you know him, Doctor?" asked the undertaker, with a gasp.

"God forbid!" was the reply. "And yet the name is a strange one; it were too much to fancy two. Tell me, landlord, is he old?"

"Well," said the host, "he's not a young man, to be sure, and his hair is white; but he looks younger than you."

"He is older, though; years older. But," with a slap upon the table, "it's the rum you see in my face—rum and sin. This man, perhaps, may have an easy conscience and a good digestion. Conscience! Hear me speak. You would think I was some good, old, decent Christian, would you not? But no, not I; I never canted. Voltaire might have canted if he'd stood in my shoes; but the brains"—with a rattling fillip on his bald head—"the brains were clear and active, and I saw and made no deductions."

"If you know this doctor," I ventured to remark, after a

somewhat awful pause, "I should gather that you do not share the landlord's good opinion."

Fettes paid no regard to me.

"Yes," he said, with sudden decision, "I must see him face to face."

There was another pause, and then a door was closed rather sharply on the first floor, and a step was heard upon the stair.

"That's the doctor," cried the landlord. "Look sharp, and you can catch him."

It was but two steps from the small parlour to the door of the Old George Inn; the wide oak staircase landed almost in the street; there was room for a Turkey rug and nothing more between the threshold and the last round of the descent; but this little space was every evening brilliantly lit up, not only by the light upon the stair and the great signal lamp below the sign, but by the warm radiance of the bar-room window. The George thus brightly advertised itself to passers-by in the cold street. Fettes walked steadily to the spot, and we, who were hanging behind, beheld the two men meet, as one of them had phrased it, face to face. Dr. Macfarlane was alert and vigorous. His white hair set off his pale and placid, although energetic, countenance. He was richly dressed in the finest of broadcloth and the whitest of linen, with a great gold watch-chain, and studs and spectacles of the same precious material. He wore a broad-folded tie, white and speckled with lilac, and he carried on his arm a comfortable driving-coat of fur. There was no doubt but he became his years, breathing, as he did, of wealth and consideration; and it was a surprising contrast to see our parlour sot—bald, dirty, pimpled, and robed in his old camlet cloak—confront him at the bottom of the stairs.

"Macfarlane!" he said somewhat loudly, more like a herald than a friend.

The great doctor pulled up short on the fourth step, as though the familiarity of the address surprised and somewhat shocked his dignity.

"Toddy Macfarlane!" repeated Fettes.

The London man almost staggered. He stared for the swiftest of seconds at the man before him, glanced behind him with a sort of scare, and then in a startled whisper, "Fettes!" he said, "you!"

"Aye," said the other, "me! Did you think I was dead too? We are not so easy shut of our acquaintance."

"Hush, hush!" exclaimed the doctor. "Hush, hush! this meeting is so unexpected—I can see you are unmanned. I hardly knew you, I confess, at first; but I am overjoyed—overjoyed to have this opportunity. For the present it must be how-d'ye-do and good-bye in one, for my fly is waiting, and I must not fail the train; but you shall—let me see—yes—you shall give me your address, and you can count on early news of me. We must do something for you, Fettes. I fear you are out at elbows; but we must see to that for auld lang syne, as once we sang at suppers."

"Money!" cried Fettes; "money from you! The money that I had from you is lying where I cast it in the rain."

Dr. Macfarlane had talked himself into some measure of superiority and confidence, but the uncommon energy of this refusal cast him back into his first confusion.

A horrible, ugly look came and went across his almost venerable countenance. "My dear fellow," he said, "be it as you please; my last thought is to offend you. I would intrude on none. I will leave you my address, however—"

"I do not wish it—I do not wish to know the roof that shelters you," interrupted the other. "I heard your name; I feared it might be you; I wished to know if, after all, there were a God; I know now that there is none. Begone!"

He still stood in the middle of the rug, between the stair and doorway; and the great London physician, in order to escape, would be forced to step to one side. It was plain that he hesitated before the thought of this humiliation. White as he was, there was a dangerous glitter in his spectacles; but while he still paused uncertain, he became aware that the driver of his fly was peering in from the street at this unusual scene and caught a glimpse at the same time of our little body from the parlour, huddled by the corner of the bar. The presence of so many witnesses decided him at once to flee. He crouched together, brushing on the wainscot, and made a dart like a serpent, striking for the door. But his tribulation was not entirely at an end, for even as he was passing Fettes clutched him by the arm and these words came in a whisper, and yet painfully distinct, "Have you seen it again?"

The great rich London doctor cried out aloud with a sharp, throttling cry; he dashed his questioner across the open space, and, with his hands over his head, fled out of the door like a detected thief. Before it had occurred to one of us to make a movement the fly was already rattling toward the station. The scene was over like a dream, but the dream had left proofs and traces of its passage. Next day the servant found the fine gold spectacles broken on the threshold, and that very night we were all standing breathless by the bar-room window, and Fettes at our side, sober, pale, and resolute in look.

"God protect us, Mr. Fettes!" said the landlord, coming first into possession of his customary senses. "What in the universe is all this? These are strange things you have been saying."

Fettes turned toward us; he looked us each in succession in the face. "See if you can hold your tongues," said he. "That man Macfarlane is not safe to cross; those that have done so already have repented it too late."

And then, without so much as finishing his third glass, far less waiting for the other two, he bade us good-bye and went forth, under the lamp of the hotel, into the black night.

We three turned to our places in the parlour, with the big red fire and four clear candles; and as we recapitulated what had passed, the first chill of our surprise soon changed into a glow of curiosity. We sat late; it was the latest session I have known in the old George. Each man, before we parted, had his theory that he was bound to prove; and none of us had any nearer business in this world than to track out the past of our condemned companion, and surprise the secret that he shared with the great London doctor. It is no great boast, but I believe I was a better hand at worming out a story than either of my fellows at the George; and perhaps there is now no other man alive who could narrate to you the following foul and unnatural events.

In his young days Fettes studied medicine in the schools of Edinburgh. He had talent of a kind, the talent that picks up swiftly what it hears and readily retails it for its own. He worked little at home; but he was civil, attentive, and intelligent in the presence of his masters. They soon picked him out as a lad who listened closely and remembered well; nay, strange as it seemed to me when I first heard it, he was in those days well favoured, and pleased by his exterior. There was, at that period, a certain extramural teacher of anatomy, whom I shall here designate by the letter K. His name was subsequently too well known. The man who bore it skulked through the streets of Edinburgh in disguise, while the mob that applauded at the execution of Burke called loudly for the blood of his employer. But Mr. K— was then at the top of his vogue; he enjoyed a popularity due partly to his own talent and address, partly to the incapacity of his rival, the university professor. The students, at least, swore by his name, and Fettes believed himself, and was believed by others, to have laid the foundations of success when he acquired the favour of this meteorically famous man. Mr. K— was a *bon vivant* as well as an accomplished teacher; he liked a sly illusion no less than a careful preparation. In both capacities Fettes enjoyed and deserved his notice, and by the second year of his attendance he held the half-regular position of second demonstrator, or sub-assistant in his class.

In this capacity the charge of the theatre and lecture-room devolved in particular upon his shoulders. He had to answer for the cleanliness of the premises and the conduct of the other students, and it was a part of his duty to supply, receive, and divide the various subjects. It was with a view to this last— at that time very delicate—affair that he was lodged by Mr. K— in the same wynd, and at last in the same building, with the dissecting-rooms. Here, after a night of turbulent pleasures, his hand still tottering, his sight still misty and confused, he would be called out of bed in the black hours before the winter dawn by the unclean and desperate interlopers who supplied the table. He would open the door to these men, since infamous throughout the land. He would help them with their tragic burden, pay them their sordid price, and remain alone, when they were gone, with the unfriendly relics of humanity. From such a scene he would return to snatch another hour or two of slumber, to repair the abuses of the night, and refresh himself for the labours of the day.

Few lads could have been more insensible to the impressions of a life thus passed among the ensigns of mortality. His mind was closed against all general considerations. He was incapable of interest in the fate and fortunes of another, the slave of his own desires and low ambitions. Cold, light, and selfish in the last resort, he had that modicum of prudence, miscalled morality, which keeps a man from inconvenient drunkenness or punishable theft. He coveted, besides, a measure of consideration from his masters and his fellow-pupils, and he had no desire to fail conspicuously in the external parts of life. Thus he made it his pleasure to gain some distinction in his studies, and day after day rendered unimpeachable eye-service to his employer, Mr. K—. For his day of work he indemnified himself by nights of roaring, blackguardly enjoyment; and when that balance had been struck, the organ that he called his conscience declared itself content.

The supply of subjects was a continual trouble to him as well as to his master. In that large and busy class, the raw material of the anatomist kept perpetually running out; and the business thus rendered necessary was not only unpleasant in itself, but threatened dangerous consequences to all who were concerned. It was the policy of Mr. K— to ask no questions in his dealings with the trade. "They bring the body, and we pay the price," he used to say, dwelling on the alliteration—"*quid pro quo*." And, again, and somewhat profanely, "Ask no questions," he would tell his assistants, "for conscience' sake." There was no understanding that the subjects were provided by the crime of murder. Had that idea been broached to him in words, he would have recoiled in horror; but the lightness of his speech upon so grave a matter was, in itself, an offence against good manners, and a temptation to the men with whom he dealt. Fettes, for instance, had often remarked to himself upon the singular freshness of the bodies. He had been struck again and again by the hangdog, abominable looks of the ruffians who came to him before the dawn; and putting things together clearly in his private thoughts, he perhaps attributed a meaning too immoral and too categorical to the unguarded counsels of his master. He understood his duty, in short, to have three branches: to take what was brought, to pay the price, and to avert the eye from any evidence of crime.

One November morning this policy of silence was put sharply to the test. He had been awake all night with a racking toothache—pacing his room like a caged beast or throwing himself in fury on his bed—and had fallen at last into that profound, uneasy slumber that so often follows on a night of pain, when he was awakened by the third or fourth angry repetition of the concerted signal. There was a thin, bright moonshine; it was bitter cold, windy, and frosty; the town had not yet awakened, but an indefinable stir already preluded the noise and business of the day. The ghouls had come later than usual, and they seemed more than usually eager to be gone. Fettes, sick with sleep, lighted them upstairs. He heard their grumbling Irish voices through a dream; and as they stripped the sack from their sad merchandise he leaned dozing, with his shoulder propped against the wall; he had to shake himself to find the men their money. As he did so his eyes lighted on the dead face. He started; he took two steps nearer, with the candle raised.

"God Almighty!" he cried. "That is Jane Galbraith!"

The men answered nothing, but they shuffled nearer the door.

"I know her, I tell you," he continued. "She was alive and hearty yesterday. It's impossible she can be dead; it's impossible you should have got this body fairly."

"Sure, sir, you're mistaken entirely," said one of the men.

But the other looked Fettes darkly in the eyes, and demanded the money on the spot.

It was impossible to misconceive the threat or to exaggerate the danger. The lad's heart failed him. He stammered some excuses, counted out the sum, and saw his hateful visitors depart. No sooner were they gone than he hastened to confirm his doubts. By a dozen unquestionable marks he identified the girl he had jested with the day before. He saw, with horror, marks upon her body that might well betoken violence. A panic seized him, and he took refuge in his room. There he reflected at length over the discovery that he had made; considered soberly the bearing of Mr. K—'s instructions and the danger to himself of interference in so serious a business, and at last, in sore perplexity, determined to wait for the advice of his immediate superior, the class assistant.

This was a young doctor, Wolfe Macfarlane, a high favourite among all the reckless students, clever, dissipated, and unscrupulous to the last degree. He had travelled and studied abroad. His manners were agreeable and a little forward. He was an authority on the stage, skilful on the ice or the links with skate or golf-club; he dressed with nice audacity, and, to put the finishing touch upon his glory, he kept a gig and a strong trotting-horse. With Fettes he was on terms of intimacy; indeed, their relative positions called for some community of life; and when subjects were scarce the pair would drive far into the country in Macfarlane's gig, visit and desecrate some lonely graveyard, and return before dawn with their booty to the door of the dissecting-room.

On that particular morning Macfarlane arrived somewhat earlier than his wont. Fettes heard him, and met him on the stairs, told him his story, and showed him the cause of his alarm. Macfarlane examined the marks on her body.

"Yes," he said, with a nod, "it looks fishy."

"Well, what should I do?" asked Fettes.

"Do?" repeated the other. "Do you want to do anything? Least said soonest mended, I should say."

"Some one else might recognise her," objected Fettes. "She was as well known as the Castle Rock."

"We'll hope not," said Macfarlane, "and if anybody does— well, you didn't, don't you see, and there's an end. The fact is, this has been going on too long. Stir up the mud, and you'll get K— into the most unholy trouble; you'll be in a shocking box yourself. So will I, if you come to that. I should like to know how any one of us would look, or what the devil we should have to say for ourselves, in any Christian witness-box. For me, you know there's one thing certain—that, practically speaking, all our subjects have been murdered."

"Macfarlane!" cried Fettes.

"Come now!" sneered the other. "As if you hadn't suspected it yourself!"

"Suspecting is one thing—"

"And proof another. Yes, I know; and I'm as sorry as you are this should have come here," tapping the body with his cane. "The next best thing for me is not to recognise it; and," he added coolly, "I don't. You may, if you please. I don't dictate, but I think a man of the world would do as I do; and I may add, I fancy that is what K— would look for at our hands. The question is, Why did he choose us two for his assistants? And I answer, Because he didn't want old wives."

This was the tone of all others to affect the mind of a lad like Fettes. He agreed to imitate Macfarlane. The body of the unfortunate girl was duly dissected, and no one remarked or appeared to recognise her.

One afternoon, when his day's work was over, Fettes dropped into a popular tavern and found Macfarlane sitting with a stranger. This was a small man, very pale and dark, with coal-black eyes. The cut of his features gave a promise of intellect and refinement which was but feebly realised in his manners, for he proved, upon a nearer acquaintance, coarse, vulgar, and stupid. He exercised, however, a very remarkable control over Macfarlane; issued orders like the Great Bashaw; became inflamed at the least discussion or delay, and commented rudely on the servility with which he was obeyed. This most offensive person took a fancy to Fettes on the spot, plied him with drinks, and honoured him with unusual confidences on his past career. If a tenth part of what he confessed were true, he was a very loathsome rogue; and the lad's vanity was tickled by the attention of so experienced a man.

"I'm a pretty bad fellow myself," the stranger remarked, "but Macfarlane is the boy—Toddy Macfarlane I call him. Toddy, order your friend another glass." Or it might be, "Toddy, you jump up and shut the door." "Toddy hates me," he said again. "Oh, yes, Toddy, you do!"

"Don't you call me that confounded name," growled Macfarlane.

"Hear him! Did you ever see the lads play knife? He would like to do that all over my body," remarked the stranger.

"We medicals have a better way than that," said Fettes. "When we dislike a dead friend of ours, we dissect him."

Macfarlane looked up sharply, as though this jest were scarcely to his mind.

The afternoon passed. Gray, for that was the stranger's name, invited Fettes to join them at dinner, ordered a feast so sumptuous that the tavern was thrown into commotion, and when all was done commanded Macfarlane to settle the bill. It was late before they separated; the man Gray was incapably drunk. Macfarlane, sobered by his fury, chewed the cud of the money he had been forced to squander and the slights he had been obliged to swallow. Fettes, with various liquors singing in his head, returned home with devious footsteps and a mind entirely in abeyance. Next day Macfarlane was absent from the class, and Fettes smiled to himself as he imagined him still squiring the intolerable Gray from tavern to tavern. As soon as the hour of liberty had struck he posted from place to place in quest of his last night's companions. He could find them, however, nowhere; so returned early to his rooms, went early to bed, and slept the sleep of the just.

At four in the morning he was awakened by the well-known signal. Descending to the door, he was filled with astonishment to find Macfarlane with his gig, and in the gig one of those long and ghastly packages with which he was so well acquainted.

"What?" he cried. "Have you been out alone? How did you manage?"

But Macfarlane silenced him roughly, bidding him turn to business. When they had got the body upstairs and laid it on the table, Macfarlane made at first as if he were going away. Then he paused and seemed to hesitate; and then, "You had better look at the face," said he, in tones of some constraint. "You had better," he repeated, as Fettes only stared at him in wonder.

"But where, and how, and when did you come by it?" cried the other.

"Look at the face," was the only answer.

Fettes was staggered; strange doubts assailed him. He looked from the young doctor to the body, and then back again. At last, with a start, he did as he was bidden. He had almost expected the sight that met his eyes, and yet the shock was cruel. To see, fixed in the rigidity of death and naked on that coarse layer of sackcloth, the man whom he had left well clad and full of meat and sin upon the threshold of a tavern, awoke, even in the thoughtless Fettes, some of the terrors of the conscience. It was a *cras tibi* which re-echoed in his soul, that two whom he had known should have come to lie upon these icy tables. Yet these were only secondary thoughts. His first concern regarded Wolfe. Unprepared for a challenge so momentous, he knew not how to look his comrade in the face. He durst not meet his eye, and he had neither words nor voice at his command.

It was Macfarlane himself who made the first advance. He

came up quietly behind and laid his hand gently but firmly on the other's shoulder.

"Richardson," said he, "may have the head."

Now Richardson was a student who had long been anxious for that portion of the human subject to dissect. There was no answer, and the murderer resumed: "Talking of business, you must pay me; your accounts, you see, must tally."

Fettes found a voice, the ghost of his own: "Pay you!" he cried. "Pay you for that?"

"Why, yes, of course you must. By all means and on every possible account, you must," returned the other. "I dare not give it for nothing, you dare not take it for nothing; it would compromise us both. This is another case like Jane Galbraith's. The more things are wrong the more we must act as if all were right. Where does old K— keep his money?"

"There," answered Fettes hoarsely, pointing to a cupboard in the corner.

"Give me the key, then," said the other calmly, holding out his hand.

There was an instant's hesitation, and the die was cast. Macfarlane could not suppress a nervous twitch, the infinitesimal mark of an immense relief, as he felt the key between his fingers. He opened the cupboard, brought out pen and ink and a paper-book that stood in one compartment, and separated from the funds in a drawer a sum suitable to the occasion.

"Now, look here," he said, "there is the payment made—first proof of your good faith: first step to your security. You have now to clinch it by a second. Enter the payment in your book, and then you for your part may defy the devil."

The next few seconds were for Fettes an agony of thought; but in balancing his terrors it was the most immediate that triumphed. Any future difficulty seemed almost welcome if he could avoid a present quarrel with Macfarlane. He set down the candle which he had been carrying all this time, and with a steady hand entered the date, the nature, and the amount of the transaction.

"And now," said Macfarlane, "it's only fair that you should pocket the lucre. I've had my share already. By-the-bye, when a man of the world falls into a bit of luck, has a few shillings extra in his pocket—I'm ashamed to speak of it, but there's a rule of conduct in the case. No treating, no purchase of expensive class-books, no squaring of old debts; borrow, don't lend."

"Macfarlane," began Fettes, still somewhat hoarsely, "I have put my neck in a halter to oblige you."

"To oblige me?" cried Wolfe. "Oh, come! You did, as near as I can see the matter, what you downright had to do in self-defence. Suppose I got into trouble, where would you be? This second little matter flows clearly from the first. Mr. Gray is the continuation of Miss Galbraith. You can't begin and then stop. If you begin, you must keep on beginning; that's the truth. No rest for the wicked."

A horrible sense of blackness and the treachery of fate seized hold upon the soul of the unhappy student.

"My God!" he cried, "but what have I done? and when did I begin? To be made a class assistant—in the name of reason, where's the harm in that? Service wanted the position; Service might have got it. Would *he* have been where *I* am now!"

"My dear fellow," said Macfarlane, "what a boy you are! What harm *has* come to you? What harm *can* come to you if you hold your tongue? Why, man, do you know what this life is? There are two squads of us—the lions and the lambs. If you're a lamb, you'll come to lie upon these tables like Gray or Jane Galbraith; if you're a lion, you'll live and drive a horse like me, like K—, like all the world with any wit or courage. You're staggered at the first. But look at K—! My dear fellow, you're clever, you have pluck. I like you, and K— likes you. You were born to lead the hunt; and I tell you, on my honour and my experience of life, three days from now you'll laugh at all these scarecrows like a High School boy at a farce."

And with that Macfarlane took his departure and drove off up the wynd in his gig to get under cover before daylight. Fettes was thus left alone with his regrets. He saw the miserable peril in which he stood involved. He saw, with inexpressible dismay, that there was no limit to his weakness, and that, from concession to concession, he had fallen from the arbiter of Macfarlane's destiny to his paid and helpless accomplice. He would have given the world to have been a little braver at the time, but it did not occur to him that he might still be brave. The secret of Jane Galbraith and the cursed entry in the day-book closed his mouth.

Hours passed; the class began to arrive; the members of the unhappy Gray were dealt out to one and to another, and received without remark. Richardson was made happy with the head; and before the hour of freedom rang Fettes trembled with exultation to perceive how far they had already gone toward safety.

For two days he continued to watch, with increasing joy, the dreadful process of disguise.

On the third day Macfarlane made his appearance. He had been ill, he said; but he made up for lost time by the energy with which he directed the students. To Richardson in particular he extended the most valuable assistance and advice, and that student, encouraged by the praise of the demonstrator, burned high with ambitious hopes, and saw the medal already in his grasp.

Before the week was out Macfarlane's prophecy had been fulfilled. Fettes had outlived his terrors and had forgotten his baseness. He began to plume himself upon his courage, and had so arranged the story in his mind that he could look back on these events with an unhealthy pride. Of his accomplice he saw but little. They met, of course, in the business of the class; they received their orders together from Mr. K—. At times they had a word or two in private, and Macfarlane was from first to last particularly kind and jovial. But it was plain that he avoided any reference to their common secret; and even when Fettes whispered to him that he had cast in his lot with the lions and forsworn the lambs, he only signed to him smilingly to hold his peace.

At length an occasion arose which threw the pair once more into a closer union. Mr. K— was again short of subjects; pupils were eager, and it was a part of this teacher's pretensions to be always well supplied. At the same time there came the news of a burial in the rustic graveyard of Glencorse. Time has little changed the place in question. It stood then, as now, upon a cross road, out of call of human habitations, and buried fathom deep in the foliage of six cedar trees. The cries of the sheep upon the neighbouring hills, the streamlets upon either hand, one loudly singing among pebbles, the other dripping furtively from pond to pond, the stir of the wind in mountainous old flowering chestnuts, and once in seven days the voice of the bell and the old tunes of the precentor, were the only sounds that disturbed the silence around the rural church. The Resurrection Man—to use a byname of the period—was not to be deterred by any of the sanctities of customary piety. It was part of his trade to despise and desecrate the scrolls and trumpets of old tombs, the paths worn by the feet of worshippers and mourners, and the offerings and the inscriptions of bereaved affection. To rustic neighbourhood, where love is more than commonly tenacious, and where some bonds of blood or fellowship unite the entire society of a parish, the body-snatcher, far from being repelled by natural respect, was attracted by the ease and safety of the task. To bodies that had been laid in earth, in joyful expectation of a far different awakening, there came that hasty, lamp-lit, terror-haunted resurrection of the spade and mattock. The coffin was forced, the cerements torn, and the melancholy relics, clad in sackcloth, after being rattled for hours on moonless byways, were at length exposed to uttermost indignities before a class of gaping boys.

Somewhat as two vultures may swoop upon a dying lamb, Fettes and Macfarlane were to be let loose upon a grave in that green and quiet resting-place. The wife of a farmer, a woman who had lived for sixty years, and been known for nothing but good butter and a godly conversation, was to be rooted from her grave at midnight and carried, dead and naked, to that far-away city that she had always honoured with her Sunday's best; the place beside her family was to be empty till the crack of doom; her innocent and almost venerable members to be exposed to that last curiosity of the anatomist.

Late one afternoon the pair set forth, well wrapped in cloaks and furnished with a formidable bottle. It rained without remission—a cold, dense, lashing rain. Now and again there blew a puff of wind, but these sheets of falling water kept it down. Bottle and all, it was a sad and silent drive as far as Penicuik, where they were to spend the evening. They stopped once, to hide their implements in a thick bush not far from the churchyard, and once again at the Fisher's Tryst, to have a toast before the kitchen fire and vary their nips of whisky with a glass of ale. When they reached their journey's end the gig was housed, the horse was fed and comforted, and the two young doctors in a private room sat down to the best dinner and the best wine the house afforded. The lights, the fire, the beating rain upon the window, the cold, incongruous work that lay before them, added zest to their enjoyment of the meal. With every glass their cordiality increased. Soon Macfarlane handed a little pile of gold to his companion.

"A compliment," he said. 'Between friends these little d—d accommodations ought to fly like pipe-lights."

Fettes pocketed the money, and applauded the sentiment to the echo. "You are a philosopher," he cried. "I was an ass till I knew you. You and K— between you, by the Lord Harry! but you'll make a man of me."

"Of course we shall," applauded Macfarlane. "A man! I tell you, it required a man to back me up the other morning. There are some big, brawling, forty-year-old cowards who would have turned sick at the look of the d—d thing; but not you—you kept your head. I watched you."

"Well, and why not?" Fettes thus vaunted himself. "It was no affair of mine. There was nothing to gain on the one side but disturbance, and on the other I could count on your gratitude,

99

don't you see?" And he slapped his pocket till the gold pieces rang.

Macfarlane somehow felt a certain touch of alarm at these unpleasant words. He may have regretted that he had taught his young companion so successfully, but he had no time to interfere, for the other noisily continued in this boastful strain:—

"The great thing is not to be afraid. Now, between you and me, I don't want to hang—that's practical; but for all cant, Macfarlane, I was born with a contempt. Hell, God, Devil, right, wrong, sin, crime, and all the old gallery of curiosities—they may frighten boys, but men of the world, like you and me, despise them. Here's to the memory of Gray!"

It was by this time growing somewhat late. The gig, according to order, was brought round to the door with both lamps brightly shining, and the young men had to pay their bill and take the road. They announced that they were bound for Peebles, and drove in that direction till they were clear of the last houses of the town; then, extinguishing the lamps, returned upon their course, and followed a by-road toward Glencorse. There was no sound but that of their own passage, and the incessant, strident pouring of the rain. It was pitch dark; here and there a white gate or a white stone in the wall guided them for a short space across the night; but for the most part it was at a foot pace, and almost groping, that they picked their way through that resonant blackness to their solemn and isolated destination. In the sunken woods that traverse the neighbourhood of the burying-ground the last glimmer failed them, and it became necessary to kindle a match and re-illumine one of the lanterns of the gig. Thus, under the dripping trees, and environed by huge and moving shadows, they reached the scene of their unhallowed labours.

They were both experienced in such affairs, and powerful with the spade; and they had scarce been twenty minutes at their task before they were rewarded by a dull rattle on the coffin lid. At the same moment, Macfarlane, having hurt his hand upon a stone, flung it carelessly above his head. The grave, in which they now stood almost to the shoulders, was close to the edge of the plateau of the graveyard; and the gig lamp had been propped, the better to illuminate their labours, against a tree, and on the immediate verge of the steep bank descending to the stream. Chance had taken a sure aim with the stone. Then came a clang of broken glass; night fell upon them; sounds alternately dull and ringing announced the bounding of the lantern down the bank, and its occasional collision with the trees. A stone or two, which it had dislodged in its descent, rattled behind it into the profundities of the glen; and then silence, like night, resumed its sway; and they might bend their hearing to its utmost pitch, but naught was to be heard except the rain, now marching to the wind, now steadily falling over miles of open country.

They were so nearly at an end of their abhorred task that they judged it wisest to complete it in the dark. The coffin was exhumed and broken open; the body inserted in the dripping sack and carried between them to the gig; one mounted to keep it in its place, and the other, taking the horse by the mouth, groped along by wall and bush until they reached the wider road by the Fisher's Tryst. Here was a faint, diffused radiancy, which they hailed like daylight; by that they pushed the horse to a good pace and began to rattle along merrily in the direction of the town.

They had both been wetted to the skin during their operations, and now, as the gig jumped among the deep ruts, the thing that stood propped between them fell now upon one and now upon the other. At every repetition of the horrid contact each instinctively repelled it with the greater haste; and the process, natural although it was, began to tell upon the nerves of the companions. Macfarlane made some ill-favoured jest about the farmer's wife, but it came hollowly from his lips, and was allowed to drop in silence. Still their unnatural burden bumped from side to side; and now the head would be laid, as if in confidence, upon their shoulders, and now the drenching sackcloth would flap icily about their faces. A creeping chill began to possess the soul of Fettes. He peered at the bundle, and it seemed somehow larger than at first. All over the countryside, and from every degree of distance, the farm dogs accompanied their passage with tragic ululations; and it grew and grew upon his mind that some unnatural miracle had been accomplished, that some nameless change had befallen the dead body, and that it was in fear of their unholy burden that the dogs were howling.

"For God's sake," said he, making a great effort to arrive at speech, "for God's sake, let's have a light!"

Seemingly Macfarlane was affected in the same direction; for, though he made no reply, he stopped the horse, passed the reins to his companion, got down, and proceeded to kindle the remaining lamp. They had by that time got no farther than the cross-road down to Auchenclinny. The rain still poured as though the deluge were returning, and it was no easy matter to make a light in such a world of wet and darkness. When at last the flickering blue flame had been transferred to the wick and began to expand and clarify, and shed a wide circle of misty brightness round the gig, it became possible for the two young men to see each other and the thing they had along with them. The rain had moulded the rough sacking to the outlines of the body underneath; the head was distinct from the trunk, the shoulders plainly modelled; something at once spectral and human riveted their eyes upon the ghastly comrade of their drive.

For some time Macfarlane stood motionless, holding up the lamp. A nameless dread was swathed, like a wet sheet, about the body, and tightened the white skin upon the face of Fettes; a fear that was meaningless, a horror of what could not be, kept mounting to his brain. Another beat of the watch, and he had spoken. But his comrade forestalled him.

"That is not a woman," said Macfarlane, in a hushed voice.

"It was a woman when we put her in," whispered Fettes.

"Hold that lamp," said the other. "I must see her face."

And as Fettes took the lamp his companion untied the fastenings of the sack and drew down the cover from the head. The light fell very clear upon the dark, well-moulded features and smooth-shaven cheeks of a too familiar countenance, often beheld in dreams of both of these young men. A wild yell rang up into the night; each leaped from his own side into the roadway: the lamp fell, broke, and was extinguished; and the horse, terrified by this unusual commotion, bounded and went off toward Edinburgh at a gallop, bearing along with it, sole occupant of the gig, the body of the dead and long-dissected Gray.

MARKHEIM

MARKHEIM

"Yes," said the dealer, "our windfalls are of various kinds. Some customers are ignorant, and then I touch a dividend on my superior knowledge. Some are dishonest," and here he held up the candle, so that the light fell strongly on his visitor, "and in that case," he continued, "I profit by my virtue."

Markheim had but just entered from the daylight streets, and his eyes had not yet grown familiar with the mingled shine and darkness in the shop. At these pointed words, and before the near presence of the flame, he blinked painfully and looked aside.

The dealer chuckled. "You come to me on Christmas Day," he resumed, "when you know that I am alone in my house, put up my shutters, and make a point of refusing business. Well, you will have to pay for that; you will have to pay for my loss of time, when I should be balancing my books; you will have to pay, besides, for a kind of manner that I remark in you today very strongly. I am the essence of discretion, and ask no awkward questions; but when a customer cannot look me in the eye, he has to pay for it." The dealer once more chuckled; and then, changing to his usual business voice, though still with a note of irony, "You can give, as usual, a clear account of how you came into the possession of the object?" he continued. "Still your uncle's cabinet? A remarkable collector, sir!"

And the little pale, round-shouldered dealer stood almost on tip-toe, looking over the top of his gold spectacles, and - nodding his head with every mark of disbelief. Markheim returned his gaze with one of infinite pity, and a touch of horror.

"This time," said he, "you are in error. I have not come to sell, but to buy. I have no curios to dispose of; my uncle's cabinet is bare to the wainscot; even were it still intact, I have done well on the Stock Exchange, and should more likely add to it than otherwise, and my errand today is simplicity itself. I seek a Christmas present for a lady," he continued, waxing more fluent as he struck into the speech he had prepared; "and certainly I owe you every excuse for thus disturbing you upon so small a matter. But the thing was neglected yesterday; I must produce my little compliment at dinner; and, as you very well know, a rich marriage is not a thing to be neglected."

There followed a pause, during which the dealer seemed to weigh this statement incredulously. The ticking of many clocks among the curious lumber of the shop, and the faint rushing of the cabs in a near thoroughfare, filled up the interval of silence.

"Well, sir," said the dealer, "be it so. You are an old customer after all; and if, as you say, you have the chance of a good marriage, far be it from me to be an obstacle.–Here is a nice thing for a lady now," he went on, "this hand-glass–fifteenth century, warranted; comes from a good collection, too; but I reserve the name, in the interests of my customer, who was just like yourself, my dear sir, the nephew and sole heir of a remarkable collector."

The dealer, while he thus ran on in his dry and biting voice, had stooped to take the object from its place; and, as he had done so, a shock had passed through Markheim, a start both of hand and foot, a sudden leap of many tumultuous passions to the face. It passed as swiftly as it came, and left no trace beyond a certain trembling of the hand that now received the glass.

"A glass," he said hoarsely, and then paused, and repeated it more clearly. "A glass? For Christmas? Surely not?"

"And why not?" cried the dealer. "Why not a glass?"

Markheim was looking upon him with an indefinable expression. "You ask me why not?" he said. "Why, look here–look in it–look at yourself! Do you like to see it? No! nor I–nor any man."

The little man had jumped back when Markheim had so suddenly confronted him with the mirror; but now, perceiving there was nothing worse on hand, he chuckled. "Your future lady, sir, must be pretty hard favoured," said he.

"I ask you," said Markheim, "for a Christmas present, and you give me this—this damned reminder of years, and sins and follies—this hand-conscience. Did you mean it? Had you a thought in your mind? Tell me. It will be better for you if you do. Come, tell me about yourself. I hazard a guess now, that you are in secret a very charitable man?"

The dealer looked closely at his companion. It was very odd, Markheim did not appear to be laughing; there was something in his face like an eager sparkle of hope, but nothing of mirth.

"What are you driving at?" the dealer asked.

"Not charitable?" returned the other gloomily. "Not charitable? not pious; not scrupulous; unloving, unbeloved; a hand to get money, a safe to keep it. Is that all? Dear God, man, is that all?"

"I will tell you what it is," began the dealer, with some sharpness, and then broke off again into a chuckle. "But I see this is a love-match of yours, and you have been drinking the lady's health."

"Ah!" cried Markheim, with a strange curiosity. "Ah, have you been in love? Tell me about that."

"I," cried the dealer. "I in love! I never had the time, nor have I the time today for all this nonsense.—Will you take the glass?"

"Where is the hurry?" returned Markheim. "It is very pleasant to stand here talking; and life is so short and insecure that I would not hurry away from any pleasure—no, not even from so mild a one as this. We should rather cling, cling to what little we can get, like a man at a cliff's edge. Every second is a cliff, if you think upon it—a cliff a mile high—high enough, if we fall, to dash us out of every feature of humanity. Hence it is best to talk pleasantly. Let us talk of each other: why should we wear this mask? Let us be confidential. Who knows?—we might become friends."

"I have just one word to say to you," said the dealer. "Either make your purchase, or walk out of my shop!"

"True, true," said Markheim. "Enough fooling. To business. Show me something else."

The dealer stooped once more, this time to replace the glass upon the shelf, his thin blond hair falling over his eyes as he did so. Markheim moved a little nearer, with one hand in the pocket of his greatcoat: he drew himself up and filled his lungs; at the same time many different emotions were depicted together on his face—terror, horror, and resolve, fascination and a physical repulsion; and through a haggard lift of his upper lip his teeth looked out.

"This, perhaps, may suit," observed the dealer: and then, as he began to re-arise, Markheim bounded from behind upon his victim. The long, skewer-like dagger flashed and fell. The dealer struggled like a hen, striking his temple on the shelf, and then tumbled on the floor in a heap.

Time had some score of small voices in that shop, some stately and slow, as was becoming to their great age; others garrulous and hurried. All these told out the seconds in an intricate chorus of tickings. Then the passage of a lad's feet, heavily running on the pavement, broke in upon these smaller voices and startled Markheim into the consciousness of his surroundings. He looked about him awfully. The candle stood on the counter, its flame solemnly wagging in a draught; and by that inconsiderable movement the whole room was filled with noiseless bustle and kept heaving like a sea: the tall shadows nodding, the gross blots of darkness swelling and dwindling as with respiration, the faces of the portraits and the china gods changing and wavering like images in water. The inner door stood ajar, and peered into that leaguer of shadows with a long slit of daylight like a pointing finger.

From these fear-stricken rovings Markheim's eyes returned to the body of his victim, where it lay both humped and sprawling, incredibly small and strangely meaner than in life. In these poor, miserly clothes, in that ungainly attitude, the dealer lay like so much sawdust. Markheim had feared to see it, and, lo! it was nothing. And yet, as he gazed, this bundle of old clothes and pool of blood began to find eloquent voices. There it must lie; there was none to work the cunning hinges or direct the miracle of locomotion—there it must lie till it was found.

Found! ay, and then? Then would this dead flesh lift up a cry that would ring over England, and fill the world with the echoes of pursuit. Ay, dead or not, this was still the enemy. "Time was that when the brains were out," he thought; and the first word struck into his mind. Time, now that the deed was accomplished–time, which had closed for the victim, had become instant and momentous for the slayer.

The thought was yet in his mind when, first one and then another, with every variety of pace and voice–one deep as the bell from a cathedral turret, another ringing on its treble notes the prelude of a waltz–the clocks began to strike the hour of three in the afternoon.

The sudden outbreak of so many tongues in that dumb chamber staggered him. He began to bestir himself, going to and fro with the candle, beleaguered by moving shadows, and startled to the soul by chance reflections. In many rich mirrors, some of home design, some from Venice or Amsterdam, he saw his face repeated and repeated, as it were an army of spies; his own eyes met and detected him; and the sound of his own steps, lightly as they fell, vexed the surrounding quiet. And still, as he continued to fill his pockets, his mind accused him, with a sickening iteration, of the thousand faults of his design. He should have chosen a more quiet hour; he should have prepared an alibi; he should not have used a knife; he should have been more cautious, and only bound and gagged the dealer, and not killed him; he should have been more bold, and killed the servant also; he should have done all things otherwise: poignant regrets, weary, incessant toiling of the mind to change what was unchangeable, to plan what was now useless, to be the architect of the irrevocable past. Meanwhile, and behind all this activity, brute terrors, like the scurrying of rats in a deserted attic, filled the more remote chambers of his brain with riot; the hand of the constable would fall heavy on his shoulder, and his nerves would jerk like a hooked fish; or he beheld, in galloping defile, the dock, the prison, the gallows, and the black coffin.

Terror of the people in the street sat down before his mind like a besieging army. It was impossible, he thought, but that some rumour of the struggle must have reached their ears and set on edge their curiosity; and now, in all the neighbouring houses, he divined them sitting motionless and with uplifted ear—solitary people, condemned to spend Christmas dwelling alone on memories of the past, and now startlingly recalled from that tender exercise; happy family parties, struck into silence round the table, the mother still with raised finger: every degree and age and humour, but all, by their own hearths, prying and hearkening and weaving the rope that was to hang him. Sometimes it seemed to him he could not move too softly; the clink of the tall Bohemian goblets rang out loudly like a bell; and alarmed by the bigness of the ticking, he was tempted to stop the clocks. And then, again, with a swift transition of his terrors, the very silence of the place appeared a source of peril, and a thing to strike and freeze the passer-by; and he would step more boldly, and bustle aloud among the contents of the shop, and imitate, with elaborate bravado, the movements of a busy man at ease in his own house.

But he was now so pulled about by different alarms, that, while one portion of his mind was still alert and cunning, another trembled on the brink of lunacy. One hallucination in particular took a strong hold on his credulity. The neighbour hearkening with white face beside his window, the passer-by arrested by a horrible surmise on the pavement—these could at worst suspect, they could not know; through the brick walls and shuttered windows only sounds could penetrate. But here, within the house, was he alone? He knew he was; he had watched the servant set forth sweethearting, in her poor best, "out for the day" written on every ribbon and smile. Yes, he was alone, of course; and yet, in the bulk of empty house above him, he could surely hear a stir of delicate footing—he was surely conscious, inexplicably conscious, of some presence. Ay, surely; to every room and corner of the house his imagination followed it; and now it was a faceless thing, and yet had eyes to see with; and again it was a shadow of himself; and yet again beheld the image of the dead dealer, reinspired with cunning and hatred.

At times, with a strong effort, he would glance at the open door which still seemed to repel his eyes. The house was tall, the skylight small and dirty, the day blind with fog; and the light that filtered down to the ground story was exceedingly faint, and showed dimly on the threshold of the shop. And yet, in that strip of doubtful brightness, did there not hang wavering a shadow?

Suddenly, from the street outside, a very jovial gentleman began to beat with a staff on the shop-door, accompanying his blows with shouts and railleries in which the dealer was continually called upon by name. Markheim, smitten into ice, glanced at the dead man. But no! he lay quite still; he was fled away far beyond ear-shot of these blows and shoutings; he was sunk beneath seas of silence; and his name, which would once have caught his notice above the howling of a storm, had become an empty sound. And presently the jovial gentleman desisted from his knocking and departed.

Here was a broad hint to hurry what remained to be done, to get forth from this accusing neighbourhood, to plunge into a bath of London multitudes, and to reach, on the other side of day, that haven of safety and apparent innocence—his bed. One visitor had come: at any moment another might follow and be more obstinate. To have done the deed, and yet not to reap the profit, would be too abhorrent a failure. The money, that was now Markheim's concern; and as a means to that, the keys.

He glanced over his shoulder at the open door; where the shadow was still lingering and shivering; and with no conscious repugnance of the mind, yet with a tremor of the belly, he drew near the body of his victim. The human character had quite departed. Like a suit half-stuffed with bran, the limbs lay scattered, the trunk doubled, on the floor; and yet the thing repelled him. Although so dingy and inconsiderable to the eye, he feared it might have more significance to the touch. He took the body by the shoulders and turned it on its back. It was strangely light and supple, and the limbs, as if they had been broken, fell into the oddest postures. The face was robbed of all expression; but it was as pale as wax, and shockingly smeared with blood about one temple. That was, for Markheim, the one displeasing circumstance. It carried him back, upon the instant, to a certain fair-day in a fishers' village: a grey day, a piping wind, a crowd upon the street, a blare of brasses, the booming of drums, the nasal voice of a ballad-singer; and a boy going to and fro, buried over-head in the crowd and divided between interest and fear, until, coming out upon the chief place of concourse, he beheld a booth and a great screen with pictures, dismally designed, garishly coloured: Brownrigg with her apprentice; the Mannings with their murdered guest; Weare in the death-grip of Thurtell; and a score besides of famous crimes. The thing was as clear as an illusion; he was once again that little boy; he was looking once again, and with the same sense of physical revolt, at these vile pictures; he was still stunned by the thumping of the drums. A bar of that day's music returned upon his memory; and at that, for the first time, a qualm came over him, a breath of nausea, a sudden weakness of the joints, which he must instantly resist and conquer.

He judged it more prudent to confront than to flee from these considerations; looking the more hardily in the dead face, bending his mind to realise the nature and greatness of his crime. So little a while ago that face had moved with every change of sentiment, that pale mouth had spoken, that body had been all on fire with governable energies; and now, and by his act, that piece of life had been arrested, as the horologist, with interjected finger, arrests the beating of the clock. So he reasoned in vain; he could rise to no more remorseful consciousness; the same heart which had shuddered before the painted effigies of crime looked on its reality unmoved. At best, he felt a gleam of pity for one who had been endowed in vain with all those faculties that can make the world a garden of enchantment, one who had never lived and who was now dead. But of penitence, no, not a tremor.

With that, shaking himself clear of these considerations, he found the keys and advanced towards the open door of the shop. Outside, it had begun to rain smartly; and the sound of the shower upon the roof had banished silence. Like some dripping cavern, the chambers of the house were haunted by an incessant echoing, which filled the ear and mingled with the ticking of the clocks. And, as Markheim approached the door, he seemed to hear, in answer to his own cautious tread, the steps of another foot withdrawing up the stair. The shadow still palpitated loosely on the threshold. He threw a ton's weight of resolve upon his muscles, and drew back the door.

The faint, foggy daylight glimmered dimly on the bare floor and stairs; on the bright suit of armour posted, halbert in hand, upon the landing: and on the dark wood-carvings, and framed pictures that hung against the yellow panels of the wainscot. So loud was the beating of the rain through all the house that, in Markheim's ears, it began to be distinguished into many different sounds. Footsteps and sighs, the tread of regiments marching in the distance, the chink of money in the counting, and the creaking of doors held stealthily ajar, appeared to mingle with the patter of the drops upon the cupola and the gushing of the water in the pipes. The sense that he was not alone grew upon him to the verge of madness. On every side he was haunted and begirt by presences. He heard them moving in the upper chambers; from the shop he heard the dead man getting to his legs; and as he began with a great effort to mount the stairs, feet fled quietly before him and followed stealthily behind. If he were but deaf, he thought, how tranquilly he would possess his soul! And then again, and hearkening with ever fresh attention, he blessed himself for that unresting sense which held the outposts and stood a trusty sentinel upon his life. His head turned continually on his neck; his eyes, which seemed starting from their orbits, scouted on every side, and on every side were half-rewarded as with the tail of something nameless vanishing. The four-and-twenty steps to the first floor were four-and-twenty agonies.

On that first story, the doors stood ajar, three of them like three ambushes, shaking his nerves like the throats of cannon. He could never again, he felt, be sufficiently immured and fortified from men's observing eyes; he longed to be home, girt in by walls, buried among bedclothes, and invisible to all but God. And at that thought he wondered a little, recollecting tales of other murderers and the fear they were said to entertain of heavenly avengers. It was not so, at least, with him. He feared the laws of nature, lest, in their callous and immutable procedure, they should preserve some damning evidence of his crime. He feared tenfold more, with a slavish, superstitious terror, some scission in the continuity of man's experience, some wilful illegality of nature. He played a game of skill, depending on the rules, calculating consequence from cause; and what if nature, as the defeated tyrant overthrew the chess-board, should break the mould of their succession? The like had befallen Napoleon (so writers said) when the winter changed the time of its appearance. The like might befall Markheim: the solid walls might become transparent and reveal his doings like those of bees in a glass hive; the stout planks might yield under his foot like quicksands and detain him in their clutch; ay, and there were soberer accidents that might destroy him: if, for instance, the house should fall and imprison him beside the body of his victim; or the house next door should fly on fire, and the firemen invade him from all sides. These things he feared; and, in a sense, these things might be called the hands of God reached forth against sin. But about God Himself he was at ease: his act was doubtless exceptional, but so were his excuses, which God knew; it was there, and not among men, that he felt sure of justice.

When he had got safe into the drawing-room, and shut the door behind him, he was aware of a respite from alarms. The room was quite dismantled, uncarpeted besides, and strewn with packing-cases and incongruous furniture; several great pier-glasses, in which he beheld himself at various angles, like an actor on a stage; many pictures, framed and unframed, standing with their faces to the wall; a fine Sheraton sideboard, a cabinet of marquetry, and a great old bed, with tapestry hangings. The windows opened to the floor; but by great good fortune the lower part of the shutters had been closed, and this concealed him from the neighbours. Here, then, Markheim drew in a packing-case before the cabinet, and began to search among the keys. It was a long business, for there were many; and it was irksome besides; for, after all, there might be nothing in the cabinet, and time was on the wing. But the closeness of the occupation sobered him. With the tail of his eye he saw the door—even glanced at it from time to time directly, like a besieged commander, pleased to verify the good estate of his defences. But in truth he was at peace. The rain falling in the street sounded natural and pleasant. Presently, on the other side, the notes of a piano were wakened to the music of a hymn, and the voices of many children took up the air and words. How stately, how comfortable was the melody! How fresh the youthful voices! Markheim gave ear to it smilingly, as he sorted out the keys; and his mind was thronged with answerable ideas and images; church-going children and the pealing of the high organ; children afield, bathers by the brookside, ramblers on the brambly common, kite-flyers in the windy and cloud-navigated sky; and then, at another cadence of the hymn, back again to church, and the somnolence of summer Sundays, and the high genteel voice of the parson (which he smiled a little to recall) and the painted Jacobean tombs, and the dim lettering of the Ten Commandments in the chancel.

And as he sat thus, at once busy and absent, he was startled to his feet. A flash of ice, a flash of fire, a bursting gush of blood, went over him, and then he stood transfixed and thrilling. A step mounted the stair slowly and steadily, and presently a hand was laid upon the knob, and the lock clicked, and the door opened.

Fear held Markheim in a vice. What to expect he knew not, whether the dead man walking, or the official ministers of human justice, or some chance witness blindly stumbling in to consign him to the gallows. But when a face was thrust into the aperture, glanced round the room, looked at him, nodded and smiled as if in friendly recognition, and then withdrew again, and the door closed behind it, his fear broke loose from his control in a hoarse cry. At the sound of this the visitant returned.

"Did you call me?" he asked pleasantly, and with that he entered the room and closed the door behind him.

Markheim stood and gazed at him with all his eyes. Perhaps there was a film upon his sight, but the outlines of the new-comer seemed to change and waver like those of the idols in the wavering candlelight of the shop; and at times he thought he knew him; and at times he thought he bore a likeness to himself; and always, like a lump of living terror, there lay in his bosom the conviction that this thing was not of the earth and not of God.

And yet the creature had a strange air of the commonplace, as he stood looking on Markheim with a smile; and when he added: "You are looking for the money, I believe?" it was in the tones of everyday politeness.

Markheim made no answer.

"I should warn you," resumed the other, "that the maid has left her sweetheart earlier than usual and will soon be here. If Mr. Markheim be found in this house, I need not describe to him the consequences."

"You know me?" cried the murderer.

The visitor smiled. "You have long been a favourite of mine," he said; "and I have long observed and often sought to help you."

"What are you?" cried Markheim, "the devil?"

"What I may be," returned the other, "cannot affect the service I propose to render you."

"It can," cried Markheim; "it does! Be helped by you? No,

never; not by you! You do not know me yet; thank God, you do not know me!"

"I know you," replied the visitant, with a sort of kind severity, or rather firmness. "I know you to the soul."

"Know me!" cried Markheim. "Who can do so? My life is but a travesty and slander on myself. I have lived to belie my nature. All men do; all men are better than this disguise, that grows about and stifles them. You see each dragged away by life, like one whom bravos have seized and muffled in a cloak. If they had their own control—if you could see their faces, they would be altogether different, they would shine out for heroes and saints! I am worse than most; myself is more overlaid; my excuse is known to me and God. But, had I the time, I could disclose myself."

"To me?" inquired the visitant.

"To you before all," returned the murderer. "I supposed you were intelligent. I thought—since you exist—you would prove a reader of the heart. And yet you would propose to judge me by my acts! Think of it; my acts! I was born and I have lived in a land of giants; giants have dragged me by the wrists since I was born out of my mother—the giants of circumstance. And you would judge me by my acts! But can you not look within? Can you not understand that evil is hateful to me? Can you not see within me the clear writing of conscience, never blurred by any wilful sophistry, although too often disregarded? Can you not read me for a thing that surely must be common as humanity—the unwilling sinner?"

"All this is very feelingly expressed," was the reply, "but it regards me not. These points of consistency are beyond my province, and I care not in the least by what compulsion you may have been dragged away, so as you are but carried in the right direction. But time flies; the servant delays, looking in the faces of the crowd and at the pictures on the hoardings, but still she keeps moving nearer; and remember, it is as if the gallows itself was striding towards you through the Christmas streets! Shall I help you; I, who know all? Shall I tell you where

119

to find the money?"

"For what price?" asked Markheim.

"I offer you the service for a Christmas gift," returned the other.

Markheim could not refrain from smiling with a kind of bitter triumph. "No," said he, "I will take nothing at your hands; if I were dying of thirst, and it was your hand that put the pitcher to my lips, I should find the courage to refuse. It may be credulous, but I will do nothing to commit myself to evil."

"I have no objection to a death-bed repentance," observed the visitant.

"Because you disbelieve their efficacy!" Markheim cried.

"I do not say so," returned the other; "but I look on these things from a different side, and when the life is done my interest falls. The man has lived to serve me, to spread black looks under colour of religion, or to sow tares in the wheat-field, as you do, in a course of weak compliance with desire. Now that he draws so near to his deliverance, he can add but one act of service—to repent, to die smiling, and thus to build up in confidence and hope the more timorous of my surviving followers. I am not so hard a master. Try me. Accept my help. Please yourself in life as you have done hitherto; please yourself more amply, spread your elbows at the board; and when the night begins to fall and the curtains to be drawn, I tell you, for your greater comfort, that you will find it even easy to compound your quarrel with your conscience, and to make a truckling peace with God. I came but now from such a death-bed, and the room was full of sincere mourners, listening to the man's last words: and when I looked into that face, which had been set as a flint against mercy, I found it smiling with hope."

"And do you, then, suppose me such a creature?" asked Markheim. "Do you think I have no more generous aspirations than to sin, and sin, and sin, and, at the last, sneak into heaven? My heart rises at the thought. Is this, then, your experience of mankind? or is it because you find me with red hands that you presume such baseness? and is this crime of murder indeed so impious as to dry up the very springs of good?"

"Murder is to me no special category," replied the other. "All sins are murder, even as all life is war. I behold your race, like starving mariners on a raft, plucking crusts out of the hands of famine and feeding on each other's lives. I follow sins beyond the moment of their acting; I find in all that the last conse-quence is death; and to my eyes, the pretty maid who thwarts her mother with such taking graces on a question of a ball, drips no less visibly with human gore than such a murderer as yourself. Do I say that I follow sins? I follow virtues also; they differ not by the thickness of a nail, they are both scythes for the reaping angel of Death. Evil, for which I live, consists not in action but in character. The bad man is dear to me; not the bad act, whose fruits, if we could follow them far enough down the hurtling cataract of the ages, might yet be found more blessed than those of the rarest virtues. And it is not because you have killed a dealer, but because you are Markheim, that I offer to forward your escape."

"I will lay my heart open to you," answered Markheim. "This crime on which you find me is my last. On my way to it I have learned many lessons; itself is a lesson, a momentous lesson. Hitherto I have been driven with revolt to what I would not; I was a bond-slave to poverty, driven and scourged. There are robust virtues that can stand in these temptations; mine was not so: I had a thirst of pleasure. But today, and out of this deed, I pluck both warning and riches—both the power and a fresh resolve to be myself. I become in all things a free actor in the world; I begin to see myself all changed, these hands the agents of good, this heart at peace. Something comes over me out of the past; something of what I have dreamed on Sabbath evenings to the sound of the church organ, of what I forecast when I shed tears over noble books, or talked, an innocent child, with my mother. There lies my life; I have wandered a few years, but now I see once more my city of destination."

"You are to use this money on the Stock Exchange, I think?" remarked the visitor; "and there, if I mistake not, you have already lost some thousands."

"Ah," said Markheim, "but this time I have a sure thing."

"This time, again, you will lose," replied the visitor quietly.

"Ah, but I will keep back the half!" cried Markheim.

"That also you will lose," said the other.

The sweat started upon Markheim's brow. "Well, then, what matter?" he exclaimed. "Say it be lost, say I am plunged again in poverty, shall one part of me, and that the worse, continue until the end to override the better? Evil and good run strong in me, haling me both ways. I do not love the one thing, I love all. I can conceive great deeds, renunciations, martyrdoms; and though I be fallen to such a crime as murder, pity is no stranger to my thoughts. I pity the poor; who knows their trials better than myself? I pity and help them; I prize love, I love honest laughter; there is no good thing nor true thing on earth but I love it from my heart. And are my vices only to direct my life, and my virtues to lie without effect, like some passive lumber of the mind? Not so; good, also, is the spring of acts."

But the visitant raised his finger. "For six-and-thirty years that you have been in this world," said he, "through many changes of fortune and varieties of humour, I have watched you steadily fall. Fifteen years ago you would have started at a theft. Three years back you would have blenched at the name of murder. Is there any crime, is there any cruelty or meanness, from which you still recoil?—five years from now I shall detect you in the fact! Downward, downward lies your way; nor can anything but death avail to stop you."

"It is true," Markheim said huskily, "I have in some degree complied with evil. But it is so with all: the very saints, in the mere exercise of living, grow less dainty, and take on the tone of their surroundings."

"I will propound to you one simple question," said the other; "and as you answer, I shall read to you your moral horoscope. You have grown in many things more lax; possibly you do right to be so; and at any account, it is the same with all men. But granting that, are you in any one particular, however trifling, more difficult to please with your own conduct, or do you go in all things with a looser rein?"

"In any one?" repeated Markheim, with an anguish of consideration. "No," he added, with despair, "in none! I have gone down in all."

"Then," said the visitor, "content yourself with what you are, for you will never change; and the words of your part on this stage are irrevocably written down."

Markheim stood for a long while silent, and indeed it was the visitor who first broke the silence. "That being so," he said, "shall I show you the money?"

"And grace?" cried Markheim.

"Have you not tried it?" returned the other. "Two or three years ago, did I not see you on the platform of revival meetings, and was not your voice the loudest in the hymn?"

"It is true," said Markheim; "and I see clearly what remains for me by way of duty. I thank you for these lessons from my soul; my eyes are opened, and I behold myself at last for what I am."

At this moment, the sharp note of the door-bell rang through the house; and the visitant, as though this were some concerted signal for which he had been waiting, changed at once in his demeanour.

"The maid!" he cried. "She has returned, as I forewarned you, and there is now before you one more difficult passage. Her master, you must say, is ill; you must let her in, with an assured but rather serious countenance—no smiles, no overacting, and I promise you success! Once the girl within, and the door closed, the same dexterity that has already rid you of the dealer will relieve you of this last danger in your path. Thenceforward you have the whole evening—the whole night, if needful—to ransack the treasures of the house and to make good your safety. This is help that comes to you with the mask of danger. Up!" he cried; "up, friend; your life hangs trembling in the scales: up, and act!"

Markheim steadily regarded his counsellor. "If I be condemned to evil acts," he said, "there is still one door of freedom open—I can cease from action. If my life be an ill thing, I can lay it down. Though I be, as you say truly, at the beck of every small temptation, I can yet, by one decisive gesture, place myself beyond the reach of all. My love of good is damned to barrenness; it may, and let it be! But I have still my hatred of evil; and from that, to your galling disappointment, you shall see that I can draw both energy and courage."

The features of the visitor began to undergo a wonderful and lovely change: they brightened and softened with a tender triumph, and, even as they brightened, faded and dislimned. But Markheim did not pause to watch or understand the transformation. He opened the door and went downstairs very slowly, thinking to himself. His past went soberly before him; he beheld it as it was, ugly and strenuous like a dream, random as chance-medley—a scene of defeat. Life, as he thus reviewed it, tempted him no longer; but on the farther side he perceived a quiet haven for his bark. He paused in the passage, and looked into the shop, where the candle still burned by the dead body. It was strangely silent. Thoughts of the dealer swarmed into his mind, as he stood gazing. And then the bell once more broke out into impatient clamour.

He confronted the maid upon the threshold with something like a smile.

"You had better go for the police," said he: "I have killed your master."

OLALLA

OLALLA

"Now," said the doctor, "my part is done, and, I may say, with some vanity, well done. It remains only to get you out of this cold and poisonous city, and to give you two months of a pure air and an easy conscience. The last is your affair. To the first I think I can help you. It falls indeed rather oddly; it was but the other day the Padre came in from the country; and as he and I are old friends, although of contrary professions, he applied to me in a matter of distress among some of his parishioners. This was a family—but you are ignorant of Spain, and even the names of our grandees are hardly known to you; suffice it, then, that they were once great people, and are now fallen to the brink of destitution. Nothing now belongs to them but the residencia, and certain leagues of desert mountain, in the greater part of which not even a goat could support life. But the house is a fine old place, and stands at a great height among the hills, and most salubriously; and I had no sooner heard my friend's tale than I remembered you. I told him I had a wounded officer, wounded in the good cause, who was now able to make a change; and I proposed that his friends should take you for a lodger. Instantly the Padre's face grew dark, as I had maliciously foreseen it would. It was out of the question, he said. Then let them starve, said I, for I have no sympathy with tatterdemalion pride. Thereupon we separated, not very content with one another; but yesterday, to my wonder, the Padre returned and made a submission: the difficulty, he said, he had found upon inquiry to be less than he had feared; or, in other words, these proud people had put their pride in their pocket. I closed with the offer; and, subject to your approval, I have taken rooms for you in the residencia. The air of these mountains will renew your blood; and the quiet in which you will there live is worth all the medicines in the world."

"Doctor," said I, "you have been throughout my good angel, and your advice is a command. But tell me, if you please, something of the family with which I am to reside."

"I am coming to that," replied my friend; "and, indeed, there is a difficulty in the way. These beggars are, as I have said, of very high descent, and swollen with the most baseless vanity; they have lived for some generations in a growing isolation, drawing away, on either hand, from the rich who had now become too high for them, and from the poor, whom they still regarded as too low; and even today, when poverty forces them to unfasten their door to a guest, they cannot do so without a most ungracious stipulation. You are to remain, they say, a stranger; they will give you attendance, but they refuse from the first the idea of the smallest intimacy."

I will not deny that I was piqued, and perhaps the feeling strengthened my desire to go, for I was confident that I could break down that barrier if I desired. "There is nothing offensive in such a stipulation," said I; "and I even sympathise with the feeling that inspired it."

"It is true they have never seen you," returned the doctor politely; "and if they knew you were the handsomest and the most pleasant man that ever came from England (where I am told that handsome men are common, but pleasant ones not so much so), they would doubtless make you welcome with a better grace. But since you take the thing so well, it matters not. To me, indeed, it seems discourteous. But you will find yourself the gainer. The family will not much tempt you. A mother, a son, and a daughter; an old woman said to be half-witted, a country lout, and a country girl, who stands very high with her confessor, and is, therefore," chuckled the physician, "most likely plain; there is not much in that to attract the fancy of a dashing officer."

"And yet you say they are high-born," I objected.

"Well, as to that, I should distinguish," returned the doctor. "The mother is; not so the children. The mother was the last representative of a princely stock, degenerate both in parts and fortune. Her father was not only poor, he was mad: and the girl ran wild about the residencia till his death. Then, much of the fortune having died with him, and the family being quite extinct, the girl ran wilder than ever, until at last she married, Heaven knows whom, a muleteer some say, others a smuggler; while there are some who uphold there was no marriage at all, and that Felipe and Olalla are bastards. The union, such as it was, was tragically dissolved some years ago; but they live in such seclusion, and the country at that time was in so much disorder, that the precise manner of the man's end is known only to the priest—if even to him."

"I begin to think I shall have strange experiences," said I.

"I would not romance, if I were you," replied the doctor; "you will find, I fear, a very grovelling and commonplace reality. Felipe, for instance, I have seen. And what am I to say? He is very rustic, very cunning, very loutish, and, I should say, an innocent; the others are probably to match. No, no, Señor commandante, you must seek congenial society among the great sights of our mountains; and in these at least, if you are at all a lover of the works of nature, I promise you will not be disappointed."

The next day Felipe came for me in a rough country cart, drawn by a mule; and a little before the stroke of noon, after I had said farewell to the doctor, the innkeeper, and different good souls who had befriended me during my sickness, we set forth out of the city by the eastern gate, and began to ascend into the Sierra. I had been so long a prisoner, since I was left behind for dying after the loss of the convoy, that the mere smell of the earth set me smiling. The country through which we went was wild and rocky, partially covered with rough woods, now of the cork-tree, and now of the great Spanish chestnut, and frequently intersected by the beds of mountain torrents. The sun shone, the wind rustled joyously; and we had advanced some miles, and the city had already shrunk into an inconsiderable knoll upon the plain behind us, before my attention began to be diverted to the companion of my drive. To the eye, he seemed but a diminutive, loutish, well-made country lad, such as the doctor had described, mighty quick and active, but devoid of any culture; and this first impression was with most observers final. What began to strike me was his familiar, chattering talk; so strangely inconsistent with the terms on which I was to be received; and partly from his imperfect enunciation, partly from the sprightly incoherence of the matter, so very difficult to follow clearly without an effort of the mind. It is true I had before talked with persons of a similar mental constitution; persons who seemed to live (as he did) by the senses, taken and possessed by the visual object of the moment and unable to discharge their minds of that impression. His seemed to me (as I sat, distantly giving ear) a kind of conversation proper to drivers, who pass much of their time in a great vacancy of the intellect and threading the sights of a familiar country. But this was not the case of Felipe; by his own account, he was a home-keeper; "I wish I was there now," he said; and then, spying a tree by the wayside, he broke off to tell me that he had once seen a crow among its branches.

"A crow?" I repeated, struck by the ineptitude of the remark, and thinking I had heard imperfectly.

But by this time he was already filled with a new idea; hearkening with a rapt intentness, his head on one side, his face puckered; and he struck me rudely, to make me hold my peace. Then he smiled and shook his head.

"What did you hear?" I asked.

"Oh, it is all right," he said; and began encouraging his mule with cries that echoed unhumanly up the mountain walls.

I looked at him more closely. He was superlatively well-built, light, and lithe and strong; he was well-featured; his yellow eyes were very large, though, perhaps, not very expressive; take him altogether, he was a pleasant-looking lad, and I had no fault to find with him, beyond that he was of a dusky hue, and inclined to hairiness; two characteristics that I disliked. It was his mind that puzzled, and yet attracted me. The doctor's phrase—an innocent—came back to me; and I was wondering if that were, after all, the true description, when the road began to go down into the narrow and naked chasm of a torrent. The waters thundered tumultuously in the bottom; and the ravine was filled full of the sound, the thin spray, and the claps of wind, that accompanied their descent. The scene was certainly impress- ive; but the road was in that part very securely walled in; the mule went steadily forward; and I was astonished to perceive the paleness of terror in the face of my companion. The voice of that wild river was inconstant, now sinking lower as if in weariness, now doubling its hoarse tones; momentary freshets seemed to swell its volume, sweeping down the gorge, raving and booming against the barrier walls; and I observed it was at each of these accessions to the clamour that my driver more particularly winced and blanched. Some thoughts of Scottish superstition and the river-kelpie passed across my mind; I won- dered if perchance the like were prevalent in that part of Spain; and turning to Felipe, sought to draw him out.

"What is the matter?" I asked.

"Oh, I am afraid," he replied.

"Of what are you afraid?" I returned. "This seems one of the safest places on this very dangerous road."

"It makes a noise," he said, with a simplicity of awe that set my doubts at rest.

The lad was but a child in intellect; his mind was like his body, active and swift, but stunted in development; and I began from that time forth to regard him with a measure of pity, and to listen at first with indulgence, and at last even with pleasure, to his disjointed babble.

By about four in the afternoon we had crossed the summit of the mountain line, said farewell to the western sunshine, and began to go down upon the other side, skirting the edge of many ravines and moving through the shadow of dusky woods. There rose upon all sides the voice of falling water, not condensed and formidable as in the gorge of the river, but scattered and sounding gaily and musically from glen to glen. Here, too, the spirits of my driver mended, and he began to sing aloud in a falsetto voice, and with a singular bluntness of musical perception, never true either to melody or key, but wandering at will, and yet somehow with an effect that was natural and pleasing, like that of the song of birds. As the dusk increased, I fell more and more under the spell of this artless warbling, listening and waiting for some articulate air, and still disappointed; and when at last I asked him what it was he sang—"Oh," cried he, "I am just singing!" Above all, I was taken with a trick he had of unweariedly repeating the same note at little intervals; it was not so monotonous as you would think, or, at least, not disagreeable; and it seemed to breathe a wonderful contentment with what is, such as we love to fancy in the attitude of trees, or the quiescence of a pool.

Night had fallen dark before we came out upon a plateau, and drew up a little after, before a certain lump of superior blackness which I could only conjecture to be the residencia. Here my guide, getting down from the cart, hooted and whistled for a long time in vain; until at last an old peasant man came towards us from somewhere in the surrounding dark, carrying a candle in his hand. By the light of this I was able to perceive a great arched doorway of a Moorish character: it was closed by iron-studded gates, in one of the leaves of which Felipe opened a wicket. The peasant carried off the cart to some outbuilding; but my guide and I passed through the wicket, which was closed again behind us; and, by the glimmer of the candle, passed through a court, up a stone stair, along a section of an open gallery, and up more stairs again, until we came at last to the door of a great and somewhat bare apartment. This room, which I understood was to be mine, was pierced by three windows, lined with some lustrous wood disposed in panels, and carpeted with the skins of many savage animals. A bright fire burned in the chimney, and shed abroad a changeful flicker; close up to the blaze there was drawn a table, laid for supper; and in the far end a bed stood ready. I was pleased by these preparations, and said so to Felipe; and he, with the same simplicity of disposition that I had already remarked in him, warmly re-echoed my praises. "A fine room," he said; "a very fine room. And fire, too; fire is good; it melts out the pleasure in your bones. And the bed," he continued, carrying over the candle in that direction—"see what fine sheets—how soft, how smooth, smooth"; and he passed his hand again and again over their texture, and then laid down his head and rubbed his cheeks among them with a grossness of content that somehow offended me. I took the candle from his hand (for I feared he would set the bed on fire) and walked back to the supper-table, where, perceiving a measure of wine, I poured out a cup and called to him to come and drink of it. He started to his feet at once and ran to me with a strong expression of hope; but when he saw the wine he visibly shuddered.

"Oh, no," he said, "not that; that is for you. I hate it."

"Very well, Señor," said I; "then I will drink to your good health, and to the prosperity of your house and family. Speaking of which," I added, after I had drunk, "shall I not have the pleasure of laying my salutations in person at the feet of the Señora, your mother?"

But at these words all the childishness passed out of his face, and was succeeded by a look of indescribable cunning and secrecy. He backed away from me at the same time, as though I were an animal about to leap or some dangerous fellow with a weapon, and when he had got near the door, glowered at me sullenly with contracted pupils. "No," he said at last, and the next moment was gone noiselessly out of the room; and I heard his footing die away downstairs as light as rainfall, and silence closed over the house.

After I had supped I drew up the table nearer to the bed and began to prepare for rest; but in the new position of the light, I was struck by a picture on the wall. It represented a woman, still young. To judge by her costume and the mellow unity which reigned over the canvas, she had long been dead; to judge by the vivacity of the attitude, the eyes and the features, I might have been beholding in a mirror the image of life. Her figure was very slim and strong, and of a just proportion; red tresses lay like a crown over her brow; her eyes, of a very golden brown, held mine with a look; and her face, which was perfectly shaped, was yet marred by a cruel, sullen, and sensual expression. Something in both face and figure, something exquisitely intangible, like the echo of an echo, suggested the features and bearing of my guide; and I stood a while unpleasantly attracted and wondering at the oddity of the resemblance. The common, carnal stock of that race, which had been originally designed for such high dames as the one now looking on me from the canvas, had fallen to baser uses, wearing country clothes, sitting on the shaft and holding the reins of a mule cart, to bring home a lodger. Perhaps an actual link subsisted; perhaps some scruple of the delicate flesh that was once clothed upon with the satin and brocade of the dead lady, now winced at the rude contact of Felipe's frieze.

The first light of the morning shone full upon the portrait, and, as I lay awake, my eyes continued to dwell upon it with growing complacency; its beauty crept about my heart insidiously, silencing my scruples one after another; and while I knew that to love such a woman were to sign and seal one's own sentence of degeneration, I still knew that, if she were alive, I should love her. Day after day the double knowledge of her wickedness and of my weakness grew clearer. She came to be the heroine of many day-dreams, in which her eyes led on to, and sufficiently rewarded, crimes. She cast a dark shadow on my fancy, and when I was out in the free air of heaven, taking vigorous exercise and healthily renewing the current of my blood, it was often a glad thought to me that my enchantress was safe in the grave, her wand of beauty broken, her lips closed in silence, her philtre spilt. And yet I had a half-lingering terror that she might not be dead after all, but re-arisen in the body of some descendant.

Felipe served my meals in my own apartment; and his resemblance to the portrait haunted me. At times it was not; at times, upon some change of attitude or flash of expression, it would leap out upon me like a ghost. It was above all in his ill tempers that the likeness triumphed. He certainly liked me; he was proud of my notice, which he sought to engage by many simple and childlike devices; he loved to sit close before my fire, talking his broken talk or singing his odd, endless, word-less songs, and sometimes drawing his hand over my clothes with an affectionate manner of caressing that never failed to cause in me an embarrassment of which I was ashamed. But for all that, he was capable of flashes of causeless anger and fits of sturdy sullenness. At a word of reproof, I have seen him upset the dish of which I was about to eat, and this not surreptitiously, but with defiance; and similarly at a hint of inquisition. I was not unnaturally curious, being in a strange place and surrounded by strange people; but at the shadow of a question he shrank back, lowering and dangerous. Then it was that, for a fraction of a second, this rough lad might have been the brother of the lady in the frame. But these humours were swift to pass; and the resemblance died along with them.

In these first days I saw nothing of any one but Felipe, unless the portrait is to be counted; and since the lad was plainly of weak mind, and had moments of passion, it may be wondered that I bore his dangerous neighbourhood with equanimity. As a matter of fact, it was for some time irksome; but it happened before long that I obtained over him so complete a mastery as set my disquietude at rest.

It fell in this way. He was by nature slothful, and much of a vagabond, and yet he kept by the house, and not only waited upon my wants, but laboured every day in the garden or small farm to the south of the residencia. Here he would be joined by the peasant whom I had seen on the night of my arrival, and who dwelt at the far end of the enclosure, about half a mile away, in a rude outhouse; but it was plain to me that of these two, it was Felipe who did most; and though I would some-times see him throw down his spade and go to sleep among the very plants he had been digging, his constancy and energy were admirable in themselves, and still more so since I was well assured they were foreign to his disposition, and the fruit of an ungrateful effort. But while I admired, I wondered what had called forth in a lad so shuttle-witted this enduring sense of duty. How was it sustained? I asked myself, and to what length did it prevail over his instincts? The priest was possibly his inspirer; but the priest came one day to the residencia. I saw him both come and go after an interval of close upon an hour, from a knoll where I was sketching, and all that time Felipe continued to labour undisturbed in the garden.

At last, in a very unworthy spirit, I determined to debauch the lad from his good resolutions, and, waylaying him at the gate, easily persuaded him to join me in a ramble. It was a fine day, and the woods to which I led him were green and pleasant and sweet-smelling, and alive with the hum of insects. Here he discovered himself in a fresh character, mounting up to heights of gaiety that abashed me, and displaying an energy and grace of movement that delighted the eye. He leaped, he ran round me in mere glee; he would stop, and look and listen, and seem to drink in the world like a cordial; and then he would suddenly spring into a tree with one bound, and hang and gambol there like one at home. Little as he said to me, and that of not much import, I have rarely enjoyed more stirring company; the sight of his delight was a continual feast; the speed and accuracy of his movements pleased me to the heart; and I might have been so thoughtlessly unkind as to make a habit of these walks, had not chance prepared a very rude conclusion to my pleasure. By some swiftness or dexterity the lad captured a squirrel in a tree top. He was then some way ahead of me, but I saw him drop to the ground and crouch there, crying aloud for pleasure like a child. The sound stirred my sympathies, it was so fresh and innocent; but as I bettered my pace to draw near, the cry of the squirrel knocked upon my heart. I have heard and seen much of the cruelty of lads, and above all, of peasants; but what I now beheld struck me into a passion of anger. I thrust the fellow aside, plucked the poor brute out of his hands, and with swift mercy killed it. Then I turned upon the torturer, spoke to him long out of the heat of my indignation, calling him names at which he seemed to wither; and at length, pointing towards the residencia, bade him begone and leave me, for I chose to walk with men, not with vermin. He fell upon his knees, and, the words coming to him with more clearness than usual, poured out a stream of the most touching supplications, begging me in mercy to forgive him, to forget what he had done, to look to the future. "Oh, I try so hard," he said. "Oh, commandante, bear with Felipe this once; he will never be a brute again!" Thereupon, much more affected than I cared to show, I suffered myself to be persuaded, and at last shook hands with him and made it up. But the squirrel, by way of penance, I made him bury; speaking of the poor thing's beauty, telling him what pains it had suffered, and how base a thing was the abuse of strength. "See, Felipe," said I, "you are strong indeed; but in my hands you are as helpless as that poor thing of the trees. Give me your hand in mine. You cannot remove it. Now suppose that I were cruel like you, and took a pleasure in pain. I only tighten my hold, and see how you suffer." He screamed aloud, his face stricken ashy and dotted with needle-points of sweat; and when I set him free, he fell to the earth and nursed his hand and moaned over it like a baby. But he took the lesson in good part; and whether from that, or from what I had said to him, or the higher notion he now had of my bodily strength, his original affection was changed into a dog-like, adoring fidelity.

Meanwhile I gained rapidly in health. The residencia stood on the crown of a stony plateau; on every side the mountains hemmed it about; only from the roof, where was a bartizan, there might be seen, between two peaks, a small segment of plain, blue with extreme distance. The air in these altitudes moved freely and largely; great clouds congregated there, and were broken up by the wind and left in tatters on the hill-tops; a hoarse and yet faint rumbling of torrents rose from all round; and one could there study all the ruder and more ancient characters of nature in something of their pristine force. I delighted from the first in the vigorous scenery and changeful weather; nor less in the antique and dilapidated mansion where I dwelt. This was a large oblong, flanked at two opposite corners by bastion-like projections, one of which commanded

139

the door, while both were loopholed for musketry. The lower story was, besides, naked of windows, so that the building, if garrisoned, could not be carried without artillery. It enclosed an open court planted with pomegranate trees. From this a broad flight of marble stairs ascended to an open gallery, running all round and resting, towards the court, on slender pillars. Thence, again, several enclosed stairs led to the upper stories of the house, which were thus broken up into distinct divisions. The windows, both within and without, were closely shuttered; some of the stonework in the upper parts had fallen; the roof, in one place, had been wrecked in one of the flurries of wind which were common in these mountains; and the whole house, in the strong, beating sunlight, and standing out above a grove of stunted cork-trees, thickly laden and discoloured with dust, looked like the sleeping palace of the legend. The court, in particular, seemed the very home of slumber. A hoarse cooing of doves haunted about the eaves; the winds were excluded, but when they blew outside, the mountain dust fell here as thick as rain, and veiled the red bloom of the pomegranates; shuttered windows and the closed doors of numerous cellars, and the vacant arches of the gallery, enclosed it; and all day long the sun made broken profiles on the four sides, and paraded the shadow of the pillars on the gallery floor. At the ground level there was, however, a certain pillared recess, which bore the marks of human habitation. Though it was open in front upon the court, it was yet provided with a chimney, where a wood fire would be always prettily blazing; and the tile floor was littered with the skins of animals.

It was in this place that I first saw my hostess. She had drawn one of the skins forward and sat in the sun, leaning against a pillar. It was her dress that struck me first of all, for it was rich and brightly coloured, and shone out in that dusty courtyard with something of the same relief as the flowers of the pome-granates. At a second look it was her beauty of person that took hold of me. As she sat back—watching me, I thought, though with invisible eyes—and wearing at the same time an expression of almost imbecile good-humour and contentment, she showed a perfectness of feature and a quiet nobility of attitude that were beyond a statue's. I took off my hat to her in passing, and her face puckered with suspicion as swiftly and lightly as a pool ruffles in the breeze; but she paid no heed to my courtesy. I went forth on my customary walk a trifle daunted, her idol-like impassivity haunting me; and when I returned, although she was still in much the same posture, I was half surprised to see that she had moved as far as the next pillar, following the sunshine. This time, however, she address-ed me with some trivial salutation, civilly enough conceived, and uttered in the same deep-chested, and yet indistinct and lisping tones, that had already baffled the utmost niceness of my hearing from her son. I answered rather at a venture; for not only did I fail to take her meaning with precision, but the sudden disclosure of her eyes disturbed me. They were unusually large, the iris golden like Felipe's, but the pupil at that moment so distended that they seemed almost black; and what affected me was not so much their size as (what was perhaps its consequence) the singular insignificance of their regard. A look more blankly stupid I have never met. My eyes dropped before it even as I spoke, and I went on my way upstairs to my own room, at once baffled and embarrassed. Yet when I came there and saw the face of the portrait, I was again reminded of the miracle of family descent. My hostess was, indeed, both older and fuller in person; her eyes were of a different colour; her face, besides, was not only free from the ill-significance that offended and attracted me in the painting; it was devoid of either good or bad—a moral blank expressing literally naught. And yet there was a likeness, not so much speaking as immanent, not so much in any particular feature as upon the whole. It should seem, I thought, as if when the master set his signature to that grave canvas, he had not only caught the image of one smiling and false-eyed woman, but stamped the essential quality of a race.

From that day forth, whether I came or went, I was sure to find the Señora seated in the sun against a pillar, or stretched on a rug before the fire; only at times she would shift her station to the top round of the stone staircase, where she lay with the same nonchalance right across my path. In all these days, I never knew her to display the least spark of energy beyond what she expended in brushing and re-brushing her copious copper-coloured hair, or in lisping out, in the rich and broken hoarseness of her voice, her customary idle salutations to myself. These, I think, were her two chief pleasures, beyond that of mere quiescence. She seemed always proud of her remarks, as though they had been witticisms: and, indeed, though they were empty enough, like the conversation of many respectable persons, and turned on a very narrow range of subjects, they were never meaningless or incoherent; nay, they had a certain beauty of their own, breathing, as they did, of her entire contentment. Now she would speak of the warmth, in which (like her son) she greatly delighted; now of the flowers of the pomegranate trees, and now of the white doves and long-winged swallows that fanned the air of the court. The birds excited her. As they raked the eaves in their swift flight, or skimmed sidelong past her with a rush of wind, she would sometimes stir, and sit a little up, and seem to awaken from her doze of satisfaction. But for the rest of her days she lay luxuriously folded on herself and sunk in sloth and pleasure. Her invincible content at first annoyed me, but I came gradually to find repose in the spectacle, until at last it grew to be my habit to sit down beside her four times in the day, both coming and going, and to talk with her sleepily, I scarce knew of what. I had come to like her dull, almost animal neighbourhood; her beauty and her stupidity soothed and amused me. I began to find a kind of transcendental good sense in her remarks, and her unfathomable good-nature moved me to admiration and envy. The liking was returned; she enjoyed my presence half-unconsciously, as a man in deep meditation may enjoy the babbling of a brook. I can scarce say

she brightened when I came, for satisfaction was written on
her face eternally, as on some foolish statue's; but I was made
conscious of her pleasure by some more intimate communication than the sight. And one day, as I sat within reach of her
on the marble step, she suddenly shot forth one of her hands
and patted mine. The thing was done, and she was back in her
accustomed attitude, before my mind had received intelligence
of the caress; and when I turned to look her in the face I could
perceive no answerable sentiment. It was plain she attached no
moment to the act, and I blamed myself for my own more
uneasy consciousness.

The sight and (if I may so call it) the acquaintance of the
mother confirmed the view I had already taken of the son. The
family blood had been impoverished, perhaps by long inbreed-
ing, which I knew to be a common error among the proud and
the exclusive. No decline, indeed, was to be traced in the body,
which had been handed down unimpaired in shapeliness and
strength; and the faces of today were struck as sharply from the
mint as the face of two centuries ago that smiled upon me
from the portrait. But the intelligence (that more precious
heirloom) was degenerate; the treasure of ancestral memory
ran low; and it had required the potent, plebeian crossing of a
muleteer or mountain *contrabandista* to raise what approached hebetude in the mother into the active oddity of the son.
Yet of the two, it was the mother I preferred. Of Felipe,
vengeful and placable, full of starts and shyings, inconstant as
a hare, I could even conceive as a creature possibly noxious. Of
the mother I had no thoughts but those of kindness. And
indeed, as spectators are apt ignorantly to take sides, I grew
something of a partisan in the enmity which I perceived to
smoulder between them. True, it seemed mostly on the
mother's part. She would sometimes draw in her breath as he
came near, and the pupils of her vacant eyes would contract as
if with horror or fear. Her emotions, such as they were, were
much upon the surface and readily shared; and this latent
repulsion occupied my mind, and kept me wondering on what

grounds it rested, and whether the son was certainly in fault.

I had been about ten days in the residencia, when there sprang up a high and harsh wind, carrying clouds of dust. It came out of malarious lowlands, and over several snowy sierras. The nerves of those on whom it blew were strung and jangled; their eyes smarted with the dust; their legs ached under the burthen of their body; and the touch of one hand upon another grew to be odious. The wind, besides, came down the gullies of the hills and stormed about the house with a great, hollow buzzing and whistling that was wearisome to the ear and dismally depressing to the mind. It did not so much blow in gusts as with the steady sweep of a waterfall, so that there was no remission of discomfort while it blew. But higher up on the mountain it was probably of a more variable strength, with accesses of fury; for there came down at times a far-off wailing, infinitely grievous to hear; and at times, on one of the high shelves or terraces, there would start up, and then disperse, a tower of dust, like the smoke of an explosion.

I no sooner awoke in bed than I was conscious of the nervous tension and depression of the weather, and the effect grew stronger as the day proceeded. It was in vain that I resisted; in vain that I set forth upon my customary morning's walk; the irrational, unchanging fury of the storm had soon beat down my strength and wrecked my temper; and I returned to the residencia, glowing with dry heat, and foul and gritty with dust. The court had a forlorn appearance; now and then a glimmer of sun fled over it; now and then the wind swooped down upon the pomegranates, and scattered the blossoms, and set the window shutter clapping on the wall. In the recess the Señora was pacing to and fro with a flushed countenance and bright eyes; I thought, too, she was speaking to herself, like one in anger. But when I addressed her with my customary salutation, she only replied by a sharp gesture and continued her walk. The weather had distempered even this impassive creature; and as I went on upstairs I was the less ashamed of my own discomposure.

All day the wind continued; and I sat in my room and made a feint of reading, or walked up and down, and listened to the riot overhead. Night fell, and I had not so much as a candle. I began to long for some society, and stole down to the court. It was now plunged in the blue of the first darkness; but the recess was redly lighted by the fire. The wood had been piled high, and was crowned by a shock of flames, which the draught of the chimney brandished to and fro. In this strong and shaken brightness the Señora continued pacing from wall to wall with disconnected gestures, clasping her hands, stretching forth her arms, throwing back her head as in appeal to heaven. In these disordered movements the beauty and grace of the woman showed more clearly; but there was a light in her eyes that struck on me unpleasantly; and when I had looked on a while in silence, and seemingly unobserved, I turned tail as I had come, and groped my way back again to my own chamber.

By the time Felipe brought my supper and lights, my nerve was utterly gone; and, had the lad been such as I was used to seeing him, I should have kept him (even by force, had that been necessary) to take off the edge from my distasteful solitude. But on Felipe, also, the wind had exercised its influence. He had been feverish all day; now that the night had come he was fallen into a low and tremulous humour that reacted on my own. The sight of his scared face, his starts and pallors and sudden hearkenings, unstrung me; and when he dropped and broke a dish, I fairly leaped out of my seat.

"I think we are all mad today," said I, affecting to laugh.

"It is the black wind," he replied dolefully. "You feel as if you must do something, and you don't know what it is."

I noted the aptness of the description; but, indeed, Felipe had sometimes a strange felicity in rendering into words the sensations of the body. "And your mother, too," said I; "she seems to feel this weather much. Do you not fear she may be unwell?"

He stared at me a little, and then said, "No," almost defiantly; and the next moment, carrying his hand to his brow, cried out

145

lamentably on the wind and the noise that made his head go round like a millwheel. "Who can be well?" he cried; and, indeed, I could only echo his question, for I was disturbed enough myself.

I went to bed early, wearied with daylong restlessness; but the poisonous nature of the wind, and its ungodly and unintermittent uproar, would not suffer me to sleep. I lay there and tossed, my nerves and senses on the stretch. At times I would doze, dream horribly, and wake again; and these snatches of oblivion confused me as to time. But it must have been late on in the night, when I was suddenly startled by an outbreak of pitiable and hateful cries. I leaped from my bed, supposing I had dreamed; but the cries still continued to fill the house, cries of pain, I thought, but certainly of rage also, and so savage and discordant that they shocked the heart. It was no illusion; some living thing, some lunatic or some wild animal, was being foully tortured. The thought of Felipe and the squirrel flashed into my mind, and I ran to the door; but it had been locked from the outside, and I might shake it as I pleased, I was a fast prisoner. Still the cries continued. Now they would dwindle down into a moaning that seemed to be articulate, and at these times I made sure they must be human; and again they would break forth and fill the house with ravings worthy of hell. I stood at the door and gave ear to them, till at last they died away. Long after that, I still lingered and still continued to hear them mingle in fancy with the storming of the wind; and when at last I crept to my bed, it was with a deadly sickness and a blackness of horror on my heart.

It was little wonder if I slept no more. Why had I been locked in? What had passed? Who was the author of these indescribable and shocking cries? A human being? It was inconceivable. A beast? The cries were scarce quite bestial; and what animal, short of a lion or a tiger, could thus shake the solid walls of the residencia? And while I was thus turning over the elements of the mystery, it came into my mind that I had not yet set eyes upon the daughter of the house. What was more probable than that the daughter of the Señora, and the sister of Felipe, should be herself insane? Or, what more likely than that these ignorant and half-witted people should seek to manage an afflicted kinswoman by violence? Here was a solution; and yet when I called to mind the cries (which I never did without a shuddering chill) it seemed altogether insufficient: not even cruelty could wring such cries from madness. But of one thing I was sure: I could not live in a house where such a thing was half conceivable, and not probe the matter home and, if necessary, interfere.

The next day came, the wind had blown itself out, and there was nothing to remind me of the business of the night. Felipe came to my bedside with obvious cheerfulness; as I passed through the court the Señora was sunning herself with her accustomed immobility; and when I passed from the gateway I found the whole face of nature austerely smiling, the heavens of a cold blue, and sown with great cloud islands, and the mountain-sides mapped forth into provinces of light and shadow. A short walk restored me to myself, and renewed within me the resolve to plumb this mystery; and when, from the vantage of my knoll, I had seen Felipe pass forth to his labours in the garden, I returned at once to the residencia to put my design in practice. The Señora appeared plunged in slumber; I stood a while and marked her, but she did not stir; even if my design were indiscreet, I had little to fear from such a guardian; and turning away, I mounted to the gallery and began my exploration of the house.

All morning I went from one door to another, and entered spacious and faded chambers, some rudely shuttered, some receiving their full charge of daylight, all empty and unhomely. It was a rich house, on which Time had breathed his tarnish and dust had scattered disillusion. The spider swung there; the bloated tarantula scampered on the cornices; ants had their crowded highways on the floor of halls of audience; the big and foul fly, that lives on carrion and is often the messenger of death, had set up his nest in the rotten woodwork, and buzzed heavily about the rooms. Here and there a stool or two, a couch, a bed, or a great carved chair remained behind, like islets on the bare floors, to testify of man's bygone habitation; and everywhere the walls were set with the portraits of the dead. I could judge, by these decaying effigies, in the house of what a great and what a handsome race I was then wandering. Many of the men wore orders on their breasts and had the port of noble offices; the women were all richly attired; the canvases, most of them, by famous hands. But it was not so much these evidences of greatness that took hold upon my mind, even contrasted, as they were, with the present depopulation and decay of that great house. It was rather the parable of family life that I read in this succession of fair faces and shapely bodies. Never before had I so realised the miracle of the continued race, the creation and re-creation, the weaving and changing and handing down of fleshly elements. That a child should be born of its mother, that it should grow and clothe itself (we know not how) with humanity, and put on inherited looks, and turn its head with the manner of one ascendant, and offer its hand with the gesture of another, are wonders dulled for us by repetition. But in the singular unity of look, in the common features and common bearing, of all these painted generations on the walls of the residencia, the miracle started out and looked me in the face. And an ancient mirror falling opportunely in my way, I stood and read my own features a long while, tracing out on either hand the filaments of descent and the bonds that knit me with my family.

At last, in the course of these investigations, I opened the door of a chamber that bore the marks of habitation. It was of large proportions and faced to the north, where the mountains were most wildly figured. The embers of a fire smouldered and smoked upon the hearth, to which a chair had been drawn close. And yet the aspect of the chamber was ascetic to the degree of sternness; the chair was uncushioned; the floor and walls were naked; and beyond the books which lay here and there in some confusion, there was no instrument of either work or pleasure. The sight of books in the house of such a family exceedingly amazed me; and I began with a great hurry, and in momentary fear of interruption, to go from one to another and hastily inspect their character. They were of all sorts, devotional, historical, and scientific, but mostly of a great age and in the Latin tongue. Some I could see to bear the marks of constant study; others had been torn across and tossed aside as if in petulance or disapproval. Lastly, as I cruised about that empty chamber, I espied some papers written upon with pencil on a table near the window. An unthinking curiosity led me to take one up. It bore a copy of verses, very roughly metred in the original Spanish, and which I may render somewhat thus—

"Pleasure approached with pain and shame,
Grief with a wreath of lilies came.
Pleasure showed the lovely sun;
Jesu dear, how sweet it shone!
Grief with her worn hand pointed on,
        Jesu dear, to Thee!"

Shame and confusion at once fell on me; and, laying down the paper, I beat an immediate retreat from the apartment. Neither Felipe nor his mother could have read the books nor written these rough but feeling verses. It was plain I had stumbled with sacrilegious feet into the room of the daughter of the house. God knows, my own heart most sharply punished me for my indiscretion. The thought that I had thus secretly pushed my way into the confidence of a girl so strangely situated, and the fear that she might somehow come to hear of it, oppressed me like guilt. I blamed myself besides for my suspicions of the night before; wondered that I should ever have attributed those shocking cries to one of whom I now conceived as of a saint, spectral of mien, wasted with maceration, bound up in the practices of a mechanical devotion, and dwelling in a great isolation of soul with her incongruous relatives; and as I leaned on the balustrade of the gallery and looked

down into the bright close of pomegranates and at the gaily
dressed and somnolent woman, who just then stretched herself and delicately licked her lips as in the very sensuality of
sloth, my mind swiftly compared the scene with the cold chamber looking northward on the mountains, where the daughter
dwelt.

That same afternoon, as I sat upon my knoll, I saw the Padre
enter the gates of the residencia. The revelation of the daughter's character had struck home to my fancy, and almost blotted
out the horrors of the night before; but at sight of this worthy
man the memory revived. I descended, then, from the knoll,
and making a circuit among the woods, posted myself by the
wayside to await his passage. As soon as he appeared I stepped
forth and introduced myself as the lodger of the residencia. He
had a very strong, honest countenance, on which it was easy to
read the mingled emotions with which he regarded me, as a
foreigner, a heretic, and yet one who had been wounded for
the good cause. Of the family at the residencia he spoke with
reserve, and yet with respect. I mentioned that I had not yet
seen the daughter, whereupon he remarked that that was as it
should be, and looked at me a little askance. Lastly, I plucked
up courage to refer to the cries that had disturbed me in the
night. He heard me out in silence, and then stopped and partly turned about, as though to mark beyond doubt that he was
dismissing me.

"Do you take tobacco-powder?" said he, offering his snuff-
box; and then, when I had refused, "I am an old man," he
added, "and I may be allowed to remind you that you are a
guest."

"I have, then, your authority," I returned, firmly enough, although I flushed at the implied reproof, "to let things take their
course, and not to interfere?"

He said "Yes," and with a somewhat uneasy salute turned
and left me where I was. But he had done two things: he had
set my conscience at rest, and he had awakened my delicacy. I
made a great effort, once more dismissed the recollections of

the night, and fell once more to brooding on my saintly poet-ess. At the same time, I could not quite forget that I had been locked in, and that night when Felipe brought me my supper I attacked him warily on both points of interest.

"I never see your sister," said I casually.

"Oh, no," said he; "she is a good, good girl," and his mind instantly veered to something else.

"Your sister is pious, I suppose?" I asked in the next pause.

"Oh!" he cried, joining his hands with extreme fervour, "a saint; it is she that keeps me up."

"You are very fortunate," said I, "for the most of us, I am afraid, and myself among the number, are better at going down."

"Señor," said Felipe earnestly, "I would not say that. You should not tempt your angel. If one goes down, where is he to stop?"

"Why, Felipe," said I, "I had no guess you were a preacher, and I may say a good one; but I suppose that is your sister's doing?"

He nodded at me with round eyes.

"Well, then," I continued, "she has doubtless reproved you for your sin of cruelty?"

"Twelve times!" he cried; for this was the phrase by which the odd creature expressed the sense of frequency. "And I told her you had done so—I remembered that," he added proudly—"and she was pleased."

"Then, Felipe," said I, "what were those cries that I heard last night? for surely they were cries of some creature in suffering."

"The wind," returned Felipe, looking in the fire.

I took his hand in mine, at which, thinking it to be a caress, he smiled with a brightness of pleasure that came near disarm-ing my resolve. But I trod the weakness down. "The wind," I repeated; "and yet I think it was this hand," holding it up, "that had first locked me in." The lad shook visibly, but answered never a word. "Well," said I, "I am a stranger and a guest. It is not my part either to meddle or to judge in your affairs; in these you shall take your sister's counsel, which I cannot doubt to be excellent. But in so far as concerns my own I will be no man's prisoner, and I demand that key." Half an hour later my door was suddenly thrown open, and the key tossed ringing on the floor.

A day or two after I came in from a walk a little before the point of noon. The Señora was lying lapped in slumber on the threshold of the recess; the pigeons dozed below the eaves like snowdrifts; the house was under a deep spell of noontide quiet; and only a wandering and gentle wind from the mountain stole round the galleries, rustled among the pomegranates, and pleasantly stirred the shadows. Something in the stillness moved me to imitation, and I went very lightly across the court and up the marble staircase. My foot was on the topmost round, when a door opened, and I found myself face to face with Olalla. Surprise transfixed me; her loveliness struck to my heart; she glowed in the deep shadow of the gallery, a gem of colour; her eyes took hold upon mine and clung there, and bound us together like the joining of hands; and the moments we thus stood face to face, drinking each other in, were sacramental and the wedding of souls. I know not how long it was before I awoke out of a deep trance, and, hastily bowing, passed on into the upper stair. She did not move, but followed me with her great, thirsting eyes; and as I passed out of sight it seemed to me as if she paled and faded.

In my own room, I opened the window and looked out, and could not think what change had come upon that austere field of mountains that it should thus sing and shine under the lofty heaven. I had seen her—Olalla! And the stone crags answered, Olalla! and the dumb, unfathomable azure answered, Olalla! The pale saint of my dreams had vanished for ever; and in her place I beheld this maiden on whom God had lavished the richest colours and the most exuberant energies of life, whom He had made active as a deer, slender as a reed, and in whose great eyes He had lighted the torches of the soul. The thrill of her young life, strung like a wild animal's, had entered into me;

the force of soul that had looked out from her eyes and conquered mine, mantled about my heart and sprang to my lips in
singing. She passed through my veins: she was one with me.

I will not say that this enthusiasm declined; rather my soul
held out in its ecstasy as in a strong castle, and was there besieged by cold and sorrowful considerations. I could not doubt
but that I loved her at first sight, and already with a quivering
ardour that was strange to my experience. What then was to
follow? She was the child of an afflicted house, the Señora's
daughter, the sister of Felipe; she bore it even in her beauty.
She had the lightness and swiftness of the one, swift as an
arrow, light as dew; like the other, she shone on the pale back-
ground of the world with the brilliancy of flowers. I could not
call by the name of brother that half-witted lad, nor by the
name of mother that immovable and lovely thing of flesh,
whose silly eyes and perpetual simper now recurred to my
mind like something hateful. And if I could not marry, what
then? She was helplessly unprotected; her eyes, in that single
and long glance, which had been all our intercourse, had confessed a weakness equal to my own; but in my heart I knew her
for the student of the cold northern chamber, and the writer of
the sorrowful lines; and this was a knowledge to disarm a
brute. To flee was more than I could find courage for; but I
registered a vow of unsleeping circumspection.

As I turned from the window, my eyes alighted on the
portrait. It had fallen dead, like a candle after sunrise; it followed me with eyes of paint. I knew it to be like, and marvelled at
the tenacity of type in that declining race; but the likeness was
swallowed up in difference. I remembered how it had seemed
to me a thing unapproachable in the life, a creature rather of
the painter's craft than of the modesty of nature, and I marvelled at the thought, and exulted in the image of Olalla.
Beauty I had seen before, and not been charmed, and I had
been often drawn to women, who were not beautiful except to
me; but in Olalla all that I desired and had not dared to imagine
was united.

I did not see her the next day, and my heart ached and my eyes longed for her, as men long for morning. But the day after, when I returned, about my usual hour, she was once more on the gallery, and our looks once more met and embraced. I would have spoken, I would have drawn near to her; but strongly as she plucked at my heart, drawing me like a magnet, something yet more imperious withheld me; and I could only bow and pass by; and she, leaving my salutation unanswered, only followed me with her noble eyes.

I had now her image by rote, and as I conned the traits in memory it seemed as if I read her very heart. She was dressed with something of her mother's coquetry and love of positive colour. Her robe, which I knew she must have made with her own hands, clung about her with a cunning grace. After the fashion of that country, besides, her bodice stood open in the middle, in a long slit, and here, in spite of the poverty of the house, a gold coin, hanging by a ribbon, lay on her brown bosom. These were proofs, had any been needed, of her inborn delight in life and her own loveliness. On the other hand, in her eyes that hung upon mine, I could read depth beyond depth of passion and sadness, lights of poetry and hope, blacknesses of despair, and thoughts that were above the earth. It was a lovely body, but the inmate, the soul, was more than worthy of that lodging. Should I leave this incomparable flower to wither unseen on these rough mountains? Should I despise the great gift offered me in the eloquent silence of her eyes? Here was a soul immured; should I not burst its prison? All side considerations fell off from me; were she the child of Herod I swore I should make her mine; and that very evening I set myself, with a mingled sense of treachery and disgrace, to captivate the brother. Perhaps I read him with more favourable eyes, perhaps the thought of his sister always summoned up the better qualities of that imperfect soul; but he had never seemed to me so amiable, and his very likeness to Olalla, while it annoyed, yet softened me.

A third day passed in vain—an empty desert of hours. I would not lose a chance, and loitered all afternoon in the court where (to give myself a countenance) I spoke more than usual with the Señora. God knows it was with a most tender and sincere interest that I now studied her; and even as for Felipe, so now for the mother, I was conscious of a growing warmth of toleration. And yet I wondered. Even while I spoke with her, she would doze off into a little sleep, and presently awake again without embarrassment; and this composure staggered me. And again, as I marked her make infinitesimal changes in her posture, savouring and lingering on the bodily pleasure of the movement, I was driven to wonder at this depth of passive sensuality. She lived in her body; and her consciousness was all sunk into and disseminated through her members, where it luxuriously dwelt. Lastly, I could not grow accustomed to her eyes. Each time she turned on me these great beautiful and meaningless orbs, wide open to the day, but closed against human inquiry—each time I had occasion to observe the lively changes of her pupils which expanded and contracted in a breath—I know not what it was came over me, I can find no name for the mingled feeling of disappointment, annoyance, and distaste that jarred along my nerves. I tried her on a variety of subjects, equally in vain; and at last led the talk to her daughter. But even there she proved indifferent; said she was pretty, which (as with children) was her highest word of commendation, but was plainly incapable of any higher thought; and when I remarked that Olalla seemed silent, merely yawned in my face and replied that speech was of no great use when you had nothing to say. "People speak much, very much," she added, looking at me with expanded pupils; and then again yawned, and again showed me a mouth that was as dainty as a toy. This time I took the hint, and, leaving her to her repose, went up into my own chamber to sit by the open window, looking on the hills and not beholding them, sunk in lustrous and deep dreams, and hearkening in fancy to the note of a voice that I had never heard.

I awoke on the fifth morning with a brightness of anticipation that seemed to challenge fate. I was sure of myself, light of heart and foot, and resolved to put my love incontinently to the touch of knowledge. It should lie no longer under the bonds of silence, a dumb thing, living by the eye only, like the love of beasts; but should now put on the spirit, and enter upon the joys of the complete human intimacy. I thought of it with wild hopes, like a voyager to El Dorado; into that unknown and lovely country of her soul, I no longer trembled to adventure. Yet when I did indeed encounter her, the same force of passion descended on me and at once submerged my mind; speech seemed to drop away from me like a childish habit; and I but drew near to her as the giddy man draws near to the margin of a gulf. She drew back from me a little as I came; but her eyes did not waver from mine, and these lured me forward. At last, when I was already within reach of her, I stopped. Words were denied me; if I advanced I could but clasp her to my heart in silence; and all that was sane in me, all that was still unconquered, revolted against the thought of such an accost. So we stood for a second, all our life in our eyes, exchanging salvos of attraction and yet each resisting; and then, with a great effort of the will, and conscious at the same time of a sudden bitterness of disappointment, I turned and went away in the same silence.

What power lay upon me that I could not speak? And she, why was she also silent? Why did she draw away before me dumbly, with fascinated eyes? Was this love? or was it a mere brute attraction, mindless and inevitable, like that of the magnet for the steel? We had never spoken, we were wholly strangers; and yet an influence, strong as the grasp of a giant, swept us silently together. On my side, it filled me with impatience; and yet I was sure that she was worthy; I had seen her books, read her verses, and thus, in a sense, divined the soul of my mistress. But on her side, it struck me almost cold. Of me, she knew nothing but my bodily favour; she was drawn to me as stones fall to the earth; the laws that rule the earth conducted her, unconsenting, to my arms; and I drew back at the thought of such a bridal, and began to be jealous for myself. It was not thus that I desired to be loved. And then I began to fall into a great pity for the girl herself. I thought how sharp must be her mortification, that she, the student, the recluse, Felipe's saintly monitress, should have thus confessed an overweening weakness for a man with whom she had never exchanged a word. And at the coming of pity, all other thoughts were swallowed up; and I longed only to find and console and reassure her; to tell her how wholly her love was returned on my side, and how her choice, even if blindly made, was not unworthy.

The next day it was glorious weather; depth upon depth of blue over-canopied the mountains; the sun shone wide; and the wind in the trees and the many fallen torrents in the mountains filled the air with delicate and haunting music. Yet I was prostrated with sadness. My heart wept for the sight of Olalla, as a child weeps for its mother. I sat down on a boulder on the verge of the low cliffs that bound the plateau to the north. Thence I looked down into the wooded valley of a stream, where no foot came. In the mood I was in, it was even touching to behold the place untenanted; it lacked Olalla; and I thought of the delight and glory of a life passed wholly with her in that strong air, and among these rugged and lovely surroundings, at first with a whimpering sentiment, and then again with such a fiery joy that I seemed to grow in strength and stature, like a Samson.

And then suddenly I was aware of Olalla drawing near. She appeared out of a grove of cork-trees, and came straight towards me; and I stood up and waited. She seemed in her walking a creature of such life and fire and lightness as amazed me; yet she came quietly and slowly. Her energy was in the slowness; but for inimitable strength, I felt she would have run, she would have flown to me. Still, as she approached, she kept her eyes lowered to the ground; and when she had drawn quite near, it was without one glance that she addressed me. At the first note of her voice I started. It was for this I had been waiting; this was the last test of my love. And lo, her enunciation was precise and clear, not lisping and incomplete like that of her family; and the voice, though deeper than usual with women, was still both youthful and womanly. She spoke in a rich chord; golden contralto strains mingled with hoarseness, as the red threads were mingled with the brown among her tresses. It was not only a voice that spoke to my heart directly; but it spoke to me of her. And yet her words immediately plunged me back upon despair.

"You will go away," she said, "today."

Her example broke the bonds of my speech; I felt as lightened of a weight, or as if a spell had been dissolved. I know not in what words I answered; but, standing before her on the cliffs, I poured out the whole ardour of my love, telling her that I lived upon the thought of her, slept only to dream of her loveliness, and would gladly forswear my country, my language, and my friends, to live for ever by her side. And then, strongly commanding myself, I changed the note; I reassured, I comforted her; I told her I had divined in her a pious and heroic spirit, with which I was worthy to sympathise, and which I longed to share and lighten. "Nature," I told her, "was the voice of God, which men disobey at peril; and if we were thus dumbly drawn together, ay, even as by a miracle of love, it must imply a divine fitness in our souls; we must be made," I said—"made for one another. We should be mad rebels," I cried out—"mad rebels against God, not to obey this instinct."

She shook her head. "You will go today," she repeated, and then with a gesture, and in a sudden, sharp note—"no, not today," she cried, "tomorrow!"

But at this sign of relenting, power came in upon me in a tide. I stretched out my arms and called upon her name; and she leaped to me and clung to me. The hills rocked about us, the earth quailed; a shock as of a blow went through me and left me blind and dizzy. And the next moment she had thrust me back, broken rudely from my arms, and fled with the speed of a deer among the cork-trees.

I stood and shouted to the mountains; I turned and went

back towards the residencia, walking upon air. She sent me away, and yet I had but to call upon her name and she came to me. These were but the weaknesses of girls, from which even she, the strangest of her sex, was not exempted. Go? Not I, Olalla—Oh, not I, Olalla, my Olalla! A bird sang near by; and in that season birds were rare. It bade me be of good cheer. And once more the whole countenance of nature, from the ponderous and stable mountains down to the lightest leaf and the smallest darting fly in the shadow of the groves, began to stir before me and to put on the lineaments of life and wear a face of awful joy. The sunshine struck upon the hills, strong as a hammer on the anvil, and the hills shook; the earth, under that vigorous insolation, yielded up heady scents; the woods smouldered in the blaze. I felt the thrill of travail and delight run through the earth. Something elemental, something rude, violent, and savage, in the love that sang in my heart, was like a key to nature's secrets; and the very stones that rattled under my feet appeared alive and friendly. Olalla! Her touch had quickened, and renewed, and strung me up to the old pitch of concert with the rugged earth, to a swelling of the soul that men learn to forget in their polite assemblies. Love burned in me like rage; tenderness waxed fierce; I hated, I adored, I pitied, I revered her with ecstasy. She seemed the link that bound me in with dead things on the one hand, and with our pure and pitying God upon the other: a thing brutal and divine, and akin at once to the innocence and to the unbridled forces of the earth.

My head thus reeling, I came into the courtyard of the residencia, and the sight of the mother struck me like a revelation. She sat there, all sloth and contentment, blinking under the strong sunshine, branded with a passive enjoyment, a creature set quite apart, before whom my ardour fell away like a thing ashamed. I stopped a moment, and, commanding such shaken tones as I was able, said a word or two. She looked at me with her unfathomable kindness; her voice in reply sounded vaguely out of the realm of peace in which she slumbered, and there fell on my mind, for the first time, a sense of respect for one so uniformly innocent and happy, and I passed on in a kind of wonder at myself that I should be so much disquieted.

On my table there lay a piece of the same yellow paper I had seen in the north room; it was written on with pencil in the same hand, Olalla's hand, and I picked it up with a sudden sinking of alarm, and read, "If you have any kindness for Olalla, if you have any chivalry for a creature sorely wrought, go from here today; in pity, in honour, for the sake of Him who died, I supplicate that you shall go." I looked at this a while in mere stupidity, then I began to awaken to a weariness and horror of life; the sunshine darkened outside on the bare hills, and I began to shake like a man in terror. The vacancy thus suddenly opened in my life unmanned me like a physical void. It was not my heart, it was not my happiness, it was life itself that was involved. I could not lose her. I said so, and stood repeating it. And then, like one in a dream, I moved to the window, put forth my hand to open the casement, and thrust it through the pane. The blood spurted from my wrist; and with an instantaneous quietude and command of myself, I pressed my thumb on the little leaping fountain, and reflected what to do. In that empty room there was nothing to my purpose; I felt, besides, that I required assistance. There shot into my mind a hope that Olalla herself might be my helper, and I turned and went downstairs, still keeping my thumb upon the wound.

There was no sign of either Olalla or Felipe, and I addressed myself to the recess, whither the Señora had now drawn quite back and sat dozing close before the fire, for no degree of heat appeared too much for her.

"Pardon me," said I, "if I disturb you, but I must apply to you for help."

She looked up sleepily and asked me what it was, and with the very words I thought she drew in her breath with a widening of the nostrils and seemed to come suddenly and fully alive.

"I have cut myself," I said, "and rather badly. See!" And I held out my two hands, from which the blood was oozing and - dripping.

Her great eyes opened wide, the pupils shrank into points; a veil seemed to fall from her face, and leave it sharply express- ive and yet inscrutable. And as I still stood, marvelling a little at her disturbance, she came swiftly up to me, and stooped and caught me by the hand; and the next moment my hand was at her mouth, and she had bitten me to the bone. The pang of the bite, the sudden spurting of blood, and the monstrous horror of the act, flashed through me all in one, and I beat her back; and she sprang at me again and again, with bestial cries, cries that I recognised, such cries as had awakened me on the night of the high wind. Her strength was like that of madness; mine was rapidly ebbing with the loss of blood; my mind besides was whirling with the abhorrent strangeness of the onslaught, and I was already forced against the wall, when Olalla ran be- twixt us, and Felipe, following at a bound, pinned down his mother on the floor.

A trance-like weakness fell upon me; I saw, heard, and felt, but I was incapable of movement. I heard the struggle roll to and fro upon the floor, the yells of that catamount ringing up to heaven as she strove to reach me. I felt Olalla clasp me in her arms, her hair falling on my face, and, with the strength of a man, raise and half drag, half carry me upstairs into my own room, where she cast me down upon the bed. Then I saw her hasten to the door and lock it, and stand an instant listening to the savage cries that shook the residencia. And then, swift and light as a thought, she was again beside me, binding up my hand, laying it in her bosom, moaning and mourning over it, with dove-like sounds. They were not words that came to her, they were sounds more beautiful than speech, infinitely touch- ing, infinitely tender; and yet as I lay there, a thought stung to my heart, a thought wounded me like a sword, a thought, like a worm in a flower, profaned the holiness of my love. Yes, they were beautiful sounds, and they were inspired by human tenderness; but was their beauty human?

All day I lay there. For a long time the cries of that nameless female thing, as she struggled with her half-witted whelp, resounded through the house, and pierced me with despairing sorrow and disgust. They were the death-cry of my love; my love was murdered; it was not only dead, but an offence to me; and yet, think as I pleased, feel as I must, it still swelled within me like a storm of sweetness, and my heart melted at her looks and touch. This horror that had sprung out, this doubt upon Olalla, this savage and bestial strain that ran not only through the whole behaviour of her family, but found a place in the very foundations and story of our love—though it appalled, though it shocked and sickened me, was yet not of power to break the knot of my infatuation.

When the cries had ceased, there came a scraping at the door, by which I knew Felipe was without; and Olalla went and spoke to him—I know not what. With that exception, she stayed close beside me, now kneeling by my bed and fervently praying, now sitting with her eyes upon mine. So then, for these six hours I drank in her beauty, and silently perused the story in her face. I saw the golden coin hover on her breaths; I saw her eyes darken and brighten, and still speak no language but that of an unfathomable kindness; I saw the faultless face, and, through the robe, the lines of the faultless body. Night came at last, and in the growing darkness of the chamber the sight of her slowly melted; but even then the touch of her smooth hand lingered in mine and talked with me. To lie thus in deadly weakness and drink in the traits of the beloved, is to re-awake to love from whatever shock of disillusion. I reasoned with myself; and I shut my eyes on horrors, and again I was very bold to accept the worst. What mattered it, if that imperious sentiment survived; if her eyes still beckoned and attached me; if now, even as before, every fibre of my dull body yearned and turned to her? Late on in the night some strength revived in me, and I spoke:—

"Olalla," I said, "nothing matters; I ask nothing; I am content: I love you."

162

She knelt down a while and prayed, and I devoutly respected her devotions. The moon had begun to shine in upon one side of each of the three windows, and make a misty clearness in the room, by which I saw her indistinctly. When she re-arose she made the sign of the cross.

"It is for me to speak," she said, "and for you to listen. I know; you can but guess. I prayed, how I prayed for you to leave this place. I begged it of you, and I know you would have granted me even this; or if not, oh let me think so!"

"I love you," I said.

"And yet you have lived in the world," she said; after a pause, "you are a man and wise; and I am but a child. Forgive me, if I seem to teach, who am as ignorant as the trees of the mountain; but those who learn much do but skim the face of knowledge; they seize the laws, they conceive the dignity of the design—the horror of the living fact fades from their memory. It is we who sit at home with evil who remember, I think, and are warned and pity. Go, rather, go now, and keep me in mind. So I shall have a life in the cherished places of your memory; a life as much my own as that which I lead in this body."

"I love you," I said once more; and reaching out my weak hand, took hers, and carried it to my lips, and kissed it. Nor did she resist, but winced a little; and I could see her look upon me with a frown that was not unkindly, only sad and baffled. And then it seemed she made a call upon her resolution; plucked my hand towards her, herself at the same time leaning somewhat forward, and laid it on the beating of her heart. "There," she cried, "you feel the very footfall of my life. It only moves for you; it is yours. But is it even mine? It is mine indeed to offer you, as I might take the coin from my neck, as I might break a live branch from a tree, and give it you. And yet not mine! I dwell, or I think I dwell (if I exist at all), somewhere apart, an impotent prisoner, and carried about and deafened by a mob that I disown. This capsule, such as throbs against the sides of animals, knows you at a touch for its master; ay, it loves you! But my soul, does my soul? I think not; I know not, fearing to ask. Yet when you spoke to me, your words were of the soul; it is of the soul that you ask—it is only from the soul that you would take me."

"Olalla," I said, "the soul and the body are one, and mostly so in love. What the body chooses, the soul loves; where the body clings, the soul cleaves; body for body, soul to soul, they come together at God's signal; and the lower part (if we can call aught low) is only the footstool and foundation of the highest."

"Have you," she said, "seen the portraits in the house of my fathers? Have you looked at my mother or at Felipe? Have your eyes never rested on that picture that hangs by your bed? She who sat for it died ages ago; and she did evil in her life. But, look again: there is my hand to the least line, there are my eyes and my hair. What is mine, then, and what am I? If not a curve in this poor body of mine (which you love, and for the sake of which you dotingly dream that you love me), not a gesture that I can frame, not a tone of my voice, not any look from my eyes, no, not even now when I speak to him I love, but has belonged to others? Others, ages dead, have wooed other men with my eyes; other men have heard the pleading of the same voice that now sounds in your ears. The hands of the dead are in my bosom; they move me, they pluck me, they guide me; I am a puppet at their command; and I but re-inform features and attributes that have long been laid aside from evil in the quiet of the grave. Is it me you love, friend? or the race that made me? The girl who does not know and cannot answer for the least portion of herself? or the stream of which she is a transitory eddy, the tree of which she is the passing fruit? The race exists; it is old, it is ever young, it carries its eternal destiny in its bosom; upon it, like waves upon the sea, individual succeeds to individual, mocked with a semblance of self-control, but they are nothing. We speak of the soul, but the soul is in the race."

"You fret against the common law," I said. "You rebel against the voice of God, which He has made so winning to convince, so imperious to command. Hear it, and how it speaks between us! Your hand clings to mine, your heart leaps at my touch, the unknown elements of which we are compounded awake and run together at a look; the clay of the earth remembers its independent life and yearns to join us; we are drawn together as the stars are turned about in space, or as the tides ebb and flow; by things older and greater than we ourselves."

"Alas!" she said, "what can I say to you? My fathers, eight hundred years ago, ruled all this province: they were wise, great, cunning, and cruel; they were a picked race of the Spanish; their flags led in war; the king called them his cousin; the people, when the rope was slung for them or when they returned and found their hovels smoking, blasphemed their name. Presently a change began. Man has risen; if he has sprung from the brutes, he can descend again to the same level. The breath of weariness blew on their humanity and the cords relaxed; they began to go down; their minds fell on sleep, their passions awoke in gusts, heady and senseless like the wind in the gutters of the mountains; beauty was still handed down, but no longer the guiding wit nor the human heart; the seed passed on, it was wrapped in flesh, the flesh covered the bones, but they were the bones and the flesh of brutes, and their mind was as the mind of flies. I speak to you as I dare; but you have seen for yourself how the wheel has gone backward with my doomed race. I stand, as it were, upon a little rising ground in this desperate descent, and see both before and behind, both what we have lost and to what we are condemned to go farther downward. And shall I—I that dwell apart in the house of the dead, my body, loathing its ways— shall I repeat the spell? Shall I bind another spirit, reluctant as my own, into this bewitched and tempest-broken tenement that I now suffer in? Shall I hand down this cursed vessel of humanity, charge it with fresh life as with fresh poison, and dash it, like a fire, in the faces of posterity? But my vow has been given; the race shall cease from off the earth. At this hour my brother is making ready; his foot will soon be on the stair; and you will go with him and pass out of my sight for ever.

Think of me sometimes as one to whom the lesson of life was very harshly told, but who heard it with courage; as one who loved you indeed, but who hated herself so deeply that her love was hateful to her; as one who sent you away and yet would have longed to keep you for ever: who had no dearer hope than to forget you, and no greater fear than to be forgotten."

She had drawn towards the door as she spoke, her rich voice sounding softer and farther away; and with the last word she was gone, and I lay alone in the moonlit chamber. What I might have done had not I lain bound by my extreme weakness, I know not; but as it was, there fell upon me a great and blank despair. It was not long before there shone in at the door the ruddy glimmer of a lantern, and Felipe, coming, charged me without a word upon his shoulders, and carried me down to the great gate, where the cart was waiting. In the moonlight the hills stood out sharply, as if they were of cardboard; on the glimmering surface of the plateau, and from among the low trees which swung together and sparkled in the wind, the great black cube of the residencia stood out bulkily, its mass only broken by three dimly lighted windows in the northern front above the gate. They were Olalla's windows, and as the cart jolted onwards I kept my eyes fixed upon them till, where the road dipped into a valley, they were lost to my view for ever. Felipe walked in silence beside the shafts, but from time to time he would check the mule and seem to look back upon me; and at length drew quite near and laid his hand upon my head. There was such kindness in the touch, and such a simplicity, as of the brutes, that tears broke from me like the bursting of an artery.

"Felipe," I said, "take me where they will ask no questions."

He said never a word, but he turned his mule about, end for end, retraced some part of the way we had gone, and, striking into another path, led me to the mountain village, which was, as we say in Scotland, the kirk-town of that thinly peopled district. Some broken memories dwell in my mind of the day

breaking over the plain, of the cart stopping, of arms that helped me down, of a bare room into which I was carried, and of a
swoon that fell upon me like sleep.

The next day and the days following, the old priest was often
at my side with his snuff-box and prayer-book, and after a
while, when I began to pick up strength, he told me that I was
now on a fair way to recovery, and must as soon as possible
hurry my departure; whereupon, without naming any reason,
he took snuff and looked at me sideways. I did not affect
ignorance; I knew he must have seen Olalla. "Sir," said I, "you
know that I do not ask in wantonness. What of that family?"

He said they were very unfortunate; that it seemed a declining race, and that they were very poor and had been much
neglected.

"But she has not," I said. "Thanks, doubtless, to yourself, she
is instructed and wise beyond the use of women."

"Yes," he said, "the Señorita is well-informed. But the family
has been neglected."

"The mother?" I queried.

"Yes, the mother too," said the Padre, taking snuff. "But
Felipe is a well-intentioned lad."

"The mother is odd?" I asked.

"Very odd," replied the priest.

"I think, sir, we beat about the bush," said I. "You must know
more of my affairs than you allow. You must know my curiosity to be justified on many grounds. Will you not be frank with
me?"

"My son," said the old gentleman, "I will be very frank with
you on matters within my competence; on those of which I
know nothing it does not require much discretion to be silent.
I will not fence with you, I take your meaning perfectly; and
what can I say, but that we are all in God's hands, and that His
ways are not our ways? I have even advised with my superiors
in the Church, but they, too, were dumb. It is a great mystery."

"Is she mad?" I asked.

"I will answer you according to my belief. She is not," returned the Padre, "or she was not. When she was young—God help me, I fear I neglected that wild lamb—she was surely sane; and yet, although it did not run to such heights, the same strain was already notable; it had been so before her in her father, ay, and before him, and this inclined me, perhaps, to think too lightly of it. But these things go on growing, not only in the individual but in the race."

"When she was young," I began, and my voice failed me for a moment, and it was only with a great effort that I was able to add, "was she like Olalla?"

"Now God forbid!" exclaimed the Padre. "God forbid that any man should think so slightingly of my favourite penitent. No, no; the Señorita (but for her beauty, which I wish most honestly she had less of) has not a hair's resemblance to what her mother was at the same age. I could not bear to have you think so; though, heaven knows, it were, perhaps, better that you should."

At this I raised myself in bed, and opened my heart to the old man; telling him of our love and of her decision; owning my own horrors, my own passing fancies, but telling him that these were at an end; and with something more than a purely formal submission, appealing to his judgment.

He heard me very patiently and without surprise; and when I had done he sat for some time silent. Then he began: "The Church," and instantly broke off again to apologise. "I had forgotten, my child, that you were not a Christian," said he. "And indeed, upon a point so highly unusual, even the Church can scarce be said to have decided. But would you have my opinion? The Señorita is, in a matter of this kind, the best judge; I would accept her judgment."

On the back of that he went away, nor was he thenceforward so assiduous in his visits; indeed, even when I began to get about again, he plainly feared and deprecated my society, not as in distaste, but much as a man might be disposed to flee from the riddling sphinx. The villagers, too, avoided me; they were unwilling to be my guides upon the mountain. I thought they looked at me askance, and I made sure that the more superstitious crossed themselves on my approach. At first I set this down to my heretical opinions; but it began at length to dawn upon me that if I was thus redoubted it was because I had stayed at the residencia. All men despise the savage notions of such peasantry; and yet I was conscious of a chill shadow that seemed to fall and dwell upon my love. It did not conquer, but I may not deny that it restrained, my ardour.

Some miles westward of the village there was a gap in the sierra, from which the eye plunged direct upon the residencia; and thither it became my daily habit to repair. A wood crowned the summit; and just where the pathway issued from its fringes, it was overhung by a considerable shelf of rock, and that, in its turn, was surmounted by a crucifix of the size of life and more than usually painful in design. This was my perch; thence, day after day, I looked down upon the plateau, and the great old house, and could see Felipe, no bigger than a fly, going to and fro about the garden. Sometimes mists would draw across the view, and be broken up again by mountain winds; sometimes the plain slumbered below me in unbroken sunshine; it would sometimes be all blotted out by rain. This distant post, these interrupted sights of the place where my life had been so strangely changed, suited the indecision of my humour. I passed whole days there, debating with myself the various elements of our position, now leaning to the suggestions of love, now giving an ear to prudence, and in the end halting irresolute between the two.

One day, as I was sitting on my rock, there came by that way a somewhat gaunt peasant wrapped in a mantle. He was a stranger, and plainly did not know me even by repute; for, instead of keeping the other side, he drew near and sat down beside me, and we had soon fallen in talk. Among other things, he told me he had been a muleteer, and in former years had much frequented these mountains; later on, he had followed the army with his mules, had realised a competence, and was now living retired with his family.

"Do you know that house?" I inquired at last, pointing to the residencia, for I readily wearied of any talk that kept me from the thought of Olalla.

He looked at me darkly and crossed himself.

"Too well," he said, "it was there that one of my comrades sold himself to Satan; the Virgin shield us from temptations! He has paid the price; he is now burning in the reddest place in hell!"

A fear came upon me; I could answer nothing; and presently the man resumed, as if to himself: "Yes," he said, "O yes, I know it. I have passed its doors. There was snow upon the pass, the wind was driving it; sure enough there was death that night upon the mountains, but there was worse beside the hearth. I took him by the arm, Señor, and dragged him to the gate; I conjured him, by all he loved and respected, to go forth with me; I went on my knees before him in the snow; and I could see he was moved by my entreaty. And just then she came out on the gallery, and called him by his name; and he turned, and there was she, standing with a lamp in her hand and smiling on him to come back. I cried out aloud to God, and threw my arms about him, but he put me by, and left me alone. He had made his choice; God help us. I would pray for him, but to what end? there are sins that not even the Pope can loose."

"And your friend," I asked, "what became of him?"

"Nay, God knows," said the muleteer. "If all be true that we hear, his end was like his sin, a thing to raise the hair."

"Do you mean that he was killed?" I asked.

"Sure enough, he was killed," returned the man. "But how? Ah, how? But these are things that it is sin to speak of."

"The people of that house ..." I began.

But he interrupted me with a savage outburst. "The people?" he cried. "What people? There are neither men nor women in that house of Satan's! What? have you lived here so long, and never heard?" And here he put his mouth to my ear and whispered, as if even the fowls of the mountain might have overheard and been stricken with horror.

What he told me was not true, nor was it even original; being, indeed, but a new edition, vamped up again by village ignorance and superstition, of stories nearly as ancient as the race of man. It was rather the application that appalled me. In the old days, he said, the Church would have burned out that nest of basilisks; but the arm of the Church was now shortened; his friend Miguel had been unpunished by the hands of men, and left to the more awful judgment of an offended God. This was wrong; but it should be so no more. The Padre was sunk in age; he was even bewitched himself; but the eyes of his flock were now awake to their own danger; and some day—ay, and before long—the smoke of that house should go up to heaven.

He left me filled with horror and fear. Which way to turn I knew not; whether first to warn the Padre, or to carry my ill news direct to the threatened inhabitants of the residencia. Fate was to decide for me; for, while I was still hesitating, I beheld the veiled figure of a woman drawing near to me up the pathway. No veil could deceive my penetration; by every line and every movement I recognised Olalla; and keeping hidden behind a corner of the rock, I suffered her to gain the summit. Then I came forward. She knew me and paused, but did not speak; I, too, remained silent; and we continued for some time to gaze upon each other with a passionate sadness.

"I thought you had gone," she said at length. "It is all that you can do for me—to go. It is all I ever asked of you. And you still stay. But do you know, that every day heaps up the peril of death, not only on your head, but on ours? A report has gone about the mountain; it is thought you love me, and the people will not suffer it."

I saw she was already informed of her danger, and I rejoiced at it. "Olalla," I said, "I am ready to go this day, this very hour, but not alone."

She stepped aside and knelt down before the crucifix to pray, and I stood by and looked now at her and now at the object of her adoration, now at the living figure of the penitent, and now at the ghastly, daubed countenance, the painted

171

wounds, and the projected ribs of the image. The silence was only broken by the wailing of some large birds that circled side-long, as if in surprise or alarm, about the summit of the hills. Presently Olalla rose again, turned towards me, raised her veil, and, still leaning with one hand on the shaft of the crucifix, looked upon me with a pale and sorrowful countenance.

"I have laid my hand upon the cross," she said. "The Padre says you are no Christian; but look up for a moment with my eyes, and behold the face of the Man of Sorrows. We are all such as He was—the inheritors of sin; we must all bear and expiate a past which was not ours; there is in all of us—ay, even in me—a sparkle of the divine. Like Him, we must endure for a little while, until morning returns, bringing peace. Suffer me to pass on upon my way alone; it is thus that I shall be least lonely, counting for my friend Him who is the friend of all the distressed; it is thus that I shall be the most happy, having taken my farewell of earthly happiness, and willingly accepted sorrow for my portion."

I looked at the face of the crucifix, and, though I was no friend to images, and despised that imitative and grimacing art of which it was a rude example, some sense of what the thing implied was carried home to my intelligence. The face looked down upon me with a painful and deadly contraction; but the rays of a glory encircled it, and reminded me that the sacrifice was voluntary. It stood there, crowning the rock, as it still stands on so many highway sides, vainly preaching to passers-by, an emblem of sad and noble truths; that pleasure is not an end, but an accident; that pain is the choice of the magnanimous; that it is best to suffer all things and do well. I turned and went down the mountain in silence; and when I looked back for the last time before the wood closed about my path, I saw Olalla still leaning on the crucifix.

THE EBB-TIDE

PART I
THE TRIO

CHAPTER 1
NIGHT ON THE BEACH

Throughout the island world of the Pacific, scattered men of many European races, and from almost every grade of society, carry activity and disseminate disease. Some prosper, some vegetate. Some have mounted the steps of thrones and owned islands and navies. Others again must marry for a livelihood; a strapping, merry, chocolate-coloured dame supports them in sheer idleness; and, dressed like natives, but still retaining some foreign element of gait or attitude, still perhaps with some relic (such as a single eye-glass) of the officer and gentleman, they sprawl in palm-leaf verandahs and entertain an island audience with memoirs of the music-hall. And there are still others, less pliable, less capable, less fortunate, perhaps less base, who continue, even in these isles of plenty, to lack bread.

At the far end of the town of Papeete, three such men were seated on the beach under a *purao*-tree.

It was late. Long ago the band had broken up and marched musically home, a motley troop of men and women, merchant clerks and navy officers, dancing in its wake, arms about waist and crowned with garlands. Long ago darkness and silence had gone from house to house about the tiny pagan city. Only the street-lamps shone on, making a glow-worm halo in the umbrageous alleys, or drawing a tremulous image on the waters of the port. A sound of snoring ran among the piles of lumber by the Government pier. It was wafted ashore from the graceful clipper-bottomed schooners, where they lay moored close in like dinghies, and their crews were stretched upon the deck under the open sky or huddled in a rude tent amidst the disorder of merchandise.

But the men under the *purao* had no thought of sleep. The same temperature in England would have passed without remark in summer; but it was bitter cold for the South Seas. Inanimate nature knew it, and the bottle of coconut oil stood frozen in every bird-cage house about the island; and the men knew it, and shivered. They wore flimsy cotton clothes, the same they had sweated in by day and run the gauntlet of the tropic showers; and to complete their evil case, they had no breakfast to mention, less dinner, and no supper at all.

In the telling South Sea phrase, these three men were *on the beach*. Common calamity had brought them acquainted, as the three most miserable English-speaking creatures in Tahiti; and beyond their misery, they knew next to nothing of each other, not even their true names. For each had made a long apprenticeship in going downward; and each, at some stage of the descent, had been shamed into the adoption of an *alias*. And yet not one of them had figured in a court of justice; two were men of kindly virtues; and one, as he sat and shivered under the *purao*, had a tattered Virgil in his pocket.

Certainly, if money could have been raised upon the book, Robert Herrick would long ago have sacrificed that last possession; but the demand for literature, which is so marked a feature in some parts of the South Seas, extends not so far as the dead tongues; and the Virgil, which he could not exchange against a meal, had often consoled him in his hunger. He would study it, as he lay with tightened belt on the floor of the old calaboose, seeking favourite passages and finding new ones only less beautiful because they lacked the consecration of remembrance. Or he would pause on random country walks; sit on the path-side, gazing over the sea on the mountains of Eimeo; and dip into the *Aeneid*, seeking *sortes*. And if the oracle (as is the way of oracles) replied with no very certain nor encouraging voice, visions of England at least would throng upon the exile's memory: the busy schoolroom, the green playing-fields, holidays at home, and the perennial roar of London, and the fireside, and the white head of his father.

For it is the destiny of those grave, restrained, and classic writers, with whom we make enforced and often painful acquaintanceship at school, to pass into the blood and become native in the memory; so that a phrase of Virgil speaks not so much of Mantua or Augustus, but of English places and the student's own irrevocable youth.

Robert Herrick was the son of an intelligent, active, and ambitious man, small partner in a considerable London house. Hopes were conceived of the boy; he was sent to a good school, gained there an Oxford scholarship, and proceeded in course to the western University. With all his talent and taste (and he had much of both) Robert was deficient in consistency and intellectual manhood, wandered in bypaths of study, worked at music or at metaphysics when he should have been at Greek, and took at last a paltry degree. Almost at the same time, the London house was disastrously wound up; Mr. Herrick must begin the world again as a clerk in a strange office, and Robert relinquish his ambitions and accept with gratitude a career that he detested and despised. He had no head for figures, no interest in affairs, detested the constraint of hours, and despised the aims and the success of merchants. To grow rich was none of his ambitions; rather to do well. A worse or a more bold young man would have refused the destiny; perhaps tried his future with his pen; perhaps enlisted. Robert, more prudent, possibly more timid, consented to embrace that way of life in which he could most readily assist his family. But he did so with a mind divided; fled the neighbourhood of former comrades; and chose, out of several positions placed at his disposal, a clerkship in New York.

His career thenceforth was one of unbroken shame. He did not drink, he was exactly honest, he was never rude to his employers, yet was everywhere discharged. Bringing no interest to his duties, he brought no attention; his day was a tissue of things neglected and things done amiss; and from place to place, and from town to town, he carried the character of one thoroughly incompetent. No man can bear the word applied to him without some flush of colour, as indeed there is none other that so emphatically slams in a man's face the door of self-respect. And to Herrick, who was conscious of talents and acquirements, who looked down upon those humble duties in which he was found wanting, the pain was the more exquisite. Early in his fall he had ceased to be able to make remittances; shortly after, having nothing but failure to communicate, he ceased writing home; and about a year before this tale begins, turned suddenly upon the streets of San Francisco by a vulgar and infuriated German Jew, he had broken the last bonds of self-respect, and, upon a sudden impulse, changed his name and invested his last dollar in a passage on the mail brigantine, the *City of Papeete*. With what expectation he had trimmed his flight for the South Seas, Herrick perhaps scarcely knew. Doubtless there were fortunes to be made in pearl and copra; doubtless others not more gifted than himself had climbed in the island world to be queen's consorts and king's ministers. But if Herrick had gone there with any manful purpose, he would have kept his father's name; the *alias* betrayed his moral bankruptcy; he had struck his flag; he entertained no hope to reinstate himself or help his straitened family; and he came to the islands (where he knew the climate to be soft, bread cheap, and manners easy) a skulker from life's battle and his own immediate duty. Failure, he had said, was his portion; let it be a pleasant failure.

It is fortunately not enough to say, "I will be base." Herrick continued in the islands his career of failure; but in the new scene and under the new name, he suffered no less sharply than before. A place was got, it was lost in the old style; from the long-suffering of the keepers of restaurants he fell to more open charity upon the wayside; as time went on, good-nature became weary, and, after a repulse or two, Herrick became shy. There were women enough who would have supported a far worse and a far uglier man; Herrick never met or never knew them: or if he did both, some manlier feeling would revolt, and he preferred starvation. Drenched with rains, broiling by day, shivering by night, a disused and ruinous prison for a bedroom, his diet begged or pilfered out of rubbish heaps, his associates two creatures equally outcast with himself, he had drained for months the cup of penitence. He had known what it was to be resigned, what it was to break forth in a childish fury of rebellion against fate, and what it was to sink into the coma of despair. The time had changed him. He told himself no longer tales of an easy and perhaps agreeable declension; he read his nature otherwise; he had proved himself incapable of rising, and he now learned by experience that he could not stoop to fall. Something that was scarcely pride or strength, that was perhaps only refinement, withheld him from capitulation; but he looked on upon his own misfortune with a growing rage, and sometimes wondered at his patience.

It was now the fourth month completed, and still there was no change or sign of change. The moon, racing through a world of flying clouds of every size and shape and density, some black as inkstains, some delicate as lawn, threw the marvel of her southern brightness over the same lovely and detested scene: the island mountains crowned with the perennial island cloud, the embowered city studded with rare lamps, the masts in the harbour, the smooth mirror of the lagoon, and the mole of the barrier reef on which the breakers whitened. The moon shone too, with bull's-eye sweeps, on his companions; on the stalwart frame of the American who called himself Brown, and was known to be a master-mariner in some disgrace; and on the dwarfish person, the pale eyes and toothless smile of a vulgar and bad-hearted cockney clerk. Here was society for Robert Herrick! The Yankee skipper was a man at least: he had sterling qualities of tenderness and resolution: he was one whose hand you could take without a blush. But there was no redeeming grace about the other, who called himself sometimes Hay and sometimes Tomkins, and laughed at the discrepancy; who had been employed in every store in Papeete, for the creature was able in his way; who had been discharged from each in turn, for he was wholly vile; who had

181

alienated all his old employers so that they passed him in the street as if he were a dog, and all his old comrades so that they shunned him as they would a creditor.

Not long before, a ship from Peru had brought an influenza, and it now raged in the island, and particularly in Papeete. From all around the *purao* arose and fell a dismal sound of men coughing, and strangling as they coughed. The sick natives, with the islander's impatience of a touch of fever, had crawled from their houses to be cool, and, squatting on the shore or on the beached canoes, painfully expected the new day. Even as the crowing of cocks goes about the country in the night from farm to farm, accesses of coughing arose and spread, and died in the distance, and sprang up again. Each miserable shiverer caught the suggestion from his neighbour, was torn for some minutes by that cruel ecstasy, and left spent and without voice or courage when it passed. If a man had pity to spend, Papeete beach, in that cold night and in that infected season, was a place to spend it on. And of all the sufferers perhaps the least deserving, but surely the most pitiable, was the London clerk. He was used to another life, to houses, beds, nursing, and the dainties of the sick-room; he lay here now, in the cold open, exposed to the gusting of the wind, and with an empty belly. He was besides infirm; the disease shook him to the vitals; and his companions watched his endurance with surprise. A profound commiseration filled them, and contended with and conquered their abhorrence. The disgust attendant on so ugly a sickness magnified this dislike; at the same time, and with more than compensating strength, shame for a sentiment so inhuman bound them the more straitly to his service; and even the evil they knew of him swelled their solicitude, for the thought of death is always the least supportable when it draws near to the merely sensual and selfish. Sometimes they held him up; sometimes, with mistaken helpfulness, they beat him between the shoulders; and when the poor wretch lay back ghastly and spent after a paroxysm of coughing, they would sometimes peer into his face, doubtfully exploring it for any mark of life. There is no one but has some virtue: that of the clerk was courage; and he would make haste to reassure them in a pleasantry not always decent.

"I'm all right, pals," he gasped once: "this is the thing to strengthen the muscles of the larynx."

"Well, you take the cake!" cried the captain.

"O, I'm good plucked enough," pursued the sufferer, with a broken utterance. "But it do seem bloomin' hard to me, that I should be the only party down with this form of vice, and the only one to do the funny business. I think one of you other parties might wake up. Tell a fellow something."

"The trouble is we've nothing to tell, my son," returned the captain.

"I'll tell you, if you like, what I was thinking," said Herrick.

"Tell us anything," said the clerk, "I only want to be reminded that I ain't dead."

Herrick took up his parable, lying on his face and speaking slowly and scarce above his breath, not like a man who has anything to say, but like one talking against time.

"Well, I was thinking this," he began: "I was thinking I lay on Papeete beach one night—all moon and squalls and fellows coughing—and I was cold and hungry, and down in the mouth, and was about ninety years of age, and had spent two hundred and twenty of them on Papeete beach. And I was thinking I wished I had a ring to rub, or had a fairy godmother, or could raise Beelzebub. And I was trying to remember how you did it. I knew you made a ring of skulls, for I had seen that in the *Freischütz:* and that you took off your coat and turned up your sleeves, for I had seen Formes do that when he was playing Kaspar, and you could see (by the way he went about it) it was a business he had studied; and that you ought to have something to kick up a smoke and a bad smell, I daresay a cigar might do, and that you ought to say the Lord's Prayer backwards. Well, I wondered if I could do that; it seemed rather a feat, you see. And then I wondered if I would say it forward,

183

and I thought I did. Well, no sooner had I got to *world without end*, than I saw a man in a *pariu*, and with a mat under his arm, come along the beach from the town. He was rather a hard-favoured old party, and he limped and crippled, and all the time he kept coughing. At first I didn't cotton to his looks, I thought, and then I got sorry for the old soul because he coughed so hard. I remembered that we had some of that cough mixture the American consul gave the captain for Hay. It never did Hay a ha'porth of service, but I thought it might do the old gentleman's business for him, and stood up. '*Yorana!*' says I. '*Yorana!*' says he. 'Look here,' I said, 'I've got some first-rate stuff in a bottle; it'll fix your cough, savvy? *Harry my* and I'll measure you a tablespoonful in the palm of my hand, for all our plate is at the bankers.' So I thought the old party came up, and the nearer he came the less I took to him. But I had passed my word, you see."

"Wot is this bloomin' drivel?" interrupted the clerk. "It's like the rot there is in tracts."

"It's a story; I used to tell them to the kids at home," said Herrick. "If it bores you, I'll drop it."

"O, cut along!" returned the sick man irritably. "It's better than nothing."

"Well," continued Herrick, "I had no sooner given him the cough mixture than he seemed to straighten up and change, and I saw he wasn't a Tahitian after all, but some kind of Arab, and had a long beard on his chin. 'One good turn deserves another,' says he. 'I am a magician out of the "Arabian Nights," and this mat that I have under my arm is the original carpet of Mohammed Ben Somebody-or-other. Say the word, and you can have a cruise upon the carpet.' 'You don't mean to say this is the Travelling Carpet?' I cried. 'You bet I do,' said he. 'You've been to America since last I read the "Arabian Nights," said I, a little suspicious. 'I should think so,' said he. 'Been everywhere. A man with a carpet like this isn't going to moulder in a semi-detached villa.' Well, that struck me as reasonable. 'All right,' I said; 'and do you mean to tell me I can get on that carpet and go straight to London, England?' I said 'London, England,' captain, because he seemed to have been so long in your part of the world. 'In the crack of a whip,' said he. I figured up the time. What is the difference between Papeete and London, captain?"

"Taking Greenwich and Point Venus, nine hours, odd minutes and seconds," replied the mariner.

"Well, that's about what I made it," resumed Herrick, "about nine hours. Calling this three in the morning, I made out I would drop into London about noon; and the idea tickled me immensely. 'There's only one bother,' I said, 'I haven't a copper cent. It would be a pity to go to London and not buy the morning *Standard*.' 'O!' said he, 'you don't realise the conveniences of this carpet. You see this pocket? you've only got to stick your hand in, and you pull it out filled with sovereigns.' "

"Double-eagles, wasn't it?" inquired the captain.

"That was what it was!" cried Herrick. "I thought they seemed unusually big, and I remember how I had to go to the money-changers at Charing Cross and get English silver."

"O, you went there?" said the clerk. "Wot did you do? Bet you had a B.-and-S.!"

"Well, you see, it was just as the old boy said—like the cut of a whip," said Herrick. "The one minute I was here on the beach at three in the morning, the next I was in front of the Golden Cross at midday. At first I was dazzled, and covered my eyes, and there didn't seem the smallest change; the roar of the Strand and the roar of the reef were like the same: hark to it now, and you can hear the cabs and 'buses rolling and the streets resound! And then at last I could look about, and there was the old place, and no mistake! With the statues in the square, and St. Martin's-in-the-Fields, and the bobbies, and the sparrows, and the hacks; and I can't tell you what I felt like. I felt like crying, I believe, or dancing, or jumping clean over the Nelson Column. I was like a fellow caught up out of Hell and flung down into the dandiest part of Heaven. Then I spotted for a hansom with a spanking horse. 'A shilling for yourself if

❧ you're there in twenty minutes!' said I to the jarvey. He went a good pace, though of course it was a trifle to the carpet; and in nineteen minutes and a half I was at the door."

"What door?" asked the captain.

"O, a house I know of," returned Herrick.

"But it was a public-house!" cried the clerk,—only these were not his words. "And w'y didn't you take the carpet there instead
❧ of trundling in a growler?"

"I didn't want to startle a quiet street," said the narrator. "Bad form. And besides, it was a hansom."

"Well, and what did you do next?" inquired the captain.

"O, I went in," said Herrick.

"The old folks?" asked the captain.

"That's about it," said the other, chewing a grass.

"Well, I think you are about the poorest 'and at a yarn!" cried the clerk. "Crikey, it's like 'Ministering Children!'. I can tell you there would be more beer and skittles about my little jaunt. I would go and have a B.-and-S. for luck. Then I would get a big ulster with astrakhan fur, and take my cane and do the la-de-da down Piccadilly. Then I would go to a slap-up restaurant, and have green peas, and a bottle of fizz, and a chump chop—O! and I forgot, I'd 'ave some devilled whitebait first—and green gooseberry tart, and 'ot coffee, and some of that form of vice in big bottles with a seal—Benedictine—that's the bloomin' nyme! Then I'd drop into a theatre, and pal on with some chappies, and do the dancing rooms and bars, and that, and wouldn't go 'ome till morning, till daylight doth appear. And the next day I'd have water-cresses, 'am, muffin, and fresh butter; wouldn't I just, O my!"

The clerk was interrupted by a fresh attack of coughing.

"Well, now, I'll tell you what I would do," said the captain: "I would have none of your fancy rigs with the man driving from the mizzen cross-trees, but a plain fore-and-aft hack cab of the highest registered tonnage. First of all, I would bring up at the market and get a turkey and a sucking-pig. Then I'd go to a wine-merchant's and get a dozen of champagne, and a dozen of some sweet wine, rich and sticky and strong, something in the port or madeira line, the best in the store. Then I'd bear up for a toy-store, and lay out twenty dollars in assorted toys for the pickaninnies; and then to a confectioner's and take in cakes and pies and fancy bread, and that stuff with the plums in it; and then to a newsagency and buy all the papers, all the picture ones for the kids, and all the story papers for the old girl about the Earl discovering himself to Anna-Mariar and the escape of the Lady Maude from the private madhouse; and then I'd tell the fellow to drive home."

"There ought to be some syrup for the kids," suggested Herrick; "they like syrup."

"Yes, syrup for the kids, red syrup at that!" said the captain. "And those things they pull at, and go pop, and have measly poetry inside. And then I tell you we'd have a thanksgiving-day and Christmas-tree combined. Great Scott, but I would like to see the kids! I guess they would like right out of the house when they saw daddy driving up. My little Adar—"

The captain stopped sharply.

"Well, keep it up!" said the clerk.

"The damned thing is, I don't know if they ain't starving!" cried the captain.

"They can't be worse off than we are, and that's one comfort," returned the clerk. "I defy the devil to make me worse off."

It seemed as if the devil heard him. The light of the moon had been some time cut off and they had talked in darkness. Now there was heard a roar, which drew impetuously nearer; the face of the lagoon was seen to whiten; and before they had staggered to their feet, a squall burst in rain upon the outcasts. The rage and volume of that avalanche one must have lived in the tropics to conceive; a man panted in its assault as he might pant under a shower-bath; and the world seemed whelmed in night and water.

They fled, groping for their usual shelter—it might be almost called their home—in the old calaboose; came drenched into its empty chambers; and lay down, three sops of humanity, on the cold coral floors, and presently, when the squall was over-past, the others could hear in the darkness the chattering of the clerk's teeth.

"I say, you fellows," he wailed, "for God's sake, lie up and try to warm me. I'm blymed if I don't think I'll die else!"

So the three crept together into one wet mass, and lay until day came, shivering and dozing off, and continually re-awakened to wretchedness by the coughing of the clerk.

CHAPTER 2
MORNING ON THE BEACH—THE THREE LETTERS

The clouds were all fled, the beauty of the tropic day was spread upon Papeete; and the wall of breaking seas upon the reef, and palms upon the islet, already trembled in the heat. A French man-of-war was going out, homeward bound; she lay in the middle distance of the port, an ant-heap for activity. In the night a schooner had come in, and now lay far out, hard by the passage; and the yellow flag, the emblem of pestilence, flew on her. From up the coast, a long procession of canoes headed round the point and towards the market, bright as a scarf with the many-coloured clothing of the natives and the piles of fruit. But not even the beauty and the welcome warmth of the morning, not even these naval movements, so interesting to sailors and to idlers, could engage the attention of the outcasts. They were still cold at heart, their mouths sour from the want of sleep, their steps rambling from the lack of food; and they strung like lame geese along the beach in a disheartened silence. It was towards the town they moved; towards the town whence smoke arose, where happier folk were breakfasting; and as they went, their hungry eyes were upon all sides, but they were only scouting for a meal.

A small and dingy schooner lay snug against the quay, with which it was connected by a plank. On the forward deck, under a spot of awning, five Kanakas, who made up the crew, were squatted round a basin of fried feis, and drinking coffee from tin mugs.

"Eight bells: knock off for breakfast!" cried the captain, with a miserable heartiness. "Never tried this craft before; positively my first appearance; guess I'll draw a bumper house."

He came close up to where the plank rested on the grassy quay; turned his back upon the schooner, and began to whistle that lively air, "The Irish Washerwoman." It caught the ears of the Kanaka seamen like a preconcerted signal; with one accord they looked up from their meal and crowded to the ship's side, fei in hand and munching as they looked. Even as a poor brown Pyrenean bear dances in the streets of English towns under his master's baton; even so, but with how much more of spirit and precision, the captain footed it in time to his own whistling, and his long morning shadow capered beyond him on the grass. The Kanakas smiled on the performance; Herrick looked on heavy-eyed, hunger for the moment conquering all sense of shame; and a little farther off, but still hard by, the clerk was torn by the seven devils of the influenza.

The captain stopped suddenly, appeared to perceive his audience for the first time, and represented the part of a man surprised in his private hour of pleasure.

"Hello!" said he.

The Kanakas clapped hands and called upon him to go on.

"No, *sir!*" said the captain. "No eat, no dance. Savvy?"

"Poor old man!" returned one of the crew. "Him no eat?"

"Lord, no!" said the captain. "Like-um too much eat. No got."

"All right. Me got," said the sailor; "you tome here. Plenty toffee, plenty fei. Nutha man him tome too."

"I guess we'll drop right in," observed the captain; and he and his companions hastened up the plank. They were welcomed on board with the shaking of hands; place was made for them round the basin; a sticky demijohn of molasses was added to the feast in honour of company, and an accordion brought from the forecastle and significantly laid by the performer's side.

"*Ariana,*" said he lightly, touching the instrument as he spoke; and he fell to on a long savoury fei, made an end of it, raised his mug of coffee, and nodded across at the spokesman of the crew. "Here's your health, old man; you're a credit to the South Pacific," said he.

With the unsightly greed of hounds they glutted themselves with the hot food and coffee; and even the clerk revived and the colour deepened in his eyes. The kettle was drained, the basin cleaned; their entertainers, who had waited on their wants throughout with the pleased hospitality of Polynesians, made haste to bring forward a dessert of island tobacco and rolls of pandanus leaf to serve as paper; and presently all sat about the dishes puffing like Indian sachems.

"When a man 'as breakfast every day, he don't know what it is," observed the clerk.

"The next point is dinner," said Herrick; and then with a passionate utterance: "I wish to God I was a Kanaka!"

"There's one thing sure," said the captain. "I'm about desperate; I'd rather hang than rot here much longer." And with the word he took the accordion and struck up "Home, sweet Home."

"O, drop that!" cried Herrick, "I can't stand that."

"No more can I," said the captain. "I've got to play something though: got to pay the shot, my son." And he struck up "John Brown's Body" in a fine sweet baritone: "Dandy Jim of Carolina" came next; "Rorin the Bold," "Swing low, Sweet Chariot," and "The Beautiful Land" followed. The captain was paying his shot with usury, as he had done many a time before; many a meal had he bought with the same currency from the melodious-minded natives, always, as now, to their delight.

He was in the middle of "Fifteen Dollars in the Inside Pocket," singing with dogged energy, for the task went sore against the grain, when a sensation was suddenly to be observed among the crew.

"*Tapena Tom harry my,*" said the spokesman, pointing.

And the three beachcombers, following his indication, saw the figure of a man in pyjama trousers and a white jumper approaching briskly from the town.

"That's Tapena Tom, is it?" said the captain, pausing in his music. "I don't seem to place the brute."

"We'd better cut," said the clerk. "'E's no good."

"Well," said the musician deliberately, "one can't most generally always tell. I'll try it on, I guess. Music has charms to soothe the savage Tapena, boys. We might strike it rich; it might amount to iced punch in the cabin."

"Hiced punch? O my!" said the clerk. "Give him something 'ot, captain. 'Way down the Swannee River': try that."

"No, *sir!* Looks Scots," said the captain; and he struck, for his life, into "Auld Lang Syne."

Captain Tom continued to approach with the same business-like alacrity; no change was to be perceived in his bearded face as he came swinging up the plank: he did not even turn his eyes on the performer.

> "We twa hae paidled in the burn,
> Frae morning tide till dine,"

went the song.

Captain Tom had a parcel under his arm, which he laid on the house roof, and then turning suddenly to the strangers: "Here, you!" he bellowed, "be off out of that!"

The clerk and Herrick stood not on the order of their going, but fled incontinently by the plank. The performer, on the other hand, flung down the instrument and rose to his full height slowly.

"What's that you say?" he said. "I've half a mind to give you a lesson in civility."

"You set up any more of your gab to me," returned the Scotsman, "and I'll show ye the wrong side of a jyle. I've heard tell of the three of ye. Ye're not long for here, I can tell ye that. The Government has their eyes upon ye. They make short work of damned beachcombers, I'll say that for the French."

"You wait till I catch you off your ship!" cried the captain; and then, turning to the crew, "Good-bye, you fellows!" he said. "You're gentlemen, anyway! The worst nigger among you would look better upon a quarter-deck than that filthy Scotsman."

Captain Tom scorned to reply. He watched with a hard smile the departure of his guests, and as soon as the last foot was off the plank, turned to the hands to work cargo.

The beachcombers beat their inglorious retreat along the shore; Herrick first, his face dark with blood, his knees trembling under him with the hysteria of rage. Presently, under the same *purao* where they had shivered the night before, he cast himself down, and groaned aloud, and ground his face into the sand.

"Don't speak to me, don't speak to me. I can't stand it," broke from him.

The other two stood over him perplexed.

"Wot can't he stand now?" said the clerk. "'Asn't he 'ad a meal? *I'm* lickin' my lips."

Herrick reared up his wild eyes and burning face. "I can't beg!" he screamed, and again threw himself prone.

"This thing's got to come to an end," said the captain, with an intake of the breath.

"Looks like signs of an end, don't it?" sneered the clerk.

"He's not so far from it, and don't you deceive yourself," replied the captain.—"Well," he added in a livelier voice, "you fellows hang on here, and I'll go and interview my representative."

Whereupon he turned on his heel, and set off at a swinging sailor's walk towards Papeete.

It was some half-hour later when he returned. The clerk was dozing with his back against the tree: Herrick still lay where he had flung himself; nothing showed whether he slept or waked.

"See, boys!" cried the captain, with that artificial heartiness of his which was at times so painful, "here's a new idea." And he produced note-paper, stamped envelopes, and pencils, three of each. "We can all write home by the mail brigantine; the consul says I can come over to his place and ink up the addresses."

"Well, that's a start, too," said the clerk. "I never thought of that."

"It was that yarning last night about going home that put me up to it," said the captain.

"Well, 'and over," said the clerk. "I'll 'ave a shy," and he retired a little distance to the shade of a canoe.

The others remained under the *purao*. Now they would write a word or two, now scribble it out; now they would sit biting at the pencil end and staring seaward, now their eyes would rest on the clerk, where he sat propped on the canoe, leering and coughing, his pencil racing glibly on the paper.

"I can't do it," said Herrick suddenly. "I haven't got the heart."

"See here," said the captain, speaking with unwonted gravity; "it may be hard to write, and to write lies at that; and God knows it is; but it's the square thing. It don't cost anything to say you're well and happy, and sorry you can't make a remittance this mail; and if you don't I'll tell you what I think it is—I think it's about the high-water mark of being a brute beast."

"It's easy to talk," said Herrick. "You don't seem to have written much yourself, I notice."

"What do you bring in me for?" broke from the captain. His voice was indeed scarce raised above a whisper, but emotion clanged in it. "What do you know about me? If you had commanded the finest barque that ever sailed from Portland; if you had been drunk in your berth when she struck the breakers in Fourteen Island Group, and hadn't had the wit to stay there and drown, but came on deck, and given drunken orders, and lost six lives—I could understand your talking then! There," he said more quietly, "that's my yarn, and now you know it. It's a pretty one for the father of a family. Five men and a woman murdered. Yes, there was a woman on board, and hadn't no business to be either. Guess I sent her to Hell, if there is such a place. I never dared go home again; and the wife and the little ones went to England to her father's place. I don't know what's come to them," he added, with a bitter shrug.

"Thank you, captain," said Herrick. "I never liked you better."

They shook hands, short and hard, with eyes averted, tenderness swelling in their bosoms.

"Now, boys! to work again at lying!" said the captain.

"I'll give my father up," returned Herrick with a writhen smile. "I'll try my sweetheart instead for a change of evils."

And here is what he wrote: —

"Emma, I have scratched out the beginning to my father, for I think I can write more easily to you. This is my last farewell to all, the last you will ever hear or see of an unworthy friend and son. I have failed in life; I am quite broken down and disgraced. I pass under a false name; you will have to tell my father that with all your kindness. It is my own fault. I know, had I chosen, that I might have done well; and yet I swear to you I tried to choose. I could not bear that you should think I did not try. For I loved you all; you must never doubt me in that, you least of all. I have always unceasingly loved, but what was my love worth? and what was I worth? I had not the manhood of a common clerk; I could not work to earn you; I have lost you now, and for your sake I could be glad of it. When you first came to my father's house—do you remember those days? I want you to—you saw the best of me then, all that was good in me. Do you remember the day I took your hand and would not let it go—and the day on Battersea Bridge, when we were looking at a barge, and I began to tell you one of my silly stories, and broke off to say I loved you? That was the beginning, and now here is the end. When you have read this letter, you will go round and kiss them all good-bye, my father and mother, and the children, one by one, and poor uncle; and tell them all to forget me, and forget me yourself. Turn the key in the door; let no thought of me return; be done with the poor ghost that pretended he was a man and stole your love. Scorn of myself grinds in me as I write. I should tell you I am well and happy, and want for nothing. I do not exactly make money, or I should send a remittance; but I am well cared for, have friends, live in a beautiful place and climate, such as we have dreamed of together, and no pity need be wasted on me. In such places, you understand, it is easy to live, and live well, but often hard to make sixpence in money. Explain this to my father, he will understand. I have no more to say; only linger, going out, like an unwilling guest. God in heaven bless you. Think of me at the last, here, on a bright beach, the sky and sea immoderately blue, and the great breakers roaring outside on a barrier reef, where a little isle sits green with palms. I am well and strong. It is a more pleasant way to die than if you were crowding me on a sick-bed. And yet I am dying. This is my last kiss. Forgive, forget the unworthy."

So far he had written, his paper was all filled, when there returned a memory of evenings at the piano, and that song, the masterpiece of love, in which so many have found the expression of their dearest thoughts. "*Einst, O Wunder!*" he added. More was not required; he knew that in his love's heart the context would spring up, escorted with fair images and harmony; of how all through life her name should tremble in his ears, her name be everywhere repeated in the sounds of nature; and when death came, and he lay dissolved, her memory lingered and thrilled among his elements.

> "Once, O wonder! once from the ashes of my heart
> Arose a blossom—"

Herrick and the captain finished their letters about the same time; each was breathing deep, and their eyes met and were averted as they closed the envelopes.

"Sorry I write so big," said the captain gruffly. "Came all of a rush, when it did come."

"Same here," said Herrick. "I could have done with a ream when I got started; but it's long enough for all the good I had to say."

They were still at the addresses when the clerk strolled up, smirking and twirling his envelope, like a man well pleased. He looked over Herrick's shoulder.

"Hullo," he said, "you ain't writing 'ome."

"I am, though," said Herrick; "she lives with my father.—O, I see what you mean," he added. "My real name is Herrick. No more Hay"—they had both used the same *alias*,—"no more Hay than yours, I daresay."

"Clean bowled in the middle stump!" laughed the clerk. "My name's 'Uish, if you want to know. Everybody has a false nyme in the Pacific. Lay you five to three the captain 'as."

"So I have too," replied the captain; "and I've never told my own since the day I tore the title-page out of my Bowditch and flung the damned thing into the sea. But I'll tell it to you, boys.

John Davis is my name. I'm Davis of the *Sea Ranger*."

"Dooce you are!" said Huish. "And what was she? a pirate or a slyver?"

"She was the fastest barque out of Portland, Maine," replied the captain; "and for the way I lost her, I might as well have bored a hole in her side with an auger."

"O, you lost her, did you?" said the clerk. "'Ope she was insured?"

No answer being returned to this sally, Huish, still brimming over with vanity and conversation, struck into another subject.

"I've a good mind to read you my letter," said he. "I've a good fist with a pen when I choose, and this is a prime lark. She was a barmaid I ran across in Northampton; she was a spanking fine piece, no end of style; and we cottoned at first sight like parties in the play. I suppose I spent the chynge of a fiver on that girl. Well, I 'appened to remember her nyme, so I wrote to her, and told her 'ow I had got rich, and married a queen in the Hislands, and lived in a blooming palace. Such a sight of crammers! I must read you one bit about my opening the nigger parliament in a cocked 'at. It's really prime."

The captain jumped to his feet. "That's what you did with the paper that I went and begged for you?" he roared.

It was perhaps lucky for Huish—it was surely in the end unfortunate for all—that he was seized just then by one of his prostrating accesses of cough; his comrades would have else deserted him, so bitter was their resentment. When the fit had passed, the clerk reached out his hand, picked up the letter, which had fallen to the earth, and tore it into fragments, stamp and all.

"Does that satisfy you?" he asked sullenly.

"We'll say no more about it," replied Davis.

CHAPTER 3
THE OLD CALABOOSE –
DESTINY AT THE DOOR

The old calaboose, in which the waifs had so long harboured, is a low, rectangular enclosure of building at the corner of a shady western avenue and a little townward of the British consulate. Within was a grassy court, littered with wreckage and the traces of vagrant occupation. Six or seven cells opened from the court: the doors, that had once been locked on mutinous whalermen, rotting before them in the grass. No mark remained of their old destination, except the rusty bars upon the windows.

The floor of one of the cells had been a little cleared; a bucket (the last remaining piece of furniture of the three caitiffs) stood full of water by the door, a half coconut shell beside it for a drinking-cup; and on some ragged ends of mat Huish sprawled asleep, his mouth open, his face deathly. The glow of the tropic afternoon, the green of sunbright foliage, stared into that shady place through door and window; and Herrick, pacing to and fro on the coral floor, sometimes paused and laved his face and neck with tepid water from the bucket. His long arrears of suffering, the night's vigil, the insults of the morning, and the harrowing business of the letter, had strung him to that point when pain is almost pleasure, time shrinks to a mere point, and death and life appear indifferent. To and fro he paced like a caged brute; his mind whirling through the universe of thought and memory; his eyes, as he went, skimming the legends of the wall. The crumbling whitewash was all full of them: Tahitian names, and French, and English, and rude sketches of ships under sail and men at fisticuffs.

It came to him of a sudden that he too must leave upon these walls the memorial of his passage. He paused before a clean space, took the pencil out, and pondered. Vanity, so hard to dislodge, awoke in him. We call it vanity at least; perhaps unjustly. Rather it was the bare sense of his existence prompted him; the sense of his life, the one thing wonderful, to which he scarce clung with a finger. From his jarred nerves there came a strong sentiment of coming change; whether good or ill he could not say: change, he knew no more—change with inscrutable veiled face, approaching noiseless. With the feeling came the vision of a concert-room, the rich hues of instruments, the silent audience, and the loud voice of the symphony. "Destiny knocking at the door," he thought; drew a stave on the plaster, and wrote in the famous phrase from the Fifth Symphony. "So," thought he, "they will know that I loved music and had classical tastes. They? He, I suppose: the unknown, kindred spirit that shall come some day and read my *memor querela*. Ha, he shall have Latin too!" And he added: *terque quaterque beati Queis ante ora patrum.*

He turned again to his uneasy pacing, but now with an irrational and supporting sense of duty done. He had dug his grave that morning; now he had carved his epitaph; the folds of the toga were composed, why should he delay the insignificant trifle that remained to do? He paused and looked long in the face of the sleeping Huish, drinking disenchantment and distaste of life. He nauseated himself with that vile countenance. Could the thing continue? What bound him now? Had he no rights?—only the obligation to go on, without discharge or furlough, bearing the unbearable? *Ich trage unerträgliches*, the quotation rose in his mind; he repeated the whole piece, one of the most perfect of the most perfect of poets; and a phrase struck him like a blow: *Du, stolzes Herz, du hast es ja gewollt.* Where was the pride of his heart? And he raged against himself, as a man bites on a sore tooth, in a heady sensuality of scorn. "I have no pride, I have no heart, no manhood," he thought, "or why should I prolong a life more shameful than the gallows? Or why should I have fallen to it? No pride, no capacity, no force. Not even a bandit! and to be starving here with worse than banditti—with this trivial hell-hound!" His rage against his comrade rose and flooded him, and he shook a trembling fist at the sleeper.

A swift step was audible. The captain appeared upon the threshold of the cell, panting and flushed, and with a foolish face of happiness. In his arms he carried a loaf of bread and bottles of beer; the pockets of his coat were bulging with cigars. He rolled his treasures on the floor, grasped Herrick by both hands, and crowed with laughter.

"Broach the beer!" he shouted. "Broach the beer, and glory hallelujah!"

"Beer?" repeated Huish, struggling to his feet.

"Beer it is!" cried Davis. "Beer, and plenty of it. Any number of persons can use it (like Lyon's tooth-tablet) with perfect propriety and neatness.—Who's to officiate?"

"Leave me alone for that," said the clerk. He knocked the necks of with a lump of coral, and each drank in succession from the shell.

"Have a weed," said Davis. "It's all in the bill."

"What is up?" asked Herrick.

The captain fell suddenly grave. "I'm coming to that," said he. "I want to speak with Herrick here. You, Hay—or Huish, or whatever your name is—you take a weed and the other bottle, and go and see how the wind is down by the *purao*. I'll call you when you're wanted!"

"Hey? Secrets? That ain't the ticket," said Huish.

"Look here, my son," said the captain, "this is business, and don't you make any mistake about it. If you're going to make trouble, you can have it your own way and stop right here. Only get the thing right: if Herrick and I go, we take the beer. Savvy?"

"O, I don't want to shove my oar in," returned Huish. "I'll cut right enough. Give me the swipes. You can jaw till you're blue in the face for what I care. I don't think it's the friendly touch, that's all." And he shambled grumbling out of the cell into the staring sun.

The captain watched him clear of the courtyard; then turned to Herrick.

"What is it?" asked Herrick thickly.

"I'll tell you," said Davis. "I want to consult you. It's a chance we've got.—What's that?" he cried, pointing to the music on the wall.

"What?" said the other. "O, that! It's music; it's a phrase of Beethoven's I was writing up. It means Destiny knocking at the door."

"Does it?" said the captain, rather low; and he went near and studied the inscription. "And this French?" he asked, pointing to the Latin.

"O, it just means I should have been luckier if I had died at home," returned Herrick impatiently. "What is this business?"

"Destiny knocking at the door," repeated the captain; and then, looking over his shoulder, "Well, Mr. Herrick, that's about what it comes to," he added.

"What do you mean? Explain yourself," said Herrick.

But the captain was again staring at the music. "About how long ago since you wrote up this truck?" he asked.

"What does it matter?" exclaimed Herrick. "I daresay half an hour."

"My God, it's strange!" cried Davis. "There's some men would call that accidental: not me. That—" and he drew his thick finger under the music—"that's what I call Providence."

"You said we had a chance," said Herrick.

"Yes, *sir!*" said the captain, wheeling suddenly face to face with his companion. "I did so. If you're the man I take you for, we have a chance."

"I don't know what you take me for," was the reply. "You can scarce take me too low."

"Shake hands, Mr. Herrick," said the captain. "I know you. You're a gentleman and a man of spirit. I didn't want to speak before that bummer there; you'll see why. But to you I'll rip it right out. I got a ship."

"A ship?" cried Herrick. "What ship?"

"That schooner we saw this morning off the passage."

"That schooner with the hospital flag?"

"That's the hooker," said Davis. "She's the *Farallone*, hundred and sixty tons register, out of 'Frisco for Sydney, in California champagne. Captain, mate, and one hand all died of the small-pox, same as they had round in the Paumotus, I guess. Captain and mate were the only white men; all the hands Kanakas; seems a queer kind of outfit from the Christian port. Three of them left and a cook; didn't know where they were; I can't think where they were either, if you come to that; Wiseman must have been on the booze, I guess, to sail the course he did. However, there *he* was, dead; and here are the Kanakas as good as lost. They bummed around at sea like the babes in the wood; and tumbled end-on upon Tahiti. The consul here took charge. He offered the berth to Williams; Williams had never had the smallpox and backed down. That was when I came in for the letter-paper; I thought there was something up when the con-sul asked me to look in again; but I never let on to you fellows, so's you'd not be disappointed. Consul tried M'Neil; scared of smallpox. He tried Capirati, that Corsican, and Leblue, or what-ever his name is, wouldn't lay a hand on it; all too fond of their sweet lives. Last of all, when there wasn't nobody else left to offer it to, he offers it to me. 'Brown, will you ship captain and take her to Sydney?' says he. 'Let me choose my own mate and another white hand,' says I, 'for I don't hold with this Kanaka crew racket; give us all two months' advance to get our clothes and instruments out of pawn, and I'll take stock tonight, fill up stores, and get to sea tomorrow before dark!' That's what I said. 'That's good enough,' says the consul, 'and you can count your-self damned lucky, Brown,' says he. And he said it pretty mean-ingful-appearing too. However, that's all one now. I'll ship Huish before the mast—of course I'll let him berth aft—and I'll ship you mate at seventy-five dollars and two months' ad-vance."

"Me mate? Why, I'm a landsman!" cried Herrick.

"Guess you've got to learn," said the captain. "You don't fancy I'm going to skip and leave you rotting on the beach, perhaps? I'm not that sort, old man. And you're handy, anyway;

I've been shipmates with worse."

"God knows I can't refuse," said Herrick. "God knows I thank you from my heart."

"That's all right," said the captain. "But it ain't all." He turned aside to light a cigar.

"What else is there?" asked the other, with a pang of undefinable alarm.

"I'm coming to that," said Davis, and then paused a little. "See here," he began, holding out his cigar between his finger and thumb, "suppose you figure up what this'll amount to. You don't catch on? Well, we get two months' advance; we can't get away from Papeete—our creditors wouldn't let us go—for less; it'll take us along about two months to get to Sydney; and when we get there, I just want to put it to you squarely: What the better are we?"

"We're off the beach at least," said Herrick.

"I guess there's a beach at Sydney," returned the captain; "and I'll tell you one thing, Mr. Herrick—I don't mean to try. No, *sir!* Sydney will never see me."

"Speak out plain," said Herrick.

"Plain Dutch," replied the captain. "I'm going to own that schooner. It's nothing new; it's done every year in the Pacific. Stephens stole a schooner the other day, didn't he? Hayes and Pease stole vessels all the time. And it's the making of the crowd of us. See here—you think of that cargo. Champagne! why, it's like as if it was put up on purpose. In Peru we'll sell that liquor off at the pier-head, and the schooner after it, if we can find a fool to buy her; and then light out for the mines. If you'll back me up, I stake my life I carry it through."

"Captain," said Herrick, with a quailing voice, "don't do it!"

"I'm desperate," returned Davis. "I've got a chance; I may never get another. Herrick, say the word: back me up; I think we've starved together long enough for that."

"I can't do it. I'm sorry. I can't do it. I've not fallen as low as that," said Herrick, deadly pale.

"What did you say this morning?" said Davis. "That you

couldn't beg? It's the one thing or the other, my son."

"Ah, but this is the gaol!" cried Herrick. "Don't tempt me. It's the gaol."

"Did you hear what the skipper said on board that schooner?" pursued the captain. "Well, I tell you he talked straight. The French have let us alone for a long time; it can't last longer; they've got their eye on us; and as sure as you live, in three weeks you'll be in gaol whatever you do. I read it in the consul's face."

"You forget, captain," said the young man. "There is another way. I can die; and to say truth, I think I should have died three years ago."

The captain folded his arms and looked the other in the face. "Yes," said he, "yes, you can cut your throat; that's a frozen fact; much good may it do you! And where do I come in?"

The light of a strange excitement came in Herrick's face. "Both of us," said he, "both of us together. It's not possible you can enjoy this business. Come," and he reached out a timid hand, "a few strokes in the lagoon—and rest!"

"I tell you, Herrick, I'm 'most tempted to answer you the way the man does in the Bible, and say, '*Get thee behind me, Satan!*'" said the captain. "What! you think I would go drown myself, and I got children starving? Enjoy it? No, by God, I do not enjoy it! but it's the row I've got to hoe, and I'll hoe it till I drop right here. I have three of them, you see, two boys and the one girl, Adar. The trouble is that you are not a parent yourself. I tell you, Herrick, I love you," the man broke out; "I didn't take to you at first, you were so Anglified and tony, but I love you now; it's a man that loves you stands here and wrestles with you. I can't go to sea with the bummer alone; it's not possible. Go drown yourself, and there goes my last chance—the last chance of a poor miserable beast, earning a crust to feed his family. I can't do nothing but sail ships, and I've no papers. And here I get a chance, and you go back on me! Ah, you've no family, and that's where the trouble is!"

"I have indeed," said Herrick.

"Yes, I know," said the captain, "you think so. But no man's got a family till he's got children. It's only the kids count. There's something about the little shavers ... I can't talk of them. And if you thought a cent about this father that I hear you talk of, or that sweetheart you were writing to this morning, you would feel like me. You would say, What matter laws, and God, and that? My folks are hard up, I belong to them, I'll get them bread, or, by God! I'll get them wealth, if I have to burn down London for it. That's what you would say. And I'll tell you more: your heart is saying so this living minute. I can see it in your face. You're thinking, Here's poor friendship for the man I've starved along of, and as for the girl that I set up to be in love with, here's a mighty limp kind of a love that won't carry me as far as 'most any man would go for a demijohn of whisky. There's not much *ro*mance to that love, anyway; it's not the kind they carry on about in song-books. But what's the good of my carrying on talking, when it's all in your inside as plain as print? I put the question to you once for all. Are you going to desert me in my hour of need?—you know if I've deserted you—or will you give me your hand, and try a fresh deal, and go home (as like as not) a millionaire? Say No, and God pity me! Say Yes, and I'll make the little ones pray for you every night on their bended knees. 'God bless Mr. Herrick!' that's what they'll say, one after the other, the old girl sitting there holding stakes at the foot of the bed, and the damned little innocents ..." he broke off. "I don't often rip out about the kids," he said; "but when I do, there's something fetches loose."

"Captain," said Herrick faintly, "is there nothing else?"

"I'll prophesy if you like," said the captain with renewed vigour. "Refuse this, because you think yourself too honest, and before a month's out you'll be gaoled for a sneak-thief. I give you the word fair. I can see it, Herrick, if you can't; you're breaking down. Don't think, if you refuse this chance, that you'll go on doing the evangelical; you're about through with your stock; and before you know where you are, you'll be right out on the other side. No, it's either this for you; or else it's

205

Caledonia. I bet you never were there, and saw those white, shaved men, in their dust-clothes and straw hats, prowling around in gangs in the lamplight at Noumea; they look like wolves, and they look like preachers, and they look like the sick; Huish is a daisy to the best of them. Well, there's your company. They're waiting for you, Herrick, and you got to go; and that's a prophecy."

And as the man stood and shook through his great stature, he seemed indeed like one in whom the spirit of divination worked and might utter oracles. Herrick looked at him, and looked away; it seemed not decent to spy upon such agitation; and the young man's courage sank.

"You talk of going home," he objected. "We could never do that."

"*We* could," said the other. "Captain Brown couldn't, nor Mr. Hay, that shipped mate with him couldn't. But what's that to do with Captain Davis or Mr. Herrick, you galoot?"

"But Hayes had these wild islands where he used to call," came the next fainter objection.

"We have the wild islands of Peru," retorted Davis. "They were wild enough for Stephens, no longer agone than just last year. I guess they'll be wild enough for us."

"And the crew?"

"All Kanakas. Come, I see you're right, old man. I see you'll stand by." And the captain once more offered his hand.

"Have it your own way then," said Herrick. "I'll do it: a strange thing for my father's son. But I'll do it. I'll stand by you, man, for good or evil."

"God bless you!" cried the captain, and stood silent. "Herrick," he added with a smile, "I believe I'd have died in my tracks if you'd said No!"

And Herrick, looking at the man, half believed so also.

"And now we'll go break it to the bummer," said Davis.

"I wonder how he'll take it," said Herrick.

"Him? Jump at it!" was the reply.

206

CHAPTER 4
THE YELLOW FLAG

The schooner *Farallone* lay well out in the jaws of the pass, where the terrified pilot had made haste to bring her to her moorings and escape. Seen from the beach through the thin line of shipping, two objects stood conspicuous to seaward: the little isle, on the one hand, with its palms and the guns and batteries raised forty years before in defence of Queen Pomare's capital; the outcast *Farallone*, upon the other, banished to the threshold of the port, rolling there to her scuppers, and flaunting the plague-flag as she rolled. A few sea-birds screamed and cried about the ship; and within easy range, a man-of-war guard-boat hung off and on and glittered with the weapons of marines. The exuberant daylight and the blinding heaven of the tropics picked out and framed the pictures.

A neat boat, manned by natives in uniform, and steered by the doctor of the port, put from shore towards three of the afternoon, and pulled smartly for the schooner. The foresheets were heaped with sacks of flour, onions, and potatoes, perched among which was Huish dressed as a foremast hand; a heap of chests and cases impeded the action of the oarsmen; and in the stern, by the left hand of the doctor, sat Herrick, dressed in a fresh rig of slops, his brown beard trimmed to a point, a pile of paper novels on his lap, and nursing the while between his feet a chronometer, for which they had exchanged that of the *Farallone*, long since run down and the rate lost.

They passed the guard-boat, exchanging hails with the boatswain's mate in charge, and drew near at last to the forbidden ship. Not a cat stirred, there was no speech of man; and the sea being exceeding high outside, and the reef close to where the schooner lay, the clamour of the surf hung round her like the sound of battle.

"*Ohé la goëlette!*" sang out the doctor, with his best voice.

Instantly, from the house where they had been stowing away

stores, first Davis, and then the ragamuffin, swarthy crew made their appearance.

"Hullo, Hay, that you?" said the captain, leaning on the rail. "Tell the old man to lay her alongside, as if she was eggs. There's a hell of a run of sea here, and his boat's brittle."

The movement of the schooner was at that time more than usually violent. Now she heaved her side as high as a deep-sea steamer's, and showed the flashing of her copper; now she swung swiftly towards the boat until her scuppers gurgled.

"I hope you have sea-legs," observed the doctor. "You will require them."

Indeed, to board the *Farallone*, in that exposed position where she lay, was an affair of some dexterity. The less precious goods were hoisted roughly; the chronometer, after repeated failures, was passed gently and successfully from hand to hand; and there remained only the more difficult business of embarking Huish. Even that piece of dead weight (shipped A.B. at eighteen dollars, and described by the captain to the consul as an invaluable man) was at last hauled on board without mishap; and the doctor, with civil salutations, took his leave.

The three co-adventurers looked at each other, and Davis heaved a breath of relief.

"Now let's get this chronometer fixed," said he, and led the way into the house. It was a fairly spacious place; two state-rooms and a good-sized pantry opened from the main cabin; the bulkheads were painted white, the floor laid with waxcloth. No litter, no sign of life remained; for the effects of the dead men had been disinfected and conveyed on shore. Only on the table, in a saucer, some sulphur burned, and the fumes set them coughing as they entered. The captain peered into the starboard state-room, where the bed-clothes still lay tumbled in the bunk, the blanket flung back as they had flung it back from the disfigured corpse before its burial.

"Now, I told these niggers to tumble that truck overboard," grumbled Davis. "Guess they were afraid to lay hands on it. Well, they've hosed the place out; that's as much as can be expected, I suppose. Huish, lay on to these blankets."

"See you blooming well far enough first," said Huish, drawing back.

"What's that?" snapped the captain. "I'll tell you, my young friend, I think you make a mistake. I'm captain here."

"Fat lot I care," returned the clerk.

"That so?" said Davis. "Then you'll berth forward with the niggers! Walk right out of this cabin."

"O, I dessay!" said Huish. "See any green in my eye? A lark's a lark."

"Well, now, I'll explain this business, and you'll see, once for all, just precisely how much lark there is to it," said Davis. "I'm captain, and I'm going to be it. One thing of three. First, you take my orders here as cabin steward, in which case you mess with us. Or, second, you refuse, and I pack you forward—and you get as quick as the word's said. Or, third and last, I'll signal that man-of-war and send you ashore under arrest for mutiny."

"And, of course, I wouldn't blow the gaff? O no!" replied the jeering Huish.

"And who's to believe you, my son?" inquired the captain. "No, sir! There ain't no larking about my captainising. Enough said. Up with these blankets."

Huish was no fool, he knew when he was beaten; and he was no coward either, for he stepped to the bunk, took the infected bed-clothes fairly in his arms, and carried them out of the house without a check or tremor.

"I was waiting for the chance," said Davis to Herrick. "I needn't do the same with you, because you understand it for yourself."

"Are you going to berth here?" asked Herrick, following the captain into the state-room, where he began to adjust the chronometer in its place at the bed-head.

"Not much!" replied he. "I guess I'll berth on deck. I don't know as I'm afraid, but I've no immediate use for confluent smallpox."

"I don't know that I'm afraid either," said Herrick. "But the thought of these two men sticks in my throat; that captain and mate dying here, one opposite to the other. It's grim. I wonder what they said last?"

"Wiseman and Wishart?" said the captain. "Probably mighty small potatoes. That's a thing a fellow figures out for himself one way, and the real business goes quite another. Perhaps Wiseman said, 'Here, old man, fetch up the gin, I'm feeling powerful rocky.' And perhaps Wishart said, 'O, hell!'"

"Well, that's grim enough," said Herrick.

"And so it is," said Davis.—"There; there's that chronometer fixed. And now it's about time to up anchor and clear out."

He lit a cigar and stepped on deck.

"Here, you! What's *your* name?" he cried to one of the hands, a lean-flanked, clean-built fellow from some far western island, and of a darkness almost approaching to the African.

"Sally Day," replied the man.

"Devil it is," said the captain. "Didn't know we had ladies on board.—Well, Sally, oblige me by hauling down that rag there. I'll do the same for you another time." He watched the yellow bunting as it was eased past the cross-trees and handed down on deck. "You'll float no more on this ship," he observed. "Muster the people aft, Mr. Hay," he added, speaking unnecessarily loud, "I've a word to say to them."

It was with a singular sensation that Herrick prepared for the first time to address a crew. He thanked his stars indeed that they were natives. But even natives, he reflected, might be critics too quick for such a novice as himself; they might perceive some lapse from that precise and cut-and-dry English which prevails on board a ship; it was even possible they understood no other; and he racked his brain, and overhauled his reminiscences of sea romance for some appropriate words.

"Here, men! tumble aft!" he said. "Lively now! all hands aft!"

They crowded in the alleyway like sheep.

"Here they are, sir," said Herrick.

For some time the captain continued to face the stern; then turned with ferocious suddenness on the crew, and seemed to enjoy their shrinking.

"Now," he said, twisting his cigar in his mouth and toying with the spokes of the wheel. "I'm Captain Brown. I command this ship. This is Mr. Hay, first officer. The other white man is cabin steward, but he'll stand watch and do his trick. My orders shall be obeyed smartly. You savvy, 'smartly'? There shall be no growling about the kaikai, which will be above allowance. You'll put a handle to the mate's name, and tack on 'sir' to every order I give you. If you're smart and quick, I'll make this ship comfortable for all hands." He took the cigar out of his mouth. "If you're not," he added, in a roaring voice, "I'll make it a floating hell.—Now, Mr. Hay, we'll pick watches, if you please."

"All right," said Herrick.

"You will please use 'sir' when you address me, Mr. Hay," said the captain. "I'll take the lady. Step to starboard, Sally." And then he whispered in Herrick's ear, "Take the old man."

"I'll take you, there," said Herrick.

"What's your name?" said the captain. "What's that you say? O, that's not English; I'll have none of your highway gibberish on my ship. We'll call you old Uncle Ned, because you've got no wool on the top of your head, just the place where the wool ought to grow. Step to port, Uncle. Don't you hear Mr. Hay has picked you? Then I'll take the white man. White Man, step to starboard. Now, which of you two is the cook? You? Then Mr. Hay takes your friend in the blue dungaree. Step to port, Dungaree. There, we know who we all are: Dungaree, Uncle Ned, Sally Day, White Man, and Cook. All F.F.V.'s I guess. And now, Mr. Hay, we'll up anchor, if you please."

"For heaven's sake, tell me some of the words," whispered Herrick.

An hour later the *Farallone* was under all plain sail, the rudder hard a-port, and the cheerfully-clanking windlass had brought the anchor home.

"All clear, sir," cried Herrick from the bow.

The captain met her with the wheel, as she bounded like a stag from her repose, trembling and bending to the puffs. The guard-boat gave a parting hail, the wake whitened and ran out; the *Farallone* was under weigh.

Her berth had been close to the pass. Even as she forged ahead Davis slewed her for the channel between the pier-ends of the reef, the breakers sounding and whitening to either hand. Straight through the narrow band of blue she shot to seaward; and the captain's heart exulted as he felt her tremble underfoot, and (looking back over the taffrail) beheld the roofs of Papeete changing position on the shore and the island mountains rearing higher in the wake.

But they were not yet done with the shore and the horror of the yellow flag. About midway of the pass there was a cry and a scurry, a man was seen to leap upon the rail, and, throwing his arms over his head, to stoop and plunge into the sea.

"Steady as she goes," the captain cried, relinquishing the wheel to Huish.

The next moment he was forward in the midst of the Kanakas, belaying-pin in hand.

"Anybody else for shore?" he cried, and the savage trumpeting of his voice, no less than the ready weapon in his hand, struck fear in all. Stupidly they stared after their escaped companion, whose black head was visible upon the water, steering for the land. And the schooner meanwhile slipped like a racer through the pass, and met the long sea of the open ocean with a souse of spray.

"Fool that I was, not to have a pistol ready!" exclaimed Davis. "Well, we go to sea short-handed; we can't help that. You have a lame watch of it, Mr. Hay."

"I don't see how we are to get along," said Herrick.

"Got to," said the captain. "No more Tahiti for me."

Both turned instinctively and looked astern. The fair island was unfolding mountain-top on mountain-top; Eimeo, on the port board, lifted her splintered pinnacles; and still the schooner raced to the open sea.

"Think!" cried the captain, with a gesture, "yesterday morning I danced for my breakfast like a poodle dog."

CHAPTER 5
THE CARGO OF CHAMPAGNE

The ship's head was laid to clear Eimeo to the north, and the captain sat down in the cabin, with a chart, a ruler, and an epitome.

"East a half no'the," said he, raising his face from his labours. "Mr. Hay, you'll have to watch your dead reckoning; I want every yard she makes on every hair's-breadth of a course. I'm going to knock a hole right straight through the Paumotus, and that's always a near touch. Now, if this South East Trade ever blew out of the S.E., which it don't, we might hope to lie within half a point of our course. Say we lie within a point of it. That'll just about weather Fakarava. Yes, sir, that's what we've got to do, if we tack for it. Brings us through this slush of little islands in the cleanest place: see?" And he showed where his ruler intersected the wide-lying labyrinth of the Dangerous Archipelago. "I wish it was night, and I could put her about right now; we're losing time and easting. Well, we'll do our best. And if we don't fetch Peru, we'll bring up to Ecuador. All one, I guess. Depreciated dollars down, and no questions asked. A remarkable fine institootion, the South American don."

Tahiti was already some way astern, the Diadem rising from among broken mountains—Eimeo was already close aboard, and stood black and strange against the golden splendour of the west—when the captain took his departure from the two islands, and the patent log was set.

Some twenty minutes later, Sally Day, who was continually leaving the wheel to peer in at the cabin clock, announced in a shrill cry "Fo' bell," and the cook was to be seen carrying the soup into the cabin.

"I guess I'll sit down and have a pick with you," said Davis to Herrick. "By the time I've done it'll be dark, and we'll clap the hooker on the wind for South America."

In the cabin at one corner of the table, immediately below

the lamp, and on the lee side of a bottle of champagne, sat Huish.

"What's this? Where did that come from?" asked the captain.

"It's fizz, and it came from the after-'old, if you want to know," said Huish, and drained his mug.

"This'll never do," exclaimed Davis, the merchant seaman's horror of breaking into cargo showing incongruously forth on board that stolen ship. "There was never any good came of games like that."

"You byby!" said Huish. "A fellow would think (to 'ear him) we were on the square! And look 'ere you've put this job up 'ansomely for me, 'aven't you? I'm to go on deck and steer, while you two sit and guzzle, and I'm to go by a nickname, and got to call you 'sir' and 'mister.' Well, you look here, my bloke: I'll have fizz *ad lib.*, or it won't wash. I tell you that. And you know mighty well, you ain't got any man-of-war to signal now."

Davis was staggered. "I'd give fifty dollars this had never happened," he said weakly.

"Well, it 'as 'appened, you see," returned Huish. "Try some; it's devilish good."

The Rubicon was crossed without another struggle. The captain filled a mug and drank.

"I wish it was beer," he said with a sigh. "But there's no denying it's the genuine stuff and cheap at the money. Now, Huish, you clear out and take your wheel."

The little wretch had gained a point, and he was gay. "Ay, ay, sir," said he, and left the others to their meal.

"Pea-soup!" exclaimed the captain. "Blamed if I thought I should taste pea-soup again!"

Herrick sat inert and silent. It was impossible after these months of hopeless want to smell the rough, high-spiced sea victuals without lust, and his mouth watered with desire of the champagne. It was no less impossible to have assisted at the scene between Huish and the captain, and not to perceive, with sudden bluntness, the gulf where he had fallen. He was a thief among thieves. He said it to himself. He could not touch the soup. If he had moved at all, it must have been to leave the table, throw himself overboard, and drown—an honest man.

"Here," said the captain, "you look sick, old man; have a drop of this."

The champagne creamed and bubbled in the mug; its bright colour, its lively effervescence, seized his eye. "It is too late to hesitate," he thought; his hand took the mug instinctively; he drank, with unquenchable pleasure and desire of more; drained the vessel dry, and set it down with sparkling eyes.

"There is something in life after all!" he cried. "I had forgot what it was like. Yes, even this is worth while. Wine, food, dry clothes—why, they're worth dying, worth hanging for! Captain, tell me one thing: why aren't all the poor folk foot-pads?"

"Give it up," said the captain.

"They must be damned good," cried Herrick. "There's something here beyond me. Think of that calaboose! Suppose we were sent suddenly back." He shuddered as stung by a convulsion, and buried his face in his clutching hands.

"Here, what's wrong with you?" cried the captain. There was no reply; only Herrick's shoulders heaved, so that the table was shaken. "Take some more of this. Here, drink this. I order you to. Don't start crying when you're out of the wood."

"I'm not crying," said Herrick, raising his face and showing his dry eyes. "It's worse than crying. It's the horror of that grave that we've escaped from."

"Come now, you tackle your soup; that'll fix you," said Davis kindly. "I told you you were all broken up. You couldn't have stood out another week."

"That's the dreadful part of it!" cried Herrick. "Another week and I'd have murdered some one for a dollar! God! and I know that? And I'm still living? It's some beastly dream."

"Quietly, quietly! Quietly does it, my son. Take your pea-soup. Food, that's what you want," said Davis.

The soup strengthened and quieted Herrick's nerves; another glass of wine, and a piece of pickled pork and fried banana completed what the soup began; and he was able once more to look the captain in the face.

"I didn't know I was so much run down," he said.

"Well," said Davis, "you were as steady as a rock all day: now you've had a little lunch, you'll be as steady as a rock again."

"Yes," was the reply, "I'm steady enough now, but I'm a queer kind of a first officer."

"Shucks!" cried the captain. "You've only got to mind the ship's course, and keep your slate to half a point. A babby could do that, let alone a college graduate like you. There ain't nothing *to* sailoring, when you come to look it in the face. And now we'll go and put her about. Bring the slate; we'll have to start our dead reckoning right away."

The distance run since the departure was read off the log by the binnacle light and entered on the slate.

"Ready about," said the captain. "Give me the wheel, White Man, and you stand by the mainsheet. Boom tackle, Mr. Hay, please, and then you can jump forward and attend head sails."

"Ay, ay, sir," responded Herrick.

"All clear forward?" asked Davis.

"All clear, sir."

"Hard a-lee!" cried the captain. "Haul in your slack as she comes," he called to Huish. "Haul in your slack, put your back into it; keep your feet out of the coils." A sudden blow sent Huish flat along the deck, and the captain was in his place. "Pick yourself up and keep the wheel hard over!" he roared. "You wooden fool, you wanted to get killed, I guess. Draw the jib," he cried a moment later; and then to Huish, "Give me the wheel again, and see if you can coil that sheet."

But Huish stood and looked at Davis with an evil countenance. "Do you know you struck me?" said he.

"Do you know I saved your life?" returned the other, not deigning to look at him, his eyes travelling instead between the compass and the sails. "Where would you have been if that boom had swung out and you bundled in the slack? No, *sir*, we'll have no more of you at the mainsheet. Seaport towns are full of mainsheet-men; they hop upon one leg, my son, what's left of them, and the rest are dead. (Set your boom tackle, Mr. Hay.) Struck you, did I? Lucky for you I did."

"Well," said Huish slowly, "I dessay there may be somethink in that. 'Ope there is." He turned his back elaborately on the captain, and entered the house, where the speedy explosion of a champagne cork showed he was attending to his comfort.

Herrick came aft to the captain. "How is she doing now!" he asked.

"East and by no'the a half no'the," said Davis. "It's about as good as I expected."

"What'll the hands think of it?" said Herrick.

"O, they don't think. They ain't paid to," says the captain.

"There was something wrong, was there not? between you and—" Herrick paused.

"That's a nasty little beast; that's a biter," replied the captain, shaking his head. "But so long as you and me hang in, it don't matter."

Herrick lay down in the weather alleyway; the night was cloudless, the movement of the ship cradled him, he was oppressed besides by the first generous meal after so long a time of famine; and he was recalled from deep sleep by the voice of Davis singing out: "Eight bells!"

He rose stupidly and staggered aft, where the captain gave him the wheel.

"By the wind," said the captain. "It comes a little puffy; when you get a heavy puff, steal all you can to windward, but keep her a good full."

He stepped towards the house, paused and hailed the fore-castle.

"Got such a thing as a concertina forward?" said he. "Bully for you, Uncle Ned. Fetch it aft, will you?"

The schooner steered very easy; and Herrick, watching the moon-whitened sails, was overpowered by drowsiness. A sharp report from the cabin startled him; a third bottle had been opened; and Herrick remembered the *Sea Ranger* and

Fourteen Island Group. Presently the notes of the accordion sounded, and then the captain's voice:

"O honey, with our pockets full of money,
We will trip, trip, trip, we will trip it on the quay,
And I will dance with Kate, and Tom will dance with Sall,
When we're all back from South Amerikee."

So it went to its quaint air; and the watch below lingered and listened by the forward door, and Uncle Ned was to be seen in the moonlight nodding time; and Herrick smiled at the wheel, his anxieties a while forgotten. Song followed song; another cork exploded; there were voices raised, as though the pair in the cabin were in disagreement: and presently it seemed the breach was healed; for it was now the voice of Huish that struck up, to the captain's accompaniment:—

"Up in a balloon, boys,
Up in a balloon,
All among the little stars
And round about the moon."

A wave a nausea overcame Herrick at the wheel. He wondered why the air, the words (which were yet written with a certain knack), and the voice and accent of the singer, should all jar his spirit like a file on a man's teeth. He sickened at the thought of his two comrades drinking away their reason upon stolen wine, quarrelling and hiccupping and waking up, while the doors of a prison yawned for them in the near future. "Shall I have sold my honour for nothing?" he thought; and a heat of rage and resolution glowed in his bosom—rage against his comrades—resolution to carry through this business if it might be carried; pluck profit out of shame, since the shame at least was now inevitable; and come home, home from South America—how did the song go?—"with his pockets full of money."

"O honey, with our pockets full of money,
  We will trip, trip, trip, we will trip it on the quay":

so the words ran in his head; and the honey took on visible form, the quay rose before him and he knew it for the lamplit Embankment, and he saw the lights of Battersea bridge bestride the sullen river. All through the remainder of his trick he stood entranced, reviewing the past. He had been always true to his love, but not always sedulous to recall her. In the growing calamity of his life, she had swum more distant, like the moon in mist. The letter of farewell, the dishonourable hope that had surprised and corrupted him in his distress, the changed scene, the sea, the night and the music—all stirred him to the roots of manhood. "I *will* win her," he thought, and ground his teeth. "Fair or foul, what matters if I win her?"

"Fo' bell, matey. I think um fo' bell"—he was suddenly recalled by these words in the voice of Uncle Ned.

"Look in at the clock, Uncle," said he. He would not look himself, from horror of the tipplers.

"Him past, matey," repeated the Hawaiian.

"So much the better for you, Uncle," he replied; and he gave up the wheel, repeating the directions as he had received them.

He took two steps forward and remembered his dead reckoning. "How has she been heading?" he thought; and he flushed from head to foot. He had not observed or had forgotten; here was the old incompetence; the slate must be filled up by guess. "Never again!" he vowed to himself in silent fury, "never again. It shall be no fault of mine if this miscarry." And for the remainder of his watch, he stood close by Uncle Ned, and read the face of the compass as perhaps he had never read a letter from his sweetheart.

All the time, and spurring him to the more attention, song, loud talk, fleering laughter, and the occasional popping of a cork, reached his ears from the interior of the house; and when the port watch was relieved at midnight, Huish and the captain appeared upon the quarter-deck with flushed faces and un-even steps, the former laden with bottles, the latter with two tin mugs. Herrick silently passed them by. They hailed him in thick voices, he made no answer; they cursed him for a churl, he paid no heed although his belly quivered with disgust and rage. He closed-to the door of the house behind him, and cast himself on a locker in the cabin—not to sleep, he thought—rather to think and to despair. Yet he had scarce turned twice on his uneasy bed, before a drunken voice hailed him in the ear, and he must go on deck again to stand the morning watch.

The first evening set the model for those that were to follow. Two cases of champagne scarce lasted the four-and-twenty hours, and almost the whole was drunk by Huish and the captain. Huish seemed to thrive on the excess; he was never sober, yet never wholly tipsy; the food and the sea air had soon healed him of his disease, and he began to lay on flesh. But with Davis things went worse. In the drooping, unbuttoned figure that sprawled all day upon the lockers, tippling and reading novels; in the fool who made of the evening watch a public carouse on the quarter-deck, it would have been hard to recognise the vigorous seaman of Papeete roads. He kept him-self reasonably well in hand till he had taken the sun and yawned and blotted through his calculations; but from the moment he rolled up the chart, his hours were passed in slavish self-indulgence or in hoggish slumber. Every other branch of his duty was neglected, except maintaining a stern discipline about the dinner-table. Again and again Herrick would hear the cook called aft, and see him running with fresh tins, or carrying away again a meal that had been totally condemned. And the more the captain became sunk in drunkenness, the more delicate his palate showed itself. Once, in the forenoon, he had a bo'sun's chair rigged over the rail, stripped to his trousers, and went overboard with a pot of paint. "I don't like the way this schooner's painted," said he, "and I've taken a down upon her name." But he tired of it in half an hour, and the schooner went on her way with an incongruous patch of colour on the stern, and the word *Farallone* part obliterated and part looking through. He refused to stand either the middle or morning watch. It was fine-weather sailing, he said; and asked, with a laugh, "Who ever heard of the old man standing watch himself?" To the dead reckoning which Herrick still tried to keep, he would pay not the least attention nor afford the least assistance.

"What do we want of dead reckoning?" he asked. "We get the sun all right, don't we?"

"We mayn't get it always, though," objected Herrick. "And you told me yourself you weren't sure of the chronometer."

"O, there ain't no flies in the chronometer!" cried Davis.

"Oblige me so far, captain," said Herrick stiffly. "I am anxious to keep this reckoning, which is a part of my duty; I do not know what to allow for current, nor how to allow for it. I am too inexperienced; and I beg of you to help me."

"Never discourage zealous officer," said the captain, unrolling the chart again, for Herrick had taken him over his day's work and while he was still partly sober. "Here it is: look for yourself; anything from west to west no'the-west, and anyways from five to twenty-five miles. That's what the A'm'ralty chart says; I guess you don't expect to get on ahead of your own Britishers?"

"I am trying to do my duty, Captain Brown," said Herrick, with a dark flush, "and I have the honour to inform you that I don't enjoy being trifled with."

"What in thunder do you want?" roared Davis. "Go and look at the blamed wake. If you're trying to do your duty, why don't you go and do it? I guess it's no business of mine to go and stick my head over the ship's rump? I guess it's yours. And I'll tell you what it is, my fine fellow, I'll trouble you not to come the dude over me. You're insolent, that's what's wrong with you. Don't you crowd me, Mr. Herrick, Esquire."

Herrick tore up his papers, threw them on the floor, and left the cabin.

"He's turned a bloomin' swot, ain't he?" sneered Huish.

"He thinks himself too good for his company, that's what ails Herrick, Esquire," raged the captain. "He thinks I don't understand when he comes the heavy swell. Won't sit down with us, won't he? won't say a civil word? I'll serve the son of a gun as he deserves. By God, Huish, I'll show him whether he's too good for John Davis!"

"Easy with the names, cap'," said Huish, who was always the more sober. "Easy over the stones, my boy!"

"All right, I will. You're a good sort, Huish. I didn't take to you at first, but I guess you're right enough. Let's open another bottle," said the captain; and that day, perhaps because he was excited by the quarrel, he drank more recklessly, and by four o'clock was stretched insensible upon the locker.

Herrick and Huish supped alone, one after the other, opposite his flushed and snorting body. And if the sight killed Herrick's hunger, the isolation weighed so heavily on the clerk's spirit, that he was scarce risen from table ere he was currying favour with his former comrade.

Herrick was at the wheel when he approached, and Huish leaned confidentially across the binnacle.

"I say, old chappie," he said, "you and me don't seem to be such pals somehow."

Herrick gave her a spoke or two in silence; his eye, as it skirted from the needle to the luff of the foresail, passed the man by without speculation. But Huish was really dull, a thing he could support with difficulty, having no resources of his own. The idea of a private talk with Herrick, at this stage of their relations, held out particular inducements to a person of his character. Drink besides, as it renders some men hyper-sensitive, made Huish callous. And it would almost have required a blow to make him quit his purpose.

"Pretty business, ain't it?" he continued; "Dyvis on the lush? Must say I thought you gave it 'im A1 to-day. He didn't like it a bit; took on hawful after you were gone.—'Ere,' says I, ''old on, easy on the lush,' I says. ''Errick was right and you know it. Give 'im a chanst,' I says.—'Uish,' sezee, 'don't you gimme no more of your jaw, or I'll knock your bloomin' eyes out.' Well, wot can I do, 'Errick? But I tell you, I don't 'arf like it. It looks to me like the *Sea Rynger* over again."

Still Herrick was silent.

"Do you 'ear me speak?" asked Huish sharply. "You're pleasant, ain't you?"

"Stand away from that binnacle," said Herrick.

The clerk looked at him long and straight and black; his figure seemed to writhe like that of a snake about to strike; then he turned on his heel, went back to the cabin and opened a bottle of champagne. When eight bells were cried he slept on the floor beside the captain on the locker; and of the whole starboard watch only Sally Day appeared upon the summons. The mate proposed to stand the watch with him, and let Uncle Ned lie down; it would make twelve hours on deck, and probably sixteen, but in this fair-weather sailing he might safely sleep between his tricks of wheel, leaving orders to be called on any sign of squalls. So far he could trust the men, between whom and himself a close relation had sprung up. With Uncle Ned he held long nocturnal conversations, and the old man told him his simple and hard story of exile, suffering, and injustice among cruel whites. The cook, when he found Herrick messed alone, produced for him unexpected and sometimes unpalatable dainties, of which he forced himself to eat. And one day, when he was forward, he was surprised to feel a caressing hand run down his shoulder, and to hear the voice of Sally Day crooning in his ear: "You gootch man!" He turned, and, choking down a sob, shook hands with the negrito. They were kindly, cheery, childish souls. Upon the Sunday each brought forth his separate Bible—for they were all men of alien speech even to each other, and Sally Day communicated with his mates in English only, each read or made-believe to read his chapter, Uncle Ned with spectacles on his nose; and they would all join together in the singing of missionary hymns. It was thus a cutting reproof to compare the islanders and the whites aboard the *Farallone*. Shame ran in

Herrick's blood to remember what employment he was on, and to see these poor souls—and even Sally Day, the child of cannibals, in all likelihood a cannibal himself—so faithful to what they knew of good. The fact that he was held in grateful favour by these innocents served like blinders to his conscience, and there were times when he was inclined, with Sally Day, to call himself a good man. But the height of his favour was only now to appear. With one voice, the crew protested; ere Herrick knew what they were doing, the cook was aroused and came a willing volunteer; all hands clustered about their mate with expostulations and caresses; and he was bidden to lie down and take his customary rest without alarm.

"He tell you true," said Uncle Ned. "You sleep. Evely man hea he do all light. Evely man he like you too much."

Herrick struggled, and gave way; choked upon some trivial words of gratitude; and walked to the side of the house, against which he leaned, struggling with emotion.

Uncle Ned presently followed him and begged him to lie down.

"It's no use, Uncle Ned," he replied. "I couldn't sleep. I'm knocked over with all your goodness."

"Ah, no call me Uncle Ned no mo'!" cried the old man. "No my name! My name Taveeta, all-e-same Taveeta King of Islael. Wat for he call that Hawaii? I think no savvy nothing—all-e-same Wise-a-mana."

It was the first time the name of the late captain had been mentioned, and Herrick grasped the occasion. The reader shall be spared Uncle Ned's unwieldy dialect, and learn in less embarrassing English the sum of what he now communicated. The ship had scarce cleared the Golden Gates before the captain and mate had entered on a career of drunkenness, which was scarcely interrupted by their malady and only closed by death. For days and weeks they had encountered neither land nor ship; and seeing themselves lost on the huge deep with their insane conductors, the natives had drunk deep of terror.

At length they made a low island and went in; and Wiseman and Wishart landed in the boat.

There was a great village, a very fine village, and plenty Kanakas in that place; but all mighty serious; and from every here and there in the back parts of the settlement, Taveeta heard the sounds of island lamentation. "I no savvy *talk* that island," said he. "I savvy hear um *cly*. I think, Hum! too many people die here!" But upon Wiseman and Wishart the significance of that barbaric keening was lost. Full of bread and drink, they rollicked along unconcerned, embraced the girls, who had scarce energy to repel them, took up and joined (with drunken voices) in the death-wail, and at last (on what they took to be an invitation) entered under the roof of a house in which was a considerable concourse of people sitting silent. They stooped below the eaves, flushed and laughing; within a minute they came forth again with changed faces and silent tongues; and as the press severed to make way for them, Taveeta was able to perceive, in the deep shadow of the house, the sick man raising from his mat a head already defeatured by disease. The two tragic triflers fled without hesitation for their boat, screaming on Taveeta to make haste; they came aboard with all speed of oars, raised anchor and crowded sail upon the ship with blows and curses, and were at sea again—and again drunk—before sunset. A week after, and the last of the two had been committed to the deep. Herrick asked Taveeta where that island was, and he replied that, by what he gathered of folks' talk as they went up together from the beach, he supposed it must be one of the Paumotus. This was in itself probable enough, for the Dangerous Archipelago had been swept that year from east to west by devastating smallpox; but Herrick thought it a strange course to lie from Sydney. Then he remembered the drink.

"Were they not surprised when they made the island?" he asked.

"Wise-a-mana he say, 'damn! what this?'" was the reply.

"O, that's it, then," said Herrick. "I don't believe they knew where they were."

"I think so too," said Uncle Ned. "I think no savvy. This one mo' betta," he added, pointing to the house, where the drunken captain slumbered: "Take-a-sun all-e-time."

The implied last touch completed Herrick's picture of the life and death of his two predecessors; of their prolonged, sordid, sodden sensuality as they sailed, they knew not whither, on their last cruise. He held but a twinkling and unsure belief in any future state; the thought of one of punishment he derided; yet for him (as for all) there dwelt a *horror* about the end of the brutish man. Sickness fell upon him at the image thus called up; and when he compared it with the scene in which he himself was acting, and considered the doom that seemed to brood upon the schooner, a horror that was almost superstitious fell upon him. And yet the strange thing was, he did not falter. He who had proved his incapacity in so many fields, being now falsely placed amid duties which he did not understand, without help, and it might be said without countenance, had hitherto surpassed expectation; and even the shameful misconduct and shocking disclosures of that night seemed but to nerve and strengthen him. He had sold his honour; he vowed it should not be in vain; "it shall be no fault of mine if this miscarry," he repeated. And in his heart he wondered at himself. Living rage no doubt supported him; no doubt also, the sense of the last cast, of the ships burned, of all doors closed but one, which is so strong a tonic to the merely weak, and so deadly a depressant to the merely cowardly.

For some time the voyage went otherwise well. They weathered Fakarava with one board; and the wind holding well to the southward, and blowing fresh, they passed between Ranaka and Ratiu, and ran some days north-east by east-half-east under the lee of Takume and Honden, neither of which they made. In about 14° south, and between 134° and 135° west, it fell a dead calm, with rather a heavy sea. The captain refused to take in sail, the helm was lashed, no watch was set, and the *Farallone* rolled and banged for three days, according to observation, in almost the same place. The fourth morning, a little before day, a breeze sprang up and rapidly freshened. The captain had drunk hard the night before; he was far from sober when he was roused; and when he came on deck for the first time at half-past eight, it was plain he had already drunk deep again at breakfast. Herrick avoided his eye; and resigned the deck with indignation to a man more than half-seas-over.

By the loud commands of the captain and the singing out of fellows at the ropes, he could judge from the house that sail was being crowded on the ship; relinquished his half-eaten breakfast; and came on deck again, to find the main and the jib topsails set, and both watches and the cook turned out to hand the staysail. The *Farallone* lay already far over; the sky was obscured with misty scud; and from the windward an ominous squall came flying up, broadening and blackening as it rose.

Fear thrilled in Herrick's vitals. He saw death hard by; and if not death, sure ruin. For if the *Farallone* lived through the coming squall, she must surely be dismasted. With that their enterprise was at an end, and they themselves bound prisoners to the very evidence of their crime. The greatness of the peril and his own alarm sufficed to silence him. Pride, wrath, and shame raged without issue in his mind; and he shut his teeth and folded his arms close.

The captain sat in the boat to windward, bellowing orders and insults, his eyes glazed, his face deeply congested; a bottle set between his knees, a glass in his hand half empty. His back was to the squall, and he was at first intent upon the setting of the sail. When that was done, and the great trapezium of canvas had begun to draw and to trail the lee-rail of the *Farallone* level with the foam, he laughed out an empty laugh, drained his glass, sprawled back among the lumber in the boat, and fetched out a crumpled novel.

Herrick watched him, and his indignation glowed red-hot. He glanced to windward where the squall already whitened the near sea and heralded its coming with a singular and dismal sound. He glanced at the steersman, and saw him clinging

227

to the spokes with a face of a sickly blue. He saw the crew were running to their stations without orders. And it seemed as if something broke in his brain; and the passion of anger, so long restrained, so long eaten in secret, burst suddenly loose and shook him like a sail. He stepped across to the captain, and smote his hand heavily on the drunkard's shoulder.

"You brute," he said, in a voice that tottered, "look behind you!"

"Wha's that?" cried Davis, bounding in the boat and up-setting the champagne.

"You lost the *Sea Ranger* because you were a drunken sot," said Herrick. "Now you're going to lose the *Farallone*. You're going to drown here the same way as you drowned others, and be damned. And your daughter shall walk the streets, and your sons be thieves like their father."

For the moment the words struck the captain white and foolish. "My God!" he cried, looking at Herrick as upon a ghost; "my God, Herrick!" "Look behind you, then!" reiterated the assailant.

The wretched man, already partly sobered, did as he was told, and in the same breath of time leaped to his feet. "Down staysail" he trumpeted. The hands were thrilling for the order, and the great sail came with a run, and fell half overboard among the racing foam. "Jib top-sail halyards! Let the stays'l be," he said again.

But before it was well uttered, the squall shouted aloud and fell, in a solid mass of wind and rain commingled, on the *Farallone*; and she stooped under the blow, and lay like a thing dead. From the mind of Herrick reason fled; he clung in the weather rigging, exulting; he was done with life, and he gloried in the release; he gloried in the wild noises of the wind and the choking onslaught of the rain; he gloried to die so, and now, amid this coil of the elements. And meanwhile, in the waist, up to his knees in water—so low the schooner lay—the captain was hacking at the foresheet with a pocket-knife. It was a question of seconds, for the *Farallone* drank deep of the encroaching seas. But the hand of the captain had the advance; the foresail boom tore apart the last strands of the sheet and crashed to leeward; the *Farallone* leaped up into the wind and righted; and the peak and throat halyards, which had long been let go, began to run at the same instant.

For some ten minutes more she careered under the impulse of the squall; but the captain was now master of himself and of his ship, and all danger at an end. And then, sudden as a trick-change upon the stage, the squall blew by, the wind dropped into light airs, the sun beamed forth again upon the tattered schooner; and the captain, having secured the foresail boom and set a couple of hands to the pump, walked aft, sober, a little pale, and with the sodden end of a cigar still stuck between his teeth even as the squall had found it. Herrick followed him; he could scarce recall the violence of his late emotions, but he felt there was a scene to go through, and he was anxious and even eager to go through with it.

The captain, turning at the house-end, met him face to face, and averted his eyes. "We've lost the two tops'ls and the stays'l," he gabbled. "Good business we didn't lose any sticks. I guess you think we're all the better without the kites."

"That's not what I'm thinking," said Herrick, in a voice strangely quiet, that yet echoed confusion in the captain's mind.

"I know that," he cried, holding up his hand. "I know what you're thinking. No use to say it now. I'm sober."

"I have to say it, though," returned Herrick.

"Hold on, Herrick; you've said enough," said Davis. "You've said what I would take from no man breathing but yourself; only I know it's true."

"I have to tell you, Captain Brown," pursued Herrick, "that I resign my position as mate. You can put me in irons or shoot me, as you please; I will make no resistance—only, I decline in any way to help or to obey you; and I suggest you should put Mr. Huish in my place. He will make a worthy first officer to your captain, sir." He smiled, bowed, and turned to walk forward.

"Where are you going, Herrick?" cried the captain, detaining him by the shoulder.

"To berth forward with the men, sir," replied Herrick, with the same hateful smile. "I've been long enough aft here with you—gentlemen."

"You're wrong there," said Davis. "Don't you be too quick with me; there ain't nothing wrong but the drink—it's the old story, man! Let me get sober once and then you'll see," he pleaded.

"Excuse me, I desire to see no more of you," said Herrick.

The captain groaned aloud. "You know what you said about my children?" he broke out.

"By rote. In case you wish me to say it you again?" asked Herrick.

"Don't!" cried the captain clapping his hands to his ears. "Don't make me kill a man I care for! Herrick, if you see me put a glass to my lips again till we're ashore, I give you leave to put a bullet through me; I beg you to it! You're the only man aboard whose carcase is worth losing; do you think I don't know that? do you think I ever went back on you? I always knew you were in the right of it—drunk or sober, I knew that. What do you want?—an oath? Man, you're clever enough to see that this is sure-enough earnest."

"Do you mean there shall be no more drinking?" asked Herrick, "neither by you nor Huish? that you won't go on stealing my profits and drinking my champagne that I gave my honour for? and that you'll attend to your duties, and stand watch and watch, and bear your proper share of the ship's work, instead of leaving it all on the shoulders of the landsman, and making yourself the butt and scoff of native seamen? Is that what you mean? If it is, be so good as say it categorically."

"You put these things in a way hard for a gentleman to swallow," said the captain. "You wouldn't have me say I was ashamed of myself? Trust me this once; I'll do the square thing, and there's my hand on it."

"Well, I'll try it once," said Herrick. "Fail me again..."

"No more now!" interrupted Davis. "No more, old man! Enough said. You've a riling tongue when your back's up, Herrick. Just be glad we're friends again, the same as what I am; and go tender on the raws; I'll see as you don't repent it. We've been mighty near death this day—don't say whose fault it was!—pretty near hell, too, I guess. We're in a mighty bad line of life, us two, and ought to go easy with each other."

He was maundering; yet it seemed as if he were maundering with some design, beating about the bush of some communication that he feared to make, or perhaps only talking against time in terror of what Herrick might say next. But Herrick had now spat his venom; his was a kindly nature, and, content with his triumph, he had now begun to pity. With a few soothing words he sought to conclude the interview, and proposed that they should change their clothes.

"Not right yet," said Davis. "There's another thing I want to tell you first. You know what you said about my children? I want to tell you why it hit me so hard; I kind of think you'll feel bad about it too. It's about my little Adar. You hadn't ought to have quite said that—but of course I know you didn't know. She—she's dead, you see."

"Why, Davis!" cried Herrick. "You've told me a dozen times she was alive! Clear your head, man! This must be the drink."

"No, *sir*," said Davis. "She's dead. Died of a bowel complaint. That was when I was away in the brig *Oregon*. She lies in Portland, Maine. 'Adar, only daughter of Captain John Davis and Mariar his wife, aged five.' I had a doll for her on board. I never took the paper off'n that doll, Herrick; it went down the way it was with the *Sea Ranger*, that day I was damned."

The captain's eyes were fixed on the horizon; he talked with an extraordinary softness, but a complete composure; and Herrick looked upon him with something that was almost terror.

"Don't think I'm crazy neither," resumed Davis. "I've all the cold sense that I know what to do with. But I guess a man that's unhappy's like a child; and this is a kind of a child's game of

231

mine. I never could act up to the plain-cut truth, you see; so I pretend. And I warn you square; as soon as we're through with this talk, I'll start in again with the pretending. Only, you see, she can't walk no streets," added the captain, "couldn't even make out to live and get that doll!"

Herrick laid a tremulous hand upon the captain's shoulder.

"Don't do that!" cried Davis, recoiling from the touch. "Can't you see I'm all broken up the way it is? Come along, then; come along, old man; you can put your trust in me right through; come along and get dry clothes."

They entered the cabin, and there was Huish on his knees prizing open a case of champagne.

"'Vast there!" cried the captain. "No more of that. No more drinking on this ship."

"Turned teetotal, 'ave you?" inquired Huish. "I'm agreeable. About time, eh? Bloomin' nearly lost another ship, I fancy." He took out a bottle and began calmly to burst the wire with the spike of a corkscrew.

"Do you hear me speak?" cried Davis.

"I suppose I do. You speak loud enough," said Huish. "The trouble is that I don't care."

Herrick plucked the captain's sleeve. "Let him free now," he said. "We've had all we want this morning."

"Let him have it, then," said the captain. "It's his last."

By this time the wire was open, the string was cut, the head of gilded paper was torn away; and Huish waited, mug in hand, expecting the usual explosion. It did not follow. He eased the cork with his thumb; still there was no result. At last he took the screw and drew it. It came out very easy and with scarce a sound.

"'Illo!" said Huish. "'Ere's a bad bottle."

He poured some of the wine into the mug; it was colourless and still. He smelt and tasted it.

"W'y, wot's this?" he said. "It's water!"

If the voice of trumpets had suddenly sounded about the ship in the midst of the sea, the three men in the house could scarcely have been more stunned than by this incident. The mug passed round; each sipped, each smelt of it; each stared at the bottle in its glory of gold paper as Crusoe may have stared at the footprint; and their minds were swift to fix upon a common apprehension. The difference between a bottle of champagne and a bottle of water is not great; between a shipload of one or of the other lay the whole scale from riches to ruin.

A second bottle was broached. There were two cases standing ready in a state-room; these two were brought out, broken open, and tested. Still with the same result: the contents were still colourless and tasteless, and dead as the rain in a beached fishing-boat.

"Crikey!" said Huish.

"Here, let's sample the hold," said the captain, mopping his brow with a back-handed sweep; and the three stalked out of the house, grim and heavy-footed.

All hands were turned out; two Kanakas were sent below, another stationed at a purchase; and Davis, axe in hand, took his place beside the coamings.

"Are you going to let the men know?" whispered Herrick.

"Damn the men!" said Davis. "It's beyond that. We've got to know ourselves."

Three cases were sent on deck and sampled in turn; from each bottle, as the captain smashed it with the axe, the champagne ran bubbling and creaming.

"Go deeper, can't you?" cried Davis to the Kanakas in the hold.

The command gave the signal for a disastrous change. Case after case came up, bottle after bottle was burst, and bled mere water. Deeper yet, and they came upon a layer where there was scarcely so much as the intention to deceive; where the cases were no longer branded, the bottles no longer wired or papered, where the fraud was manifest and stared them in the face.

"Here's about enough of this foolery!" said Davis. "Stow back the cases in the hold, Uncle, and get the broken crockery overboard. Come with me," he added to his co-adventurers, and led the way back into the cabin.

CHAPTER 6
THE PARTNERS

Each took a side of the fixed table; it was the first time they had sat down at it together, but now all sense of incongruity, all memory of differences, was quite swept away by the presence of the common ruin.

"Gentlemen," said the captain, after a pause, and with very much the air of a chairman opening a board meeting, "we're sold."

Huish broke out in laughter. "Well, if this ain't the 'ighest old rig!" he cried. "And Dyvis 'ere, who thought he had got up so bloomin' early in the mornin'! We've stolen a cargo of spring water! O, my crikey!" and he squirmed with mirth.

The captain managed to screw out a phantom smile.

"Here's Old Man Destiny again," said he to Herrick, "but this time I guess he's kicked the door right in."

Herrick only shook his head.

"O Lord, it's rich!" laughed Huish. "It would really be a scrumptious lark if it 'ad 'appened to somebody else! And what are we to do next? O, my eye! with this bloomin' schooner, too?"

"That's the trouble," said Davis. "There's only one thing certain: it's no use carting this old glass and ballast to Peru. No, *sir*, we're in a hole."

"O my, and the merchant!" cried Huish; "the man that made this shipment! He'll get the news by the mail brigantine; and he'll think of course we're making straight for Sydney."

"Yes, he'll be a sick merchant," said the captain. "One thing: this explains the Kanaka crew. If you're going to lose a ship, I would ask no better myself than a Kanaka crew. But there's one thing it don't explain; it don't explain why she came down Tahiti-ways."

"W'y, to lose her, you byby!" said Huish.

"A lot you know," said the captain. "Nobody wants to lose a

schooner; they want to lose her *on her course*, you skeezicks! You seem to think underwriters haven't got enough sense to come in out of the rain."

"Well," said Herrick, "I can tell you (I am afraid) why she came so far to the eastward. I had it of Uncle Ned. It seems thee two unhappy devils, Wiseman and Wishart, were drunk on the champagne from the beginning—and died drunk at the end."

The captain looked on the table.

"They lay in their two bunks, or sat here in this damned house," he pursued, with rising agitation, "filling their skins with the accursed stuff, till sickness took them. As they sickened and the fever rose, they drank the more. They lay here howling and groaning, drunk and dying, all in one. They didn't know where they were; they didn't care. They didn't even take the sun, it seems."

"Not take the sun?" cried the captain, looking up. "Sacred Billy! what a crowd!"

"Well, it don't matter to Joe!" said Huish. "Wot are Wiseman and t'other buffer to us?"

"A good deal, too," said the captain. "We're their heirs, I guess."

"It is a great inheritance," said Herrick.

"Well, I don't know about that," returned Davis. "Appears to me as if it might be worse. 'Tain't worth what the cargo would have been, of course, at least not money down. But I'll tell you what it appears to figure up to. Appears to me as if it amounted to about the bottom dollar of the man in 'Frisco."

"'Old on," said Huish. "Give a fellow time; 'ow's this, umpire?"

"Well, my sons," pursued the captain, who seemed to have recovered his assurance, "Wiseman and Wishart were to be paid for casting away this old schooner and its cargo. We're going to cast away the schooner right enough; and I'll make it my private business to see that we get paid. What were W. and W. to get? That's more'n I can tell. But W. and W. went into this business themselves, they were on the crook. Now *we're* on the square, *we* only stumbled into it; and that merchant has just got to squeal, and I'm the man to see that he squeals good. No, *sir!* there's some stuffing to this *Farallone* racket after all."

"Go it, cap'!" cried Huish. "Yoicks! Forrard! 'Old 'ard! There's your style for the money! Blow me if I don't prefer this to the hother."

"I do not understand," said Herrick. "I have to ask you to excuse me; I do not understand."

"Well, now, see here, Herrick," said Davis. "I'm going to have word with you anyway upon a different matter, and it's good that Huish should hear it too. We're done with this boozing business, and we ask your pardon for it right here and now. We have to thank you for all you did for us while we were making hogs of ourselves; you'll find me turn-to all right in future; and as for the wine, which I grant we stole from you, I'll take stock and see you paid for it. That's good enough, I believe. But what I want to point out to you is this. The old game was a risky game. The new game's as safe as running a Vienna bakery. We just put this *Farallone* before the wind, and run till we're well to looard of our port of departure, and reasonably well up with some other place, where they have an American consul. Down goes the *Farallone*, and good-bye to her! A day or so in the boat; the consul packs us home, at Uncle Sam's expense, to 'Frisco; and if that merchant don't put the dollars down, you come to me!"

"But I thought—" began Herrick; and then broke out: "O, let's get on to Peru!"

"Well, if you're going to Peru for your health, I won't say no!" replied the captain. "But for what other blame' shadow of a reason you should want to go there gets me clear. We don't want to go there with this cargo; I don't know as old bottles is a lively article anywheres; leastways, I'll go my bottom cent, it ain't Peru. It was always a doubt if we could sell the schooner; I never rightly hoped to, and now I'm sure she ain't worth a hill of beans; what's wrong with her I don't know; I only know it's something, or she wouldn't be here with this truck in her inside. Then again, if we lose her, and land in Peru, where are we?

We can't declare the loss, or how did we get to Peru? In that case the merchant can't touch the insurance; most likely he'll go bust; and don't you think you see the three of us on the beach of Callao?"

"There's no extradition there," said Herrick.

"Well, my son, and we want to be extraded," said the captain. "What's our point? We want to have a consul extrade us as far as San Francisco and that merchant's office door. My idea is that Samoa would be found an eligible business centre. It's dead before the wind; the States have a consul there, and 'Frisco steamers call, so's we could skip right back and interview the merchant."

"Samoa?" said Herrick. "It will take us for ever to get there."

"O, with a fair wind!" said the captain.

"No trouble about the log, eh?" asked Huish.

"No, *sir*," said Davis. "*Light airs and baffling winds. Squalls and calms. D. R.: five miles. No obs. Pumps attended.* And fill in the barometer and thermometer off of last year's trip. 'Never saw such a voyage,' says you to the consul. 'Thought I was going to run short ...'" He stopped in mid career. "Say," he began again, and once more stopped. "Beg your pardon, Herrick," he added with undisguised humility, "but did you keep the run of the stores?"

"Had I been told to do so it should have been done, as the rest was done, to the best of my little ability," said Herrick. "As it was, the cook helped himself to what he pleased."

Davis looked at the table.

"I drew it rather fine, you see," he said at last. "The great thing was to clear right out of Papeete before the consul could think better of it. Tell you what: I guess I'll take stock."

And he rose from table and disappeared with a lamp in the lazarette.

"'Ere's another screw loose," observed Huish.

"My man," said Herrick, with a sudden gleam of animosity, "it is still your watch on deck, and surely your wheel also?"

"You come the 'eavy swell, don't you, ducky?" said Huish.

"Stand away from that binnacle. Surely your w'eel, my man. Yah."

He lit a cigar ostentatiously, and strolled into the waist with his hands in his pockets.

In a surprisingly short time the captain reappeared; he did not look at Herrick, but called Huish back and sat down.

"Well," he began, "I've taken stock—roughly." He paused as if for somebody to help him out; and none doing so, both gazing on him instead with manifest anxiety, he yet more heavily resumed: "Well, it won't fight. We can't do it; that's the bed-rock. I'm as sorry as what you can be, and sorrier. But the game's up. We can't look near Samoa. I don't know as we could get to Peru."

"Wot-ju mean?" asked Huish brutally.

"I can't 'most tell myself," replied the captain. "I drew it fine; I said I did; but what's been going on here gets me! Appears as if the devil had been around. That cook must be the holiest kind of fraud. Only twelve days too! Seems like craziness. I'll own up square to one thing: I seem to have figured too fine upon the flour. But the rest—my land! I'll never understand it! There's been more waste on this twopenny ship than what there is to an Atlantic Liner." He stole a glance at his companions: nothing good was to be gleaned from their dark faces; and he had recourse to rage. "You wait till I interview that cook!" he roared, and smote the table with his fist. "I'll interview the son of a gun so's he's never been spoken to before. I'll put a bead upon the—!"

"You will not lay a finger on the man," said Herrick. "The fault is yours, and you know it. If you turn a savage loose in your storeroom, you know what to expect. I will not allow the man to be molested."

It is hard to say how Davis might have taken this defiance; but he was diverted to a fresh assailant.

"Well," drawled Huish, "you're a plummy captain, ain't you? You're a blooming captain! Don't you set up any of your chat to me, John Dyvis: I know you now; you ain't any more use

239

than a blooming dawl! O, you 'don't know,' don't you? O, it 'gets you,' do it? O, I dessay! W'y, weren't you 'owling for fresh tins every blessed day? 'Ow often 'ave I 'eard you send the 'ole bloomin' dinner off and tell the man to chuck it in the swill-tub? And breakfast? O, my crikey! breakfast for ten, and you 'ollerin' for more! And now you 'can't most tell'! Blow me if it ain't enough to make a man write an insultin' letter to Gawd! You dror it mild, John Dyvis: don't 'andle me; I'm dyngerous."

Davis sat like one bemused; it might even have been doubted if he heard, but the voice of the clerk rang about the cabin like that of a cormorant among the ledges of the cliff.

"That will do, Huish," said Herrick.

"O, so you tyke his part, do you? you stuck-up, sneerin' snob. Tyke it then. Come on, the pair of you. But as for John Dyvis, let him look out! He struck me the first night aboard, and I never took a blow yet but wot I gave as good. Let him knuckle down on his marrow-bones and beg my pardon. That's my last word."

"I stand by the captain," said Herrick. "That makes us two to one, both good men; and the crew will all follow me. I hope I shall die very soon; but I have not the least objection to killing you before I go. I should prefer it so; I should do it with no more remorse than winking. Take care—take care—you little cad!"

The animosity with which these words were uttered was so marked in itself, and so remarkable in the man who uttered them, that Huish stared, and even the humiliated Davis reared up his head and gazed at his defender. As for Herrick, the successive agitations and disappointments of the day had left him wholly reckless; he was conscious of a pleasant glow, an agreeable excitement; his head seemed empty, his eyeballs burned as he turned them, his throat was dry as a biscuit; the least dangerous man by nature, except in so far as the weak are always dangerous, at that moment he was ready to slay or to be slain with equal unconcern.

Here at least was the gage thrown down, and battle offered; he who should speak next would bring the matter to an issue there and then; all knew it to be so and hung back; and for many seconds by the cabin clock the trio sat motionless and silent.

Then came an interruption, welcome as the flowers in May.

"Land ho!" sang out a voice on deck. "Land a weatha bow!"

"Land!" cried Davis, springing to his feet. "What's this? There ain't no land here."

And as men may run from the chamber of a murdered corpse, the three ran forth out of the house and left their quarrel behind them undecided.

The sky shaded down at the sea-level to the white of opals; the sea itself, insolently, inkily blue, drew all about them the uncompromising wheel of the horizon. Search it as they pleased, not even the practised eye of Captain Davis could descry the smallest interruption. A few filmy clouds were slowly melting overhead; and about the schooner, as around the only point of interest, a tropic bird, white as a snow-flake, hung, and circled, and displayed, as it turned, the long vermilion feather of its tail. Save the sea and the heaven, that was all.

"Who sang out land?" asked Davis. "If there's any boy playing funny-dog with me, I'll teach him sky-larking!"

But Uncle Ned contentedly pointed to a part of the horizon where a greenish, filmy iridescence could be discerned floating like smoke on the pale heavens.

Davis applied his glass to it, and then looked at the Kanaka. "Call that land?" said he. "Well, it's more than I do."

"One time long ago," said Uncle Ned, "I see Anaa all-e-same that, four five hours befo' we come up. Capena he say sun go down, sun go up again; he say lagoon all-e-same milla."

"All-e-same *what?*" asked Davis.

"Milla, sah," said Uncle Ned.

"O, ah! mirror," said Davis. "I see; reflection from the lagoon. Well, you know, it is just possible, though it's strange I never heard of it. Here, let's look at the chart."

They went back to the cabin, and found the position of the schooner well to windward of the archipelago in the midst of

241

a white field of paper.

"There! you see for yourselves," said Davis.

"And yet I don't know," said Herrick; "I somehow think there's something in it. I'll tell you one thing too, captain: that's all right about the reflection; I heard it in Papeete."

"Fetch up that Findlay, then!" said Davis. "I'll try it all ways. An island wouldn't come amiss the way we're fixed."

The bulky volume was handed up to him, broken-backed as is the way with Findlay; and he turned to the place and began to run over the text, muttering to himself and turning over the pages with a wetted finger.

"Hullo!" he exclaimed. "How's this?" And he read aloud: "'*New Island.* According to M. Delille this island, which from private interests would remain unknown, lies, it is said, in lat. 12° 49´ 10˝ S., long. 133° 6´ W. In addition to the position above given, Commander Matthews, H.M.S. *Scorpion*, states that an island exists in lat 12° 0´ S., long. 133° 16´ W. This must be the same, if such an island exists, which is very doubtful, and totally disbelieved in by South Sea traders.'"

"Golly!" said Huish.

"It's rather in the conditional mood," said Herrick.

"It's anything you please," cried Davis, "only there it is! That's our place, and don't you make any mistake."

"'Which from private interests would remain unknown,'" read Herrick, over his shoulder. "What may that mean?"

"It should mean pearls," said Davis. "A pearling island the Government don't known about? That sounds like real estate. Or suppose it don't mean anything. Suppose it's just an island; I guess we could fill up with fish, and coconuts, and native stuff, and carry out the Samoa scheme hand over fist. How long did he say it was before they raised Anaa? Five hours, I think?"

"Four or five," said Herrick.

Davis stepped to the door. "What breeze had you that time you made Anaa, Uncle Ned?" said he.

"Six or seven knots," was the reply.

"Thirty or thirty-five miles," said Davis. "High time we were shortening sail, then. If it is an island, we don't want to be butting our head against it in the dark; and if it isn't an island, we can get through it just as well by daylight. Ready about!" he roared.

And the schooner's head was laid for that elusive glimmer in the sky, which began already to pale in lustre and diminish in size, as the stain of breath vanishes from a window pane. At the same time she was reefed close down.

PART II
THE QUARTETTE

CHAPTER 7
THE PEARL-FISHER

About four in the morning, as the captain and Herrick sat together on the rail, there arose from the midst of the night in front of them the voice of breakers. Each sprang to his feet and stared and listened. The sound was continuous, like the passing of a train; no rise or fall could be distinguished; minute by minute the ocean heaved with an equal potency against the invisible isle; and as time passed, and Herrick waited in vain for any vicissitude in the volume of that roaring, a sense of the eternal weighed upon his mind. To the expert eye the isle itself was to be inferred from a certain string of blots along the starry heaven. And the schooner was laid to and anxiously observed till daylight.

There was little or no morning bank. A brightening came in the east; then a wash of some ineffable, faint, nameless hue between crimson and silver; and then coals of fire. These glimmered a while on the sea-line, and seemed to brighten and darken and spread out, and still the night and the stars reigned undisturbed; it was as though a spark should catch and glow and creep along the foot of some heavy and almost incombustible wall-hanging, and the room itself be scarce menaced. Yet a little after, and the whole east glowed with gold and scarlet, and the hollow of heaven was filled with the daylight.

The isle—the undiscovered, the scarce-believed in—now lay before them and close aboard; and Herrick thought that never in his dreams had be beheld anything more strange and delicate. The beach was excellently white, the continuous barrier of trees inimitably green; the land perhaps ten feet high, the trees thirty more. Every here and there, as the schooner coast-

245

ed northward, the wood was intermitted; and he could see clear over the inconsiderable strip of land (as a man looks over a wall) to the lagoon within—and clear over that again to where the far side of the atoll prolonged its pencilling of trees against the mourning sky. He tortured himself to find analogies. The isle was like the rim of a great vessel sunken in the waters; it was like the embankment of an annular railway grown upon with wood: so slender it seemed amidst the outrageous breakers, so frail and pretty, he would scarce have wondered to see it sink and disappear without a sound, and the waves close smoothly over its descent.

Meanwhile the captain was in the four cross-trees, glass in hand, his eyes in every quarter, spying for an entrance, spying for signs of tenancy. But the isle continued to unfold itself in joints, and to run out in indeterminate capes, and still there was neither house nor man, nor the smoke of fires. Here a multitude of sea-birds soared and twinkled, and fished in the blue waters; and there, and for miles together, the fringe of coco-palm and pandanus extended desolate, and made desirable green bowers for nobody to visit, and the silence of death was only broken by the throbbing of the sea.

The airs were very light, their speed was small; the heat intense. The decks were scorching underfoot, the sun flamed overhead, brazen, out of a brazen sky; the pitch bubbled in the seams, and the brains in the brain-pan. And all the while the excitement of the three adventurers glowed about their bones like a fever. They whispered, and nodded, and pointed, and put mouth to ear, with a singular instinct of secrecy, approaching that island underhand like eavesdroppers and thieves; and even Davis from the cross-trees gave his orders mostly by gestures. The hands shared in this mute strain, like dogs, without comprehending it; and through the roar of so many miles of breakers, it was a silent ship that approached an empty island.

At last they drew near to the break in that interminable gangway. A spur of coral sand stood forth on the one hand; on the other a high and thick tuft of trees cut off the view; between was the mouth of the huge laver. Twice a day the ocean crowded in that narrow entrance and was heaped between these frail walls; twice a day, with the return of the ebb, the mighty surplusage of water must struggle to escape. The hour in which the *Farallone* came there was the hour of the flood. The sea turned (as with the instinct of the homing pigeon) for the vast receptacle, swept eddying through the gates, was transmuted, as it did so, into a wonder of watery and silken hues, and brimmed into the inland sea beyond. The schooner looked up close-hauled, and was caught and carried away by the influx like a toy. She skimmed; she flew; a momentary shadow touched her decks from the shoreside trees; the bottom of the channel showed up for a moment and was in a moment gone; the next, she floated on the bosom of the lagoon, and below, in the transparent chamber of waters, a myriad of many-coloured fishes were sporting, a myriad pale flowers of coral diversified the floor.

Herrick stood transported. In the gratified lust of his eye he forgot the past and the present; forgot that he was menaced by a prison on the one hand and starvation on the other; forgot that he was come to that island, desperately foraging, clutching at expedients. A drove of fishes, painted like the rainbow and billed like parrots, hovered up in the shadow of the schooner, and passed clear of it, and glinted in the submarine sun. They were beautiful, like birds, and their silent passage impressed him like a strain of song.

Meanwhile, to the eye of Davis in the cross-trees, the lagoon continued to expand its empty waters, and the long succession of the shoreside trees to be paid out like fishing-line of a reel. And still there was no mark of habitation. The schooner, immediately on entering, had been kept away to the nor'ard where the water seemed to be the most deep; and she was now skimming past the tall grove of trees, which stood on that side of the channel and denied further view. Of the whole of the lower shores of the island only this bight remained to be revealed. And suddenly the curtain was raised; they began to open out a haven, snugly elbowed there, and beheld, with an astonishment beyond words, the roofs of men.

The appearance, thus "instantaneously disclosed" to those on the deck of the *Farallone*, was not that of a city, rather of a substantial country farm with its attendant hamlet: a long line of sheds and store-houses; apart, upon the one side, a deep-verandah'd dwelling-house; on the other, perhaps a dozen native huts; a building with a belfry and some rude offer at architectural features that might be thought to mark it out for a chapel; on the beach in front some heavy boots drawn up, and a pile of timber running forth into the burning shallows of the lagoon. From a flagstaff at the pierhead the red ensign of England was displayed. Behind, about, and over, the same tall grove of palms, which had masked the settlement in the beginning, prolonged its roof of tumultuous green fans, and turned and ruffled overhead, and sang its silver song all day in the wind. The place had the indescribable but unmistakable appearance of being in commission; yet there breathed from it a sense of desertion that was almost poignant, no human figure was to be observed going to and fro about the houses, and there was no sound of human industry or enjoyment. Only, on the top of the beach, and hard by the flagstaff, a woman of exorbitant stature and as white as snow was to be seen beckoning with uplifted arm. The second glance identified her as a piece of naval sculpture, the figure-head of a ship that had long hovered and plunged into so many running billows, and was now brought ashore to be the ensign and presiding genius of that empty town.

The *Farallone* made a soldier's breeze of it; the wind, besides, was stronger inside than without under the lee of the land; and the stolen schooner opened out successive objects with the swiftness of a panorama, so that the adventurers stood speechless. The flag spoke for itself; it was no frayed and weathered trophy that had beaten itself to pieces on the post, flying over desolation; and to make assurance stronger, there was to be descried in the deep shade of the verandah a glitter of crystal and the fluttering of white napery. If the figurehead at the pier-end, with its perpetual gesture and its leprous whiteness, reigned alone in that hamlet as it seemed to do, it would not have reigned long. Men's hands had been busy, men's feet stirring there, within the circuit of the clock. The *Farallones* were sure of it; their eyes dug in the deep shadow of the palms of some one hiding; if intensity of looking might have prevailed, they would have pierced the walls of houses; and there came to them, in these pregnant seconds, a sense of being watched and played with, and of a blow impending, that was hardly bearable.

The extreme point of palms they had just passed enclosed a creek, which was thus hidden up to the last moment from the eyes of those on board; and from this a boat put suddenly and briskly out, and a voice hailed.

"Schooner ahoy!" it cried. "Stand in for the pier! In two cables' lengths you'll have twenty fathoms water and good holding-ground."

The boat was manned with a couple of brown oarsmen in scanty kilts of blue. The speaker, who was steering, wore white clothes, the full dress of the tropics; a wide hat shaded his face; but it could be seen that he was of stalwart size, and his voice sounded like a gentleman's. So much could be made out. It was plain, besides, that the *Farallone* had been descried some time before at sea, and the inhabitants were prepared for its reception.

Mechanically the orders were obeyed, and the ship berthed; and the three adventurers gathered aft beside the house and waited, with galloping pulses and a perfect vacancy of mind, the coming of the stranger who might mean so much to them. They had no plan, no story prepared; there was no time to make one; they were caught red-handed and must stand their chance. Yet this anxiety was chequered with hope. The island being undeclared, it was not possible the man could hold any office or be in a position to demand their papers. And beyond that, if there was any truth in Findlay, as it now seemed there should be, he was the representative of the "private reasons," he must see their coming with a profound disappointment; and perhaps (hope whispered) he would be willing and able to purchase their silence.

The boat was by that time forging alongside, and they were able at last to see what manner of man they had to do with. He was a huge fellow, six feet four in height, and of a build proportionately strong, but his sinews seemed to be dissolved in a listlessness that was more than languor. It was only the eye that corrected this impression; an eye of an unusual mingled brilliancy and softness, sombre as coal and with lights that outshone the topaz; an eye of unimpaired health and virility; an eye that bid you beware of the man's devastating anger. A complexion, naturally dark, had been tanned in the island to a hue hardly distinguishable from that of a Tahitian; only his manners and movements, and the living force that dwelt in him, like fire in flint, betrayed the European. He was dressed in white drill, exquisitely made; his scarf and tie were of tender-coloured silks; on the thwart beside him there leaned a Winchester rifle.

"Is the doctor on board?" he cried as he came up. "Dr. Symonds, I mean? You never heard of him? Nor yet of the *Trinity Hall*? Ah!"

He did not look surprised, seemed rather to affect it in politeness; but his eye rested on each of the three white men in succession with a sudden weight of curiosity that was almost savage. "Ah, *then*!" said he, "there is some small mistake, no doubt, and I must ask you to what I am indebted for this pleasure?"

He was by this time on the deck, but he had the art to be quite unapproachable; the friendliest vulgarian, three parts drunk, would have known better than take liberties; and not one of the adventurers so much as offered to shake hands.

"Well," said Davis, "I suppose you may call it an accident. We had heard of your island, and read that thing in the Directory about the *private reasons*, you see; so when we saw the lagoon reflected in the sky, we put her head for it at once, and so here we are."

"'Ope we don't intrude!" said Huish.

The stranger looked at Huish with an air of faint surprise, and looked pointedly away again. It was hard to be more offensive in dumb show.

"It may suit me, your coming here," he said. "My own schooner is overdue, and I may put something in your way in the meantime. Are you open to a charter?"

"Well, I guess so," said Davis; "it depends."

"My name is Attwater," continued the stranger. "You, I presume, are the captain?"

"Yes, sir. I am the captain of this ship: Captain Brown," was the reply.

"Well, see 'ere!" said Huish; "better begin fair! 'E's skipper on deck right enough, but not below. Below, we're all equal, all got a lay in the adventure; when it comes to business I'm as good as 'e; and what I say is, let's go into the 'ouse and have a lush, and talk it over among pals. We've some prime fizz," he said, and winked.

The presence of the gentleman lighted up like a candle the vulgarity of the clerk; and Herrick instinctively, as one shields himself from pain, made haste to interrupt.

"My name is Hay," said he, "since introductions are going. We shall be very glad if you will step inside."

Attwater leaned to him swiftly. "University man?" said he.

"Yes, Merton," said Herrick, and the next moment blushed scarlet at his indiscretion.

"I am of the other lot," said Attwater: "Trinity Hall, Cambridge. I called my schooner after the old shop. Well! this is a queer place and company for us to meet in, Mr. Hay," he pursued, with easy incivility to the others. "But do you bear out ... I beg this gentleman's pardon, I really did not catch his name."

"My name is 'Uish, sir," returned the clerk, and blushed in turn.

"Ah!" said Attwater. And then turning again to Herrick, "Do you bear out Mr. Whish's description of your vintage? or was it only the unaffected poetry of his own nature bubbling up?"

Herrick was embarrassed; the silken brutality of their visitor made him blush; that he should be accepted as an equal, and the others thus pointedly ignored, pleased him in spite of himself, and then ran through his veins in a recoil of anger.

"I don't know," he said. "It's only California; it's good enough, I believe."

Attwater seemed to make up his mind. "Well, then, I'll tell you what: you three gentlemen come ashore this evening and bring a basket of wine with you; I'll try and find the food," he said. "And by the by, here is a question I should have asked you when I came on board: have you had smallpox?"

"Personally, no," said Herrick. "But the schooner had it."

"Deaths?" from Attwater.

"Two," said Herrick.

"Well, it is a dreadful sickness," said Attwater.

"'Ad you any deaths?" asked Huish, "'ere on the island?'

"Twenty-nine," said Attwater. "Twenty-nine deaths and thirty-one cases, out of thirty-three souls upon the island.— That's a strange way to calculate, Mr. Hay, is it not? Souls! I never say it but it startles me."

"O, so that's why everything's deserted?" said Huish.

"That is why, Mr. Whish," said Attwater; "that is why the house is empty and the graveyard full."

"Twenty-nine out of thirty-three!" exclaimed Herrick. "Why, when it came to burying—or did you bother burying?"

"Scarcely," said Attwater; "or there was one day at least when we gave up. There were five of the dead that morning, and thirteen of the dying, and no one able to go about except the sexton and myself. We held a council of war, took the ... empty bottles ... into the lagoon, and ... buried them." He looked over his shoulder, back at the bright water. "Well, so you'll come to dinner, then? Shall we say half-past six? *So* good of you!"

His voice, in uttering these conventional phrases, fell at once into the false measure of society; and Herrick unconsciously followed the example.

"I am sure we shall be glad," he said. "At half-past six? Thank you so very much."

> "'For my voice has been tuned to the note of the gun
> That startles the deep when the combat's begun,'"

quoted Attwater, with a smile, which instantly gave way to an air of funereal solemnity, "I shall particularly expect Mr. Whish," he continued.—"Mr. Whish, I trust you understand the invitation?"

"I believe you, my boy!" replied the genial Huish.

"That is right, then; and quite understood, is it not?" said Attwater. "Mr. Whish and Captain Brown at six-thirty without fault—and you, Hay, at four sharp."

And he called his boat.

During all this talk a load of thought or anxiety had weighed upon the captain. There was no part for which nature had so liberally endowed him as that of the genial ship-captain. But today he was silent and abstracted. Those who knew him could see that he hearkened closely to every syllable, and seemed to ponder and try it in balances. It would have been hard to say what look there was, cold, attentive, and sinister, as of a man maturing plans, which still brooded over the unconscious guest; it was here, it was there, it was nowhere; it was now so little that Herrick chid himself for an idle fancy; and anon it was so gross and palpable that you could say every hair on the man's head talked mischief.

He woke up now, as with a start. "You were talking of a charter," said he.

"Was I?" said Attwater. "Well, let's talk of it no more at present."

"Your own schooner is overdue, I understand?" continued the captain.

"You understand perfectly, Captain Brown," said Attwater; "thirty-three days overdue at noon today."

"She comes and goes, eh? Plies between here and ...?" hinted the captain.

"Exactly; every four months; three trips in the year," said Attwater.

"You go in her ever?" asked Davis.

"No; one stops here," said Attwater; "one has plenty to attend to."

"Stop here, do you?" cried Davis. "Say, how long?"

"How long, O Lord," said Attwater, with perfect, stern gravity. "But it does not seem so," he added, with a smile.

"No, I daresay not," said Davis. "No, I suppose not. Not with all your gods about you, and in as snug a berth as this. For it is a pretty snug berth," said he, with a sweeping look.

"The spot, as you are good enough to indicate, is not entirely intolerable," was the reply.

"Shell, I suppose?" said Davis.

"Yes, there was shell," said Attwater.

"This is a considerable big beast of a lagoon, sir," said the captain. "Was there a—was the fishing—would you call the fishing anyways *good?*"

"I don't know that I would call it anyways anything," said Attwater, "if you put it to me direct."

"There were pearls, too?" said Davis.

"Pearls too," said Attwater.

"Well, I give out!" laughed Davis, and his laughter rang cracked like a false piece. "If you're not going to tell, you're not going to tell, and there's an end to it."

"There can be no reason why I should affect the least degree of secrecy about my island," returned Attwater; "that came wholly to an end with your arrival; and I am sure, at any rate, that gentlemen like you and Mr. Whish I should have always been charmed to make perfectly at home. The point on which we are now differing—if you can call it a difference—is one of times and seasons. I have some information which you think I might impart, and I think not. Well, we'll see to-night! By-by, Whish!" He stepped into his boat and shoved off. "All understood, then?" said he. "The captain and Mr. Whish at six-thirty, and you, Hay, at four precise. You understand that, Hay? Mind, I take no denial. If you're not there by the time named, there will be no banquet; no song, no supper, Mr. Whish!"

White birds whisked in the air above, a shoal of parti-coloured fishes in the scarce denser medium below; between, like Mahomet's coffin, the boat drew away briskly on the surface, and its shadow followed it over the glittering floor of the lagoon. Attwater looked steadily back over his shoulders as he sat; he did not once remove his eyes from the *Farallone* and the group on her quarter-deck beside the house, till his boat ground upon the pier. Thence, with an agile pace, he hurried ashore, and they saw his white clothes shining in the chequered dusk of the grove until the house received him.

The captain, with a gesture and a speaking countenance, called the adventurers into the cabin.

"Well," he said to Herrick, when they were seated, "there's one good job at least. He's taken to you in earnest."

"Why should that be a good job?" said Herrick.

"O, you'll see how it pans out presently," returned Davis. "You go ashore and stand in with him, that's all! You'll get lots of pointers; you can find out what he has, and what the charter is, and who's the fourth man—for there's four of them, and we're only three."

"And suppose I do, what next?" cried Herrick. "Answer me that!"

"So I will, Robert Herrick," said the captain. "But first, let's see all clear. I guess you know," he said, with imperious solemnity, "I guess you know the bottom is out of this *Farallone* specula-tion? I guess you know it's *right* out? and if this old island hadn't been turned up right when it did, I guess you know where you and I and Huish would have been?"

"Yes, I know that," said Herrick. "No matter who's to blame, I know it. And what next?"

"No matter who's to blame, you know it, right enough," said the captain, "and I'm obliged to you for the reminder. Now, here's this Attwater: what do you think of him?"

"I do not know," said Herrick. "I am attracted and repelled. He was insufferably rude to you."

"And you, Huish?" said the captain.

Huish sat cleaning a favourite briar-root; he scarce looked up from that engrossing task. "Don't ast me what I think of him!" he said. "There's a day comin', I pray Gawd, when I can tell it him myself."

"Huish means the same as what I do," said Davis. "When that man came stepping around, and saying, 'Look here, I'm Attwater'—and you knew it was so, by God!—I sized him right straight up. He's the real article, I said, and I don't like it; here's the real, first-rate, copper-bottomed aristocrat. '*Aw! don't know ye, do I? God damn ye, did God make ye?*' No, that couldn't be nothing but genuine; a man got to be born to that, and notice! smart as champagne and hard as nails; no kind of a fool; no, *sir*! not a pound of him! Well, what's he here upon this beastly island for? I said. *He's* not here collecting eggs. He's a palace at home, and powdered flunkeys; and if he don't stay there, you bet he knows the reason why! Follow?"

"O yes, I 'ear you," said Huish.

"He's been doing good business here, then," continued the captain. "For ten years he's been doing a great business. It's pearl and shell, of course; there couldn't be nothing else in such a place, and no doubt the shell goes off regularly by this *Trinity Hall*, and the money for it straight into the bank, so that's no use to us. But what else is there? Is there nothing else he would be likely to keep here? Is there nothing else he would be bound to keep here? Yes, sir; the pearls! First, because they're too valuable to trust out of his hands. Second, because pearls want a lot of handling and matching; and the man who sells his pearls as they come in one here, one there, instead of hanging back and holding up—well, that man's a fool, and it's not Attwater.'

"Likely," said Huish, "that's w'at it is; not proved, but likely."

"It's proved," said Davis bluntly.

"Suppose it was?" said Herrick. "Suppose that was all so, and he had these pearls—a ten years' collection of them?—Suppose he had? There's my question."

The captain drummed with his thick hands on the board in front of him; he looked steadily in Herrick's face, and Herrick as steadily looked up the table and the pattering fingers; there was a gentle oscillation of the anchored ship, and a big patch of sunlight travelled to and fro between the one and the other.

"Hear me!" Herrick burst out suddenly.

"No, you better hear me first," said Davis. "hear me and understand me. *We*'ve got no use for that fellow, whatever you may have. He's your kind, he's not ours; he's took to you, and he's wiped his boots on me and Huish. Save him if you can!"

"Save him?" repeated Herrick.

"Save him, if you're able!" reiterated Davis, with a blow of his clenched fist. "Go ashore, and talk him smooth; and if you get him and his pearls aboard, I'll spare him. If you don't, there's going to be a funeral. Is that so, Huish? does that suit you?"

"I ain't a forgiving man," said Huish, "but I'm not the sort to spoil business neither. Bring the bloke on board and bring his pearls along with him, and you can have it your own way; maroon him where you like,—I'm agreeable."

"Well, and if I can't?" cried Herrick, while the sweat streamed upon his face. "You talk to me as if I was God Almighty, to do this and that! But if I can't?"

"My son," said the captain, "you better do your level best, or you'll see sights!"

"O yes," said Huish. "O crikey, yes!" He looked across at Herrick with a toothless smile that was shocking in its savagery; and, his ear caught apparently by the trivial expression he had used, broke into a piece of the chorus of a comic song which he must have heard twenty years before in London: meaningless gibberish that, in that hour and place, seemed hateful as a blasphemy: "Hikey, pikey, crikey, fikey, chillingawallaba dory."

The captain suffered him to finish; his face was unchanged.

"The way things are, there's many a man that wouldn't let

you go ashore," he resumed. "But I'm not that kind. I know you'd never go back on me, Herrick! Or if you choose to,—go, and do it, and be damned!" he cried, and rose abruptly from the table.

He walked out of the house; and as he reached the door turned and called Huish, suddenly and violently, like the barking of a dog. Huish followed, and Herrick remained alone in the cabin.

"Now, see here!" whispered Davis. "I know that man. If you open your mouth to him again, you'll ruin all."

CHAPTER 8
BETTER ACQUAINTANCE

The boat was gone again, and already half-way to the *Farallone*, before Herrick turned and went unwillingly up the pier. From the crown of the beach, the figurehead confronted him with what seemed irony, her helmeted head tossed back, her formidable arm apparently hurling something, whether shell or missile, in the direction of the anchored schooner. She seemed a defiant deity from the island, coming forth to its threshold with a rush as of one about to fly, and perpetuated in that dashing attitude. Herrick looked up at her, where she towered above him head and shoulders, with singular feelings of curiosity and romance, and suffered his mind to travel to and fro in her life-history. So long she had been the blind conductress of a ship among the waves; so long she had stood here idle in the violent sun, that yet did not avail to blister her; and was even this the end of so many adventures? he wondered, or was more behind? And he could have found it in his heart to regret that she was not a goddess, nor yet he a pagan, that he might have bowed down before her in that hour of difficulty.

When he now went forward, it was cool with the shadow of many well-grown palms; draughts of the dying breeze swung them together overhead; and on all sides, with a swiftness beyond dragon-flies or swallows, the spots of sunshine flitted, and hovered, and returned. Underfoot, the sand was fairly solid and quite level, and Herrick's steps fell there noiseless as in new-fallen snow. It bore the marks of having been once weeded like a garden alley at home; but the pestilence had done its work, and the weeds were returning. The buildings of the settlement showed here and there through the stems of the colonnade, fresh painted, trim and dandy, and all silent as the grave. Only here and there in the crypt, there was a rustle and scurry and some crowing of poultry; and from behind the house with the verandahs he saw smoke arise and heard the crackling of a fire.

The stone houses were nearest him upon his right. The first was locked; in the second he could dimly perceive, through a window, a certain accumulation of pearl-shell piled in the far end; the third, which stood gaping open on the afternoon, seized on the mind of Herrick with its multiplicity and disorder of romantic things. Therein were cables, windlasses, and blocks of every size and capacity; cabin-windows and ladders; rusty tanks, a companion hatch; a binnacle with its brass mountings and its compass idly pointing, in the confusion and dusk of that shed, to a forgotten pole; ropes, anchors, harpoons; a blubber-dipper of copper, green with years; a steering-wheel, a tool-chest with the vessel's name upon the top, the *Asia*: a whole curiosity-shop of sea-curios, gross and solid, heavy to lift, ill to break, bound with brass and shod with iron. Two wrecks at the least must have contributed to this random heap of lumber; and as Herrick looked upon it, it seemed to him as if the two ships' companies were there on guard, and he heard the tread of feet and whisperings, and saw with the tail of his eye the commonplace ghosts of sailor men.

This was not merely the work of an aroused imagination, but had something sensible to go upon; sounds of a stealthy approach were no doubt audible; and while he still stood staring at the lumber, the voice of his host sounded suddenly, and with even more than the customary softness of enunciation, from behind.

"Junk," it said, "only old junk! And does Mr. Hay find a parable?"

"I find at least a strong impression," replied Herrick, turning quickly, lest he might be able to catch, on the face of the speaker, some commentary on the words.

Attwater stood in the doorway, which he almost wholly filled; his hands stretched above his head and grasping the architrave. he smiled when their eyes met, but the expression was inscrutable.

"Yes, a powerful impression. You are like me; nothing so affecting as ships!" said he. "The ruins of an empire would leave me frigid, when a bit of an old rail that an old shellback leaned on in the middle watch, would bring me up all standing. But come, let's see some more of the island. It's all sand and coral and palm-trees; but there's a kind of a quaintness in the place."

"I find it heavenly," said Herrick, breathing deep, with head bared in the shadow.

"Ah, that's because you're new from sea," said Attwater. "I daresay, too, you can appreciate what one calls it. It's a lovely name. It has a flavour, it has a colour, it has a ring and fall to it; it's like its author—it's half Christian! Remember your first view of the island, and how it's only woods and woods and water; and suppose you had asked somebody for the name, and he had answered—*nemorosa Zacynthos*."

"*Jam medio apparet fluctu!*" exclaimed Herrick. "Ye gods, yes, how good!"

"If it gets upon the chart, the skippers will make nice work of it," said Attwater. "But here, come and see the diving-shed."

He opened a door, and Herrick saw a large display of apparatus neatly ordered: pumps and pipes, and the leaded boots, and the huge snouted helmets shining in rows along the wall; ten complete outfits.

"The whole eastern half of my lagoon is shallow, you must understand," said Attwater; "so we were able to get in the dress to great advantage. It paid beyond belief, and was a queer sight when they were at it, and these marine monsters"—tapping the nearest of the helmets—"kept appearing and reappearing in the midst of the lagoon. Fond of parables?" he asked abruptly.

"Oh yes!" said Herrick.

"Well, I saw these machines come up dripping and go down again, and come up dripping and go down again, and all the while the fellow inside as dry as toast!" said Attwater; "and I thought we all wanted a dress to go down into the world in, and come up scatheless. What do you think the name was?" he inquired.

"Self-conceit," said Herrick.

261

"Ah, but I mean seriously!" said Attwater.

"Call it self-respect, then!" corrected Herrick, with a laugh.

"And why not Grace? Why not God's Grace, Hay?" asked Attwater. "Why not the grace of your Maker and Redeemer, He who died for you, He who upholds you, He whom you daily crucify afresh? There is nothing here"—striking on his bosom,—"nothing there"—smiting the wall,—"and nothing there,"—stamping—"nothing but God's Grace! We walk upon it, we breathe it; we live and die by it; it makes the nails and axles of the universe; and a puppy in pyjamas prefers self-conceit!" The huge dark man stood over against Herrick by the line of the divers' helmets, and seemed to swell and glow; and the next moment the life had gone from him—"I beg your pardon," said he; "I see you don't believe in God?"

"Not in your sense, I am afraid," said Herrick.

"I never argue with young atheists or habitual drunkards," said Attwater flippantly.—"Let us go across the island to the outer beach."

It was but a little way, the greatest width of that island scarce exceeding a furlong, and they walked gently. Herrick was like one in a dream. He had come there with a mind divided; come prepared to study that ambiguous and sneering mask, drag out the essential man from underneath, and act accordingly; decision being till then postponed. Iron cruelty, an iron insensibility to the suffering of others, the uncompromising pursuit of his own interests, cold culture, manners without humanity: these he had looked for, these he still thought he saw. But to find the whole machine thus glow with the reverberation of religious zeal surprised him beyond words; and he laboured in vain, as he walked, to piece together into any kind of whole his odds and ends of knowledge—to adjust again into any kind of focus with itself his picture of the man beside him.

"What brought you here to the South Seas?" he asked presently.

"Many things," said Attwater. "Youth, curiosity, romance, the love of the sea, and (it will surprise you to hear) an interest in missions. That has a good deal declined, which will surprise you less. They go the wrong way to work; they are too parson-ish, too much of the old wife, and even the old apple-wife. *Clothes, clothes,* are their idea; but clothes are not Christianity, any more than they are the sun in heaven, or could take the place of it! They think a parsonage with roses, and church bells, and nice old women bobbing in the lanes, are part and parcel of religion. But religion is a savage thing, like the universe it illuminates; savage, cold, and bare, but infinitely strong."

"And you found this island by an accident?" said Herrick.

"As you did!" said Attwater. "And since then I have had a business, and a colony, and a mission of my own. I was a man of the world before I was a Christian; I'm a man of the world still, and I made my mission pay. No good ever came of coddling. A man has to stand up in God's sight and work up to his weight avoirdupois: then I'll talk to him, but not before. I gave these beggars what they wanted: a judge in Israel, the bearer of the sword and scourge; I was making a new people here; and behold, the angel of the Lord smote them and they were not!"

With the very uttering of the words, which were accom-panied by a gesture, they came forth out of the porch of the palm wood by the margin of the sea and full in front of the sun, which was near setting. Before them the surf broke slowly. All around, with an air of imperfect wooden things inspired with wicked activity, the crabs trundled and scuttled into holes. On the right, whither Attwater pointed and abruptly turned, was the cemetery of the island, a field of broken stones from the bigness of a child's hand to that of his head, diversified by many mounds of the same material, and walled by a rude rect-angular enclosure. Nothing grew there but a shrub or two with some white flowers; nothing but the number of the mounds, and their disquieting shape, indicated the presence of the dead.

"The rude forefathers of the hamlet sleep!" quoted Attwater, as he entered by the open gateway into that unholy close.

"Coral to coral, pebbles to pebbles," he said; "this has been the main scene of my activity in the South Pacific. Some were good, and some bad, and the majority (of course and always) null. Here was a fellow, now, that used to frisk like a dog; if you had called him he came like an arrow from a bow; if you had not, and he came unbidden, you should have seen the deprecating eye and the little intricate dancing step. Well, his trouble is over now, he has lain down with kings and councillors; the rest of his acts, are they not written in the book of the chronicles? That fellow was from Penrhyn; like all the Penrhyn islanders he was ill to manage; heady, jealous, violent: the man with the nose! He lies here quiet enough. And so they all lie. 'And darkness was the burier of the dead!'"

He stood, in the strong glow of the sunset, with bowed head; his voice sounded now sweet and now bitter with the varying sense.

"You loved these people?" cried Herrick, strangely touched.

"I?" said Attwater. "Dear no! Don't think me a philanthropist. I dislike men, and hate women. If I like the islanders at all, it is because you see them here plucked of their lendings, their dead birds and cocked hats, their petticoats and coloured hose. Here was one I liked though," and he set his foot upon a mound. "He was a fine savage fellow; he had a dark soul; yes, I liked this one. I am fanciful," he added, looking hard at Herrick, "and I take fads. I like you."

Herrick turned swiftly and looked far away to where the clouds were beginning to troop together and amass themselves round the obsequies of day. "No one can like me," he said.

"You are wrong there," said the other, "as a man usually is about himself. You are attractive, very attractive."

"It is not me," said Herrick; "no one can like me. If you knew how I despised myself—and why!" His voice rang out in the quiet graveyard.

"I knew that you despised yourself," said Attwater. "I saw the blood come into your face today when you remembered

Oxford. And I could have blushed for you myself, to see a man, a gentleman, with these two vulgar wolves."

Herrick faced him with a thrill. "Wolves?" he repeated.

"I said wolves, and vulgar wolves," said Attwater. "Do you know that today, when I came on board, I trembled?"

"You concealed it well," stammered Herrick.

"A habit of mine," said Attwater. "But I was afraid, for all that: I was afraid of the two wolves." He raised his hand slowly. "And now, Hay, you poor lost puppy, what do you do with the two wolves?"

"What do I do? I don't do anything," said Herrick. "There is nothing wrong; all is above-board; Captain Brown is a good soul; he is a ... he is ..." the phantom voice of Davis called in his ear: "There's going to be a funeral"; and the sweat burst forth and streamed on his brow. "He is a family man," he resumed again, swallowing; "he has children at home and a wife."

"And a very nice man?" said Attwater. "And so is Mr. Whish, no doubt?"

"I won't go so far as that," said Herrick. "I do not like Huish. And yet ... he has his merits too."

"And, in short, take them for all in all, as good a ship's company as one would ask?" said Attwater.

"O yes," said Herrick, "quite."

"So then we approach the other point of why you despise yourself?" said Attwater.

"Do we not all despise ourselves?" cried Herrick. "Do not you?"

"O, I say I do. But do I?" said Attwater. "One thing I know at least: I never gave a cry like yours. Hay! it came from a bad conscience! Ah, man, that poor diving-dress of self-conceit is sadly tattered! Today, if ye will hear my voice. Today, now, while the sun sets, and here in this burying-place of brown innocents, fall on your knees and cast your sins and sorrows on the Redeemer. Hay—"

"Not Hay!" interrupted the other, strangling. "Don't call me that! I mean ... For God's sake, can't you see I'm on the rack?"

"I see it, I know it, I put and keep you there; my fingers are on the screws!" said Attwater. "Please God, I will bring a penitent this night before His throne. Come, come to the mercy-seat! He waits to be gracious, man—waits to be gracious!"

He spread out his arms like a crucifix; his face shone with the brightness of a seraph's; in his voice, as it rose to the last word, the tears seemed ready.

Herrick made a vigorous call upon himself. "Attwater," he said, "you push me beyond bearing. What am I to do? I do not believe. It is living truth to you: to me, upon my conscience, only folk-lore. I do not believe there is any form of words under heaven by which I can lift the burthen from my shoulders. I must stagger on to the end with the pack of my responsibility; I cannot shift it; do you suppose I would not if I thought I could? I cannot—cannot—cannot—and let that suffice."

The rapture was all gone from Attwater's countenance; the dark apostle had disappeared; and in his place there stood an easy, sneering gentleman, who took off his hat and bowed. It was pertly done, and the blood burned in Herrick's face.

"What do you mean by that?" he cried.

"Well, shall we go back to the house?" said Attwater. "Our guests will soon be due."

Herrick stood his ground a moment with clenched fists and teeth; and as he so stood, the fact of his errand there slowly swung clear in front of him, like the moon out of clouds. He had come to lure that man on board; he was failing, even if it could be said that he had tried; he was sure to fail now, and knew it, and knew it was better so. And what was to be next?

With a groan he turned to follow his host, who was standing with polite smile, and instantly and somewhat obsequiously led the way in the now darkened colonnade of palms. There they went in silence, the earth gave up richly of her perfume, the air tasted warm and aromatic in the nostrils; and from a great way forward in the wood, the brightness of lights and fire marked out the house of Attwater.

Herrick meanwhile resolved and resisted an immense temptation to go up, to touch him on the arm and breathe a word in
his ear: "Beware, they are going to murder you." There would
be one life saved; but what of the two others? The three lives
went up and down before him like buckets in a well, or like the
scales of balances. It had come to a choice, and one that must
be speedy. For certain invaluable minutes, the wheels of life
ran before him, and he could still divert them with a touch to
the one side or the other, still choose who was to live and who
was to die. He considered the men. Attwater intrigued,
puzzled, dazzled, enchanted and revolted him; alive, he
seemed but a doubtful good; and the thought of him lying
dead was so unwelcome that it pursued him, like a vision, with
every circumstance of colour and sound. Incessantly he had
before him the image of that great mass of man stricken down
in varying attitudes and with varying wounds; fallen prone,
fallen supine, fallen on his side; or clinging to a doorpost with
the changing face and the relaxing fingers of the death-agony.
He heard the click of the trigger, the thud of the ball, the cry of
the victim; he saw the blood flow. And this building up of
circumstance was like a consecration of the man, till he
seemed to walk in sacrificial fillets. Next he considered Davis,
with his thick-fingered, coarse-grained, oat-bread commonness
of nature, his indomitable valour and mirth in the old days of
their starvation, the endearing blend of his faults and virtues,
the sudden shining forth of a tenderness that lay too deep for
tears; his children, Ada and her bowel complaint, and Ada's
doll. No, death could not be suffered to approach that head
even in fancy; with a general heat and a bracing of his muscles,
it was borne in on Herrick that Ada's father would find in him
a son to the death. And even Huish showed a little in that
sacredness; by the tacit adoption of daily life they were
become brothers; there was an implied bond of loyalty in their
cohabitation of the ship and their past miseries; to which
Herrick must be a little true or wholly dishonoured. Horror of
sudden death for horror of sudden death, there was here no

hesitation possible: it must be Attwater. And no sooner was the thought formed (which was a sentence) than his whole mind of man ran in a panic to the other side: and when he looked within himself, he was aware only of turbulence and inarticulate outcry.

In all this there was no thought of Robert Herrick. He had complied with the ebb-tide in man's affairs, and the tide had carried him away; he heard already the roaring of the maelstrom that must hurry him under. And in his bedevilled and dishonoured soul there was no thought of self.

For how long he walked silent by his companion Herrick had no guess. The clouds rolled suddenly away; the orgasm was over; he found himself placid with the placidity of despair; there returned to him the power of commonplace speech; and he heard with surprise his own voice say: "What a lovely evening!"

"Is it not?" said Attwater. "Yes, the evenings here would be very pleasant if one had anything to do. By day, of course, one can shoot."

"You shoot?" asked Herrick.

"Yes, I am what you would call a fine shot," said Attwater. "It is faith; I believe my balls will go true; if I were to miss once, it would spoil me for nine months."

'You never miss, then?" said Herrick.

"Not unless I mean to," said Attwater. "But to miss nicely is the art. There was an old king one knew in the western islands, who used to empty a Winchester all round a man, and stir his hair or nick a rag out of his clothes with every ball except the last; and that went plump between the eyes. It was pretty practice."

"You could do that?" asked Herrick, with a sudden chill.

"O, I can do anything," returned the other. "You do not understand: what must be, must."

They were now come near to the back part of the house. One of the men was engaged about the cooking-fire, which burned with the clear, fierce, essential radiance of coconut shells. A fragrance of strange meats was in the air. All round in the verandahs lamps were lighted, so that the place shone abroad in the dusk of the trees with many complicated patterns of shadow.

"Come and wash your hands," said Attwater, and led the way into a clean, matted room with a cot bed, a safe, a shelf or two of books in a glazed case, and an iron washing-stand. Presently he cried in the native, and there appeared for a moment in the doorway a plump and pretty young woman with a clean towel.

"Hullo!" cried Herrick, who now saw for the first time the fourth survivor of the pestilence, and was startled by the recollection of the captain's orders.

'Yes," said Attwater, "the whole colony lives about the house, what's left of it. We are all afraid of devils, if you please! and Taniera and she sleep in the front parlour, and the other boy on the verandah."

"She is pretty," said Herrick.

"Too pretty," said Attwater. "That was why I had her married. A man never knows when he may be inclined to be a fool about women; so when we were left alone I had the pair of them to the chapel and performed the ceremony. She made a lot of fuss. I do not take at all the romantic view of marriage," he explained.

"And that strikes you as a safeguard?" asked Herrick with amazement.

"Certainly. I am a plain man and very literal. *Whom God hath joined together* are the words, I fancy. So one married them, and respects the marriage," said Attwater.

"Ah!" and Herrick.

"You see, I may look to make an excellent marriage when I go home," began Attwater confidentially. "I am rich. This safe alone"—laying his hands upon it—"will be a moderate fortune, when I have the time to place the pearls upon the market. Here are ten years' accumulation from a lagoon, where I have had as many as ten divers going all day long; and I went further than people usually do in these waters, for I rotted a lot of shell and did splendidly. Would you like to see them?"

This confirmation of the captain's guess hit Herrick hard, and he contained himself with difficulty. "No, thank you, I think not," said he. "I do not care for pearls. I am very indifferent to all these..."

"Gewgaws?" suggested Attwater. "And yet I believe you ought to cast an eye on my collection, which is really unique, and which—O! it is the case with all of us and everything about us!—hangs by a hair. Today it groweth up and flourisheth; tomorrow it is cut down and cast into the oven. Today it is here and together in this safe; tomorrow—tonight!—it may be scattered. Thou fool, this night thy soul shall be required of thee."

"I do not understand you," said Herrick.

"Not?" said Attwater.

"You seem to speak in riddles," said Herrick unsteadily. "I do not understand what manner of man you are, nor what you are driving at."

Attwater stood with his hands upon his hips, and his head bent forward. "I am a fatalist," he replied, "and just now (if you insist on it) an experimentalist. Talking of which, by the by, who painted out the schooner's name?" he said, with mocking softness, "because, do you know? one thinks it should be done again. It can still be partly read; and whatever is worth doing is surely worth doing well. You think with me? That is so nice! Well, shall we step on the verandah? I have a dry sherry that I would like your opinion of."

Herrick followed him forth to where, under the light of the hanging lamps, the table shone with napery and crystal; followed him as the criminal goes with the hangman, or the sheep with the butcher; took the sherry mechanically, drank it, and spoke mechanical words of praise. The object of his terror had become suddenly inverted; till then he had seen Attwater trussed and gagged, a helpless victim, and had longed to run in and save him; he saw him now tower up mysterious and menacing, the angel of the Lord's wrath, armed with knowledge and threatening judgement. He set down his glass again,

270

and was surprised to see it empty.

"You go always armed?" he said, and the next moment could have plucked his tongue out.

"Always," said Attwater. "I have been through a mutiny here; that was one of my incidents of missionary life."

And just then the sound of voices reached them, and looking forth from the verandah they saw Huish and the captain drawing near.

CHAPTER 9
THE DINNER PARTY

They sat down to an island dinner, remarkable for its variety and excellence: turtle-soup and steak, fish, fowls, a suckling-pig, a coconut salad, and sprouting coconut roasted for dessert. Not a tin had been opened; and save for the oil and vinegar in the salad, and some green spears of onion which Attwater cultivated and plucked with his own hand, not even the condiments were European. Sherry, hock, and claret succeeded each other, and the *Farallone* champagne brought up the rear with the dessert.

It was plain that, like so many of the extremely religious in the days before teetotalism, Attwater had a dash of the epicure. For such characters it is softening to eat well; doubly so to have designed and had prepared an excellent meal for others; and the manners of their host were agreeably mollified in consequence. A cat of huge growth sat on his shoulder purring, and occasionally, with a deft paw, capturing a morsel in the air. To a cat he might be likened himself, as he lolled at the head of his table, dealing out attentions and innuendos, and using the velvet and the claw indifferently. And both Huish and the captain fell progressively under the charm of his hospitable freedom.

Over the third guest the incidents of the dinner may be said to have passed for long unheeded. Herrick accepted all that was offered him, ate and drank without tasting, and heard without comprehending. His mind was singly occupied in contemplating the horror of the circumstances in which he sat. What Attwater knew, what the captain designed, from which side treachery was to be first expected, these were the ground of his thoughts. There were times when he longed to throw down the table and flee into the night. And even that was debarred him; to do anything, to say anything, to move at all, were only to precipitate the barbarous tragedy; and he sat spell-

bound, eating with white lips. Two of his companions observed him narrowly, Attwater with raking, sidelong glances that
did not interrupt his talk, the captain with a heavy and anxious
consideration.

"Well, I must say this sherry is a really prime article," said
Huish. "'Ow much does it stand you in, if it's a fair question?"

"A hundred and twelve shillings in London, and the freight to
Valparaiso, and on again," said Attwater. "It strikes one as really
not a bad fluid."

"A 'undred and twelve!" murmured the clerk, relishing the
wine and the figures in a common ecstasy: "O my!"

"So glad you like it," said Attwater. "Help yourself, Mr. Whish,
and keep the bottle by you."

"My friend's name is Huish and not Whish, sir," said the
captain, with a flush.

"I beg your pardon, I am sure. Huish and not Whish; certainly," said Attwater. "I was about to say that I have still eight
dozen," he added, fixing the captain with his eye.

"Eight dozen what?" said Davis.

"Sherry," was the reply. "Eight dozen excellent sherry. Why, it
seems almost worth it in itself—to a man fond of wine."

The ambiguous words struck home to guilty consciences,
and Huish and the captain sat up in their places and regarded
him with a scare.

"Worth what?" said Davis.

"A hundred and twelve shillings," replied Attwater.

The captain breathed hard for a moment. He reached out far
and wide to find any coherency in these remarks; then, with a
great effort, changed the subject.

"I allow we are about the first white men upon this island,
sir," said he.

Attwater followed him at once, and with entire gravity, to the
new ground. "Myself and Dr. Symonds excepted, I should say
the only ones," he returned. "And yet who can tell? In the
course of the ages some one may have lived here, and we
sometimes think that some one must. The coco-palms grow all

round the island, which is scarce like nature's planting. We found besides, when we landed, an unmistakable cairn upon the beach; use unknown; but probably erected in the hope of gratifying some mumbo-jumbo whose very name is forgotten, by some thick-witted gentry whose very bones are lost. Then the island (witness the Directory) has been twice reported; and since my tenancy, we have had two wrecks, both derelict. The rest is conjecture."

"Dr. Symonds is your partner, I guess?" said Davis.

"A dear fellow, Symonds! How he would regret it, if he knew you had been here!" said Attwater.

"'E's on the *Trinity 'All*, ain't he?" asked Huish.

"And if you could tell me where the *Trinity 'All* was, you would confer a favour, Mr. Whish!" was the reply.

"I suppose she has a native crew?" said Davis.

"Since the secret has been kept ten years, one would suppose she had," replied Attwater.

"Well, now, see 'ere!" said Huish. "You have everythink about you in no end style, and no mistake, but I tell you it wouldn't do for me. Too much of 'the old rustic bridge by the mill'; too retired by 'alf. Give me the sound of Bow Bells!"

"You must not think it was always so," replied Attwater. "This was once a busy shore, although now, hark! you can hear the solitude. I find it stimulating. And talking of the sound of bells, kindly follow a little experiment of mine in silence." There was a silver bell at his right hand to call the servants; he made them a sign to stand still, struck the bell with force, and leaned eagerly forward. The note rose clear and strong; it rang out clear and far into the night and over the deserted island; it died into the distance until there only lingered in the porches of the ear a vibration that was sound no longer. "Empty house, empty sea, solitary beaches!" said Attwater. "And yet God hears the bell! And yet we sit in this verandah on a lighted stage with all heaven for spectators! And you call that solitude?"

There followed a bar of silence, during which the captain sat mesmerised.

Then Attwater laughed softly. "These are the diversions of a lonely man," he resumed, "and possibly not in good taste. One tells oneself these little fairy tales for company. If there *should* happen to be anything in folk-lore, Mr. Hay? But here comes the claret. One does not offer you Lafitte, captain, because I believe it is all sold to the railroad dining-cars in your great country; but this Brâne-Mouton is of a good year, and Mr. Whish will give me news of it."

"That's a queer idea of yours!" cried the captain, bursting with a sigh from the spell that had bound him. "So you mean to tell me now, that you sit here evenings and ring up ... well, ring on the angels ... by yourself?"

"As a matter of historic fact, and since you put it directly, one does not," said Attwater. "Why ring a bell, when there flows out from oneself and everything about one a far more momentous silence? the least beat of my heart and the least thought in my mind echoing into eternity for ever and for ever and for ever."

"O, look 'ere," said Huish, "turn down the lights at once, and the Band of 'Ope will oblige! This ain't a spiritual séance."

"No folk-lore about Mr. Whish—I beg your pardon, captain: Huish, not Whish, of course," said Attwater.

As the boy was filling Huish's glass, the bottle escaped from his hand and was shattered, and the wine spilt on the verandah floor. Instant grimness as of death appeared in the face of Attwater; he smote the bell imperiously, and the two brown natives fell into the attitude of attention and stood mute and trembling. There was just a moment of silence and hard looks; then followed a few savage words in the native; and, upon a gesture of dismissal, the service proceeded as before.

None of the party had as yet observed upon the excellent bearing of the two men. They were dark, undersized, and well set up; stepped softly, waited deftly, brought on the wines and dishes at a look, and their eyes attended studiously on their master.

"Where do you get your labour from anyway?" asked Davis.

"Ah, where not?" answered Attwater.

"Not much of a soft job, I suppose?" said the captain.

"If you will tell me where getting labour is!" said Attwater, with a shrug. "And of course, in our case, as we could name no destination, we had to go far and wide and do the best we could. We have gone as far west as the Kingsmills and as far south as Rapa-iti. Pity Symonds isn't here! He is full of yarns. That was his part, to collect them. Then began mine, which was the educational."

"You mean to run them?" said Davis.

"Ay! to run them," said Attwater.

"Wait a bit," said Davis; "I'm out of my depth. How was this? Do you mean to say you did it single-handed?"

"One did it single-handed," said Attwater, "because there was nobody to help one."

"By God, but you must be a holy terror!" cried the captain, in a glow of admiration.

"One does one's best," said Attwater.

"Well, now!" said Davis, "I have seen a lot of driving in my time, and been counted a good driver myself. I fought my way, third mate, round the Cape Horn with a push of packet-rats that would have turned the devil out of hell and shut the door on him; and I tell you, this racket of Mr. Attwater's takes the cake. In a ship, why, there ain't nothing to it! You've got the law with you, that's what does it. But put me down on this blame' beach alone, with nothing but a whip and a mouthful of bad words, and ask me to ... no, *sir*! it's not good enough! I haven't got the sand for that!" cried Davis. "It's the law behind," he added; "it's the law does it, every time!"

"The beak ain't as black as he's sometimes pynted," observed Huish humorously.

"Well, one got the law after a fashion," said Attwater. "One had to be a number of things. It was sometimes rather a bore."

"I should smile!" said Davis. "Rather lively, I should think!"

"I daresay we mean the same thing," said Attwater. "However, one way or another, one got it knocked into their heads that they *must* work, and they *did* ... until the Lord took them!"

"'Ope you made 'em jump," said Huish.

"When it was necessary, Mr. Whish, I made them jump," said Attwater.

"You bet you did," cried the captain. He was a good deal flushed, but not so much with wine as admiration; and his eyes drank in the huge proportions of the other with delight. "You bet you did, and you bet that I can see you doing it! By God, you're a man, and you can say I said so."

"Too good of you, I'm sure," said Attwater.

"Did you—did you ever have crime here?" asked Herrick, breaking his silence with a pungent voice.

"Yes," said Attwater, "we did."

"And how did you handle that, sir?" cried the eager captain.

"Well, you see, it was a queer case," replied Attwater. "It was a case that would have puzzled Solomon. Shall I tell it you? yes?"

The captain rapturously accepted.

"Well," drawled Attwater, "here is what it was. I daresay you know two types of natives, which may be called the obsequious and the sullen? Well, one had them, the types themselves, detected in the fact; and one had them together. Obsequiousness ran out of the first like wine out of a bottle, sullenness congested in the second. Obsequiousness was all smiles; he ran to catch your eye, he loved to gabble; and he had about a dozen words of beach English, and an eighth-of-an-inch veneer of Christianity. Sullens was industrious; a big down-looking bee. When he was spoken to, he answered with a black look and a shrug of one shoulder, but the thing would be done. I don't give him to you for a model of manners; there was nothing showy about Sullens; but he was strong and steady, and ungraciously obedient. Now Sullens got into trouble; no matter how; the regulations of the place were broken, and he was punished accordingly—without effect. So, the next day, and the next, and the day after, till I began to be weary of the business, and Sullens (I am afraid) particularly so. There came a day when he was in fault again, for the—O perhaps the thirtieth time; and he rolled a dull eye upon me, with a spark in it, and appeared to speak. Now the regulations of the place are formal upon one point: we allow no explanations; none are received, none allowed to be offered. So one stopped him instantly, but made a note of the circumstances. The next day he was gone from the settlement. There could be nothing more annoying; if the labour took to running away, the fishery was wrecked. There are sixty miles of this island, you see, all in length like the Queen's highway; the idea of pursuit in such a place was a piece of single-minded childishness, which one did not entertain. Two days later, I made a discovery; it came in upon me with a flash that Sullens had been unjustly punished from beginning to end, and the real culprit throughout had been Obsequiousness. The native who talks, like the woman who hesitates, is lost. You set him talking and lying; and he talks, and lies, and watches your face to see if he has pleased you; till, at last, out comes the truth! It came out of Obsequiousness in the regular course. I said nothing to him; I dismissed him; and late as it was, for it was already night, set off to look for Sullens. I had not far to go: about two hundred yards up the island and moon showed him to me. He was hanging in a coco-palm—I'm not botanist enough to tell you how—but it's the way, in nine cases out of ten, these natives commit suicide. His tongue was out, poor devil, and the birds had got at him, I spare you details: he was an ugly sight! I gave the business six good hours of thinking in this verandah. My justice had been made a fool of; I don't suppose that I was ever angrier. Next day, I had the conch sounded and all hands out before sunrise. One took one's gun, and led the way, with Obsequiousness. He was very talkative; the beggar supposed that all was right now he had confessed; in the old schoolboy phrase he was plainly 'sucking up' to me; full of protestations of good-will and good behviour; to which one answered one really can't remember what. Presently the tree came in sight, and the hang-ed man. They all burst out lamenting for their comrade in the island way, and Obsequiousness was the loudest of the mourners. He was quite genuine; a noxious creature without any consciousness of guilt. Well, presently—to make a long story short—one told him to go up the tree. He stared a bit, looked at one with a trouble in his eye, and had rather a sickly smile; but went. He was obedient to the last; he had all the pretty virtues, but the truth was not in him. So soon as he was up he looked down, and there was the rifle covering him; and at that he gave a whimper like a dog. You could hear a pin drop; no more keening now. There they all crouched upon the ground with bulging eyes; there was he in the tree-top, the colour of lead; and between was the dead man, dancing a bit in the air. He was obedient to the last, recited his crime, recommended his soul to God. And then...'

Attwater paused, and Herrick, who had been listening attentively, made a convulsive movement which upset his glass.

"And then?" said the breathless captain.

"Shot," said Attwater. "They came to the ground together."

Herrick sprang to his feet with a shriek and an insensate gesture.

"It was a murder!" he screamed, "a cold-hearted, bloody-minded murder! You monstrous being! Murderer and hypo-crite—murderer and hypocrite—murderer and hypocrite—" he repeated, and his tongue stumbled among the words.

The captain was by him in a moment. "Herrick!" he cried, "behave yourself! Here, don't be a blame' fool!"

Herrick struggled in his embrace like a frantic child, and suddenly bowing his face in his hands, choked into a sob, the first of many, which now convulsed his body silently, and now jerked from him indescribable and meaningless sounds.

"Your friend appears over-excited," remarked Attwater, sitting unmoved but all alert at table.

"It must be the wine," replied the captain. "He ain't no drink-ing man, you see. I—I think I'll take him away. A walk'll sober him up, I guess."

He led him without resistance out of the verandah and into the night, in which they soon melted; but still for some time, as

279

they drew away, his comfortable voice was to be heard soothing and remonstrating, and Herrick answering, at intervals,
with the mechanical noises of hysteria.

"'E's like a bloomin' poultry yard!" observed Huish, helping
himself to wine (of which he spilled a good deal) with gentle-
manly ease. "A man should learn to behave at table," he added.

"Rather bad form, is it not?" said Attwater. "Well, well, we are
left *tête-à-tête*. A glass of wine with you, Mr. Whish!"

CHAPTER 10
THE OPEN DOOR

The captain and Herrick meanwhile turned their back upon the lights in Attwater's verandah, and took a direction towards the pier and the beach of the lagoon.

The isle, at this hour, with its smooth floor of sand, the pillared roof overhead, and the prevalent illumination of the lamps, wore an air of unreality, like a deserted theatre or a public garden at midnight. A man looked about him for the statues and tables. Not the least air of wind was stirring among the palms, and the silence was emphasised by the continuous clamour of the surf from the seashore, as it might be of traffic in the next street.

Still talking, still soothing him, the captain hurried his patient on, brought him at last to the lagoon side, and leading him down the beach, laved his head and face with the tepid water. The paroxysm gradually subsided, the sobs became less convulsive and then ceased; by an odd but not quite unnatural conjunction, the captain's soothing current of talk died away at the same time and by proportional steps, and the pair remained sunk in silence. The lagoon broke at their feet in petty wavelets, and with a sound as delicate as a whisper; stars of all degrees looked down on their own images in that vast mirror; and the more angry colour of the *Farallone's* riding lamp burned in the middle distance. For long they continued to gaze on the scene before them, and hearken anxiously to the rustle and tinkle of that miniature surf, or the more distant and loud reverberations from the outer coast. For long speech was denied them; and when the words came at last, they came to both simultaneously.

"Say, Herrick ..." the captain was beginning.

But Herrick, turning swiftly towards his companion, bent him down with the eager cry: "Let's up anchor, captain, and to sea!"

"Where to, my son?" said the captain. "Up anchor's easy saying. But where to?"

"To sea," responded Herrick. "The sea's big enough! To sea—away from this dreadful island and that, O! that sinister man!"

'O, we'll see about that," said Davis. "You brace up, and we'll see about that. You're all run down, that's what's wrong with you; you're all nerves, like Jemimar; you've got to brace up good and be yourself again, and then we'll talk."

"To sea," reiterated Herrick, "to sea tonight—now—this moment!"

"It can't be, my son," replied the captain firmly. "No ship of mine puts to sea without provisions; you can take that for settled."

"You don't seem to understand," said Herrick. "The whole thing is over, I tell you. There is nothing to do here, when he knows all. That man there with the cat knows all; can't you take it in?"

"All what?" asked the captain, visibly discomposed. "Why, he received us like a perfect gentleman and treated us real handsome, until you began with your foolery—and I must say I seen men shot for less, and nobody sorry! What more do you expect anyway?"

Herrick rocked to and fro upon the sand, shaking his head.

"Guying us," he said; "he was guying us—only guying us; it's all we're good for."

"There was one queer thing, to be sure," admitted the captain, with a misgiving of the voice; "that about the sherry. Damned if I caught on to that. Say, Herrick, you didn't give me away?"

"O! give you away!" repeated Herrick with weary, querulous scorn. "What was there to give away? We're transparent; we've got rascal branded on us: detected rascal—detected rascal! Why, before he came on board, there was the name painted out, and he saw the whole thing. He made sure we would kill him there and then, and stood guying you and Huish on the chance. He calls that being frightened! Next he had me ashore; a fine time

I had! *The two wolves*, he calls you and Huish. *What is the puppy doing with the two wolves?* he asked. He showed me his pearls; he said they might be dispersed before morning, and *all hung by a hair*—and smiled as he said it, such a smile! O, it's no use, I tell you! He knows all, he sees through all; we only make him laugh with our pretences—he looks at us and laughs like God!"

There was a silence. Davis stood with contorted brows, gazing into the night.

"The pearls?" he said suddenly. "He showed them to you? He has them?"

"No, he didn't show them; I forgot: only the safe they were in," said Herrick. "But you'll never get them!"

"I've two words to say to that," said the captain.

"Do you think he would have been so easy at table, unless he was prepared?" said Herrick. "The servants were both armed. He was armed himself; he always is; he told me. You will never deceive his vigilance. Davis, I know it! It's all up, I tell you, and keep telling you and proving it. All up; all up. There's nothing for it, there's nothing to be done: all gone: life, honour, love. O my God, why was I born?"

Another pause followed upon this outburst.

The captain put his hands to his brow.

"Another thing!" he broke out. "Why did he tell you all this? Seems like madness to me!"

Herrick shook his head with gloomy iteration. "You wouldn't understand if I were to tell you," said he.

"I guess I can understand any blame' thing that you can tell me," said the captain.

"Well, then, he's a fatalist," said Herrick.

"What's that? a fatalist?" said Davis.

"O, it's a fellow that believes a lot of things," said Herrick; "believes that his bullets go true; believes that all falls out as God chooses, do as you like to prevent it; and all that."

"Why, I guess I believe right so myself," said Davis.

"You do?" said Herrick.

"You bet I do!" says Davis.

Herrick shrugged his shoulders. "Well, you must be a fool," said he, and he leaned his head upon his knees.

The captain stood biting his hands.

"There's one thing sure," he said at last. "I must get Huish out of that. *He's* not fit to hold his end up with a man like you describe."

And he turned to go away. The words had been quite simple; not so the tone; and the other was quick to catch it.

"Davis!" he cried, "no! Don't do it. Spare *me*, and don't do it—spare yourself, and leave it alone—for God's sake, for your children's sake!"

His voice rose to a passionate shrillness; another moment, and he might be overheard by their not distant victim. But Davis turned on him with a savage oath and gesture; and the miserable young man rolled over on his face and the sand, and lay speechless and helpless.

The captain meanwhile set out rapidly for Attwater's house. As he went, he considered with himself eagerly, his thoughts racing. The man had understood, he had mocked them from the beginning; he would teach him to make a mockery of John Davis! Herrick thought him a god; give him a second to aim in, and the god was overthrown. He chuckled as he felt the butt of his revolver. It should be done now, as he went in. From behind? It was difficult to get there. From across the table? No, the captain preferred to shoot standing, so as you could be sure to get your hand upon your gun. The best would be to summon Huish, and when Attwater stood up and turned—ah, then would be the moment. Wrapped in this ardent prefiguration of events, the captain posted towards the house with his head down.

"Hands up! Halt!" cried the voice of Attwater.

And the captain, before he knew what he was doing, had obeyed. The surprise was complete and irremediable. Coming on the top crest of his murderous intentions, he had walked straight into an ambuscade, and now stood, with his hands impotently lifted, staring at the verandah.

The party was now broken up. Attwater leaned on a post, and kept Davis covered with a Winchester. One of the servants was hard by with a second at the port arms, leaning a little forward, round-eyed with eager expectancy. In the open space at the head of the stair, Huish was partly supported by the other native; his face wreathed in meaningless smiles, his mind seemingly sunk in the contemplation of an unlighted cigar.

"Well," said Attwater, "you seem to be a very twopenny pirate!"

The captain uttered a sound in his throat for which we have no name; rage choked him.

"I am going to give you Mr. Whish—or the wine-sop that remains of him," continued Attwater. "He talks a great deal when he drinks, Captain Davis of the *Sea Ranger*. But I have quite done with him—and return the article with thanks. Now," he cried sharply; "another false movement like that, and your family will have to deplore the loss of an invaluable parent; keep strictly still, Davis."

Attwater said a word in the native, his eye still undeviatingly fixed on the captain; and the servant thrust Huish smartly forward from the brink of the stair. With an extraordinary simultaneous dispersion of his members, that gentleman bounded forth into space, struck the earth, ricocheted, and brought up with his arms about a palm. His mind was quite a stranger to these events; the expression of anguish that deformed his countenance at the moment of the leap was probably mechanical; and he suffered these convulsions in silence; clung to the tree like an infant; and seemed, by his dips, to suppose himself engaged in the pastime of bobbing for apples. A more finely sympathetic mind or a more observant eye might have remarked, a little in front of him on the sand and still quite beyond reach, the unlighted cigar.

"There is your Whitechapel carrion!" said Attwater. "And now you might very well ask me why I do not put a period to you at once, as you deserve. I will tell you why, Davis. It is because I have nothing to do with the *Sea Ranger* and the people you drowned, or the *Farallone* and the champagne that you stole. That is your account with God; He keeps it, and He will settle it when the clock strikes. In my own case, I have nothing to go on but suspicion, and I do not kill on suspicion, not even vermin like you. But understand: if ever I see any of you again, it is another matter, and you shall eat a bullet. And now take yourself off. March! and as you value what you call your life, keep your hands up as you go!"

The captain remained as he was, his hands up, his mouth open: mesmerised with fury.

"March!" said Attwater. "One—two—three!"

And Davis turned and passed slowly away. But even as he went, he was meditating a prompt, offensive return. In the twinkling of an eye he had leaped behind a tree; and was crouching there, pistol in hand, peering from either side of his place of ambush with bared teeth; a serpent already poised to strike. And already he was too late. Attwater and his servants had disappeared; and only the lamps shone on the deserted table and the bright sand above the house, and threw into the night in all directions the strong and tall shadows of the palms.

Davis ground his teeth. Where were they gone, the cowards? to what hole had they retreated beyond reach? It was in vain he should try anything, he, single and with a second-hand revolver, against three persons, armed with Winchesters, and who did not show an ear out of any of the apertures of that lighted and silent house. Some of them might have already ducked below it from the rear, and be drawing a bead upon him at that moment from the low-browed crypt, the receptacle of empty bottles and broken crockery. No, there was nothing to be done but to bring away (if it were still possible) his shattered and demoralised forces.

"Huish," he said, "come along."

"'S lose my ciga'," said Huish, reaching vaguely forward.

The captain let out a rasping oath. "Come right along here," said he.

"'S all righ'. Sleep here 'th Atty-Attwa. Go boar' t'morr'," replied the festive one.

"If you don't come, and come now, by the living God, I'll shoot you!" cried the captain.

It is not to be supposed that the sense of these words in any way penetrated to the mind of Huish; rather that, in a fresh attempt upon the cigar, he overbalanced himself and came flying erratically forward: a course which brought him within reach of Davis.

"Now you walk straight," said the captain, clutching him, "or I'll know why not!"

"'S lose my ciga'," replied Huish.

The captain's contained fury blazed up for a moment. He twisted Huish round, grasped him by the neck of the coat, ran him in front of him to the pier-end, and flung him savagely forward on his face.

"Look for your cigar then, you swine!" said he, and blew his boat-call till the pea in it ceased to rattle.

An immediate activity responded on board the *Farallone*; far-away voices, and soon the sound of oars, floated along the surface of the lagoon; and at the same time, from nearer hand, Herrick aroused himself and strolled languidly up. He bent over the insignificant figure of Huish, where it grovelled, apparently insensible, at the base of the figure-head.

"Dead?" he asked.

"No, he's not dead," said Davis.

"And Attwater?" asked Herrick.

"Now you just shut your head!" replied Davis. "You can do that, I fancy, and by God, I'll show you how! I'll stand no more of your drivel."

They waited accordingly in silence till the boat bumped on the farthest piers; then raised Huish, head and heels, carried him down the gangway, and flung him summarily in the bottom. On the way out he was heard murmuring of the loss of his cigar; and after he had been handed up the side like baggage, and cast down in the alleyway to slumber, his last audible expression was: "Splen'l fl' Attwa'!" This the expert construed into "Splendid fellow, Attwater"; with so much innocence had this great spirit issued from the adventures of the evening.

The captain went and walked in the waist with brief irate turns; Herrick leaned his arms on the taffrail; the crew had all turned in. The ship had a gentle, cradling motion; at times a block piped like a bird. On shore, through the colonnade of palm stems, Attwater's house was to be seen shining steadily with many lamps. And there was nothing else visible, whether in the heaven above or in the lagoon below, but the stars and their reflections. It might have been minutes, or it might have been hours, that Herrick leaned there, looking in the glorified water and drinking peace. "A bath of stars," he was thinking; when a hand was laid at last on his shoulder.

"Herrick," said the captain, "I've been walking off my trouble."

A sharp jar passed through the young man, but he neither answered nor so much as turned his head.

"I guess I spoke a little rough to you on shore," pursued the captain; "the fact is, I was real mad; but now it's over, and you and me have to turn to and think."

"I will *not* think," said Herrick.

"Here, old man!" said Davis kindly; "this won't fight, you know! You've got to brace up and help me get things straight. You're not going back on a friend? That's not like you, Herrick!"

'O yes, it is," said Herrick.

"Come, come!" said the captain, and paused as if quite at a loss. "Look here," he cried, "you have a glass of champagne. *I* won't touch it, so that'll show you if I'm in earnest. But it's just the pick-me-up for you; it'll put an edge on you at once."

"O, you leave me alone!" said Herrick, and turned away.

The captain caught him by the sleeve; and he shook him off and turned on him, for the moment like a demoniac.

"Go to hell in your own way!" he cried.

And he turned away again, this time unchecked, and stepped forward to where the boat rocked alongside and ground occasionally against the schooner. He looked about him. A corner of the house was interposed between the captain and himself; all was well; no eye must see him in that last act. He slid silently into the boat; thence, silently, into the starry water. Instinctively he swam a little; it would be time enough to stop by and by.

The shock of the immersion brightened his mind immediately. The events of the ignoble day passed before him in a frieze of pictures, and he thanked "whatever Gods there be" for that open door of suicide. In such a little while he would be done with it, the random business at an end, the prodigal son come home. A very bright planet shone before him and drew a trenchant wake along the water. He took that for his line and followed it.

That was the last earthly thing that he should look upon; that radiant speck, which he had soon magnified into a City of Laputa, along whose terraces there walked men and women of awful and benignant features, who viewed him with distant commiseration. These imaginary spectators consoled him; he told himself their talk, one to another; it was of himself and his sad destiny.

From such flights of fancy he was aroused by the growing coldness of the water. Why should he delay? Here, where he was now, let him drop the curtain, let him seek the ineffable refuge, let him lie down with all races and generations of men in the house of sleep. It was easy to say, easy to do. To stop swimming: there was no mystery in that, if he could do it. Could he? And he could not. He knew it instantly. He was aware instantly of an opposition in his members, unanimous and invincible, clinging to life with a single and fixed resolve, finger by finger, sinew by sinew; something that was at once he and not he—at once within and without him; the shutting of some miniature valve in his brain, which a single manly thought should suffice to open—and the grasp of an external fate ineluctable as gravity. To any man there may come at times a consciousness that there blows, through all the articulations of his body, the wind of a spirit not wholly his; that his mind rebels; that another girds him and carries him whither he would not. It came now to Herrick, with the authority of a revelation. There was no escape possible. The open door was closed in his recreant face. He must go back into the world and amongst men without illusion. He must stagger on to the end with the pack of his responsibility and his disgrace, until a cold, a blow, a merciful chance ball, or the more merciful hangman, should dismiss him from his infamy. There were men who could commit suicide; there were men who could not; and he was one who could not.

For perhaps a minute there raged in his mind the coil of this discovery; then cheerless certitude followed; and, with an incredible simplicity of submission to ascertained fact, he turned round and struck out for shore. There was a courage in this which he could not appreciate; the ignobility of his cowardice wholly occupying him. A strong current set against him like a wind in his face; he contended with it heavily, wearily, without enthusiasm, but with substantial advantage; making his progress the while, without pleasure, by the outline of the trees. Once he had a moment of hope. He heard to the southward of him, towards the centre of the lagoon, the wallowing of some great fish, doubtless a shark, and paused for a little, treading water. Might not this be the hangman? he thought. But the wallowing died away; mere silence succeeded; and Herrick pushed on again for the shore, raging as he went at his own nature. Ay, he would wait for the shark; but if he had heard him coming! ... His smile was tragic. He could have spat upon himself.

About three in the morning, chance, and the set of the current, and the bias of his own right-handed body so decided it between them that he came to shore upon the beach in front of Attwater's. There he sat down, and looked forth into a world without any of the lights of hope. The poor diving-dress of self-conceit was sadly tattered! With the fairy tale of suicide, of a refuge always open to him, he had hitherto beguiled and supported himself in the trials of life; and behold! that also was only a fairy tale, that also was folk-lore. With the consequences of his acts he saw himself implacably confronted for the duration of life: stretched upon a cross, and nailed there with the iron bolts of his own cowardice. He had no tears; he told himself no stories. His disgust with himself was so complete, that even the process of apologetic mythology had ceased. He was like a man cast down from a pillar, and every bone broken. He lay there, and admitted the facts, and did not attempt to rise.

Dawn began to break over the far side of the atoll, the sky brightened, the clouds became dyed with gorgeous colours, the shadows of the night lifted. And, suddenly, Herrick was aware that the lagoon and the trees wore again their daylight livery; and he saw, on board the *Farallone*, Davis extinguishing the lantern, and smoke rising from the galley.

Davis, without doubt, remarked and recognised the figure on the beach; or perhaps hesitated to recognise it; for after he had gazed a long while from under his hand, he went into the house and fetched a glass. It was very powerful; Herrick had often used it. With an instinct of shame, he hid his face in his hands.

"And what brings you here, Mr. Herrick-Hay, or Mr. Hay-Herrick?" asked the voice of Attwater. "Your back view from my present position is remarkably fine, and I would continue to present it. We can get on very nicely as we are, and if you were to turn round, do you know? I think it would be awkward."

Herrick slowly rose to his feet; his heart throbbed hard, a hideous excitement shook him, but he was master of himself. Slowly he turned and faced Attwater and the muzzle of a pointed rifle. "Why could I not do that last night?" he thought.

"Well, why don't you fire?" he said aloud, in a voice that trembled.

Attwater slowly put his gun under his arm, then his hands in his pockets.

"What brings you here?" he repeated.

"I don't know," said Herrick; and then, with a cry: "can you do anything with me?"

"Are you armed?" said Attwater. "I ask for the form's sake."

"Armed? No!" said Herrick. "O yes, I am, too!"

And he flung upon the beach a dripping pistol.

"You are wet," said Attwater.

"Yes, I am wet," said Herrick. "Can you do anything with me?"

Attwater read his face attentively.

"It would depend a good deal upon what you are," said he.

"What I am? A coward!" said Herrick.

"There is very little to be done with that," said Attwater. "And yet the description hardly strikes one as exhaustive."

"O, what does it matter?" cried Herrick. "Here I am. I am broken crockery; I am a burst drum; the whole of my life is gone to water; I have nothing left that I believe in, except my living horror of myself. Why do I come to you? I don't know; you are cold, cruel, hateful; and I hate you, or I think I hate you. But you are an honest man, an honest gentleman. I put myself, helpless, in your hands. What must I do? If I can't do anything, be merciful and put a bullet through me; it's only a puppy with a broken leg!"

"If I were you, I would pick up that pistol, come up to the house, and put on some dry clothes," said Attwater.

"If you really mean it?" said Herrick. "You know they—we—they ... But you know all."

"I know quite enough," said Attwater. "Come up to the house."

And the captain, from the deck of the *Farallone*, saw the two men pass together under the shadow of the grove.

CHAPTER 11
DAVID AND GOLIATH

Huish had bundled himself up from the glare of the day—his face to the house, his knees retracted. The frail bones in the thin tropical raiment seemed scarce more considerable than a fowl's; and Davis, sitting on the rail with his arm about a stay, contemplated him with gloom, wondering what manner of counsel that insignificant figure should contain. For since Herrick had thrown him off and deserted to the enemy, Huish, alone of mankind, remained to him to be a helper and oracle.

He considered their position with a sinking heart. The ship was a stolen ship; the stores, whether from initial carelessness or ill administration during the voyage, were insufficient to carry them to any port except back to Papeete; and there retribution waited in the shape of a gendarme, a judge with a queer-shaped hat, and the horror of distant Noumea. Upon that side there was no glimmer of hope. Here, at the island, the dragon was roused; Attwater with his men and his Winchesters watched and patrolled the house; let him who dare approach it. What else was then left but to sit there, inactive, pacing the decks, until the *Trinity Hall* arrived and they were cast into irons, or until the food came to an end, and the pangs of famine succeeded? For the *Trinity Hall* Davis was prepared; he would barricade the house, and die there defending it, like a rat in a crevice. But for the other? The cruise of the *Farallone*, into which he had plunged, only a fortnight before, with such golden expectations, could this be the nightmare end of it? The ship rotting at anchor, the crew stumbling and dying in the scuppers? It seemed as if any extreme of hazard were to be preferred to so grisly a certainty; as if it would be better to up-anchor after all, put to sea at a venture, and, perhaps, perish at the hands of cannibals on one of the more obscure Paumotus. His eye roved swiftly over sea and sky in quest of any promise of wind, but the fountains of the Trade were empty. Where it had run yesterday and for weeks before, a roaring blue river charioting clouds, silence now reigned; and the whole height of the atmosphere stood balanced. On the endless ribbon of island that stretched out to either hand of him its array of golden and green and silvery palms, not the most volatile frond was to be seen stirring; they dropped to their stable images in the lagoon like things carved of metal, and already their long line began to reverberate heat. There was no escape possible that day, none probable on the morrow. And still the stores were running out!

Then came over Davis, from deep down in the roots of his being, or at least from far back among his memories of childhood and innocence, a wave of superstition. This run of ill-luck was something beyond natural; the chances of the game were in themselves more various: it seemed as if the devil must serve the pieces. The devil? He heard again the clear note of Attwater's bell ringing abroad into the night, and dying away. How if God...?

Briskly he averted his mind. Attwater: that was the point. Attwater had food and a treasure of pearls; escape made possible in the present, riches in the future. They must come to grips with Attwater; the man must die. A smoky heat went over his face, as he recalled the impotent figure he had made last night, and the contemptuous speeches he must bear in silence. Rage, shame, and the love of life, all pointed the one way; and only invention halted: how to reach him? had he strength enough? was there any help in that misbegotten packet of bones against the house?

His eyes dwelled upon him with a strange avidity, as though he would read into his soul; and presently the sleeper moved, stirred uneasily, turned suddenly round, and threw him a blinking look. Davis maintained the same dark stare, and Huish looked away again and sat up.

"Lord, I've an 'eadache on me!" said he. "I believe I was a bit swipey last night. W'ere's that crybyby 'Errick?"

"Gone," said the captain.

"Ashore?" cried Huish. "O, I say! I'd 'a gone too."

"Would you?" said the captain.

"Yes, I would," replied Huish. "I like Attwater. 'E's all right; we got on like one o'clock when you were gone. And ain't his sherry in it, rather? It's like Spiers and Pond's Amontillado! I wish I 'ad a drain of it now." He sighed.

"Well, you'll never get no more of it—that's one thing," said Davis gravely.

"'Ere, wot's wrong with you, Dyvis? Coppers 'ot? Well, look at *me*! *I* ain't grumpy," said Huish; "I'm as plyful as a canary-bird, I am."

"Yes," said Davis, "you're playful; I own that; and you were playful last night, I believe, and a damned fine performance you made of it."

"'Allo!" said Huish. "'Ow's this? Wot performance?"

"Well, I'll tell you," said the captain, getting slowly off the rail.

And he did: at full length, with every wounding epithet and absurd detail repeated and emphasised; he had his own vanity and Huish's upon the grill, and roasted them; and as he spoke he inflicted and endured agonies of humiliation. It was a plain man's masterpiece of the sardonic.

"What do you think of it?" said he, when he had done, and looked down at Huish, flushed and serious, and yet jeering.

"I'll tell you wot it is," was the reply: "you and me cut a pretty dicky figure."

"That's so," said Davis, "a pretty measly figure, by God! And, by God, I want to see that man at my knees."

"Ah!" said Huish. "'Ow to get him there?"

"That's it!" cried Davis. "How to get hold of him! They're four to two; though there's only one man among them to count, and that's Attwater. Get a bead on Attwater, and the others would cut and run and sing out like frightened poultry—and old man Herrick would come round with his hat for a share of the pearls. No, *sir*! it's how to get hold of Attwater! And we daren't even go ashore; he would shoot us in the boat like dogs."

"Are you particular about having him dead or alive?" asked Huish.

"I want to see him dead," said the captain.

"Ah, well!" said Huish, "then I believe I'll do a bit of breakfast."

And he turned into the house.

The captain doggedly followed him.

"What's this?" he asked. "What's your idea, anyway?"

"O, you let me alone, will you?" said Huish, opening a bottle of champagne. "You'll 'ear my idea soon enough. Wyte till I pour some cham on my 'ot coppers." He drank a glass off, and affected to listen. "'Ark!" said he, "'ear it fizz. Like 'am frying, I declyre. 'Ave a glass, do, and look sociable."

"No!" said the captain, with emphasis; "no, I will not! there's business."

"You p'ys your money and you tykes your choice, my little man," returned Huish. "Seems rather a shyme to me to spoil your breakfast for wot's really ancient 'istory."

He finished three parts of a bottle of champagne, and nibbled a corner of biscuit, with extreme deliberation; the captain sitting opposite and champing the bit like an impatient horse. Then Huish leaned his arms on the table and looked Davis in the face.

"W'en you're ready!" said he.

"Well, now, what's your idea?" said Davis, with a sigh.

"Fair play!" said Huish. "What's yours?"

"The trouble is that I've got none," replied Davis; and wandered for some time in aimless discussion of the difficulties of their path, and useless explanations of his own fiasco.

"About done?" said Huish.

"I'll dry up right here," replied Davis.

"Well, then," said Huish, "you give me your 'and across the table, and say, 'Gawd strike me dead if I don't back you up.'"

His voice was hardly raised, yet it thrilled the hearer. His face seemed the epitome of cunning, and the captain recoiled from it as from a blow.

"What for?" said he.

"Luck," said Huish. "Substantial guarantee demanded."

And he continued to hold out his hand.

"I don't see the good of any such tomfoolery," said the other.

"I do, though," returned Huish. "Gimme your 'and and say the words; then you'll 'ear my view of it. Don't, and you don't."

The captain went through the required form, breathing short, and gazing on the clerk with anguish. What to fear he knew not, yet he feared slavishly what was to fall from the pale lips.

"Now, if you'll excuse me 'alf a second," said Huish, "I'll go and fetch the byby."

"The baby?" said davis. "What's that?"

"Fragile. With care. This side up," replied the clerk with a wink, as he disappeared.

He returned, smiling to himself, and carrying in his hand a silk handkerchief. The long stupid wrinkles ran up Davis's brow as he saw it. What should it contain? He could think of nothing more recondite than a revolver.

Huish resumed his seat.

"Now," said he, "are you man enough to take charge of 'Errick and the niggers? Because I'll take care of Hattwater."

"How?" cried Davis. "You can't!"

"Tut, tut!" said the clerk. "You gimme time. Wot's the first point? The first point is that we can't get ashore, and I'll make you a present of that for a 'ard one. But 'ow about a flat of truce? Would that do the trick, d'ye think? or would Attwater simply blyze aw'y at us in the bloomin' boat like dawgs?"

"No," said Davis, "I don't believe he would."

"No more do I," said Huish; "I don't believe he would either; and I'm sure I 'ope he won't! So then you can call us ashore. Next point is to get near the managin' direction. And for that I'm going to 'ave you write a letter, in w'ich you s'y you're ashymed to meet his eye, and that the bearer, Mr. J. L. 'Uish, is empowered to represent you. Armed with w'ich seemin'ly simple expedient, Mr. J. L. 'Uish will proceed to business."

He paused, like one who had finished, but still held Davis with his eye.

"How?" said Davis. "Why?"

"Well, you see, you're big," returned Huish; "'e knows you 'ave a gun in your pocket, and anybody can see with 'alf an eye that you ain't the man to 'esitate about usin' it. So it's no go with you, and never was; you're out of the runnin', Dyvis. But he won't be afryde of me, I'm such a little 'un! I'm unarmed—no kid about that—and I'll hold my 'ands up right enough." He paused. "If I can manage to sneak up nearer to him as we talk," he resumed, "you look out and back me up smart. If I don't, we go aw'y again, and nothink to 'urt. See?"

The captain's face was contorted by the frenzied effort to comprehend.

"No, I don't see," he cried; "I can't see. What do you mean?"

"I mean to do for the beast!" cried Huish, in a burst of venomous triumph. "I'll bring the 'ulkin bully to grass. He's 'ad his larks out of me; I'm goin' to 'ave my lark out of 'im, and a good lark too!"

"What is it?" said the captain, almost in a whisper.

"Sure you want to know?" asked Huish.

Davis rose and took a turn in the house.

"Yes, I want to know," he said at last with an effort.

"W'en your back's at the wall, you do the best you can, don't you?" began the clerk. "I s'y that, because I 'appen to know there's a prejudice against it; it's considered vulgar, awf'ly vulgar." He unrolled the handkerchief and showed a four-ounce jar. "This 'ere's vitriol, this is," said he.

The captain stared upon him with a whitening face.

"This is the stuff!" he pursued, holding it up. "This'll burn to the bone; you'll see it smoke upon 'im like 'ell-fire! One drop upon 'is bloomin' heyesight, and I'll trouble you for Attwater!"

"No, no, by God!" exclaimed the captain.

"Now, see 'ere, ducky," said Huish, "this is my bean feast, I believe? I'm goin' up to that man single-'anded, I am. 'E's about seven foot high, and I'm five foot one. 'E's a rifle in his 'and, 'e's on the look-out, 'e wasn't born yesterday. This is Dyvid and Goliar, I tell you! If I'd ast you to walk up and face the music I could understand. But I don't. I on'y ast you to stand by and spifflicate the niggers. It'll all come in quite natural; you'll see, else! Fust thing, you know, you'll see him running round and 'owling like a good 'un...."

"Don't!" said Davis. "Don't talk of it!"

"Well, you *are* a juggins!" exclaimed Huish. "What did you want? You wanted to kill him, and tried to last night. You wanted to kill the 'ole lot of them, and tried to, and 'ere I show you 'ow; and because there's some medicine in a bottle you kick up this fuss!"

"I suppose that's so," said Davis. "It don't seem someways reasonable, only there it is."

"It's the happlication of science, I suppose?" sneered Huish.

"I don't know what it is," cried Davis, pacing the floor; "it's there! I draw the line at it. I can't put a finger to no such piggishness. It's too damned hateful!"

"And I suppose it's all your fancy pynted it," said Huish, "w'en you take a pistol and a bit o' lead, and copse a man's brains all over him? No accountin' for tystes."

"I'm not denying it," said Davis; "it's something here, inside of me. It's foolishness; I daresay it's dam foolishness. I don't argue; I just draw the line. Isn't there no other way?"

"Look for yourself," said Huish. "I ain't wedded to this, if you think I am; I ain't ambitious; I don't make a point of playin' the lead; I offer to, that's all, and if you can't show me better, by Gawd, I'm goin' to!"

"Then the risk!" cried Davis.

"If you ast me straight, I should say it was a case of seven to one, and no takers," said Huish. "But that's my look-out, ducky, and I'm gyme. Look at me, Dyvis, there ain't any shilly-shally about me. I'm gyme, that's wot I am: gyme all through."

The captain looked at him. Huish sat there preening his sinister vanity, glorifying in his precedency in evil; and the villainous courage and readiness of the creature shone out of him like a candle from a lantern. Dismay and a kind of respect seized hold on Davis in his own despite. Until that moment he had seen the clerk always hanging back, always listless, uninterested, and openly grumbling at a word of anything to do; and now, by the touch of an enchanter's wand, he beheld him sitting girt and resolved, and his face radiant. He had raised the devil, he thought; and asked who was to control him, and his spirits quailed.

"Look as long as you like," Huish was going on. "You don't see any green in my eye! I ain't afryde of Attwater, I ain't afryde of you, and I ain't afryde of words. You want to kill people, that's wot *you* want; but you want to do it in kid gloves, and it can't be done that w'y. Murder ain't genteel, it ain't easy, it ain't safe, and it tykes a man to do it. 'Ere's the man."

"Huish!" began the captain with energy; and then stopped, and remained staring at him with corrugated brows.

"Well, hout with it!" said Huish. "'Ave you anything else to put up? Is there any other chanst to try?"

The captain held his peace.

"There you are then!" said Huish, with a shrug.

Davis fell again to his pacing.

"O, you may do sentry-go till you're blue in the mug, you won't find anythink else," said Huish.

There was a little silence; the captain, like a man launched on a swing, flying dizzily among extremes of conjecture and refusal.

"But see," he said, suddenly pausing. "Can you? Can the thing be done? It—it can't be easy."

"If I get within twenty foot of 'im it'll be done; so you look out," said Huish, and his tone of certainty was absolute.

"How can you know that?" broke from the captain in a choked cry. "You beast, I believe you've done it before!"

"O, that's private affyres," returned Huish; "I ain't a talking man."

A shock of repulsion struck and shook the captain; a scream rose almost to his lips; had he uttered it, he might have cast himself at the same moment on the body of Huish, might have picked him up, and flung him down, and wiped the cabin with him, in a frenzy of cruelty that seemed half moral. But the moment passed; and the abortive crisis left the man weaker. The stakes were so high—the pearls on the one hand—starvation and shame on the other. Ten years of pearls! the imagination of Davis translated them into a new, glorified existence for himself and his family. The seat of this new life must be in London; there were deadly reasons against Portland, Maine; and the pictures that came to him were of English manners. He saw his boys marching in the procession of a school, with gowns on, an usher marshalling them and reading as he walked in a great book. He was installed in a villa, semi-detached; the name, "Rosemore," on the gateposts. In a chair on the gravel walk he seemed to sit smoking a cigar, a blue ribbon in his buttonhole, victor over himself and circumstances and the malignity of bankers. He saw the parlour, with red curtains, and shells on the mantelpiece—and, with the fine inconsistency of visions, mixed a grog at the mahogany table ere he turned in. With that the *Farallone* gave one of the aimless and nameless movements which (even in an anchored ship, and even in the most profound calm) remind one of the mobility of fluids; and he was back again under the cover of the house, the fierce daylight besieging it all round and glaring in the chinks, and the clerk in a rather airy attitude, awaiting his decision.

He began to walk again. He aspired after the realisation of these dreams, like a horse nickering for water; the lust of them burned in his inside. And the only obstacle was Attwater, who had insulted him from the first. He gave Herrick a full share of the pearls, he insisted on it; Huish opposed him, and he trod the opposition down; and praised himself exceedingly. He was not going to use vitriol himself; was he Huish's keeper? It was a pity he had asked, but after all! ... he saw the boys again in the school procession, with the gowns he had thought to be so "tony" long since.... And at the same time the incomparable shame of the last evening blazed up in his mind.

"Have it your own way!" he said hoarsely.

"O, I knew you would walk up," said Huish. "Now for the letter. There's paper, pens, and ink. Sit down and I'll dictyte."

The captain took a seat and the pen, looked a while helplessly at the paper, then at Huish. The swing had gone the other way; there was a blur upon his eyes. "It's a dreadful business," he said, with a strong twitch of his shoulders.

"It's rather a start, no doubt," said Huish. "Tyke a dip of ink. That's it. *William John Hattwater, Esq. Sir:*" he dictated.

"How do you know his name is William John?" asked Davis.

"Saw it on a packing-case," said Huish. "Got that?"

"No," said Davis. "But there's another thing. What are we to write?"

"O my folly!" cried the exasperated Huish. "Wot kind of man do *you* call yourself? *I'm* goin' to tell you wot to write; that's *my* pitch; if you'll just be so bloomin' condescendin' as to write it down! *William John Attwater, Esq., Sir:*" he reiterated. And, the captain at last beginning half mechanically to move his pen, the dictation proceeded: "*It is with feelings of shyme and 'art-felt contrition that I approach you after the yumiliatin' events of last night. Our Mr. 'Errick has left the ship, and will have doubtless communicated to you the nature of our 'opes. Needless to s'y, these are no longer possible: Fate 'as declyred against us, and we bow the 'ead. Well awyre as I am of the just suspicions with w'ich I am regarded, I do not venture to solicit the fyvour of an interview for myself, but in order to put an end to a situytion w'ich must be equally pyneful to all, I 'ave deputed my friend and partner, Mr. J. L. Huish, to l'y before you my proposals, and w'ich by their moderytion, will, I trust, be found to merit your attention. Mr. J. L. Huish is entirely unarmed, I swear to Gawd! and will 'old 'is 'ands over 'is 'ead from the moment he begins to approach you. I am your fytheful servant, John Dyvis.*"

Huish read the letter with the innocent joy of amateurs, chuckled gustfully to himself, and reopened it more than once after it was folded, to repeat the pleasure, Davis meanwhile sitting inert and heavily frowning.

Of a sudden he rose; he seemed all abroad. "No!" he cried. "No! it can't be! It's too much; it's damnation. God would never forgive it."

"Well, and 'oo wants Him to?" returned Huish, shrill with fury. "You were damned years ago for the *Sea Rynger*, and said so yourself. Well then, be damned for something else, and 'old your tongue."

The captain looked at him mistily. "No," he pleaded, "no, old man! don't do it."

"'Ere now, said Huish, "I'll give you my ultimytum. Go or st'y w'ere you are; I don't mind; I'm goin' to see that man and chuck this vitriol in his eyes. If you st'y I'll go alone; the niggers will likely knock me on the 'ead, and a fat lot you'll be the better! But there's one thing sure: I'll 'ear no more of your moonin' mullygrubbin' rot, and tyke it stryte."

The captain took it with a blink and a gulp. Memory, with phantom voices, repeated in his ears something similar, something he had once said to Herrick—years ago it seemed.

"Now, gimme over your pistol," said Huish. "I 'ave to see all clear. Six shots, and mind you don't wyste them."

The captain, like a man in a nightmare, laid down his revolver on the table, and Huish wiped the cartridges and oiled the works.

It was close on noon, there was no breath of wind, and the heat was scarce bearable, when the two men came on deck, had the boat manned, and passed down, one after another, into the stern-sheets. A white shirt at the end of an oar served as flag of truce; and the men, by direction, and to give it the better chance to be observed, pulled with extreme slowness. The isle shook before them like a place incandescent; on the face of the lagoon blinding copper suns, no bigger than sixpences, danced and stabbed them in the eyeballs: there went up from sand and sea, and even from the boat, a glare of scathing brightness; and as they could only peer abroad from

303

between closed lashes, the excess of light seemed to be changed into a sinister darkness, comparable to that of a thundercloud before it bursts.

The captain had come upon this errand for any one of a dozen reasons, the last of which was desire for its success. Superstition rules all men; semi-ignorant and gross natures, like that of Davis, it rules utterly. For murder he had been prepared; but this horror of the medicine in the bottle went beyond him, and he seemed to himself to be parting the last strands that united him to God. The boat carried him on to reprobation, to damnation; and he suffered himself to be carried passively consenting, silently bidding farewell to his better self and his hopes.

Huish sat by his side in towering spirits that were not wholly genuine. Perhaps as brave a man as ever lived, brave as a weasel, he must still reassure himself with the tones of his own voice; he must play his part to exaggeration, he must out-Herod Herod, insult all that was respectable, and brave all that was formidable, in a kind of desperate wager with himself.

"Golly, but it's 'ot!" said he. "Cruel 'ot, I call it. Nice d'y to get your gruel in! I s'y, you know, it must feel awf'ly peculiar to get bowled over on a d'y like this. I'd rather 'ave it on a cowld and frosty morning, wouldn't you? (Singing) *'Ere we go round the mulberry bush on a cowld and frosty mornin'.'* (Spoken) Give you my word, I 'aven't thought o' that in ten year; used to sing it at a hinfant school in 'Ackney, 'Ackney Wick it was. (Singing) *'This is the way the tyler does, the tyler does.'* (Spoken) Bloomin' 'umbug.—'Ow are you off now, for the notion of a future styte? Do you cotton to the tea-fight views, or the old red-'ot bogey business?"

"O, dry up!" said the captain.

"No, but I want to know," said Huish. "It's within the sp'ere of practical politics for you and me, my boy; we may both be bowled over, one up, t'other down, within the next ten minutes. It would be rather a lark, now, if you only skipped across, came up smilin' t'other side, and a hangel met you with a B. and S. under his wing. 'Ullo, you'd s'y: come, I tyke this kind."

The captain groaned. While Huish was thus airing and exercising his bravado, the man at his side was actually engaged in prayer. Prayer, what for? God knows. But out of his inconsistent, illogical, and agitated spirit, a stream of supplication was poured forth, inarticulate as himself, earnest as death and judgment.

"Thou Gawd seest me!" continued Huish. "I remember I had that written in my Bible. I remember the Bible too, all about Abinadab and parties.—Well, Gawd!" apostrophising the meridian, "you're goin' to see a rum start presently, I promise you that!"

The captain bounded.

"I'll have no blasphemy!" he cried, "no blasphemy in my boat."

"All right, cap'," said Huish. "Anythink to oblige. Any other topic you would like to sudgest, the ryne-gyge, the lightnin'-rod, Shykespeare, or the musical glasses? 'Ere's conversation on tap. Put a penny in the slot, and ... 'ullo! 'ere they are!" he cried. "Now or never! is 'e goin' to shoot?"

And the little man straightened himself into an alert and dashing attitude, and looked steadily at the enemy.

But the captain rose half up in the boat with eyes protruding.

"What's that?" he cried.

"Wot's wot?" said Huish.

"Those—blamed things," said the captain.

And indeed it was something strange. Herrick and Attwater, both armed with Winchesters, had appeared out of the grove behind the figure-head; and to either hand of them, the sun glistened upon two metallic objects, locomotory like men, and occupying in the economy of these creatures the places of heads—only the heads were faceless. To Davis, between wind and water, his mythology appeared to have come alive and Tophet to be vomiting demons. But Huish was not mystified a moment.

"Divers' 'elmets, you ninny. Can't you see?" he said.

"So they are," said Davis, with a gasp. "And why? O, I see it's for armour."

"Wot did I tell you?" said Huish. "Dyvid and Goliar all the w'y and back."

The two natives (for they it was that were equipped in this unusual panoply of war) spread out to right and left, and at last lay down in the shade, on the extreme flank of the position. Even now that the mystery was explained, Davis was hatefully preoccupied, stared at the flame on their crests, and forgot, and then remembered with a smile, the explanation.

Attwater withdrew again into the grove, and Herrick, with his gun under his arm, came down the pier alone.

About halfway down he halted and hailed the boat.

"What do you want?," he cried.

"I'll tell that to Mr. Attwater," replied Huish, stepping briskly on the ladder. "I don't tell it to you, because you played the trucklin' sneak. Here's a letter for him: tyke it, and give it, and be 'anged to you!"

"Davis, is this all right?" said Herrick.

Davis raised his chin, glanced swiftly at Herrick and away again, and held his peace. The glance was charged with some deep emotion, but whether of hatred or of fear, it was beyond Herrick to divine.

"Well," he said, "I'll give the letter." He drew a score with his foot on the boards of the gangway. "Till I bring the answer, don't move a step past this."

And he returned to where Attwater leaned against a tree, and gave him the letter. Attwater glanced it through.

"What does that mean?" he asked, passing it to Herrick. "Treachery?"

"O, I suppose so!" said Herrick.

"Well, tell him to come on," said Attwater. "One isn't a fatalist for nothing. Tell him to come on and to look out."

Herrick returned to the figure-head. Half-way down the pier the clerk was waiting, with Davis by his side.

"You are to come along, Huish," said Herrick. "He bids you to look out—no tricks."

Huish walked briskly up the pier, and paused face to face with the young man.

"W'ere is 'e?" said he, and to Herrick's surprise, the low-bred, insignificant face before him flushed suddenly crimson and went white again.

"Right forward," said Herrick, pointing. "Now, your hands above your head."

The clerk turned away from him and towards the figure-head, as though he were about to address to it his devotions; he was seen to heave a deep breath; and raised his arms. In common with many men of his unhappy physical endow-ments, Huish's hands were disproportionately long and broad, and the palms in particular enormous; a four-ounce jar was nothing in that capacious fist. The next moment he was plodding steadily forward on his mission.

Herrick at first followed. Then a noise in his rear startled him, and he turned about to find Davis already advanced as far as the figure-head. He came, crouching and open-mouthed, as the mesmerised may follow the mesmeriser; all human con-siderations, and even the care of his own life, swallowed up in one abominable and burning curiosity.

"Halt!" cried Herrick, covering him with his rifle. "Davis, what are you doing, man? *You* are not to come."

Davis instinctively paused, and regarded him with a dreadful vacancy of eye.

"Put your back to that figure-head—do you hear me?—and stand fast!" said Herrick.

The captain fetched a breath, stepped back against the figure-head, and instantly redirected his glances after Huish.

There was a hollow place of the sand in that part, and, as it were, a glade among the coco-palms in which the direct noon-day sun blazed intolerably. At the far end, in the shadow, the tall figure of Attwater was to be seen leaning on a tree; towards him, with his hands over his head, and his steps smothered in

307

the sand, the clerk painfully waded. The surrounding glare threw out and exaggerated the man's smallness; it seemed no less perilous an enterprise, this that he was gone upon, than for a whelp to besiege a citadel.

"There, Mr. Whish. That will do," cried Attwater. "From that distance, and keeping your hands up, like a good boy, you can very well put me in possession of the skipper's views."

The interval betwixt them was perhaps forty feet; and Huish measured it with his eye, and breathed a curse. He was already distressed with labouring in the loose sand, and his arms ached bitterly from their unnatural position. In the palm of his right hand the jar was ready; and his heart thrilled, and his voice choked, as he began to speak.

"Mr. Hattwater," said he, "I don't know if ever you 'ad a mother...."

"I can set your mind at rest: I had," returned Attwater; "and henceforth, if I may venture to suggest it, her name need not recur in our communications. I should perhaps tell you that I am not amenable to the pathetic."

"I am sorry, sir, I 'ave seemed to tresparse on your private feelin's," said the clerk, cringing and stealing a step. "At least, sir, you will never pe'suade me that you are not a perfec' gentleman; I know a gentleman when I see him; and as such, I 'ave no 'esitation in throwin' myself on your merciful consideration. It *is* 'ard lines, no doubt; it's 'ard lines to have to hown yourself beat; it's 'ard lines to 'ave to come and beg to you for charity."

"When, if things had only gone right, the whole place was as good as your own?" suggested Attwater. "I can understand the feeling."

"You are judging me, Mr. Attwater," said the clerk, "and God knows how unjustly! *Thou Gawd seest me*, was the tex' I 'ad in my Bible, w'ich my father wrote it in with 'is own 'and upon the fly-leaf."

'I am sorry I have to beg your pardon once more," said Attwater; "but, do you know, you seem to me to be a trifle nearer, which is entirely outside of our bargain. And I would venture to suggest that you take one—two—three—steps back; and stay there."

The devil, at this staggering disappointment, looked out of Huish's face, and Attwater was swift to suspect. He frowned, he stared on the little man, and considered. Why should he be creeping nearer? The next moment his gun was at his shoulder.

"Kindly oblige me by opening your hands. Open your hands wide—let me see the fingers spread, you dog—throw down that thing you're holding!" he roared, his rage and certitude increasing together.

And then, at almost the same moment, the indomitable Huish decided to throw, and Attwater pulled a trigger. There was scarce the difference of a second between the two resolves, but it was in favour of the man with the rifle; and the jar had not yet left the clerk's hand before the ball shattered both. For the twinkling of an eye the wretch was in hell's agonies, bathed in liquid flames, a screaming bedlamite; and then a second and more merciful bullet stretched him dead.

The whole thing was come and gone in a breath. Before Herrick could turn about, before Davis could complete his cry of horror, the clerk lay in the sand, sprawling and convulsed.

Attwater ran to the body; he stooped and viewed it; he put his finger in the vitriol, and his face whitened and hardened with anger.

Davis had not yet moved; he stood astonished, with his back to the figure-head, his hands clutching it behind him, his body inclined forward from the waist.

Attwater turned deliberately and covered him with his rifle.

"Davis," he cried, in a voice like a trumpet, "I give you sixty seconds to make your peace with God!"

Davis looked, and his mind awoke. He did not dream of self-defence, he did not search for his pistol. He drew himself up instead to face death, with a quivering nostril.

"I guess I'll not trouble the Old Man," he said; "considering the job I was on, I guess it's better business to just shut my face."

Attwater fired; there came a spasmodic movement of the victim, and immediately above the middle of his forehead a black hole marred the whiteness of the figure-head. A dreadful pause; then again the report, and the solid sound and jar of the bullet in the wood; and this time the captain had felt the wind of it along his cheek. A third shot, and he was bleeding from one ear; and along the levelled rifle Attwater smiled like a red Indian.

The cruel game of which he was the puppet was now clear to Davis; three times he had drunk of death, and he must look to drink of it seven times more before he was despatched. He held up his hand.

"Steady!" he cried; "I'll take your sixty seconds."

"Good!" said Attwater.

The captain shut his eyes tight like a child: he held his hands up at last with a tragic and ridiculous gesture.

"My God, for Christ's sake, look after my two kids," he said, and then, after a pause and a falter, "for Christ's sake. Amen."

And he opened his eyes and looked down the rifle with a quivering mouth.

"But don't keep fooling me long!" he pleaded.

"That's all your prayer?" asked Attwater, with a singular ring in his voice.

"Guess so," said Davis.

"So?" said Attwater, resting the butt of his rifle on the ground, "is that done? Is your peace made with Heaven? Because it is with me. Go, and sin no more, sinful father. And remember that whatever you do to others, God shall visit it again a thousandfold upon your innocents."

The wretched Davis came staggering forward from his place against the figure-head, fell upon his knees, and waved his hands, and fainted.

When he came to himself again, his head was on Attwater's arm, and close by stood one of the men in diver's helmets, holding a bucket of water, from which his late executioner now laved his face. The memory of that dreadful passage returned upon him in a clap; again he saw Huish lying dead, again he seemed to himself to totter on the brink of an unplumbed eternity. With trembling hands he seized hold of the man whom he had come to slay; and his voice broke from him like that of a child among the nightmares of fever: "O! isn't there no mercy? O! what must I do to be saved?"

"Ah!" thought Attwater, "here is the true penitent."

CHAPTER 12
A TAIL-PIECE

On a very bright, hot, lusty, strongly-blowing noon, a fortnight after the events recorded, and a month since the curtain rose upon this episode, a man might have been spied praying on the sand by the lagoon beach. A point of palm-trees isolated him from the settlement; and from the place where he knelt, the only work of man's hand that interrupted the expanse was the schooner *Farallone*, her berth quite changed, and rocking at anchor some two miles to windward in the midst of the lagoon. The noise of the Trade ran very boisterous in all parts of the island; the nearer palm-trees crashed and whistled in the gusts, those farther off contributed a humming bass like the roar of cities, and yet, to any man less absorbed, there must have risen at times over this turmoil of the winds the sharper note of the human voice from the settlement. There all was activity. Attwater, stripped to his trousers, and lending a strong hand of help, was directing and encouraging five Kanakas; from his lively voice, and their more lively efforts, it was to be gathered that some sudden and joyful emergency had set them in this bustle; and the Union Jack floated once more on its staff. But the suppliant on the beach, unconscious of their voices, prayed on with instancy and fervour, and the sound of his voice rose and fell again, and his countenance brightened and was deformed with changing moods of piety and terror.

Before his closed eyes the skiff had been for some time tacking towards the distant and deserted *Farallone*; and presently the figure of Herrick might have been observed to board her, to pass for a while into the house, thence forward to the forecastle, and at last to plunge into the main hatch. In all these quarters his visit was followed by a coil of smoke; and he had scarce entered his boat again and shoved off, before flames broke forth upon the schooner. They burned gaily; kerosene had not been spared, and the bellows of the Trade incited the conflagration. About half-way on the return voyage, when Herrick looked back, he beheld the *Farallone* wrapped to the topmasts in leaping arms of fire, and the voluminous smoke pursuing him along the face of the lagoon. In one hour's time, he computed, the waters would have closed over the stolen ship.

It so chanced that, as his boat flew before the wind with much vivacity, and his eyes were continually busy in the wake, measuring the progress of the flames, he found himself embayed to the northward of the point of palms, and here became aware at the same time of the figure of Davis immersed in his devotion. An exclamation, part of annoyance, part of amusement, broke from him; and he touched the helm and ran the prow upon the beach not twenty feet from the unconscious devotee. Taking the painter in his hand, he landed, and drew near, and stood over him. And still the voluble and incoherent stream of prayer continued unabated. It was not possible for him to overhear the suppliant's petitions, which he listened to some while in a very mingled mood of humour and pity: and it was only when his own name began to occur and to be conjoined with epithets, that he at last laid his hand on the captain's shoulder.

"Sorry to interrupt the exercise," said he; "but I want you to look at the *Farallone*."

The captain scrambled to his feet, and stood gasping and staring. "Mr. Herrick, don't startle a man like that!" he said. "I don't seem someways rightly myself since ..." He broke off. "What did you say anyway? O, the *Farallone*," and he looked languidly out.

"Yes," said Herrick. "There she burns! and you may guess from that what the news is."

"The *Trinity Hall*, I guess," said the captain.

"The same," said Herrick; "sighted half an hour ago, and coming up hand over fist."

"Well, it don't amount to a hill of beans," said the captain, with a sigh.

"O, come, that's rank ingratitude!" cried Herrick.

"Well," replied the captain meditatively, "you mayn't just see the way that I view it in, but I'd 'most rather stay here upon this island. I found peace here, peace in believing. Yes, I guess this island is about good enough for John Davis."

"I never heard such nonsense!" cried Herrick. "What! with all turning out in your favour the way it does, the *Farallone* wiped out, the crew disposed of, a sure thing for your wife and family, and you, yourself, Attwater's spoiled darling and pet penitent!"

"Now, Mr. Herrick, don't say that," said the captain gently; "when you know he don't make no difference between us. But, O! why not be one of us? why not come to Jesus right away, and let's meet in yon beautiful land? That's just the one thing wanted; just say, 'Lord, I believe, help Thou mine unbelief!' and He'll fold you in His arms. You see, I know! I been a sinner myself!"

NOTES

The text of this edition is based on that edited by Edmund Gosse and published in London in 1906. A few words (*today, countryside, twopenny* etc.) have been shorn of Stevenson's hyphen, no longer wanted in contemporary usage; a very few minor printing errors have been silently corrected; but otherwise the text is that passed by Gosse. In these notes, slang or archaic or otherwise unfamiliar words as well as references are glossed, but words given in good dictionaries are not.   *Ed.*

STRANGE CASE OF DR. JEKYLL AND MR. HYDE

This tale was written at Skerryvore, the house at Bournemouth that Robert Louis Stevenson and his wife Fanny were then living in, apparently in early December 1885. Most of the story came to Stevenson in a dream, and he wrote his first draft in three days; but Fanny felt the first version was too much a thriller, too little a tale of moral substance, and Stevenson destroyed the draft and began again, now paying greater attention to "the allegory which was palpable, and yet had been missed, probably from haste and the compelling influence of the dream" (as Fanny later put it). "In another three days the book, except for a few minor corrections, was ready for the press. The amount of work this involved was appalling. That an invalid in my husband's condition of health should have been able to perform the manual labour alone of putting 60,000 words on paper in six days seems incredible. He was suffering from continual haemorrhages, and was hardly allowed to speak, his conversation being usually carried on by means of a slate and pencil." Despite Stevenson's exertions, the first edition (published in London by Longman, without the definite article which later editors often prefix to the title) came too late to interest the Christmas book trade and was therefore postponed till January 1886 (the date 1885 being hand-corrected to

1886 in printed copies). The book carried a dedication to Stevenson's cousin, Katharine de Mattos.

Stevenson's tale was controversial, and the sermons preached against it from many a pulpit, including that of St. Paul's cathedral, doubtless abetted its success. Within a year of publication there was a stage adaptation by T.R. Sullivan, starring Richard Mansfield, and later, with the arrival of motion pictures, there were film versions starring John Barrymore, Frederic March, and Spencer Tracy. One incidental effect of these films has been to popularize what seems to be a mispronunciation of Jekyll's name; Richard Aldington (in *Portrait of a Rebel,* London, 1957) reported that Stevenson himself pronounced it "Jeekyl".

p.11   *Queer Street:* financial difficulty, debt, or crooked dealing.

p.15   *Damon and Pythias:* presumably Damon and Phintias, often taken to symbolize constant friendship.

p.19   *Dr. Fell:* the reference is less to the historical divine John Fell (1625–1686), chaplain to King Charles II, vice-chancellor of Oxford, and later bishop of Oxford, a man of formidable organizational energies, than to the Dr. Fell of four well-known lines of verse. J.T. Browne, on the brink of expulsion from Oxford, was offered pardon by Fell if he could translate into English extempore the thirty-third epigram of Martial —

Non amo te, Sabidi, nec possum dicere quare;
Hoc tantum possum dicere, non amo te.
Browne instantly shot back four lines which (not only to Stevenson) have come to define irrational aversion:

I do not love thee, Doctor Fell,
The reason why I cannot tell;
But this alone I know full well,
I do not love thee, Doctor Fell.

p.21   *pede claudo:* on halting foot, i.e. with some delay.

p.30   *cheval-glass:* a tall mirror swung on a frame, long enough to reflect the entire figure.

p.56   *bull's-eye:* the lantern carried by 19th century police, so called from the thick bull's-eye glass in its panels.

THE BODY-SNATCHER

This tale, one of what Stevenson referred to as "crawlers", was begun at Kinnaird Cottage at Pitlochry in Scotland in June 1881. Stevenson had his doubts about it and laid it aside "in a justifiable   disgust, the tale being horrid" (as he wrote to Sidney Colvin that July), but completed it in the winter of 1884 when Charles Morley, editor of the *Pall Mall Gazette,* asked him for a story for the Christmas issue. To Morley, Stevenson decribed the tale as "blood-curdling enough – and ugly enough – to chill the blood of a grenadier." Morley's aggressive advertising of the tale disquieted him, though: "He has sent me (for my opinion) the most truculent advertisement I ever saw," he wrote to Gosse, "in which the white hairs of Mr. Gladstone are gragged round Troy behind my chariot wheels." Gosse reported that the police had shared Stevenson's misgivings about the advertising and had orderd it to be toned down. Stevenson's unhappiness about the story seems to have persisted, as he would not accept the full payment he had negotiated. First published in the *Pall Mall Gazette*'s Christmas extra in December 1884, it was reprinted widely before being first collected in a New York edition of Stevenson's works in 1902, and in England for the first time in the 1906 edition from which this text is taken. Scholarship has shown that parts of the tale dealing with Jane Galbraith were adapted by Stevenson from William Burke's confession, printed in the *Edinburgh Evening Courant* on 21 January 1829.

p.83   *camlet:* a fine eastern fabric, formerly perhaps made of silk and camel hair, later of Angora wool. (The deriva-

p.84   *canted:* made sanctimonious religious talk.

p.86   *fly:* a one-horse covered hired carriage.

p.88   *a certain extramural teacher of anatomy:* Dr. Robert Knox (1791–1862), whose anatomy classes at Edinburgh university drew hundreds of students. Knox paid well for human subjects for dissection, and was thus a good market for body-snatchers such as Burke and Hare.

p.88   *Burke:* William Burke (1792–1829) from County Cork in Ireland, and his partner William Hare from Londonderry, were the most infamous of the body-snatcher murderers. They sold their first corpse to Dr. Knox in november 1827 when an old pensioner died (of natural causes) in the lodging-house Hare kept in Edinburgh. Subsequently they murdered at least fifteen people and sold the bodies to Dr. Knox's school of anatomy. They were caught on 31 October 1828 and Burke was hanged on 28 January 1829; Hare, who had turned king's evidence, subsequently disappeared without trace.

p.94   *cras tibi:* the Latin words, literally meaning "tomorrow to thee likewise", have the weight of a memento mori in this context.

p.98   *precentor:* one who leads the singing of a choir or congregation.

p.98   *Resurrection Man:* a slang term for a body-snatcher, first recorded by the OED (second edn.) in 1781.

MARKHEIM

This story was written at Bournemouth in 1884 and offered to the *Pall Mall Gazette* for the Christmas issue, but it was too short and Stevenson therefore completed *The Body-Snatcher* for Morley instead, and published *Markheim* in Unwin's 1886 annual *The Broken Shaft* ("stories of dread") and subsequently in his own collection of stories, *The Merry Men,* in 1887. James Hogg's *Private Memoirs and Confessions of a Justified Sinner* is widely seen as an influence, as is Dostoyevsky's *Crime and Punishment.*

p.114 *Brownrigg ... the Mannings ... Thurtell:* Elizabeth Brownrigg, a midwife, was arrested when her apprentice Mary Clifford died of injuries. Brownrigg had practised various cruelties on Clifford, finally tying her to a hook fixed into a beam in the kitchen and flogging her. She was hanged at Tyburn on 14 September 1767 and her skeleton was later put on display at the Old Bailey. Swiss-born Marie Manning (1821–1849) and her husband Frederick George murdered their dinner guest Patrick O'Connor and buried him under the flagstones in their kitchen. They were executed at Horsemonger Lane Gaol in London on 13 November 1849. Marie Manning, a maid in the service of Lady Blantyre, suggested to Dickens the character of Lady Dedlock's waiting-woman Mademoiselle Hortense in *Bleak House.* John Thurtell (1794–1824) had a chequered career as boxer (George Borrow described him in *Lavengro*), innkeeper and gambler, and his brutal murder of William Weare resulted from Thurtell's belief that Weare had cheated him of £300 at cards. Thurtell was hanged at Hertford on 9 January 1824. Thurtell was so eloquent and self-possessed that for some time he was almost a popular hero, and Hazlitt and Scott were among those who shared the fascination.

p.117 *Sheraton:* the furniture designer Thomas Sheraton (1751–1806).

OLALLA

Olalla was first published in the 1885 Christmas number of *The Court and Society Review* (17 December 1885) and later collected in *The Merry Man.* The story has rarely been given its due, no doubt partly because Stevenson himself came to feel that "*Markheim* is true; *Olalla* false". In a persuasive analysis in *Robert Louis Stevenson and Romantic Tradition* (Princeton, 1966, pp. 201–211), Edwin M. Eigner argues that the story was influenced by Hawthorne's *The Marble Faun.*

p.133   *river-kelpie:* a kelpie, in Lowland Scottish lore, is an imp haunting lakes and rivers, prone to drown travellers.

p.139   *bartizan:* a battlemented parapet or turret.

p.161   *catamount:* the European wild cat. In *The Merry Wives of Windsor* (II, ii, 27) Shakespeare uses the word to mean a wild man.

THE EBB-TIDE

This novella was begun in summer 1889 in Honolulu by Lloyd Osbourne. He showed his draft to Stevenson, who was so taken with it that the two men collaborated on the continuation of the book. Osbourne was later adamant that the early chapters of *The Ebb-Tide,* the chapters Stevenson had been enthusiastic about, remained almost entirely his own work in the final version. Some readers may agree with André Gide's feeling, in his journal in 1905, that those opening chapters make for rather laborious reading, whereas later the tale "becomes excellent and remains so almost to the end" – the concluding chapters being mainly Stevenson's work. Stevenson and Osbourne resumed work on *The Ebb-Tide* in 1890, and Stevenson descibed it to Marcel Schwob as "a black, ugly, tramping, violent story, full of strange scenes and striking characters". A plan to write a second part set in Bloomsbury, after the return of Herrick, was abandoned. *The Ebb-Tide,* "about as grim a tale as ever was written, and as grimy, and as hateful" (in Stevenson's words), was finished on 5 June 1893, sent off for publication on 18 June, and serialized in *To-Day* from 11 November 1893 to 3 February 1894 before being published by Heinemann in London in September 1894 – the last of Stevenson's works to appear within his lifetime. The novella carries as epigraph the line, "There is a tide in the affairs of men", from Brutus's speech in IV, iii of Shakespeare's *Julius Caesar:*

> There is a tide in the affairs of men,
> Which, taken at the flood, leads on to fortune;
> Omitted, all the voyage of their life
> Is bound in shallows and in miseries.

In a post-colonial time, criticism has increasingly become sensitive to the affinities between *The Ebb-Tide* and Conrad's *Heart of Darkness.* A useful account of *The Ebb-Tide* is in Robert Kiely's *Robert Louis Stevenson and the Fiction of Adventure,* Cambridge (Mass.), 1965.

p.177 *Papeete:* the principal town on Tahiti. Other names in the tale – Eimeo, the Paumotus or Dangerous Archipelago, the Kingsmills, Rapa-iti, etc. – are islands or atolls in the Pacific. Point Venus (p. 185), near Papeete, was so named to mark the scientific reason for James Cook's 1765 voyage, to observe the passage of Venus across the sun.

p.177 *purao:* a small evergreen tropical tree, *Hibiscus tiliaceus,* with pale yellow flowers fading to deep red.

p.178 *on the beach:* washed up, down and out.

p.178 *calaboose:* a prison or lock-up.

p.178 *sortes:* i.e. *sortes Virgilianae,* the practice of divination by chance selection of passages in Virgil.

p.183 *Freischütz:* Weber's opera (1821).

p.184 *pariu:* a skirt made of a single piece of cloth, worn by men and women in Polynesia.

p.184 *Harry my:* come here (Stevenson's note).

p.185 *B.-and-S.:* brandy and soda.

p.185   *hacks:* hackney cabs (horse-drawn hired carriages).

p.186   *jarvey:* a hackney cab driver.

p.186   *growler:* a hackney cab.

p.189   *feis:* fei is the hill banana (Stevenson's note).

p.190   *Ariana:* by-and-by (Stevenson's note).

p.191   *pandanus:* a tropical tree or shrub. The modern Latin name is a coinage from Malay *pandan.*

p.191   *sachems:* the chiefs of American Indian tribes.

p.191   *Tapena Tom harry my:* Captain Tom is coming (Stevenson's note).

p.192   *We twa hae paidled ....:* from the fourth stanza of Burns' "Auld Lang Syne".

p.196   *Einst, O Wunder!:* from Beethoven's "Adelaide", op. 46, a favourite of Stevenson's.

p.199   *the Fifth Symphony:* Beethoven's.

p.199   *memor querela:* the phrase *et nostri memorem sepulcro scalpe querellam* occurs in Horace, Odes, Book Three, xi, and means "and scratch on our tomb a lament in our memory". The quotation from Virgil's *Aeneid* (I, 94–5), *terque quaterque beati Queis ante ora patrum,* is rendered by Jackson Knight as "How fortunate were you, thrice fortunate and more, whose luck it was to die under the high walls of Troy before your parents' eyes!"

p.199   *Ich trage unerträgliches:* I bear the unbearable. This and the following quotation, which means "You, proud heart, you wanted it thus", are from Heine's *Die Heimkehr (The Homecoming).*

p.200   *swipes:* beer.

p.206   *Caledonia:* the French penal colony at Noumea on New Caledonia was notorious.

p.206   *galoot:* U.S. 19th century slang for an inexperienced or clumsy person (especially at sea).

p.207   *slops:* cheap ready-made clothing.

p.207   *Ohé la goëlette!:* schooner ahoy.

p.208   *A.B.:* able-bodied seaman.

p.211   *trick:* time on duty at the helm.

p.211 *kaikai:* food.

p.213 *epitome:* a maritime compendium.

p.233 *Crusoe:* in Defoe's novel *Robinson Crusoe* (1719).

p.236 *skeezicks:* a good-for-nothing or rogue (U.S. 19th century slang).

p.242 *Findlay:* a navigational directory for the South Pacific, by Alexander Findlay, first published in 1851.

p.245 *morning bank:* i.e. of cloud.

p.253 *For my voice has been tuned ...:* the source of this quotation has not yet been traced. The lines may be by Stevenson himself.

p.261 *nemorosa Zacynthos:* the line *Iam medio apparet flucto nemoroso Zacynthos,* from Virgil's *Aeneid* (III, 270), is rendered by Jackson Knight as "And now the wave-girt wooded island of Zacynthus came into view".

p.263 *The rude forefathers of the hamlet sleep:* from Thomas Gray's "Elegy Written in a Country Churchyard".

p.264 *And darkness was the burier of the dead:* Shakespeare, *Henry IV Part Two,* I, i, 160.

p.270 *Gewgaws:* baubles, trifles.

p.270 *Thou fool, this night thy soul shall be required of thee:* Luke, 12, 20.

p.282 *all nerves, like Jemimar:* in Beatrix Potter's *The Tale of Jemima Puddle-duck* (1908) the titular heroine also complains of her nerves, in a joke doubtless meant for adults. Probably both allusions are to a popular figure named Jemima, but I have been unable to trace the source.

p.289 *Laputa:* the flying island in Book III of Swift's *Gulliver's Travels* (1726).

p.304 *out-Herod Herod:* Shakespeare, *Hamlet,* III, ii, 16.

p.305 *Tophet:* originally a Phoenician place of sacrifice, but here identified with Hell.